POWER STRUGGLE

The two huge Gan-Tir turned toward the main control board—toward Keenan, in the pilot's seat. Keenan hit the ship's alarm. The clang was loud enough to hurt his ears, but it didn't stop the Gan-Tir. They moved toward him.

"You can't stay here," he said. "You must leave!"

They kept advancing. The aliens might mean no harm, but even the most innocent of acts around the controls could result in death for everyone. Keenan could not let them advance any farther.

He stood, blocking the path to the control board. The Gan-Tir paused, and two sets of hot violet eyes looked upon him. Then the larger of the two lifted her arm. Her black-and-white tentacle uncoiled and moved past his shoulder, toward the emergency shutdown controls. She was one sweep of her tentacle away from disabling the ship and killing them all.

Her tentacle dipped . . .

By Margaret Davis
Published by Ballantine Books:

MIND LIGHT
MINDS APART

MINDS APART

Margaret Davis

A Del Rey® Book
BALLANTINE BOOKS • NEW YORK

A Del Rey® Book
Published by Ballantine Books

Library of Congress Catalog Card Number: 94-94030

ISBN 0-345-38875-5

Manufactured in the United States of America

First Edition: June 1994

10 9 8 7 6 5 4 3 2 1

For Jim and Kathy,
who brighten the present

and for

Sarah and Corie,
who are the future

Chapter 1

Daniel Keenan hated Resurrection.

The religious fundamentalists who had built the station had not placed a high value on diversity or imagination. Neither paint, murals, nor plants had been used to relieve the miles of monotonous gray corridors. There were few shops and they carried only basic goods, with little choice of brands. The only store that would order offworld book and entertainment disks charged outrageous fees for the service, and it had a disconcerting tendency to report that selected works were "unavailable," though "unwanted" might have been a more accurate term.

Bad as that was, though, what Keenan really hated about Resurrection was the restriction that made this remote, inhospitable place the only human port where the ship upon which he traveled, the *Widdon Galaxy*, could dock.

Keenan lifted the shot glass of amorth from the table and downed the remaining contents in one fiery gulp. The background noise in the bar hit him like a physical blow as the synthetic alcohol rocked his senses. He'd had enough, he told himself firmly, putting down the empty glass. People might be able to drink amorth twenty-four hours a day without damaging a cell in their bodies, but it was still an intoxicant. He stood, swayed, and had to grab the edge of the table to keep from overbalancing. He had definitely had enough.

The room was full; he had to clear a passage to the door using his shoulders and elbows. The narrow corridor outside the bar was nearly as crowded as the room inside. After months of petitions and heated debate, Resurrection's council had finally

conceded to offworlders' demands and licensed one recreation-
al facility—located in the most remote, undesirable corner of
the station they could find. But if the council had hoped to discourage patrons that way, the plan was not working. Within
minutes of docking at the station, newcomers knew where the
bar was and most of them went there. On Resurrection, there
was nowhere else to go.

Keenan worked his way through the crush as politely as he
could, but others were not so considerate. Just as he reached
the main corridor, someone pushed him in the back and sent
him stumbling forward, directly into the path of a local.
Keenan caught the man's arm, trying to keep their balance, but
the dark-clothed native shoved him away violently. "Drunken
slime!" the man exclaimed.

For a moment, Keenan thought the native might actually
strike him. He started to apologize, but the man was already
striding away as quickly as he could, as if to distance himself
from the outsiders who defiled his world.

The native was wrong, Keenan told himself as he wove his
way down the corridor. He wasn't drunk. He wasn't even
close. There had been times lately when he had wanted to be,
but even if his psychiatric training hadn't told him that was unwise, common sense would have. Drinking didn't solve any
problems—it just added one more to the list. He hadn't really
wanted the amorth. He'd only ordered it so he would have an
excuse to stay in the bar.

What had he been looking for there? Anonymity? Casual
conversation? A way to postpone returning to the ship? Whatever he had been seeking, it had not been oblivion—at least,
not at first. That impulse had come only after the room fell silent as he made his way to the sole empty table. Conversations
started up again hurriedly, but the voices were too loud and
covert glances too frequent to be ignored. The people in the
bar might be newcomers to Resurrection, but they knew who
he was and they regarded him with nearly as much wariness as
did the locals.

Consort with aliens and become an alien yourself, the looks
seemed to say. No one trusted the *Widdon Galaxy*'s crew—not

the newcomers, not the Corps, and most of all, not the planet's natives. The religious faction that had settled the planet had been looking for a quiet backwater where they could live according to their beliefs. They had never imagined they would find themselves squarely on the path to Miquiri space. Some would have seen that position as the opportunity of a lifetime; Resurrection's natives saw it as an affliction and prayed that the Miquiri, the Corps, and the newcomers would all go away.

They would not, and sooner or later, the locals were going to have to accept that.

At present, only one ship was permitted to travel between human and Miquiri space—the *Widdon Galaxy*, an aging freighter owned by the Michaelson family and contracted to supply the Corps ship stationed at the Miquiri outpost called Sumpali. The Michaelsons were free to haul any Miquiri cargo they could find, but everything they carried was subject to Corps seizure and so far they had made little profit.

The Michaelsons did not like the restrictions placed upon them, but they accepted them. So did Greg Lukas, the ship's backup pilot, who was not even permitted to leave the ship while they were docked at Resurrection. Keenan had expected him to display signs of restlessness as the months wore on, but he had not. Lukas was not yet ready to push against the restraints that bound him.

That left Daniel Keenan the only fundamentally unhappy person on the ship. He took care to hide his discontent, but he did not think he succeeded completely. The Michaelsons were quick to spot false notes in others; so was Lukas, who knew Keenan too well to be misled for long. Still, if any of them had noticed anything amiss, they had said nothing.

Perhaps they were giving him time to work matters out for himself. Then again, maybe they didn't want him to think they were withdrawing their welcome. The Michaelsons had offered him a berth on the *Widdon Galaxy* for as long as he wished to stay. But while Greg Lukas had earned a place in the family, Keenan was still an outsider and probably always would be.

He thought about leaving often. It was Greg Lukas and the *Widdon Galaxy* who were prohibited from traveling beyond

Resurrection, not him; Keenan could go anywhere he chose. He had resigned his Corps commission six months before, but he still had his medical credentials. He could start a practice on the world of his choice. Good psychiatrists were always in demand, and he was very good.

Or he had been. Once.

Keenan turned a corner and almost ran into two men and a woman wearing Corps uniforms. He pulled up warily, giving the patrol a wide berth. So did everyone else around him, locals and offworlders alike. A second patrol, two security gates, and a triple-length access tube awaited him at the *Widdon Galaxy*'s dock. Someone in security had decided those precautions would give them time to react if the Quayla, the alien life-form that lived on the Michaelsons' ship, tried to cross over to the station. They were wrong, but no one on the ship was about to tell them that. Neither was the Corps. The vessel's docking privileges were precarious enough as it was.

The security guards didn't check Keenan's ID—they just waved him through the gates. So much for anonymity, Keenan thought as the last barrier shut behind him. He might dream of walking in a place where he wasn't recognized, but it wasn't going to happen on Resurrection.

His footsteps echoed hollowly on the empty dock. There should have been ships in the adjoining berths, crew members coming and going, and machinery whirring as goods were offloaded. There should have been brokers and customs officials, but there was no one, nothing. The ship might have been carrying the plague, so completely had she been isolated.

Keenan's feet slowed as he reached the access tube. The passage was long and dimly lit, and the air inside stale; he had to fight a sudden impulse to turn around and go back. Bad as the station was, there were times when the ship seemed worse.

The *Widdon Galaxy*'s main corridor was deserted, the lights turned down low. He had been gone longer than he had thought. No matter; no one would worry about him. A person couldn't get lost on Resurrection. He turned at the first cross corridor and headed toward his cabin, keeping his eyes focused straight ahead and doing his best to ignore the pink glow surrounding him. Visible only as a sheet of light, the Quayla was brighter than it had been a few months ago, and faint patterns could sometimes be seen rippling along the walls. The alien had spread to every passageway and room on the ship—every one save Keenan's. The walls there remained solidly, chillingly gray.

The door to the galley opened as he walked past and Greg Lukas came out, wearing the unofficial uniform of dark blue pants and a light blue shirt favored by commercial pilots. His black hair was neatly combed and his gray eyes were bright and clear.

"Daniel, you're back!" he said warmly. "I was beginning to think you'd decided to stay onstation all night."

"Not likely—not on Resurrection."

"Is it really that bad?"

"It's not great." Keenan held out the bag he was carrying. "Here, I brought back the things you asked for."

Lukas gave the sack's contents a cursory inspection, then looked up again. "Is everything all right?"

"Yes, of course."

"Are you sure? You look upset. Jon Robert said he had problems at one of the stores today—a place called Brekman's. The clerks refused to serve him. He didn't make an issue out of it because other stores will, but it was an unpleasant experience. I thought something similar might have happened to you."

"No." Keenan turned toward his cabin.

"Daniel, wait," Lukas said, putting a hand on Keenan's arm. Keenan tore free with a violent gesture that took them both by surprise. He caught himself at once, but too late—Lukas's eyes had gone wide with shock.

"Daniel, what's wrong with you?" the pilot demanded.

Keenan started to say "Nothing," but made the mistake of looking at the Quayla. Lukas followed his gaze and went still.

The Quayla might have spread itself throughout the ship, but it was Lukas to whom it was truly attached. A vividly colored, glowing pool of light followed the pilot wherever he went. Under normal conditions, the Quayla pulsed slowly, its color changing from pink, to peach, to yellow, and back again. When Lukas was upset, however, it throbbed rapidly, its soft colors darkening. As Keenan watched, the light turned a violent reddish orange. Even though he knew it couldn't harm him, he took an involuntary step back.

There were scientists on the *North Star* who said the alien being was not a living organism—not as humans defined the term. Lukas insisted that it was, and claimed that it thought and felt like any other intelligent being. But by every definition Daniel Keenan knew, it was a parasite. Unable to experience physical sensations itself, the Quayla shared those of its host. At the moment, that host was Greg Lukas, and it had formed a mental bond with him that could be broken only by Lukas's death.

There were indications that the bond between the two was not solely mental. Since joining with the Quayla, Lukas had neither gained nor lost weight, no matter how much he ate. He slept less than he had before, and when he did, he sank so far into unconsciousness that he did not wake for anything less than a blaring alarm. Keenan didn't mean to respond to the Quayla with suspicion, but after seeing all the changes Lukas had undergone, he couldn't seem to help himself.

"I'm sorry," he said miserably, trying to repair the newest crack in their relationship before it had a chance to widen. "You startled me. I reacted without thinking."

Lukas did not believe him, but he was too polite—or too kind—to say so. "I'm sorry, too," he said, forcing himself to relax. "I should have known better than to touch you without warning. I keep forgetting all those self-defense lessons your mother gave you. You can't develop deeply ingrained protective reflexes and then forget them at will." He glanced down the corridor. "If you'll excuse me, I have to go to the bridge and start the preflight checks. Kiley decided she wanted to pull out as soon as you came back."

"I thought we weren't leaving until morning."

"We finished loading the last piece of cargo an hour ago. No one wanted to stay here any longer, so she moved up our departure time."

"Do you want any help?" Keenan asked as Lukas started down the corridor. "I'll be glad to give you a hand."

"No, thanks. Kiley's going to meet me on the bridge. Besides, you need to rest—you're scheduled to stand first watch after we jump tomorrow morning."

Lukas continued on, the Quayla flowing in his wake. Keenan wanted to follow, to say whatever words it would take to heal the breach between them, but he couldn't get his feet to move. When he finally did, they took him across the hall, into his cabin.

He had left the room lights on their lowest setting, and he could barely distinguish the outlines of his bed and desk. He started to reach for the control panel to turn them up, but then let his hand drop and sagged back against the wall. The cold metal chilled his spine, but he did not pull away. Instead, he stared at the shadowy reflection of himself in the bathroom mirror. Memory colored his face, showing him curly black hair, blue eyes, and a scattering of freckles across his nose. Memory even filled in the weight he'd lost. It wasn't much, but it was enough to make his stocky frame look slender for the first time in his life.

He had hurt Lukas. The pilot had covered his reaction, but he could not hide it completely.

How could he have done that? he demanded of himself. As a psychiatrist and a friend, he should have been reaching out to Lukas. He should have been doing his best to help him through what must be a difficult period of adjustment. Instead, he had rejected him openly—and not just once, but repeatedly. His doubts had damaged their relationship so badly that he feared it was beyond repair.

He should leave the ship at once. The Corps might detain him for a short time and insist that he undergo a debriefing and medical exam, but afterward he would be free. He might feel like a prisoner at times, but he was not. Freedom was only one decision away.

So why couldn't he take that final step? Why did he seem to be incapable of taking a single, positive action? Why had he turned on his best friend? His training told him that his behavior was not normal. He needed help, but instead of seeking it, he went on as he was, day after miserable day. Why?

What was wrong with him?

Chapter 2

His name was Sensar Kaikiel Anara, but his students called him Scholar.

"Scholar, I wish to study with you. Will you accept me as your pupil?"

"Scholar, I have a question."

"Scholar, I regret to inform you that I must end my studies. Other duties require my attention."

They came, they studied for a time, and then they left. They were intelligent, all of them, but they were not true scholars, and his was an esoteric field. He had given up hope of finding another who shared his passion for alien cultures and artifacts.

Only three of his generation had become academics. The other two had devoted themselves to biological research, hoping to find a solution to their people's impending extinction. Sensar had studied the past instead, trying to find the key to their survival there. He had not succeeded. Neither had the others. Only they were surprised; their elders had long since given up finding answers or cures. So had they, finally. But life went on, even so and one had to do something. By nature and training, he was a scholar, so a scholar he remained.

Sensar opened the door to his quarters and stepped in. Lights came on. "Welcome," the voice of his room cooed to him. He ignored it, turning instead to the givitch, who tumbled down the walls to embrace him. He stroked it for a time, forgetting the tensions of the day, then freed himself and changed out of his scholar's gown into a casual robe.

He was smaller than average for an adult Gan-Tir and the loose-fitting garment hung from his shoulders. He did not

mind. The gown covered him while still allowing free movement of his arms, legs, and the tentacles that wrapped around
each of his limbs. He might have chosen to call attention to his
short stature and attractively patterned black and white skin by
wearing transparent materials or robes with revealing cuts, but
Sensar had no personal vanity. He was a scholar. He left fash-
ion to the exhibitionists among his people, of whom there were
many.

Sensar pulled the gown's hood up to keep his smooth, bare
head warm, and crossed the room to the kitchen area to prepare his dinner. His quarters were as unpretentious as his clothing and consisted of a single, large room. "Student's quarters,"
the other scholars at the university called it, mocking his pref-
erence for austerity. He ignored their taunts. Like his plain
clothing, the room met all of his needs. A bed took up one
wall, and the tiny kitchen filled another. The long shelf that
was his work space ran along the third wall. The fourth contained a floor-to-ceiling window, outside of which the sun had
set several minutes before. Lights were starting to come on in
the city below; they would stay on for five or six hours, then
go out one by one. Sometime before dawn, the city would van-
ish. If he was still awake then, Sensar would be able to look
up at the sky and see the stars.

He loved the view. He loved his room. When others derided
him for being content with so little, he smiled. He had everything he wanted and needed. Everything, that is, save a pupil
to carry on his work when he was gone. In that, however, he
was no different from any other scholar at the university. There
were few students. Thanks to the Ytavi, there would soon be
none.

Even now, centuries later, no one fully understands how the
alien species had taken away the Gan-Tir's ability and desire to
procreate. Females had fewer and fewer periods of fertility, and
males had become less responsive to the attractors females
produced to stimulate their sexuality. The changes went beyond their own bodies; the Ytavi had altered their entire food
chain. They were different because the food they ate and the
water they drank was different.

At first, Gan-Tir researchers had worked frantically to synthesize chemicals that induced fertility and increased a female's natural attractors. They had found a few drugs that worked, but all were difficult to manufacture and could not be produced in large quantities. They devoted the resources of an entire generation to their production, and succeeded only in slowing the population decline. By that time, however, it wasn't the physical changes that were proving destructive, but the social ones.

As females found they had fewer and fewer opportunities to conceive, each became more important. They began taking attraction-enhancing chemicals in larger and larger doses, making themselves virtually irresistible. Males found themselves compelled to respond, whether they wished to or not. And in greater and greater numbers, they did not. Reproduction became a matter of warfare, with females determined to insure the survival of their species at any cost, and males equally determined to resist. But sexual restraint required a level of control that young males had difficulty achieving. Not believing their elders' warnings, the least wary among them agreed to enter into liaisons with fertile females. By the time they realized what was happening, it was too late; they were trapped and were not released until the female passed her period of fertility. Not all of them fathered children, but enough did to insure the continued survival of a species turned against itself—at least for a time.

Now, however, even those radical tactics were failing. Despite chemicals, females were no longer becoming fertile, and there had been no new children in years. The Ytavi had destroyed the Gan-Tir. They had not fired a single weapon in centuries, but they continued to kill as surely as if they were taking aim on each and every one of them.

Sensar had spent most of his adult life trying to understand the Ytavi. Shortly after dealing the Gan-Tir a death blow they had disappeared, leaving few records and artifacts behind. Some physical structures remained, but most of the contents had been removed. Little could be deduced from the few overlooked odds and ends, though generations of Gan-Tir scholars had done their best. So had Sensar, but he would be the last. None of his students cared. They were older hobbyists for the most part, indulging brief curiosities that quickly passed. The few scholars who became his pupils worked in other fields; they sought information for research projects of their own. None of them studied the Ytavi with more than a passing interest.

Finished with his quick meal, Sensar sat down at the long counter that served as his desk, wishing there had been one— just one—against whom he could sharpen his wits. There had not, and now there never would be. His was the last generation; when it had failed to procreate, a sense of doom had settled over his people.

He had messages waiting. He shook off his dark thoughts and forced himself to scan the list on the screen that filled the center of his worktable. All but two were from students. Without reading the contents, he knew what each of them had written. They were so predictable. So boringly predictable. Just once, he would like to receive a message with an unexpected question or argument, anything to show a student was really thinking.

He shunted his students' messages to one side; he would respond to them later. He called for the two anonymous messages. What did they contain? Hate letters from his fellow colleagues? Invitations to liaisons that might prove professionally or financially rewarding, but morally debilitating? Malicious gossip about those who had engaged in such liaisons? He scanned them quickly. They were both extracts of the same story that had appeared in the day's news. He rarely read the news; usually it contained more gossip than fact. Whoever had sent the extracts must have known that and wanted to be certain he did not miss the story. But why? Because they thought it would interest him? Or because they hoped he would respond to the article for reasons of their own?

"Miquiri report contact with previously unknown species," the first sentence read. There were no pictures, just a text summary of a story told by a trader. Sensar read the article once, then read it again. A new species, and a young, vigorously growing one, at that. How unexpected. How unsettling. Not that they posed any danger: how could they kill that which was already dead? Still, the self-elected government was calling for a mission to meet the newcomers and assess their potential threat. Any diplomats, linguists, or scholars interested in participating were invited to submit an inclusion request.

Sensar read the brief report a third time, then sat back in his chair, thinking. Jejola, a fellow scholar at the university, had probably sent one of the extracts. She was a linguist specializing in Miquiri studies. Though their fields overlapped only marginally, they were the only two who were qualified to assume the Master of Xenological Studies title once the current master died. He had not accepted a new student in years, and rumors that he was close to death had been circulating for weeks.

Jejola had studied the Miquiri because knowing their customs and language was profitable, not because she had any scholastic interest in them. She frequently acted as a consultant and translator for those who traded with the aliens, but it was no secret that she disdained them. Still, she coveted the title of master, and might believe she could lobby successfully for it if Sensar were not there. She knew him well enough to guess he would not pass up an opportunity to meet aliens firsthand.

Unlike many Gan-Tir, he had no hesitation about traveling; he had visited other worlds several times in search of Ytavi artifacts. He was also comfortable dealing with the Miquiri. He had studied them extensively, seeking to further his understanding of alien behavior patterns. Jejola knew all that and had almost certainly sent one of the messages. But who had sent the other?

It had not come from one of his students or a friendlier colleague. Such a person would have signed his or her name. Someone else must want him away from Gan-Tir. But who? Why? And most importantly, should he go? Sensar turned and stared out the window at the city that lay below him.

The lights had all gone out by the time he finally reached a conclusion. He turned back to his worktable, wrote a formal request for inclusion, and transmitted it before he could reconsider.

Jejola might disdain going among those she studied, but he did not. Nor did he care about titles, though he would not have given her the satisfaction of knowing that. Let her think she had outmaneuvered him. Let her have the title for now. It would be his soon enough; once Jejola died, he would be the only one left to assume it.

Chapter 3

The Miquiri outpost, Sumpali, orbited an Earth-class planet. There were no visible structures on the formerly uninhabited moon, but its surface swirled and pulsed with light. The colors were soft pink and yellow on the dark side of the moon, but wherever sunlight struck and energized the outpost's Quayla, they turned fiery red and orange.

Kiley Michaelson, captain of the *Widdon Galaxy*, risked a quick look at the hypnotic patterns the light formed, then forced her eyes away from the viewscreens and back to the control board. The human station at Sumpali loomed dead ahead; little more than a hastily joined assembly of modular chambers, it had a raw, unfinished look. The Miquiri had not wanted humans roaming their station, so they had given the Corps permission to construct a temporary facility to serve as a dock and site for the talks being held by the two groups' diplomats.

Despite the negotiations, the humans and Miquiri had yet to reach an accord on the boundary lines dividing the territory that lay between them. Both were reluctant to sign an agreement before they had surveyed the space in question and were certain they were not giving up rare or vital resources.

Kiley wished they would hurry up with the mapping so talks about trade agreements could begin. Most people envied her family for having exclusive access to the Miquiri port, but she was tired of making the same boring run, trip after trip, and she chafed at the Corps' restrictions.

Kiley glanced at the pool of light on the floor beside her. Six months ago, she could not have conceived of circumstances that would bring her to welcome an alien life-form on board the *Widdon Galaxy*. But that was before she'd met Greg Lukas and hired him on as the ship's backup pilot.

Lukas's flight from his past had taken them all beyond known space, into a meeting with the Miquiri. Looking for a sister ship that had never returned home, the aliens had emerged from jump to find themselves in the same unstable region of space that had claimed their fellow vessel. They were luckier than she had been—they survived the encounter—but the *Nieti*'s Quayla had lost control of the vessel's environmental systems and many of the crew had died, including the Quayla's companion.

Partially disabled, the *Nieti* had been unable to jump far enough to return to her starting coordinates, and the Miquiri were forced to search for a way around the barrier. But they hadn't found one, and when they spotted the *Widdon Galaxy*, they had waylaid her, hoping she would prove friendly and helpful.

The encounter had not gone well. The two groups had been on the verge of hostilities when the *Nieti*'s Quayla had crossed over to the *Widdon Galaxy* and joined with Lukas. That merging had threatened to shatter Lukas's mind, but he had survived. Together, he and the Quayla had convinced the Miquiri that the humans meant them no harm, and then persuaded them to accept Corps assistance in finding a safe route home. The Corps search went much faster than the Miquiri's had: they mapped the boundaries of the barrier, found an end to it, and gave the Miquiri the star charts that would take them back to their own people. The Miquiri showed their gratitude by agreeing to diplomatic talks and the establishment of trade relations.

Unable to desert the Quayla, Lukas had traveled with the aliens to Sumpali, the closest Miquiri outpost. The Michaelsons had followed him there. As soon as another companion could be found, the *Nieti*'s Quayla had divided; most of it had stayed on the Miquiri vessel, but a portion had accompanied Lukas back to the *Widdon Galaxy*.

The Michaelsons had known they would not be allowed to travel human space freely while their ship harbored an alien creature capable of dividing itself at will. If Kiley had not loved Lukas, they might have refused to let him back on board.

Initially, the Corps had refused to let the *Widdon Galaxy* dock at any human port, but they had been forced to back down when the Miquiri named the Michaelsons' ship as the only human vessel permitted to travel in their space until formal agreements were signed. The Miquiri did not completely trust the Michaelsons, but they did trust their Quayla. It would know if the family was carrying dangerous or unauthorized cargo. Despite the Corps' initial doubts about the family's reliability, the arrangement had worked out well for everyone. The Corps had someone to transport goods and personnel, the Miquiri did not have to worry about potentially hostile ships entering their space, and the Michaelsons were making a profit for the first time in years.

The *North Star* had not carried the raw materials needed to build a space station. Moreover, her initial crew had been chosen with a heavy emphasis on physical and astrological sciences, and only a few were capable of studying an alien species and conducting negotiations with them. So over the past six months, most of the scientists had been rotated out. In their place had come diplomats, linguists, and specialists in the behavioral sciences. And everyone and everything had traveled on the *Widdon Galaxy*.

When they weren't carrying Corps personnel and goods, the Michaelsons transported anything the Miquiri were willing to trade. There had not been much to haul at first. Originally constructed as a research station and staging area for colonization of the planet below, Sumpali made no pretense of being a marketplace. The few goods the Miquiri had agreed to exchange had to be brought in from other worlds.

The most profitable loads so far had also been the smallest: data disks that contained all the literature and factual information the Miquiri were willing to release. Kiley had been told there were several hundred linguists on Resurrection studying the documents. Lukas said that nearly as many Miquiri were studying the human documents the Corps had agreed to release.

"We're down to twenty percent power on the main engines," Lukas said from the copilot's seat. "Do you want me to take her into dock?"

Kiley jerked back to the bridge with a start. "I'll do it," she said quickly, forcing her attention back to the work at hand. She must be more fatigued than she realized. Pilots could not afford to let their thoughts wander—not when a single moment's inattention could mean death for everyone on board the ship. And Kiley's case of Wycker's Syndrome made her even more determined to stay in control at all times. The flaw that had washed her out of the Academy and a career in the Corps only affected her when the ship went through two or more jumps in quick succession, but the resulting disorientation and faintness made her a less than perfect captain, and she was always aware of her weakness.

Docking was not as hazardous as jumping, but the operation required a number of finely coordinated, precisely timed bursts of thruster fire. She gave a sigh of relief when they finally bumped home.

"Docking confirmed," Lukas said as they locked on to the tube that connected the ship with the station. He began to switch off all the sensors and monitors on his side of the control board, bedding the ship down for their stay at Sumpali.

Kiley went to work on her side, shutting down everything but the ship's environmental systems. She stretched and yawned when she finished, releasing the last of the tension from her muscles. Lukas gave his darkened board a final inspection, then stood.

"Ready?" He offered her a hand up.

Kiley nodded and they went down the corridor to the dining room. Her sister Lia usually cooked dinner for everyone their first night in port. Lia and her husband, Reese Sybern, were carrying platters in from the galley when Kiley and Lukas entered. Keenan was helping them.

The psychiatrist had originally been sent to the ship to investigate claims that Lukas had been falsely court-martialed by his former commanding officer. After proving Lukas's innocence, he had surprised everyone by resigning from the Corps and agreeing to stay on the *Widdon Galaxy* until Kiley's niece, Hope, was born. But three months had passed since the baby's arrival, and he was still with them. Not that Kiley objected—he had learned to pilot the ship and was standing a regular watch. His help on the bridge gave her precious time with Lukas that she would not have had otherwise.

The door to the dining room started to close, then opened again as Kiley's sister-in-law, Holly, came in carrying Hope. It was still too early to be certain of the baby's coloring, but they thought she would have fair hair and blue eyes. Her birth had meant extra work for the entire family, but it had also given them a sense of continuity. They had lived day to day before she arrived, just trying to survive. Now they were being forced to plan ahead for her future, if not their own. That necessity had an unexpected benefit: for the first time in years, they all believed they had a future.

"Jon Robert isn't here yet?" Holly looked around the room for her husband.

"No," Lia said.

"If someone will watch Hope, I'll go to the engine room and see if I can hurry him up."

"I will," Reese offered. He took the baby, his face lighting up with a wide smile; he could not have loved her more if she had been his own. Sometimes, Kiley thought he wished she was. More than once, she had seen a look of deep regret cross his face as he returned Hope to Holly's arms. Lia had seen the look, too, and Kiley had been shocked by the depth of the jealousy and anger her sister had struggled to conceal.

Lia had never had a child, though she and Reese had been married for years. Kiley had assumed neither of them wanted any. It wasn't until she saw Reese with Hope that she realized he might have been suppressing his own desires out of respect for her sister's. Lia did not want to die as her mother had, miscarrying during transition and then hemorrhaging to death.

"Do you need help carrying the food in?" Keenan asked Lia

quickly. Kiley wasn't the only one worried about Lia's jealousy—Keenan had been watching her, too.

Lia dragged her attention back to the table. "Yes, please."

Keenan had to pass in front of Kiley and Lukas to reach the galley, and he hesitated as he approached, giving Lukas a wider berth than necessary. Kiley gave him a startled glance. What was wrong with him? Had they had a disagreement? She started to ask Lukas, but Jon Robert and Holly came through the door. By the time they were all seated at the table and the confusion had died down, she'd forgotten what had happened. She didn't remember until late that night, after she and Lukas had gone to bed. She had been drifting on the edge of sleep, but the recollection brought her awake again.

"Greg, did you and Daniel have an argument?" She turned over and propped herself up on one elbow.

"Argument?" he mumbled, his voice slurred with sleep. "No."

"Are you sure?" she persisted. "For a minute this evening, I thought he was avoiding you."

" 'magining things," he muttered. He exhaled and slid over the edge of consciousness into sleep, his long body relaxing against hers.

Who did he think was imagining things—she or Keenan? Kiley started to shake Lukas awake to demand an answer, then subsided against her pillow with an exasperated sigh. Once he'd closed his eyes, nothing short of an emergency would rouse him.

What was wrong with Keenan? Were the months of confinement beginning to wear on the psychiatrist's nerves? Cabin fever might be a joke that spacers bandied about, but some people simply could not adapt to life in a restricted, artificial environment. To the best of her knowledge, Keenan had not spent a prolonged period on a ship before. If he was having trouble adjusting, she needed to talk to him, and soon. His condition was not likely to improve with time.

Then again, perhaps his problem resulted from some other cause entirely. Kiley looked up at the ceiling, watching the soft light change color as the Quayla slowly pulsed. Keenan had always been wary of the alien. At first, she had believed that his status as a Corps officer had been the cause of his suspicion; he had felt a responsibility to see the Quayla in terms of a potential threat. But he was no longer in the Corps, and any initial concerns he had experienced should have faded long ago. He himself had said the joining had benefited Lukas: with the Quayla, the pilot might never have overcome mental scars left by an illegal attempt to block his memory. It had helped Lukas, not hurt him. There was no reason to believe it posed a threat to him.

Or was there? Had something happened to renew Keenan's concern, something she had missed? Though she saw Lukas every day, it had been months since she had truly looked at him. Changes were what humans noticed, and even changes went unnoticed if they happened gradually enough—or if the observer did not wish to see them.

Was that what had happened to her? Had she stopped seeing Lukas clearly? She knew that she had consciously ignored a great deal in the beginning. It did not do to dwell on the fact that the man she loved was attached to an alien being—one that shared his every thought and emotion. One that was a party to all that passed between them. Most of the time she coped with the lack of privacy by pretending the Quayla wasn't there. Since it could not communicate with anyone but Lukas, that had been easy to do.

Had it been too easy?

Kiley turned over and studied the pilot. He lay on his side, his dark head buried deep in his pillow. The room lights were on their lowest setting, and she could make out little more than the outline of his jaw, brow, and nose. He was not classically handsome, but his smile could still take her breath away. She wasn't the only one who found him attractive, either—he had drawn interested looks on every station they had visited.

Sometimes she wondered why he had chosen her when he could have had so many other women. She wasn't ugly, but she wasn't beautiful, either, and most men found her brisk speech and movements off-putting. More interested in being respected as captain of the *Widdon Galaxy* than in men's attention, she had deliberately cultivated a businesslike manner. Lukas hadn't been deceived by her air of brusque efficiency, though. He had taken her orders and given her the same respect he'd have shown any commanding officer, but at the same time he had made her feel young, awkward, and thoroughly uncomfortable.

That wasn't the way he made her feel now. His love and respect had given her a confidence she had never had before—and a vulnerability. Some women might be able to afford the luxury of abandoning themselves to love, but starship captains could not. Kiley was responsible for the lives of everyone who traveled on the *Widdon Galaxy*.

Lukas had been captain of his own ship once; he knew that duty had to come first for her. Still, there were times when she caught him searching her eyes, as if seeking something more. If she disappointed him, though, he didn't say so. He just brushed the hair back from her face and kissed her again, sometimes lightly, sometimes deeply. The moment would pass and be forgotten until the next time.

Did he think she doubted him? If so, she should reassure him. Joining with the Quayla had made him whole again in a way he could never have been otherwise. How could she question it or him? Keenan might have reservations, but she did not. She couldn't afford them.

Kiley turned over abruptly. She had resolved her conflicts about Lukas and the Quayla long ago, and she wasn't going to seek new reasons for doubting them—not when she had everything to lose in the process and nothing to gain.

She and Lukas were already too far apart, for all they lay so close.

Chapter 4

Kiley was asleep when Lukas woke. He lay still for a time, savoring the feel of her body against his and the sound of her soft, steady breathing. They rarely had more than a few hours together while they were away from port, and they had those only because Keenan had volunteered to sit a shift on the bridge.

The former psychiatrist had no real interest in piloting the ship, but he insisted on earning his way. He sat one full six-hour watch each day. He had offered to take another, shorter shift as well, but Kiley had turned him down. Though willing, he did not have a true aptitude for piloting. He could scan the boards effectively for a few hours, but after that, his eyes dulled and his concentration lapsed. Keenan had appealed Kiley's decision to Lukas, but Lukas sided with her. No amount of desire or training could overcome an incompatible temperament, and neither he nor Kiley wanted to push Keenan beyond his abilities. They took the hours he could give them and considered themselves lucky.

You could have had more if this had been a Miquiri ship.

The Quayla flowed into Lukas's mind, welcoming him back to consciousness with such intense joy that a wave of heat suffused his body. On a Miquiri ship, that greeting would have been accompanied by a tumbling flow of images and information designed to bring him up to date on the ship's status. The data would have come so fast that he would have been able to sort it out only in retrospect. What computers did for human ships, a Quayla did for Miquiri vessels. The alien being was more than a computer, though—much more.

23

The first Quayla had been found on the remnants of a wrecked Ytavi ship, on the verge of nonexistence. Either it had been damaged as a result of whatever calamity had overtaken the vessel, or years of isolation had reduced it to a fragment of consciousness. But the arrival of a Miquiri exploration team stimulated it; it searched among the party until it found one who was receptive, and the two joined minds.

The Miquiri did not know what to make of the Quayla at first, but it didn't take them long to discover its abilities. It could make calculations faster than the most sophisticated machines, and it could absorb and process information from thousands of sources simultaneously. It also had a mind of its own. While it could theoretically replace any computer system, there was only one place it wished to live: on board a starship. A few consented to remain on stations, but only so they could gather and disseminate the experiences of other Quaylas.

At first, the Miquiri had been disappointed to realize the alien life-form had limitations, but they recovered quickly after it showed them how to redesign their ships to take advantage of its ability to operate them. They discovered only one major complication to working with Quaylas: their need for companions.

A Quayla could communicate with a ship's crew through displays, or even by writing on the walls with letters formed of light, but that contact did nothing to ease its loneliness or provide it with the sensory stimulation it craved. Since it had no physical body, it could touch, taste, and feel only through another being, and then only if the two were joined by a deep mental bond.

Few Miquiri had been able to establish mental contact with Quaylas, and fewer still had the ability to form a bond deep enough to maintain constant communication. Those who did became the most highly valued and respected people in the Miquiri civilization. Even Lukas, a human, had received special consideration after becoming a Quayla's companion.

Humanity's reception had been somewhat less enthusiastic. It hadn't taken Lukas long to realize that he was a freak to the rest of his species, and always would be. Joined to the Quayla, who knew what he might do, or what kind of monster he might become?

You are no monster, the Quayla said. High, clear laughter echoed as it called up an image of a misshapen, hulking Frankenstein and walked it across Lukas's mind. The Miquiri did not have horror films or monsters, and the Quayla found humanity's fascination with such dark creations at once fascinating and amusing. *If you were truly a monster, you would look like this.*

Not necessarily, Lukas replied. *The best monsters always looked perfectly normal on the outside. That's what made them so horrible.*

Are you saying contact with me has made you horrible? the Quayla asked, sobering.

No, of course not, but some people would. Some do.

Not the ones who count. Not the Miquiri. Not Kiley or her family.

No, but there are others— Lukas broke off, but the Quayla caught the image in his mind before he could bury it: Keenan's face as he recoiled from Lukas's touch the day before. Lukas had tried to hide the stab of pain that moment caused from Keenan, but he could not hide it from the Quayla.

I thought he was your akia, it said angrily. *How can he doubt you? It would not be so among the Miquiri.*

Human friends can be very close, but not even the best of them offers the total acceptance of an akia.

Keenan had come as close as a human being could, though. They had been roommates and best friends at the Academy the year they entered the Corps. Circumstances had separated them after that, but when Keenan had learned that Lukas might have been falsely convicted of entering a restricted zone without authorization, he had agreed to investigate the case.

Lukas's memories of the incident had been blocked. Keenan restored them. The psychiatrist steadfastly denied that he had saved Lukas's life in the process, but Lukas knew better. Tortured by recurring nightmares and irrational bursts of panic, he had been on the brink of self-destruction when Keenan found him on the *Widdon Galaxy*. Lukas owed Keenan a debt he could never repay, even if Keenan had been willing to let him try.

He fears you, doesn't he? the Quayla asked. *He is uncomfortable around me and avoids you in consequence. At first, I thought he only needed time to accept me, but I have begun to doubt that he ever can or will.* The Quayla could not conceal its disappointment, any more than Lukas had been able to conceal his response to Keenan's rejection. Despite moments of intense joy, theirs had not always been a happy relationship. Thanks to the Quayla, Lukas had lost the trust of his own species. Thanks to Lukas, it had lost its purpose in life. Though it did not say so, he knew it missed the *Nieti*. Much as the Quayla enjoyed sharing his mind and sensations, they were no substitute for the challenge of running a starship.

Unfortunately, there was no going back, not for either of them. Lukas had spent a few weeks on a Miquiri ship, but he could not survive on their food and water, and he had been extremely uncomfortable in the lower temperatures they considered normal. He belonged among humans, whether they wanted him or not.

With the exception of the Michaelsons, most of them did not.

The Quayla's sigh was the sound of dry leaves blowing before a restless fall wind. *It is not easy,* it said, *but we will survive, both of us. We must.*

Lukas gave a mental nod of agreement, then moved abruptly, lifting his arm from Kiley's waist and pushing back the covers. *I think I'll visit Chirith,* he said. *It's been days since I've been off the ship—no wonder we're both so gloomy.*

Now? the Quayla asked, brightening immediately. To appease the Corps, it had promised that it would not leave the *Widdon Galaxy*, but it could travel with him in mind, if not body.

Now, Lukas said. He eased his way out of bed, then went to the bathroom to shower and dress. The rest of the family was still sleeping, and he didn't see anyone as he left the ship. The station was equally deserted. It was early morning, and no one would be moving around for several hours.

Lukas walked down the short access tube that connected the *Widdon Galaxy* to the station. He gave silent thanks as he went that he had watched the facility being built; otherwise he couldn't have found his way through the labyrinth of randomly connected sections. As it was, he made one wrong turn. The *North Star*'s engineers had been at work again, and instead of the module he expected to see on the far side of the station, he found himself in an empty room that led to two more connecting tubes. Uncertain which to take, he tried the corridor on his left. It led to a sealed door marked UNDER CONSTRUCTION. He backtracked, went down the right-hand corridor, and was rewarded by the sight of a red and white striped door at the end.

He pressed the control plate on the wall and the door opened immediately. The Miquiri had shown him honor in that—he was the only human who had free access to their quarters. Cool air rushed out, carrying a strong, spicy scent reminiscent of cinnamon.

The Miquiri smelled. Under most circumstances, the odor was pleasant, but when they were upset, they emitted a stench so foul that it made humans gag. The crews of the *Widdon Galaxy* and the *North Star* took great care not to upset the Miquiri, though not only for that reason. Humanity had roamed the stars for a millennium, but the Miquiri had been a spacegoing people for twice as long. The least of their ships was far superior to the best humans could offer. The Corps had little doubt about which side would prevail should they come to battle.

The Miquiri section of the station consisted of several linked modules. The first served as a common meeting room. To the left was a tube leading to cooking and dining facilities. The module off the back wall was the largest of the three, and had been partitioned into private rooms for the small contingent that stayed on the station permanently.

Since it was so early, Lukas was surprised to find a group of nine Miquiri already up and clustered together in the meeting room. Several inches shorter than humans, they were covered with thick, short hair that ranged in color from black to gray, or brown to auburn. They wore no clothing or ornamentation, and even though Lukas had spent weeks living among them, he still had difficulty distinguishing one from the other.

Their language consisted of a series of high-pitched whistles, supplemented by a large vocabulary of hand signals. The group had been holding an animated discussion when Lukas entered. One of them glanced up, saw him, and gave a shrill warning cry. Lukas's hands went to his ears in self-defense. He had worn protective earplugs during his stay on the *Nieti*; he wished he had thought to bring a pair on this excursion.

He stood still, giving the Miquiri time to identify him. They, too, had their problems recognizing individual humans. Even knowing that, he was uncomfortable in the silence. He did not relax until a gray Miquiri broke away from the edge of the group and hurried toward him.

Lukas, you are back! Chirith signaled excitedly. *Come in. Be welcome here.*

The tension broke as Lukas returned Chirith's welcome with a greeting of his own. He repeated the sign to the group as a whole. A few returned his gesture, but their interest in him was cursory. They turned away and huddled together again, continuing the conversation he had interrupted.

What's wrong? Lukas asked Chirith. *The others seem to be upset.*

The Gan-Tir are coming.

The Gan-Tir?

Chirith glanced at the rest of the group, then motioned Lukas to follow him. *Come. We will go to my room. I will explain there.*

Lukas hesitated, giving the agitated group an uneasy look, then followed the alien into the next chamber and down the long corridor that divided it in half. Chirith's room was the last one on the left. He opened the door with a touch and led the way in.

On Miquiri ships, chairs and beds were constructed of a rubbery, fluid substance that rose up out of the floor and hardened, molding itself to a person's body and offering perfect support. On the human station, the Miquiri's beds and chairs were made of similar, equally flexible materials, and were more comfortable than anything humans had to offer. Chirith motioned Lukas to a chair in the corner of the room. Lukas sat cautiously, knowing from experience that he would find the seat too low and small at first. The chair began oozing around him as soon as he was down, fitting itself to his body. He didn't relax until the chair stopped moving.

It is good to see you again, Chirith said warmly. He stopped at Lukas's side and pressed his arm, welcoming him again in the third and most intimate of the Miquiri languages—the language of touch. More an expression of feelings than actual words, touch was usually reserved for one's mate, young children, or one's *akia*. Chirith offered Lukas a great honor by speaking so intimately. Lukas responded with a quick touch of his own, reciprocating the greeting.

The Quayla's previous companion, Hinfalla, had been Chirith's *akia*, and many of Hinfalla's memories had still been present in the Quayla's mind when Lukas had joined with it. He had not been surprised to find he felt a special closeness to Chirith, but he had been startled to find that the alien shared his feelings. Chirith could have liked him for himself, but Lukas suspected that much of the Miquiri's regard resulted from the parts of Hinfalla Chirith saw living on in him.

You are well? Chirith asked, sitting on the bed.

Very. Sometimes, Lukas thought Chirith worried about him more than his own people did—and that was saying a lot.

You are not experiencing undue fatigue or difficulty sleeping? No difficulty concentrating?

I am fine, Chirith.

The Miquiri studied Lukas, as if attempting to measure the truth of that assertion. Lukas doubted that he could. Even aided by Hinfalla's and the Quayla's memories, Lukas noticed few changes in a Miquiri's appearance. Chirith might see gross physical differences, such as Lukas's hair turning blond, or a massive loss or gain of weight, but he would have a difficult time detecting the subtle alterations he sought.

The Miquiri must have reached that conclusion himself, for he sat back unhappily. *I expect you think me foolish to ask such questions each time we meet,* he said, making a deprecating gesture. *Perhaps I am, but problems can arise after a joining, even among Miquiri. The danger to a human is much greater for being unknown. I worry about you, Lukas. I do not wish to see you or the Quayla suffer in any manner.*

Lukas smiled. *Neither do I. I assure you, Chirith, we are both quite well. Your concern is appreciated, but* bekith. He used the Miquiri term deliberately; literally, it meant "Earth-based." The original definition of the term had been "without vision," and it had often been used to refer to those Miquiri who would not leave their homes for a life of trade among the stars. Colloquially, the word had come to mean "without sense or justification."

Chirith gave a short, high-pitched cry—the sound of laughter. *You have learned our language well, Lukas. If you say you are well, then I accept that. What about the Quayla? Does it prosper? Has it found a way to stay occupied?*

We have been working our way through the ship's library. The Quayla would have finished long ago if it had been able to access the computer directly, but we don't know what would happen if it tried, so it has to see through my eyes. It hasn't complained, but waiting for me to read everything word by word must be excruciating. It admits it is somewhat bored, but it has been idle before and survived. It will this time, too.

The last time you were here, you said the Michaelsons were planning to refit their ship soon. Have they made the arrangements yet?

Yes. We'll lay over at Resurrection on our next trip out.

Lukas, have you talked to them about giving the Quayla access to the ship's sensor system?

Yes.

Did they agree?

They had, but only after a long debate. Lukas and the Quayla had been studying starship design ever since the joining. They thought they had found a way to let the alien being interface with human sensors without interfering with the readings. As soon as Kiley had announced that the ship would undergo a refitting, Lukas had approached her.

"Can we talk?" he asked when they were alone in their cabin.

"Of course," Kiley said. She sat down on the edge of the bunk, leaving room for him to join her. He stayed in the center of the room.

"It's about the refitting," he began.

"Yes?"

"I was wondering if you would consider a few modifications to the ship's data-gathering systems when we install the new instrumentation."

"What kind of modifications?" Kiley had stiffened and her voice was a shade too neutral for comfort.

"Nothing major," he told her quickly. "I'll be happy to go over the details with Jon Robert, but basically they amount to installing a series of reflectors that duplicate the data stream along a second path—one the Quayla could enter. It's bored, Kiley. It needs to have some other source of input besides me, and it would like to feel that it's a part of the ship, not just a passenger on her."

"And for that you want us to create a second sensor system?"

"In essence, yes. It wouldn't cost much," he added hastily, guessing what her immediate objection would be. "It would mean a little extra work during the refitting, and we'd have to buy a few more parts, but in return we'd have a complete backup for all the sensors on board." He saw her expression start to harden and rushed on. "We aren't planning anything dangerous, Kiley. The Quayla would only attach itself to one sensor at a time, and it would be very careful to stay out of the primary system. Jon Robert can check every reading every step of the way to be certain it isn't affecting the data flow in any manner."

"What good will it do for the Quayla to read the sensors? It won't be able to act on anything it learns. It won't, will it?"

"No, of course not. I'm not talking about letting it into the ship's computers—just the sensors. We don't have any ulterior motives, in case that's what you're thinking," he added, flushing. "The Quayla will spend a great deal of time analyzing the data it's receiving, just as it would if it were operating the ship, but that's all it will do."

"What if one of the readings it gathered showed an anomaly, or grounds for concern? What would it do then?"

"Alert me. I'd tell you or Jon Robert right away, just as I would if I saw a warning light on the control board." Lukas took a step forward. "Kiley, I'm not trying to force you or the rest of the family into a decision you aren't ready for— honestly. It took the Miquiri years of engineering to develop computer systems the Quayla could interact with safely; we'll need just as long. All we're asking is that you let it have some source of input to occupy its mind."

"Assuming we did agree to this, can you guarantee that your idea will work without compromising any existing systems?"

"We'd have to run a few tests," he said eagerly, sensing victory, "but I don't foresee any problems. The Quayla hasn't affected anything else it's touched so far; I don't believe there will be any danger."

"Jon Robert told me that you'd been adding engineering manuals to the ship's library. Is this why? To find a way to let the Quayla read the sensors?"

"In the beginning? No. It was just interested in learning about human ships. It couldn't help seeing the possibilities, though."

"And now it wants to act on them," Kiley said. She sighed. "I guess I can't blame it for that. We knew what it was and what it needed when it came on board. That doesn't mean we're going to take chances for its sake, though—or that everyone will agree to proceed. I want you to go over your plan with Jon Robert. If he says it sounds reasonable, then I'll put it to a family vote."

"I'll talk to him first thing tomorrow."

"I'm not making promises," Kiley warned. "Even if you can convince him to give the Quayla a chance, the rest of the family could veto the idea. So could the Corps. We'll have to have their permission, if only because it's their people who will be installing the new parts."

"I understand that."

"What about the Quayla? Does it understand that even if we agree, the Corps might not?"

"Yes."

"Will it be upset if the decision doesn't go its way?"

"It would feel regret, but it would not be angry, if that's what you're suggesting."

"How much regret?" Kiley persisted. "Enough to want to go back to a Miquiri ship?"

"No. It can't go back, even if it did want to. It has to stay where I am—that's the obligation our bond imposes on it. It might decide to return to a Miquiri ship after I die, but not before." Lukas was still standing in the center of the room. He took a step toward her. "You don't have to worry about it, Kiley. The Quayla was idle for centuries before the Miquiri found it, and it survived. Time isn't the same for it as for us. If it has nothing to do, it can shut itself down to a minimal level of awareness. It's done it before, and it can do it again."

"But it wouldn't want to?"

"Of course not. Would you? But it will do what it has to."

She looked unhappy. "You don't give us any easy choices, do you?"

"I'm sorry. I don't mean to cause problems, honestly."

"I know." She sighed.

He sat down on the bunk. "I do love you," he said softly, putting his arms around her.

"And I love you," she said, turning to him. "That's what makes this all so very difficult."

It took Lukas two days to convince Jon Robert that his plan was sound, but the engineer finally had to admit he could find no technical objection to the modifications. Kiley called a family meeting. To Lukas's surprise, the debate was not as long or heated as he had feared. After a brief discussion, Kiley took the vote. With the exception of Keenan, who steadfastly abstained on the grounds he wasn't family, the agreement to proceed was unanimous.

Now Lukas told Chirith the outcome of the vote, then added, *We still don't have final approval from the Corps, though, and they have the ultimate say. Kiley is going to talk to Admiral Bergstrom today.* Admiral Partelli, the fleet commander at Resurrection, had had no objection to having his people do the additional work, but he had told Kiley that Admiral Bergstrom, the commanding officer at Sumpali, held the final authority to approve or disapprove the changes.

Surely he will agree? Chirith asked now. *The scientists on the* North Star *have been very curious about the Quaylas. I would be surprised if they passed up an opportunity to learn more about them.*

Your ships don't carry Corps personnel or dock at human stations. We do. Your people didn't learn to trust the Quayla overnight; mine will need time, too. Lukas shifted uneasily, thinking that was an understatement. He changed subjects abruptly. *How have you been? Are you adjusting to station life after so many years on a ship? Are you having any regrets about leaving the* Nieti?

The *Nieti* had been Chirith's home for his entire adult life, its crewmates his family. But after his *akia* died, Chirith had decided he wanted a change. Chirith hesitated before answering, as if unwilling to abandon the talk of the Quaylas and the Corps. *A few regrets, perhaps. Leaving one's family is always difficult, but sometimes it must be done. I could still give the* Nieti *my mind, but my heart was no longer with her. It was best to let someone else take over as* tsiri. *A wise captain knows when it is time to step aside.*

Will you ever go back to your ship? Lukas asked.

I might, someday, when there are not so many memories. For now, I am content to spend my days talking to you humans, learning your ways. I am curious about what you will make of the Gan-Tir.

You have spoken of them before. They're your closest neighbors, right? Why are they coming? To look us over?

It appears so, though with the Gan-Tir, one can never be certain. They learned about you from one of our ships. They decided to send an official delegation to meet you. It should arrive shortly.

And that isn't good? Some of the others appeared to be upset.

Chirith raised his hands and let them fall, giving the Miquiri equivalent of a shrug. *We have always maintained good relations with the Gan-Tir, and much of our trade is with them, but there is no real liking between us. They regard us with contempt. We, in turn, find them largely incomprehensible. They are old, Lukas, both individually and as a species. Most of them are past middle age, and they bear fewer and fewer children each year. They are a mercurial people and their actions often appear irrational. On one trip a Gan-Tir will be an ascetic, and the next a complete hedonist. A trader must determine their mood quickly and bring out the appropriate goods. They are easily insulted and slow to forgive offenses, either real or imagined. We treat them with great respect and wariness. Your people would be wise to do the same.*

Have you told the human diplomats this?

We tried, but Pitar says your people won't listen. He says they trust too much in their own judgment. Lukas, would you speak to them? Would you tell them we would not offer warnings without good cause?

I'll pass along what you've said, but I doubt they'll listen to me any more than to you.

All I ask is that you try. Dealing with the Gan-Tir has always been difficult, but it will be even more complicated now that you humans are part of the equation. The arrival of any new species upsets existing relationships. Ties are strained, particularly if new alliances are forged. We do not wish hostilities with you or them. A misunderstanding between any of us could mean disaster for all.

Chapter 5

Chirith talked to Lukas a short while longer before the human went back to his ship. Chirith saw him to the door, then turned around to face Pitar, the head of the Miquiri diplomatic team. He rose as soon as the door closed and came to Chirith. "Did you tell Lukas about the Gan-Tir?" Pitar asked anxiously.

"Yes," Chirith said. "He promised to convey our warning, but he has little confidence his people will listen to him, either."

"If they do not, they will soon discover their error," Pitar said harshly. "Unfortunately for us all, that knowledge may come too late."

"The humans are not without reason, Pitar, for all they are overly emotional. They have dealt cautiously with us; I do not believe they will treat the Gan-Tir any less carefully."

"We can hope," Pitar said, dismissing the subject with a short, chopping gesture. "What about Lukas and the Quayla? Did you ask how they are?"

"Yes. Lukas says that he is well. The Quayla is bored, but that is not unexpected under the circumstances. He says it accepts its position on the human's ship and does not chafe."

"It is not pressuring him, then?"

"I do not believe so, though he could be concealing much. He says his companions plan to modify their ship when they refit so the Quayla can read some of their instruments."

"It would be best if they did. Quaylas require constant stimulation. Without a ship to occupy their attention, they must live solely in the mind and body of their companion. Human emotions are volatile and their nervous systems are overly sensi-

36

tive. It would be most dangerous if Lukas's Quayla decided to explore the full range of human awareness and feelings out of boredom."

"You still fear human sensitivity, then?"

"The Quayla on the *Nieti* took months to overcome its longing for the excessive sensory input. Its new companion is not certain it will ever recover completely. It is not healthy to focus so strongly on the physical. It would have been better for us all if humans had proven unreceptive."

"Perhaps, but they are. The matter is out of our hands now."

"Is it?" Pitar asked. "The joining between Lukas and Quayla is still new. He could fail at any time. I know you have faith in him, and I am inclined to agree with your assessment, but the Assembly is not so certain. Their instructions are to watch him closely and to act if necessary."

Chirith did not answer. His hands fell to his sides, feeling suddenly weighted. Though it had not happened often, Quaylas and their companions had sometimes ceased to function normally. Usually the failure resulted from damage to the ship they traveled on, but on at least two occasions, a companion had lost rationality and taken its Quayla down the road to madness. The Miquiri had had no choice but to destroy the companion, the Quayla, and the ship upon which they traveled. Quaylas moved freely between ships docked in port, merging with each other and sharing all they had experienced; they could not chance a damaged one infecting others. If a Quayla failed, experience had taught them the only safe course was to eradicate it as ruthlessly as a virulent infection.

The very idea of taking life was repellent to the Miquiri. But as difficult as the decision was, there wasn't a *tsiri* who wouldn't issue the order if the need arose. Nor would it matter whether the ship being attacked was Miquiri or human. If a Quayla failed—any Quayla—it would be annihilated swiftly and resolutely, without regard to lives lost or diplomatic repercussions.

Pitar touched Chirith's shoulder. The gesture was so unexpected, Chirith jumped.

"I am afraid for you," Pitar said. "You have become at-

tached to the human. I am compelled to remind you that you
are here to observe and evaluate, not befriend. I know you feel
lost and lonely without your *akia*, but you will not find a re-
placement for him among humans."

"I do not seek another *akia*, Pitar."

"You should. You have held yourself apart from the group
too long. It is time to stop mourning Hinfalla and look to those
who still live." Pitar touched Chirith's arm. *I am here,* he said
in the third language. *I would come closer. Will you let me?*

Chirith jerked away before he could stop himself, his un-
thinking rejection so immediate and forceful that it could only
be construed as an insult. Except, perhaps, by one who understood what he felt. He was not the only one who had lost an
akia recently; Pitar had, too. Knowing that, Chirith forced himself to stand still as Pitar touched his arm again.

I, too, grieve, the diplomat said, *but it does not have to be
thus for either of us. Will you think upon that, Chirith? Please?*

It was not good to be alone. Pitar knew that; so did Chirith.
Even so, he could not bring himself to offer the response Pitar
wanted.

I will think about what you have said, he told Pitar in the
second language. It was language of communication, not of
feelings, or sharing, or closeness. It was the language of strangers, not *akia*s. Pitar stiffened. He pretended he was not hurt,
but excused himself immediately and left. Chirith wanted to
run after him and tell him that he had not meant to offer rejection. Instead, he stood still. His thoughts were not happy as he
stared down the empty corridor, and his feelings, as at all too
many other times recently, were too heavy to bear.

Kiley met the *North Star*'s commanding officer, Admiral
Paul Bergstrom, in a reception room just off the main entrance
to the Corps ship.

A tall, angular man, he had fair skin, pale blue eyes, and
hair so light that it was hard to tell how much was blond and
how much white. She had spoken with him several times before, and he always made her uncomfortable. He radiated determination and authority, and had little tolerance for dissent.

You could argue with him, but you had better be certain of your ground before taking a stand; otherwise, he would cut you off at the knees.

Bergstrom motioned her to a chair near the door and Kiley sat down, wishing there were someone else she could ask for assistance. But there wasn't. Every private contractor on Resurrection had refused to take on the job of refitting the *Widdon Galaxy*. Bergstrom and Partelli had agreed to supply a work crew, but in return they wanted the *Widdon Galaxy* to make three runs between Sumpali and Resurrection at no charge to the Corps. The terms had been steep, but not beyond the family's resources, so Kiley had agreed. Getting Bergstrom to approve Lukas's modifications, however, was another matter. He heard her out, then answered with a single word.

"No."

"Admiral, I can understand your concern." Kiley struggled to contain a flash of panic. She had come prepared for an argument, but she had not expected such a flat refusal. "I hesitated, too, at first. But the Quayla won't be interacting with any of the ship's systems. Both Greg and my brother have gone over the modifications carefully and agree that they don't constitute a risk. The *Widdon Galaxy* is my family's home—believe me, none of us are about to take chances with her. Won't you at least have your chief engineer look over the idea before you reject it out of hand? I promise, if she can find any reason not to proceed, I'll let the matter drop immediately."

Bergstrom was a busy man. He weighed the stubborn jut of Kiley's chin against the merits of foisting her off on a junior officer, and decided.

"Very well, Captain. I will ask Ms. Radik to talk with your brother and Lukas. I will withhold my final decision until I've heard her report, but I warn you, I do not anticipate changing my mind."

Kiley didn't argue. She was lucky to have won that large a concession.

Bergstrom kept his word. He sent his chief engineer, Kathryn Radik, over to the *Widdon Galaxy* later that day, and she spent several hours with Jon Robert and Lukas. They must have made a convincing case, because she went away promising to speak to Bergstrom immediately. Even so, it was the next day before Kiley was summoned back to the *North Star.* Bergstrom met her in the same reception room.

"Captain, sit down," he said by way of greeting. Kiley sat. Bergstrom did not. But if he expected her to feel cowed at the sight of him standing over her, he failed. She had learned the tricks of command from a master—her father. Some he had taught her deliberately, but others, including the choice of physical position, she had learned from observation.

"Ms. Radik was very impressed by your proposal," Bergstrom went on. "So much so, she and several of my scientists have convinced me that we should allow you to proceed. There will, however, be several conditions."

"Which are?"

"First, that you convert one of your holds into passenger cabins, as we discussed previously. Nearly half your revenue is coming from passengers; it isn't fair to ask them to put up with your current makeshift accommodations. You will be carrying civilian researchers soon, and I can guarantee they won't be as tolerant of your facilities as Corps personnel have been."

"Adding the cabins is no problem, Admiral. We've already drawn up plans to convert one of the holds."

"Good. My second condition is that you let Corps engineers conduct a thorough inspection of your ship and systems after the Quayla has attached itself, both at Resurrection and here. I want to be absolutely certain it's not affecting them."

"I have no objection to that," Kiley agreed. She didn't welcome the intrusion, but the temporary loss of privacy was a small price to pay. Bergstrom's final request, however, had a more tangible impact.

"While the modifications are minimal, they will entail additional work for the refitters. With that in mind, I am going to ask that you make a fourth run at no charge to the Corps as reimbursement for our laborers' time."

"You want us to make four runs for free? Admiral, I don't want to plead financial hardship, but we can't afford that! We can barely afford the three we've already agreed to. To make another, we'd have to take out a lien on the ship. Even if I were willing to do that—and I'm not—no one on Resurrection would give us one."

"Sorry, Captain, but four is my final offer. I will, however, be flexible about the timing of the last one. If you will make three runs immediately, I will give you one calendar year to complete the fourth. That should allow you sufficient time to rebuild your financial reserves. Will that be acceptable?"

Reese would have a fit over the additional lost revenue, but Kiley couldn't see an alternative. If she tried to bargain with Bergstrom, he was likely to withdraw his offer completely.

"That will be acceptable," she said, swallowing.

She rose and they shook hands on the deal. Bergstrom's grip was one vise twist short of crushing. Kiley massaged her hand all the way back to the *Widdon Galaxy*.

"You've been losing weight," the *North Star*'s chief medical officer said accusingly at the end of Keenan's physical examination. The Corps insisted on checking at least one of the ship's crew after every run, and Keenan's name had come to the top of the list again.

"Just trying to keep in shape," Keenan replied casually. This was the first time Elderbrandt had examined him. He had assumed that meant the *North Star*'s scientific team was losing interest in him and the rest of the *Widdon Galaxy*'s crew after months of exhaustive tests. But if he'd imagined that being transferred to the ship's regular physician meant a slacking of official concern, he'd been very much mistaken.

A big man, Elderbrandt had a broad, bony forehead, deep-set eyes, a fleshy nose, and huge hands with thick, stubby fingers. But though his body would have looked more at ease in a gymnasium than a sick bay, his manner was thoroughly professional; he gave Keenan the most comprehensive examination he had had in months. When he finished, his expression was ominous.

"Are you certain you're feeling well?" he demanded.

"Positive," Keenan replied, sitting up.

"Well, I'm not. If you're losing weight, there must be a reason. And don't feed me any more stories about trying to get in shape, either, because they won't wash. You're not building muscle tone—you're losing it. I'm going to order a complete workup. It will take the rest of the day. You don't have any pressing duties on your ship, do you?"

"No," Keenan answered, wishing he did.

"Good. Come with me. We'll get started right away."

Elderbrandt ran him through every diagnostic test the *North Star*'s technicians could perform. There wasn't a part of his body that someone didn't check at least once. And when the physical inspection was over, he was given a series of psychological tests. Keenan was surprised that Elderbrandt even considered them, given his familiarity with the questions. Elderbrant must have reached the same conclusion, because he took one look at the report and then shut his computer off in disgust.

"I should have known better than to expect honest answers from a psychiatrist," he said, turning around to scrutinize Keenan. "I don't care what you or the tests say—my instincts tell me something is wrong. The problem isn't physical, so I can only conclude you're suffering from mental or emotional stress. I want to know what's wrong."

"I told you, Doctor, I'm fine."

Elderbrandt obviously didn't believe him. "Daniel, I can understand that you may be reluctant to confide in a physician you've never seen before," he said, deliberately softening his manner, "but I am genuinely concerned about you. I assure you, I will hold anything you say in strictest confidence. If something is troubling you, I want you to tell me."

"You're imagining things, Doctor. I've lost a few pounds I should have taken off years ago. That's all."

Elderbrandt gave Keenan a long look. "Very well," he said at last. "I can't force you to talk to me. On the other hand, I *can* order you to report back here after your next run. If you've lost so much as one more pound, I will have you confined to the *North Star*'s sick bay until I find out what's wrong—and I will find out, doctor. You have my word on that."

Chapter 6

One week into the refitting, Kiley decided they must have been out of their minds to open their ship and their lives to strangers.

The work had begun as soon as they returned to Resurrection. A pressurized enclosure was rigged around the *Widdon Galaxy*'s assigned dock; then the ship's aging engines were detached, leaving huge openings in her stern. Kiley had nightmares about the protective enclosure failing until the new engines were in place and the ship had been sealed again.

A constant flow of people came and went through the access tube. All belonged to the Corps, and all had security clearances, but Kiley was still uncomfortable about having so many strangers on board. They were uncomfortable, too. At Lukas's prompting, the Quayla had retreated deep inside the ship's bulkheads for the duration of the refitting, but the military personnel knew it was on board and looked for it everywhere. Rumors about the alien light circulated freely, and the men and women jumped at every unexpected sound or movement. Jon Robert had expressed understandable concern about the quality of the work being done.

As the ship's engineer, he was officially in charge of the refitting. Still, Kiley spent a good portion of her day walking around the *Widdon Galaxy*, checking on the work crews' progress and observing the installation of the new equipment. When she wasn't doing that, she sat in the common room or the cabin she shared with Lukas, studying.

Ship's systems had changed significantly in the years since the *Widdon Galaxy* had been built. Everything was different:

the terminology in the manuals, command sequences, the arrangement of monitors and buttons on the boards ... It was going to take weeks to become comfortable with the new systems, and months to know them so well that she no longer had to think before reaching for a control. If she had had any idea how sweeping the changes would be, she didn't think she would have had the courage to proceed with the refitting. But it was too late to change her mind now, so she struggled hour after hour to cram in as much information as she could.

Lukas had to study, too, but he had trained on newer systems at the Academy, so nothing was quite so unfamiliar to him. He also had a distinct advantage in the Quayla: it absorbed everything he read on the first pass and made the information available to him again instantly if he needed it. He still had to go through the material, but he didn't have to memorize it. Kiley did.

Lukas finished reading the pilot's manuals in two days, then moved on to the engineering documentation. Kiley didn't object. Jon Robert was familiarizing himself with the new systems as they were being set into place, but he did not have time to read the accompanying manuals. Lukas's familiarity with the written documentation meant that he and the Quayla would have an encyclopedic store of information available for instant recall if Kiley's brother needed assistance. She appreciated the benefits of that, but she wasn't entirely sure that Jon Robert did.

"Time for a break," Lukas said one evening shortly before the refitting was finished. Kiley had been concentrating so intently on the screen before her that she started when he spoke. He crossed the room to the desk and looked over her shoulder. "What are you working on?"

She tilted the screen so he could see it. "External monitor systems. There are three hundred external cameras," she recited from memory, "and over two thousand short- and long-range sensors. There are nearly four thousand internal sensors. The main computer can generate two thousand standard reports, and we can add an additional six thousand customized reports. Greg, how am I ever going to learn all this?" Her voice rose in despair.

"One report at a time," he said calmly. "The same way you learned the old ones."

"But you and the Quayla are already working on the engineering systems and I haven't even mastered the control board layout!"

"So? By the time the new systems are installed, the ship will practically run herself. That was one of the reasons for the refitting. I do wish we had access to a simulation board, though. You'd find it much easier to retain so much detail if you could see and touch the controls you're reading about. Learning in a vacuum can't help but be frustrating."

"It is that," she said grimly, switching off the monitor. She expected Lukas to back up as she rose, but instead he put his arms around her and kissed her. When she did not respond, he leaned back and studied her face.

"Kiley, relax," he urged. "You're trying to learn everything all at once, and you can't. No one can. Absorb what you can, but don't worry about the rest. You can pick up the details as we go along."

"And in the meantime, I should rely on you to run the ship?"

"Would that be so very terrible?" he asked, tilting his head to one side.

"Yes, it would! This is my ship. I don't like relying on anyone else to operate her, not even you."

Lukas sighed. "Somehow, that doesn't come as a great surprise—you wouldn't be captain if you did. I can't deny that I don't like seeing you push yourself so hard when it isn't necessary, but I can't blame you, either. I expect I'd feel the same way if our positions were reversed." He let go of her. "Come on. We're late for dinner, and you need to eat if you're going to stay up half the night studying."

They headed for the door, but before Lukas could go into the hall, she stopped him with a hand to his forearm and gave him a quick kiss. "Thank you for understanding. It won't be this way forever, I promise."

He smiled. "It won't be this way past midnight."

He was right.

Gareth Hastings was fifteen minutes late for work, but no one commented; the entire shift had been held up by a crowd of locals protesting at the security gate. The people had not carried signs, chanted, barricaded the gates, or otherwise harassed those who tried to enter. They had simply milled about, impeding traffic and offering a silent, stubborn protest against the *Widdon Galaxy*, the Corps, and all the strangers who had invaded their home.

The security guard at the ship's personnel hatch recognized Hastings and waved him on board without checking his ID, and he threaded his way through the maze of cables and people that lined the main corridor. The deck plates along both bulkheads had been raised, revealing the channels beneath. Men and women sat or squatted all along the openings, checking out pipes, tubes, and sensor relays. Piles of equipment and tools were scattered everywhere. As always, Hastings had difficulty believing that order could arise from such chaos, but it did. It had to, or the ship would never run again.

"Evening, Gareth," the operations chief in charge of the refitting said as he walked on the bridge.

Hastings nodded to Zeller, returning the greeting, but his eyes were on the new control board. Zeller had been worried about the fit, but the measurements they'd received had been correct to the millimeter. The board hugged the bulkhead so tightly that there was no telling where the ship ended and it began.

Hastings crossed the bridge, sat in the pilot's seat, and scanned the unlit controls. At the rate they were going, they would complete work on the ship in another two days. After that she would make an initial shakedown cruise, then depart for Sumpali again, leaving in far better condition than she'd arrived.

"The day shift finished work in the computer room this afternoon," Zeller said, coming over to stand beside Hastings. "You can install the programs tonight, if you brought them."

Zeller's eyes roamed the boards critically as he spoke, look-ing for the slightest dent, the tiniest flaw. He did not aim for perfection—he achieved it, one hundred percent of the time. That uncompromising attitude made him the most sought-after chief in the fleet—and a class-A bastard to work for if you didn't give him your best. Hastings did, and as a result, he was Zeller's first choice among systems specialists.

Hastings gestured to the soft-sided brown bag he carried over one shoulder. "They're right here."

"Have at it, then. The sooner we finish this job, the happier I'll be."

You and me both, Hastings thought as Zeller turned to an-other worker and started quizzing him on his progress. Hastings had never seen the chief so edgy before, and his ner-vousness was contagious. They all couldn't wait to get off the ship.

Hastings stood and went to the computer room across the passage from the bridge. There was hardly space to slip be-tween the banks of newly installed cabinets. A steady elec-tronic hum filled the air with the sound of life, and cool air brushed past his face as he inspected the rows of equipment. He took a deep breath and relaxed for the first time that day. Like all computer rooms, this one spoke of order and purpose. The pure functionality of the cabinets and the intricate systems they housed were the closest thing to perfect beauty that Gar-eth Hastings knew.

He closed his eyes momentarily, savoring his solitude. Only he and Zeller had access to the room now that the computers were up and running, and Zeller would not disturb him. The operations chief knew that any lapse of concentration during software installation could lead to a critical mistake, and he trusted Hastings to do the job and do it right. That was more than he could say about others on his crew. He would be too busy overseeing them to spare a second thought for Hastings.

To work, then.

Hastings opened the bag he had carried on board. Inside were seventeen round, flat disks that contained all the code needed to operate the ship's main, navigation, engineering, and environmental computers. He lifted the first one with long, sure fingers and held it up to the light, examining it. The gold surface gleamed softly. The code on it and the next fifteen disks was faultless. The same instructions had been installed on nearly ten thousand ships, and it had never failed. Not once. The seventeenth disk was another matter. It contained recent updates to the original programs and a new one that was all his own.

Hastings turned to the control board at his right. Gibberish filled the row of monitors before him, but that would change soon. He touched a panel on the wall and it slid open, revealing a small niche. He set the first disk inside the opening and it disappeared, as if sliding down an invisible throat. A moment later, symbols started to fill the first monitor in the row. They moved slowly at first, but they were soon scrolling by too quickly to be read. When the scrolling stopped, the program prompted him to choose the first of over seven hundred setup options he would decide upon that night. He pressed a key, entering his instruction, and the scrolling started again.

The first disk popped out and he inserted the second, then later the third. One hour passed, and another. The screen had stopped scrolling so rapidly by the time he reached the tenth disk, and he had to enter more and more preferences. He did so without hesitation. He had performed this installation so many times that he could have done it in his sleep.

The shift was nearly over by the time the sixteenth disk re-emerged from the computer. He picked up the seventeenth. His fingers paused on the brink of releasing it; then he let it fall into the niche. The screen scrolled, stopped, then scrolled a final time. The disk popped out.

It was done.

There had been only one risky moment, and it had passed. He was safe. Hastings put the disk back and slung the bag over his shoulder. He took one last look around the room. Orderly displays lit all the monitors, and the computers hummed softly. He loved them. He always had. Electronic extensions of the human brain, computers quietly oversaw the mundane details of existence, leaving people free to concentrate on more important matters.

A thousand years and millions of lives had gone into the design of the systems people relied on. Not all of the programmers had been benevolent. In their own self-interest, those who were had banded together, forming the most rigid code of ethics known to any professional group in history. Before they were permitted to study advanced courses, each would-be programmer took an oath that he or she would never write or knowingly implement any code that restricted the basic rights accorded every human being at birth. They swore to delete upon discovery any program that violated that oath. That second promise was the reason for the lines of additional code Hastings had written.

The officer who had briefed the work crew assembled to refit the *Widdon Galaxy* had warned them that the vessel harbored an alien being. He said it had no physical body and assured them that it constituted no threat to human life or health. Gareth Hastings disagreed.

He had heard about the Quayla within weeks of its discovery. Though wary, the Corps officers who had spoken about it were already claiming that it would prove to be a technological advance as great, or greater than, jump. They were so busy expounding the Quayla's potential that they overlooked the threat it represented. However much they likened it to a computer, there was a vital difference between it and the systems Gareth Hastings helped create and maintain: the Quayla was alive. It did not operate according to carefully written code that could be examined and altered by any programmer—it had a mind and will of its own. It might be far more powerful and efficient than any machine humans could design, but it could not be trusted.

What could not be programmed could not be controlled, and that which could not be controlled could not be allowed to control. The sum of human history could be stated in one simple admonition: Surrender the least right, the least freedom, and before you know it, oppression will be knocking at your door.

The Michaelsons wanted to give the Quayla control of their ship. There was no other explanation for some of the modifications they had insisted on making. And the Corps, which should have been the most outspoken defender of human liberty, was letting them proceed. No one had sounded a single note of caution or alarm. Someone had to stop the madness before it spread and did irreparable harm.

Someone would. Gareth Hastings had seen to that.

Chapter 7

Sensar had no difficulty obtaining a position on the contact mission; he was the only scholar to request inclusion. The rest of the group consisted of diplomatic personnel. Since the diplomatic community on Gan-Tir was quite small, the others knew each other well, and he felt out of place among them. He did not share their interests and he was not familiar with their rivalries, past and present. He had little to say to them, or they to him. He ate with them, but he spent the rest of his time in his cabin on the ship's third deck.

Traveling on a spaceship did not disturb him, as it did some Gan-Tir, but he did require privacy. Unlike the diplomats, he had no tolerance for frequent, incidental contact. The ship's captain had not wanted him so far from the others, and had objected that the berths on the third deck were not fit for a man of Sensar's stature. Sensar persisted. The captain, who had more pressing concerns, had finally conceded.

Sensar chose a cabin at random, selecting one halfway down the corridor. The furnishings were few and austere: a bed, a closet, and a few built-in shelves. He felt at home immediately. Several of the diplomats followed his lead and investigated the third-deck quarters. To his relief, they all decided to remain in their original cabins, which were larger and more luxurious. They were also closer to the ship's crew.

Few Gan-Tir traveled the star roads any longer, and those who did were considered nearly as exotic as the aliens with whom they dealt. For most Gan-Tir, exotic was synonymous with fascinating. Several in the mission had already engaged in liaisons with crew members. They had not lasted long; relationships built on a fascination for the unknown rarely proved fulfilling. Lasting unions required the kind of contempt that came only with familiarity. One's worse enemies almost always made one's best lovers.

Sensar Kaikiel Anara's worst enemy was on the ship.

He had met Rairea Tayturin a year before he achieved scholar's rank, while working as a translator to support himself and finishing his studies at the university. From time to time, he was called upon to attend governmental gatherings, and it was at one of those that he met Rairea.

A born manipulator, she had turned her skills to diplomacy as soon as she left school. She was the youngest person ever chosen to serve as an official government representative. Her enemies—and they were many—claimed that her skills were of the body, not the mind. They said she used chemicals that enhanced her natural attractors so that those who faced her across the table could no longer reason clearly. They might have been believed had she not had the same impact on Miquiri, who were theoretically immune to Gan-Tir attractors. Her skills were as much mental as physical, and they were phenomenal.

Sensar had taken one look at her and decided she was the most dazzling person he had ever seen. There wasn't a male or female in the room who didn't immediately feel drawn to her. She could have had anyone at the gathering, but she had chosen him. She had chosen him because he turned his back on her.

Young males were taught from the day they came of age that sexual encounters were degrading and demoralizing. Sensar had resolved never to be drawn by a female, and until that evening his determination had been sufficient to discourage almost all who had pursued him. A few had persisted, but not for long. Their fertile periods were too short to waste time chasing males who resisted their advances. Rairea, however, was not fertile, and she loved nothing better than the conquest and domination of unwilling males.

He could have escaped her so easily. A casual tilt of the head, a token acknowledgment of her power, and she would have immediately lost interest. But he had been too naive to understand that, and had pretended a complete lack of interest. His defiance captured her attention. She pursued him relentlessly, both that evening and in the days that followed. She placed herself in his path wherever he went, filling the air between them with attractors so powerful that he was still feeling the effects hours later. Within a week, he could not work, eat, or sleep. By the time she took him into her quarters, he offered a prayer of thanksgiving that his torment would soon be over.

Except that it wasn't. He expected Rairea to lose interest in him after their first time together, but she did not. She liked him. She liked the taste of his body. She liked the sound of his voice, begging her to end his humiliation and set him free.

She broke him. He would have done anything for her, any place, any time. Would and did. And then, as quickly as she had been drawn to him, she lost all interest—he was no longer a challenge. When she told him to go, he clung to her, his body flooded with chemicals, desperate for the release only she could give him. He begged for just one more day. Just one. But she laughed and closed the door in his face.

He had not seen her again until he boarded the ship and found that she was the third ranking diplomat on the mission to Sumpali.

He had been unable to hide his dismay when he caught sight of her. She had been waiting for his reaction, and her smile was not pleasant. They were formally introduced a short time later. Sensar bowed to her as if she were a stranger. She uncoiled her left *elith* from her arm and extended it. He hesitated, then touched her tentacle with his, offering the formal greeting he would have given any new acquaintance. He expected her to settle for touching tips—a polite tasting—but as the head of the delegation turned away, Rairea's *elith* shot up the long, loose sleeve of his robe. She wrapped her tentacle around his limbs with a speed and strength that stunned him. She squeezed gently, then began stroking his *elith*. She paused over the joint where it separated from his arm, found the point she wanted, and squeezed again, much harder.

Was it agony or ecstasy he felt? He had never been able to

decide, nor had any other Gan-Tir. Sensation drove all reason from his mind. His legs buckled and he only just choked back a cry that would have resulted in public humiliation. By the time he recovered, Rairea had released him and was stepping away, acting as if nothing had happened. "It is good to see you again, Sensar Kaikiel," she said.

"And you, Rairea Tayturin," he replied, his mind recovering faster than his body. He bowed his head deferentially. He had learned his lesson; he knew better than to offer challenge.

"I was delighted to find your name on the list of delegates. I hope we will see much of each other on the trip."

She mocked him. She always had. But he was not without resources of his own. He called on years of discipline and replied calmly. "Rairea, I cannot, of course, be certain of the intention implicit in your statement, but if you believe that you can resume our relationship where we left off, you are wrong. I now follow the ways of *jis*."

She laughed. "You? Abstentious? You might deceive others, Sensar Kaikiel, but you cannot pretend with me. You want me. You always did. You always will. I believe I want you, too. It has been some time since I enjoyed a lover with your reticence. I have been looking forward to the opportunity to renew our acquaintance."

"Rairea, I am *jis*," he said, proud that his voice was firm and calm. "You cannot have what I do not choose to give. I have no interest in you and I will not respond."

"No? You may think so, but I know you, Sensar Kaikiel. I know you better than you know yourself. You may have held to the ways of *jis* with other females, but you will not with me. Still, try if you wish. It has been my experience that denial only increases the pleasure of the ultimate union."

And then, without another word, she had turned aside to speak with another member of the mission. He had seen her only once since that evening, and she had not so much as looked at him. He wondered if she thought she was tormenting him. If so, she was not succeeding. He had spent years learning to control his body and mind, and she could not compel him to respond against his will again. He would not let her.

He didn't dare.

Chapter 8

The *Widdon Galaxy* made a short shakedown cruise to test the new engines and computer systems, then returned to Resurrection and spent another three days in port while the Quayla attached itself to the set of parallel sensors. Jon Robert watched the process every step of the way, but despite his best efforts, he could find no sign that the alien life-form was affecting any of the readings feeding into the computers.

Without giving the matter much thought, both he and Kiley had assumed the Quayla would automatically understand the information it could now access, and they were surprised to learn that this was not the case. Lukas had to monitor the readings on the boards and compare them with the impressions the Quayla was receiving before it could turn what it perceived into meaningful information. Lukas said it would take days, possibly even weeks, before the Quayla would be able to interpret all the data available to it, let alone begin to analyze it and provide him with detailed reports.

Jon Robert relaxed after that, but Lukas did not. He had not slept more than two or three consecutive hours since the Quayla began reading the data from the sensors, and he had developed a disconcerting habit of going completely blank at unexpected intervals, turning his attention inward for minutes at a time. When he came back, he would pick up where he'd left off, as if unaware he had been gone. He insisted he was fine, but the night before they were due to leave for Sumpali, Kiley told him she wanted him to see Keenan for a physical examination.

"Why?" Lukas demanded. "I admit that I'd forgotten how

tiring it can be to receive a constant flow of information, but I'll get used to it. The Quayla was doing much more on the *Nieti* than it is here, and I didn't have any problem once I'd adjusted. I'll be fine."

Kiley wanted to believe him, but she remembered the man who had come back from the Miquiri ship. Lukas had been gaunt and utterly fatigued. At the time, he had attributed his condition to difficulties adjusting to an alien environment and the hours he had spent being questioned by the Miquiri on Sumpali. There had also been the stress he'd undergone when the Quayla separated, part of it coming with him and part staying behind with its new companion. Any one of those factors could have explained his condition, and she had accepted them as the cause of his fatigue. Now, however, she found herself wondering whether he had been completely honest—not only with her, but with himself.

"That's probably true," she said, holding her ground, "but I'll still feel better if Daniel looks you over."

"I had a checkup last month. I don't need another one so soon."

"I'm sorry, Greg, but I think you do. I don't want to be difficult, but if I have to, I'll relieve you from duty until I'm convinced you're fit."

"Kiley—"

"I mean that, Greg. Go see Daniel. He's waiting for you in his cabin."

Keenan had been dreading Lukas's visit all afternoon. He had debated leaving the ship for days, and had finally reached a decision that morning. The hours he had spent reading the manuals for the new flight-control systems had convinced him that he could not stay on the ship any longer. He was a psychiatrist, not a pilot, and it was time he got on with his life. The Corps might detain him temporarily, but afterward he would be free to go where he wanted and do what he wanted.

Most of all, if he left, he would not have to see Elderbrandt again. The physician was too perceptive. Keenan did not think he would be put off by further assertions that nothing was wrong—not when something so patently was.

He was reaching into his closet for his duffel bag when Kiley called to tell him that Lukas was on the way. The pilot arrived a few minutes later. He was not happy. Keenan told him to undress and lie down, then pulled a bioscanner out of his medical kit and began running it over him.

"Kiley tells me you haven't been sleeping well."

"Kiley worries too much," Lukas said shortly. His fingers were clenched and his heartbeat increased as he spoke.

"Does she?" Keenan asked absently, moving the scanner to the other side of Lukas's chest.

"Generally speaking, yes."

Keenan's eyes flickered to Lukas's face, measuring the depth of his hostility. Seeing nothing more than momentary irritation, he relaxed. "Captains have a lot to worry about," he said mildly.

Lukas did not reply. He continued to stare up at the ceiling, his expression a study in exaggerated patience. He did not move until Keenan finished, but then he stood quickly and started pulling on his pants and shirt.

Keenan dumped the bioscanner readings into the portable medical computer on his desk. He sat down and spent the next few minutes studying them.

"Well?" Lukas demanded after Keenan had gone through the results for the second time.

Keenan gave the screen a final look, then turned to him. "As usual, you are in excellent physical condition. Your heart, lungs, kidneys, liver, and motor functions are all within normal tolerances."

"I told you this was a waste of time."

"So you did."

"And you'll tell Kiley that I'm fit for duty?"

"Yes."

Lukas nodded stiffly and started for the door.

"Greg, wait," Keenan said, gathering up his courage.

Lukas swung back, impatient again. "Yes?"

"There's something I need to tell you." He took a deep

breath. "I've decided to leave the ship. I was starting to pack when Kiley called to say she was sending you down."

"You're leaving?" Lukas repeated, looking stunned. "Daniel, why?"

"It's time I got on with my own life. I never meant to stay past Hope's birth. The refitting reminded me I'm not a pilot—I'm a psychiatrist. I don't want to spend months learning the new systems. I need to get back to the work I care about, the work I chose to do and trained for."

"I know that learning the new boards isn't easy," Lukas said, "but it won't be long before they're as familiar as the old ones. It's not as if you're alone—we're all having to relearn everything we took for granted a few weeks ago."

"The only difference is that you and Kiley want to learn. I don't. No, don't bother arguing. I've made up my mind. I'm going."

"Daniel, what's really wrong?" Lukas searched his face. "Something is—you've been avoiding me for weeks. It can't be this refitting. If I know you, you have the control manuals memorized by now, even if you aren't exactly sure how to apply all you've learned. It's the Quayla, isn't it? You're leaving because of it."

"No! The Quayla has nothing to do with this!"

"Doesn't it?" Lukas demanded roughly. He took a step forward. "I should have talked to you weeks ago. I knew I needed to, but I was afraid I'd make matters worse."

"Greg, I don't know what you're talking about, but whatever it is doesn't matter. I'm leaving the ship because I want to, not because of you or the Quayla."

"That's not true. If you really wanted to go, you'd have left after Hope was born. Instead, you stayed on. I wasn't surprised about that. The Michaelsons are good people, and you were in a position to do something you always said you'd wanted to do—speak to aliens. I remember how excited you were about the possibility back at the Academy. You were fascinated by the concept of biological blinders. You always said that if the culture in which we're raised shapes our perceptions, how much more of what we see and believe is controlled by our physical nature? You said we would never know the answer to that until we could look out through the eyes of another species. Only now that you have an opportunity to do that, you're ignoring it. You haven't made a single attempt to talk to the Miquiri. You haven't because you're afraid, and it's all my fault."

"Your fault?" Keenan repeated, startled. "I don't know what makes you think that, but whatever it is, you're wrong."

"Am I?" Lukas took a breath and said, "Daniel, have you ever wondered why the Quayla doesn't come into your cabin?"

Keenan's eyes flickered to the bare walls before he could stop them. It was true—even when Lukas came in, the Quayla stayed out. His cabin was the only place on the ship that it did not go. The only place.

"I—maybe I have," he admitted reluctantly.

"It doesn't come in because you don't want it."

"You knew that and told it to stay out?"

"No, not me. You."

"Me?" Keenan exclaimed. "How?"

"Whether you realize it or not, you're projecting a great deal of hostility toward the Quayla. So much so, it is acutely uncomfortable around you."

"Are you trying to tell me that it knows what I feel?"

Lukas hesitated. "Yes. At least, to a certain extent."

"Do the others know it can sense their feelings?"

"No—because it can't. The only person it's aware of besides me is you. I don't know quite how to say this, Daniel, but the fact is, you appear to share that awareness. Not consciously, perhaps, but on some level. In retrospect, I think that's why you reacted so strongly to the Quayla the first time you saw it. Initial hostility is one of the first signs of receptivity. I should have realized that at the time, but I didn't; too many other things were going on. It was only recently, when your feelings seemed to be strengthening instead of subsiding, that I started to wonder. I should have said something to you weeks ago, but I was afraid I'd upset you more. I was wrong not to talk to you, though. If I had explained—"

"Greg, are you saying that the Quayla might actually be able to talk to me?" Keenan interrupted, staring at Lukas in horror. "Are you saying that it could join with me the way it joined with you?"

"No! It has only one companion at a time. For now, that's me. At most, you could probably only share a few simple emotions, or impressions. Before you could even do that much, though, you would have to indicate your willingness to do it. I know this is upsetting, but I swear, you don't have to worry about the Quayla approaching you. Communication requires more than physical ability—it demands a mental and emotional openness that you simply do not have."

"If I did, would it try to talk to me?" Keenan asked warily.

"It might. It's very curious about humans. It wouldn't forgo an opportunity to explore someone else's mind and perceptions easily."

"Is it upset with me?" Keenan asked abruptly. "It must be, if it perceives me as being hostile."

"No, of course not. It understands that not everyone welcomes contact with it. That's true among Miquiri, as well as humans. I admit that it would like to have access to your room so it could read the sensors, but that isn't vital since it doesn't have to control the air or temperature in here. It is uncomfortable about the gap in its awareness, but it can live with that. It won't come in unless you invite it."

"Good," Keenan said vehemently, "because I don't want anything to do with it."

"I know." Lukas hesitated, then said carefully, "Daniel, if you truly want to leave, then I won't say another word to stop you, but I wish you'd reconsider. I think you've found something on this ship—something you only just realized you were missing. I think that's why you've stayed this long, and I don't want to see you lose it."

"Lose what?"

"Life in the Corps can be very lonely," Lukas replied obliquely. "I learned that when I became commanding officer of the *Kelsoe Moran*. I think you discovered that, too, after you went to work for Section Two. You traveled constantly, and working for internal affairs meant you were in an adversarial position with virtually everyone you met. I'd be willing to bet that you didn't have a single close friend, with the possible exception of Hal Omanu—but as your commander he didn't really count. Well, you have them here. The Michaelsons like you. What's more, they need you, and not only as a physician—you've worked hard to become a good pilot. They aren't letting you stay out of the goodness of their hearts! You're here because they want you to be. So do I. Please, Daniel, will you reconsider your decision? Will you stay on?"

Keenan started to say "No," but he couldn't bring himself to utter the word. Lukas was right—he had been lonely in the Corps. Worse, there had been times when he hadn't recognized the person he had become, let alone liked him. Omanu had tried to convince him that he was suffering from a simple case of job burnout, but his problem had run much deeper than that and he'd known it.

It hadn't been only himself or his work that he could no longer face, either—it had been the Corps itself. Learning that the Admiralty had known about the Miquiri for years and kept that knowledge secret out of fear had forced him to take another look at the organization. So had Admiral Sorseli's treatment of Greg Lukas.

Sorseli, Lukas's commanding officer, had ordered Lukas into a restricted zone to recover alien artifacts and then courtmartialed him for the act. Attempting to insure that Lukas would never raise awkward questions, the admiral asked the court to sentence him to rehabilitation therapy, to be conducted by the psychiatrist of Sorseli's choice. What had followed during those sessions had had nothing to do with therapy, and everything to do with the suppression of memory. The psychiatrist had done his best to destroy Lukas's mind and personality, and had nearly succeeded.

Fortunately for Lukas, the Corps contained self-correcting mechanisms, one of which was Section Two. Keenan had been sent to investigate questions that had been raised about Lukas's case, and it hadn't taken him long to realize that something was wrong. But correcting the injustice had been more difficult than simply proving it had occurred.

In the end, it had taken the Quayla to effect a complete cure, but its action had left him vulnerable in another manner: the Corps did not know what Lukas had become after joining, and they did not trust him. So great was their concern that they questioned Daniel Keenan for six very long days, ordering him to relate everything he knew about the pilot and Quayla. Keenan had had no hesitation telling them most of what he knew, but he had refused to discuss several therapy sessions, claiming they fell under the seal of patient confidentiality.

The Corps had been more worried about security than medical ethics. They had ordered him to undergo a drug-assisted interrogation, and made him break the only oath he held more sacred than his vow to serve and protect the Consolidated Alliance of Planets Space Corps. He had known that he could not stay in the Corps after that, but starting a new life had proved more difficult than he had anticipated. Some people might see starting over in a new place and making friends of strangers as an adventure, but he saw it as an ordeal.

On top of that, no matter how much he wanted to help people, he was dogged by a nagging feeling that he had nothing left to offer others, personally or professionally. He might be able to cover the missing dimension for a time, but even if his patients did not notice the difference, he couldn't live with it. But he couldn't go on living with the Michaelsons forever, either.

"I can't stay," he finally said. "This was never intended to be a long-term arrangement."

"Has anyone asked you to go? Well, have they? Kiley and her family like you. They want you here. If you won't take my word on that, ask her. She won't lie. If she says she wants you to stay on, then you can be certain she means it. Will you do that? Will you talk to her?"

Keenan did not want to, but the force of Lukas's appeal was so strong that he found himself unable to refuse. "I'll think about it," he said eventually.

Lukas looked like he wanted to say more, but he didn't. Was he afraid to push too hard, or could it be that he shared Keenan's sudden sense of fatigue? Keenan hadn't felt so drained since he'd walked his last patient through an emotional firestorm that had gone on for hours and threatened to engulf them both.

His last patient had been Greg Lukas.

"Please do," Lukas urged. He went to the door, but stopped and turned around. "If you do decide to go, you will tell me, won't you? I won't try to stop you again—you have my word—but I would like to say good-bye. Will you at least let me do that much?"

"Yes, of course."

Lukas nodded and left. Keenan did not move. He was staring at the blank walls in a complete daze. Could Lukas be right? Could some unsuspected receptivity to the Quayla be responsible for his feelings toward it? He didn't see how, but one thing he did know—he had hated the Quayla from the moment he realized what it was. Worse, no matter how hard he tried to control his aversion to the alien being, some of his feelings about it had spilled over to Lukas and even the Miquiri.

Keenan closed his eyes, trying to sense something—anything—that might be emanating from the light. He felt nothing. To the best of his knowledge, he never had. Lukas was wrong—he had to be—and a good thing, too. The pilot might be willing to let an alien being invade his mind, but Daniel Keenan had no intention of following suit. Not in any manner whatsoever.

Keenan spent most of the night trying to decide what to do. By the next morning, he still had not made up his mind, so he rose, showered, dressed, and then went to the bridge. He expected to find Lukas and Kiley to be in the middle of their preflight checks, but instead he found Kiley standing in the center of the chamber alone, her hands clenched into fists.

"What's going on?" Keenan asked, looking past her to the lifeless monitors.

"Traffic control," Kiley said shortly.

"I take it they're being uncooperative again?" Keenan ventured.

"Uncooperative—!" Kiley broke off, choking down her simmering anger. "It appears they have a heavy schedule this morning," she said sarcastically. "They've delayed our clearance until twelve hundred hours. Heavy schedule! They've had exactly one incoming Corps cruiser and one outgoing freighter in the past three hours."

"Where's Greg?"

"I sent him back to bed. He only slept a few hours last night, and I have plenty of time to run the flight checks myself. Daniel, are you sure he's all right?" she asked, worry replacing frustration momentarily.

"The bioscanner didn't register any anomalies," he answered, choosing his words carefully.

"And you believed it?"

"There's no reason not to."

She sighed. "I must be overreacting, but I can't shake the feeling something's wrong. Ever since the Quayla started attaching itself to the ship's sensors, Greg's been different. Something's changed—I know it has!"

"Kiley, I couldn't find a single abnormal reading, and I did my best. He's as healthy as he ever was, and probably more fit than you, given your current state of mind."

"It shows, does it?" She tried to smile, but the light didn't reach her eyes. "There was no reason for traffic control to delay our departure. They just wanted to inconvenience us."

"Did you tell them that?"

"And let them know they'd upset me? Of course not! I have to admit, though, I only held back at the last moment." She grinned, finally letting go of the tension strumming through her body.

Keenan smiled back, but Kiley gave him a troubled look. "Daniel, are you all right?" she asked. "I don't mean to pry, but there have been a few times lately when you haven't seemed entirely happy. You've been with us longer than you originally intended; are you ready to leave? If so, please tell me. We'll miss you, all of us, but we'll understand. We've imposed on you long enough."

"Has Greg been talking to you about me?"

"Greg? No. Why, should he have?"

"No," Keenan said quickly. "It's just that I said something about leaving last night. I thought he might have mentioned the conversation to you."

"All he said was that you'd cleared him for duty. Was I right, then? Are you ready to go?"

"Not exactly." Keenan swallowed, fighting panic. "Kiley, I know this was never supposed to be a long-term arrangement, but I was wondering . . ."

"Yes?"

"Even though I've talked about starting my own psychiatric practice, I'm not sure that's what I really want. I was wondering if you would let me stay on with you a while longer. I know I'm not the best pilot you could hire," he added in a rush, "but I was hoping you would consider my medical training a trade-off for my lack of aptitude."

"Daniel, I'd keep you on even if you weren't a doctor," Kiley replied. "You're a willing worker and you're already a better pilot than Reese, which is to say you're more than adequate." She gave him a close look. "I have to admit, though, I have wondered whether you were suited to shipboard life. Some people have trouble adapting to long periods of confinement."

"And you were worried that I might be one?"

"The thought had crossed my mind."

He wondered himself for a moment, thinking about the sense of oppression he had felt when he returned to the ship on their last trip to Resurrection, but then shook his head. "I don't think so. I've just been feeling, well, restless. I doubt I'd want to live on a ship for the rest of my life, but I'm not suffering from claustrophobia."

"You're sure about that?" Kiley searched his face. "It can be a serious problem, Daniel."

"I know. Believe me, I do know. If I thought that was the case I wouldn't even consider staying on."

She nodded. Then, thinking fast, she said abruptly, "You're going to need a contract."

"What?"

"We've been carrying you on the ship's log as a passenger,

but we can't go on doing that much longer. I'm surprised Resurrection's dockmaster hasn't challenged your status before now." She glanced at the chronometer. "Come on. We still have time to have one drawn up before we go."

"Kiley, wait! I don't need a contract. I don't want one."

She was already halfway across the bridge. "It's not a matter of want or need, Daniel—it's the law. The only people who are exempt are passengers, dependents, and partowners. Don't look so worried. The contract is for your protection, not ours. It guarantees your personal rights and gives you legal recourse in case we fail to reimburse you for your labor."

"I don't need—" he started, but she cut him off.

"You do," she said emphatically. "We've been negligent by not paying you all along. You've been standing a regular shift for two months; you should have received something in return besides room and board. I'll transfer back wages to your card while we're onstation."

"Kiley, you don't—"

"I do. I think we'll give you the same contract Greg had before he became partowner of the ship," she added. "I'll take a copy of it along; that should speed up the processing considerably. Come on. We don't have much time, and the dockmaster's office is liable to stall us on general principles."

He didn't want to go, but she was right. Like it or not, he needed legal papers if he intended to stay on the ship. He balked, though, when he read the finished agreement and saw the terms of payment.

"Kiley, you're offering me a one-seventh share of the ship's profits! That's more than the captain of a commercial ship earns, and I'm only the second backup pilot. The most I'm entitled to is fixed wages."

"You contribute as much as the rest of us; you deserve an equal share in the profits," Kiley replied firmly. When he still hesitated, she said, "If it's any consolation, that won't amount to much for some time—our next three runs for the Corps will be all expense."

"But there will be other runs after that, and the rest of the family might not want to be so free with the proceeds from them. They should have a say in this, Kiley."

"There isn't time for a vote, but they'd back me if we had one." She tilted her head to one side and gave him a long look. "If I didn't know you better, I'd say you were having second thoughts. Are you?"

"No."

"Then prove it. Sign the contract."

He hesitated, then picked up the lightpen and wrote his name. Kiley signed hers, and the dockmaster's clerk registered the document. It was done.

Daniel Keenan, former psychiatrist and captain in the Consolidated Alliance of Planets Space Corps, was now officially the second backup pilot on the *Widdon Galaxy*. Most people would have been congratulating themselves on their good fortune if they'd just signed the agreement he had. But as he walked back to the ship, his only thought was *What have I done?*

Chapter 9

The *Widdon Galaxy* left Resurrection at midday, carrying three
weeks' worth of freight and five passengers. Two of the passengers were military officers; the other three were civilians.
Faced with mounting pressure, the Corps had finally buckled
under and agreed to let a few more scholars and scientists
travel out to the *North Star.*

The trip went smoothly until they exited jump at Sumpali
and received orders to stand off from the station.

"*Widdon Galaxy*, this is *North Star* control. Do not dock.
Repeat, do not dock. Come to an immediate stop and hold
your position awaiting further instructions."

Kiley scrambled to comply, but slowing the ship took time.
They were within monitor view of Sumpali by the time she
brought the ship to a dead stop.

Another vessel was docked at the human station. It was not
of Miquiri design.

"*North Star* control, this is the *Widdon Galaxy*," Kiley reported, not taking her eyes off the monitor. "We are holding
position, as instructed."

"We confirm your stop, Captain," the traffic controller said.
Then a different woman spoke. "Captain, this is Lieutenant
Commander Sevren. As you may have noticed, we have visi-
tors. They would like to look you over before you come any
closer. Be advised that their scanning may disrupt your sensors
and communications temporarily."

"Understood," Kiley replied.

The image on their monitors broke apart, turning into a
montage of random, silvery dots. The sensors went crazy and

alarms started going off. Kiley silenced them, then looked around the bridge. She could neither see nor feel a beam sweeping the ship, but something obviously was.

"Kiley, what's going on?" Jon Robert demanded. "The readings on the engineering boards just went crazy!"

"We're being scanned," she told him, watching the images on the monitors return to normal. "There's another ship docked at Sumpali. An alien ship."

"The Gan-Tir?" Jon Robert asked. Lukas had told them about the impending visit, and they had speculated about the aliens on the trip to Resurrection, but they'd forgotten about them during the refitting.

"Presumably so," Kiley said.

"*Widdon Galaxy*, you are clear to dock," Sevren said. "The Gan-Tir are not, repeat, not hostile, but they may insist on inspecting your ship after you've docked. If they do, please grant them access. Do you copy?"

"We copy," Kiley replied. They had been boarded and inspected several times in the past by both the Miquiri and the Corps. They had resented the invasions nearly as much as they resented the repeated exams the *North Star*'s medical staff insisted on giving them, but they had complied. Admission to Sumpali did not come free of charge.

The Gan-Tir ship was nearly as large as the *North Star*. Six decks radiated from a central core. Given their dimensions, the Gan-Tir either believed in spaciousness or were taller than humans.

Kiley kept an uneasy eye on the alien vessel as they approached the station, but it did not move. She bumped the *Widdon Galaxy* gently into place and shut off the docking thrusters.

The *North Star* controller hailed her again. "Captain Michaelson, Admiral Bergstrom requests your immediate presence on the *North Star*. Also, Dr. Elderbrandt would like Daniel Keenan to report to medical immediately. The rest of your crew is confined to ship until further notice. I repeat, the station is off limits to your crew on this trip. Do you copy, Captain?"

"I do," Kiley answered. "What about our passengers? Do you want them to stay here for the time being?"

There was a moment's silence before Sevren came back on. "The passengers can accompany you and Keenan to the *North Star.* Have them leave all but their personal kits on board your ship; we'll transfer the rest of their belongings later. A security detachment is on the way to meet you, Captain. They'll escort you over."

"I wonder why medical wants to see Daniel again?" Lukas asked as Kiley started shutting down her side of the control board. "He did his stint the last time we were here. And why right away, when all the rest of us are confined to the ship?"

"I don't know," Kiley said absently. "Most likely, they muffed some test and wanted to run it again. That would constitute an emergency for most of them."

Nevertheless, she gave Keenan a quick look when they met at the personnel hatch. He didn't look ill, and she could testify that his job performance was unimpaired. Since he'd decided to stay on the ship, he'd been cramming in information until he knew the new systems nearly as well as she and Lukas. It was as if, having made the commitment, he had decided to become the best pilot this side of Aumarleen. If so, he had his work cut out for him. Lukas was the best Kiley had ever seen, and she was no slouch. Still, Keenan hadn't become an officer in the Corps without learning how to push himself to his personal limits and beyond.

"Do you know why medical wants to see you again?" Kiley asked as they started across the station.

Keenan glanced at the passengers accompanying them to the *North Star.* They were too busy looking around the station to pay attention to their conversation.

"They probably just want to run some follow-up tests," he said, not looking at her. "It's nothing," he added quickly. "You know how closely they monitor us. If they'd thought anything was wrong, they'd never have let me make the last run."

That was true enough. In any case, they were coming up on the *North Star* quickly. The three security guards standing just outside the ship's hatch were already standing at attention. One of them claimed the *Widdon Galaxy*'s passengers and led them on board.

"Captain Michaelson, Dr. Keenan, this way," a second said. She took Kiley and Keenan up the access tube, to a bank of elevators, and motioned them into the first in a row of five.

They traveled up two floors, then stopped to let Keenan off at medical. Kiley caught a glimpse of a technician coming forward to meet him before the doors closed and she and the guard continued up toward the *North Star*'s bridge.

"Captain Michaelson, it's good to see you again." Admiral Bergstrom met her in a small conference room just off the bridge. Kiley took his hand gingerly; his grip was as firm as ever.

"You wanted to see me, Admiral?" she asked.

"I did, Captain. Come in, sit down."

A round table with a shiny black top stood in the center of the room, surrounded by six black chairs. The floor and ceiling were white, but the walls were covered with the same dark reflective material as the tabletop. Display panels? If so, they were some new technology that had not yet been made public.

Kiley took a seat on one side of the table. Bergstrom turned the chair beside her around and sat down facing her. "How did your refitting go?" he asked.

"Very well, sir. The work crews did an excellent job."

"I received a message from the quadrant commander, Admiral Partelli. He said that his teams inspected your ship after the Quayla attached itself to the sensors and they could detect no indication of its presence. Did you have any trouble on the way out?"

"No, sir."

"How is Lukas holding up? If I remember correctly, he found receiving a constant stream of information a strain while he was on the *Nieti*."

"He's been sleeping less than usual, but he says that it's a temporary condition. I did ask Dr. Keenan to check him over before we left port. He assured me Greg was perfectly normal."

"Whatever that constitutes," Bergstrom said dryly. "My people have been pressuring me to let him on the *North Star*," he went on. "They'd like to ask him a few questions and conduct an examination of their own. Dr. Keenan has been very good about sharing his scanner readings, but he doesn't have their equipment and there are a few tests they'd like to run."

"I'll bet there are," Kiley said under her breath. So far all that had kept the Corps doctors from inviting Lukas over was a fear that the Quayla might accompany him and somehow contaminate the *North Star.* It appeared that curiosity had finally overcome their apprehension.

"I was reluctant to agree at first," Bergstrom continued, ignoring her comment. "But since none of the Quaylas on the Miquiri ships that have docked here have shown an interest in this ship, I've decided any risk is minimal."

"I'm sure Greg would have no objection to a standard physical and psychological profile," Kiley said. "But I must tell you that I cannot and will not advise him to place himself in your staff's hands unconditionally. There's no reason for him to undergo the sort of ordeal I suspect they have in mind. As a matter of fact, I believe your crew has passed the point of overzealousness with all of us. If anything were going to happen, it would have by now. I don't object to a quick checkup from time to time, but the extended examinations your scientists have been conducting are ridiculous, and I want them stopped."

Kiley didn't expect her protest to do any good, so she was surprised when Bergstrom said, "I can sympathize with that. I'll pass your comments along to my staff. If they can convince me they need to continue the current testing schedule, then I'll let you know the reasons why. If not, I'll ask them to limit themselves to one brief examination every other month. Would that be acceptable, Captain?"

Kiley gave him a suspicious look. Bergstrom was in an unusually genial mood. If he was offering concessions, then he must want something in return. "It would," she replied cautiously.

"Consider it done, then. Is anything else troubling you or your crew?"

"Aside from moderate boredom at making the same run trip after trip? No, sir." She spoke calmly, but her stomach muscles tightened. The admiral had never been this solicitous before. What did he want?

Bergstrom nodded, then glanced down at the table as if he were consulting an agenda only he could see. "You saw the Gan-Tir ship as you came in?" he asked.

"Yes, sir."

"Their arrival has not been propitious, to say the least. We were on the brink of signing a boundary agreement with the Miquiri, but the talks broke down the day the Gan-Tir arrived. They insisted on being a party to any concords we might sign. The Miquiri are unhappy about the intrusion, but they haven't offered any overt opposition. Some of my people think they're frightened of the Gan-Tir."

"The Miquiri may prefer trade to war, but I don't believe they're cowards," Kiley said, watching Bergstrom closely. "If they're wary of the Gan-Tir, then they must have good cause."

Bergstrom nodded, his jaw tightening. He stood abruptly and paced to the far side of the room, then turned around to face Kiley. "Captain, we know that Miquiri technology is superior to ours. If they wanted to shut the *North Star* down completely, they could do it. We wouldn't even have time to fire on them. If the Miquiri have that capability and are still afraid of the Gan-Tir, then it follows that we should be, too."

"I believe Greg sent you a message saying something to that effect before we left for Resurrection."

"He did. We were inclined to discount his warning at first, but after a few experiences with the Gan-Tir, we've reconsidered. They aren't openly hostile, but they haven't gone out of their way to be friendly, either. They insisted on inspecting the *North Star* as soon as they arrived, but they refused to give us permission to board their ship. They said they want to be a party to our discussions with the Miquiri, but they don't want to deal with the diplomats onstation. They've demanded to speak to the Corps director, Admiral Vladic." Bergstrom sighed tiredly. "They asked for Everest's coordinates, but we refused to reveal them—we said we weren't ready to have alien vessels visiting the Admiralty. Fortunately, the Miquiri backed us on that point, but the Gan-Tir pressed. We finally agreed to arrange a meeting with the director at Resurrection, with the understanding the aliens would travel there on human ships." He glanced at Kiley, then went on. "We don't want potentially dangerous vessels entering our space, any more than the Miquiri. The aliens can meet with the director, be assured that we speak for him, and then return here to continue the talks."

"Why doesn't Vladic just come here?"

"I wasn't comfortable about placing him in such a vulnerable position. The Gan-Tir weren't enthusiastic about that idea either. If you ask me, what they really want is to see something of our civilization and technology. Resurrection was a compromise. They won't learn much about us by going there, but they don't know that."

"The Gan-Tir accepted those terms?"

"They did, provided we agree to arrange the meeting immediately."

"And you're going to?"

"I'm going to do my best," Bergstrom said, sitting down again. "I've prepared a report for the director, telling him I consider his presence crucial at this stage and asking him to travel out to Resurrection. We don't know how sophisticated the Gan-Tir's electronic surveillance equipment is, so I'd like you to carry the message to Admiral Partelli. He can then relay it on to Admiral Vladic. How soon can you leave?"

She thought quickly. "We'll need a minimum of two hours to restart our main engines and run our pre-flight checks. Our cargo has to be unloaded, too."

"I'll send a work crew over immediately. They can transfer the supplies while you're preparing to depart."

Kiley nodded. "Will that be all, sir?"

"Not quite. Once the meeting has been arranged, someone will have to take the aliens to Resurrection. That means you.

And, since Resurrection's council is hardly likely to welcome aliens on the station, and we don't want the Gan-Tir spending a prolonged period of time on one of our ships for security reasons, we'll need a site for the talks. I am recommending your ship."

"You're asking us to take the aliens to Resurrection, then stay there with them on board while they meet with the director?" Kiley's tone was incredulous.

"I am. For the record, I did ask the Miquiri to make an exception and let a Corps ship come here to Sumpali to transport the Gan-Tir to Resurrection, but they refused. They don't want any more alien vessels in the area. They're afraid of a misunderstanding that could escalate into open conflict. If that happened, their station and the world below would be in jeopardy."

"Admiral, I don't think we—"

"I am not interested in what you think, Captain," Bergstrom said bluntly. "We have an agreement. In return for the fine work I'm certain our refitters did, you promised to make four runs for the Corps. Taking my message to Resurrection will count as one. Taking the Gan-Tir will be your second."

"Admiral, there was never any suggestion that one of those trips might involve alien passengers!"

"Nor was there any exclusion." Bergstrom was up and pacing again. "I can appreciate your reluctance to take the Gan-Tir on, but we need you, Captain Michaelson, and quite frankly you are in no position to refuse. Our agreement aside, you operate out of Resurrection by special Corps permit. That permit is subject to cancellation at any time. If that happened, you could return to your old runs, but you'd have to leave Lukas behind—we're not about to have him and the Quayla roaming human space. Your only alternative would be to stay on the Miquiri side of the boundary—assuming you could work out some sort of agreement to haul freight for them that didn't take revenues away from one of their own ships."

That wasn't likely and Bergstrom knew it. The admiral had Kiley right where he wanted her, she realized grimly. That did not, however, mean that she had no room left for bargaining.

"Two," she said. "If we have to lay over at Resurrection with the aliens on board, that's going to count as two runs." She was taking a chance, but Bergstrom must have been more uncomfortable about the orders he was issuing than his manner suggested, because he acquiesced.

"Very well, two."

Kiley gave him a doubtful look. That had been too easy for comfort. What wasn't he telling her? There had to be something. "Admiral, are you sure we can carry the Gan-Tir?" she asked. "Can they breathe our air? What about food and water?"

"Our oxygen levels are a little low for the Gan-Tir's comfort, but that shouldn't be a major problem. My engineers say they can convert one of your remaining cargo holds into temporary living quarters for them with no major difficulty. You can control airflow to the holds, so increasing the oxygen level in one and lowering the temperature in another won't be difficult."

"They need two holds? Each with different conditions?"

"The second will be for the Miquiri."

"The Miquiri?" Kiley asked, feeling like she had walked into a complicated movie halfway through and couldn't pick up the plot. "Some of them will be going, too?"

"They're worried the Gan-Tir will try to start a separate set of negotiations. They insisted on sending a delegation of their own along to make certain the Gan-Tir don't forge any secret agreements with us." Bergstrom's expression hovered somewhere between disgust and frustration. "I don't mind saying that the past few weeks have been a political nightmare. The Miquiri and Gan-Tir don't trust each other, despite their trade agreements, and each seems determined to win our support. Why they think they need it is beyond me—they both appear to be far superior to us militarily. But whatever their reasons, they each seem to think we've altered some status quo. It's entirely possible that neither group wants us to side with them so much as make certain we don't side with the other. Tensions are running quite high. It's only fair to warn you that some of that uneasiness may spill over onto your ship. If so, I'm counting on you to handle the aliens with the utmost care and diplomacy."

"Of course, sir. That goes without saying."

"You won't need to worry about provisions for the Miquiri or Gan-Tir. They'll supply their own food and any furnishings necessary for their comfort. They will need water for drinking and washing, but ours should suffice after it has been purified and filtered to remove all trace elements. That won't be difficult to do, but waste recycling is another matter entirely. We've decided that the safest course will be to send all waste to special holding tanks that can be off-loaded later. Since you won't be able to recycle the water the aliens use, you'll have to carry an additional supply. I've prepared a second message for Admiral Partelli, asking him to rig temporary partitions for the aliens' quarters in your cargo holds and to install the extra tanks you'll need. As soon as that's done, I want you to return here."

"So we can head straight back out with the delegations?"

"Yes, unless that would pose a problem for you or your crew?"

"We aren't used to spending this much time in port. A few back-to-back runs will hardly incapacitate us."

Bergstrom gave her a sharp look, then continued on. "I have one final request. The Gan-Tir have told us they wish to inspect your ship. I apologize for the intrusion, but they want to assure themselves that the *Widdon Galaxy* is both safe and hospitable. I'll give you fifteen minutes to go back and warn your family that they will be coming, then I'll advise them that they can proceed." Bergstrom stood. "Captain, one warning. The Gan-Tir are quite large by human standards, and evolved under higher gravity conditions than we did. They are extremely powerful. Their behavior can also be unpredictable. Be careful around them. Whatever you do, don't touch them. They either have some taboo against incidental contact, or they just don't like aliens. One of our scientists bumped into one of them accidentally and she ended up in the infirmary with a broken clavicle. Be careful of everything you do and say around them. Everything."

"You've gained two pounds," Elderbrandt said as he dumped his scanner readings into the ship's medical computer. He had finished his examination, but had not given Keenan permission to dress again. Keenan stood anyway and started pulling on his clothes. Elderbrandt gave him a disapproving look, then went back to the report he'd been studying and keyed in a request. Was he rechecking the readings he'd just taken, or asking for some sort of long-term comparison? Keenan angled his head, trying to read the display, but it was indecipherable from his position.

Elderbrandt scanned the information he'd requested, then switched the computer off and crossed the room. He motioned Keenan to sit on the examination table, then pulled up a stool, sat, and gave him a close look.

"Can I take it that your weight gain is evidence that you have resolved whatever problem was troubling you?"

Keenan hesitated, then nodded.

"I'm glad to hear that. The ship's psychiatric officer, Dr. Altos, and I spent some time after you left going over your medical records and the last battery of tests we gave you. We were both worried that you might be having trouble adapting to civilian life."

Keenan started to offer a denial, then stopped. Elderbrandt was offering him an easy out and he took it. "Maybe I have. A little."

"That's nothing to be ashamed of, Doctor. Midlife career changes are not uncommon, but they can be very unsettling. Dr. Altos and I felt your decision might have been more hastily reached than most, and perhaps you found yourself floundering in consequence. In fact, we wondered if you might not be regretting your decision to leave the Corps. Are you?"

"No."

"You're sure?"

"I'm positive," he said, and he was.

"That's good. I'm not so certain that staying on the

Michaelsons' ship is a good idea, though. It's hard to imagine how a man with your abilities and drive can settle for being—what, second pilot on a freighter? No matter how fond you might be of Greg Lukas or the Michaelsons, that doesn't strike me or Dr. Altos as normal behavior for you."

"Maybe I've changed."

Elderbrandt considered, then nodded. "That's possible, of course—and not necessarily bad. Still, I would be feel better about your decision if you seemed to be happier. You were a good psychiatrist and a good officer, Daniel. The Corps was sorry to lose you. If you did want to return, I'm sure you could do so with no difficulty."

"I don't."

"All right," Elderbrandt said easily, rising. "I've kept you long enough. You may go now." He waited until Keenan was at the door, then said quietly, "Daniel, I hope you'll remember that both Dr. Altos and I are here. If you do need help, or simply someone to talk to, remember us, will you?"

Keenan nodded, then left as quickly as his feet would take him. As much as he appreciated Elderbrandt's offer, he wanted nothing more to do with the physician or the Corps.

A security guard was standing watch outside the access tube leading to the *Widdon Galaxy*. He held up his hand as Keenan approached and ordered him to stand back. A moment later, Keenan saw his first Gan-Tir.

Huge.

That was his first impression of the aliens. They stood nearly two feet higher than the average human. They were taller than they were wide, but their bodies were much thicker than a human's. For all their size, though, they moved with surprising fluidity. That grace could have been an innate physical characteristic, or it could have resulted from the swirling movement of the loose, flowing robes that covered them from neck to foot. The robes had hoods, but the aliens had all pushed them back, baring large, smooth heads. They had short, thick necks—nothing longer would have supported their heavy skulls. Their eyes were nearly lost beneath the prominent ridges that formed their brows. They had similar ridges of bone high on either side of their heads, possibly marking the site of ears. Their noses were pointed risings at the center of their faces. And their mouths were large ovals, held closed by thick, pursed lips.

Keenan took all that in on his first glance, but what he noticed most was the aliens' pigmentation. They were startling combinations of obsidian black and quartz white, and their skin shone like polished rock. Though they all had the same coloring, the patches of black and white came in a variety of patterns, from large, irregular splotches to round, thumbnail-sized dots.

He could not see the Gan-Tir's legs, but they had to have them because they took distinct steps as they moved. The deck quivered with each one. He did see their arms, though calling them that was stretching the definition of the word. When they gestured to one another, the sleeves of their robes fell back, revealing long, thick limbs that terminated in six stubby appendages. Wrapped around both arms were longer, thinner limbs that resembled nothing so much as tentacles. One of them uncoiled its second appendage as it left the tube and began swinging it back and forth in the air. Whether the movement was part of a conversation or something else entirely, Keenan couldn't say.

The security guard stepped back as the group of aliens approached, giving them plenty of room. Keenan did the same. Though they moved slowly and made no hostile gestures, their sheer bulk was intimidating. So was the look one of them gave him as it passed less than two feet away. Its violet eyes met his and he found himself taking another, involuntary step back, his skin crawling. The alien stopped abruptly, taking a longer look at him. Keenan met that burning stare for several seconds, then hastily averted his eyes, not wanting to offer any sort of inadvertent challenge. He regretted even that brief contact as the alien moved toward him, its right tentacle uncoiling and reaching for him.

Keenan stumbled back. "Hold still!" the guard ordered. He grabbed Keenan's arm, steadying him.

The warning was unnecessary. Keenan froze as the tentacle came within an inch of his face. It moved from side to side, a restless snake considering a strike. The top side was black, the underside white; it did not appear to be wet, but the skin glistened. The tip came closer and closer. It touched his cheek.

Keenan made a strangled sound and closed his eyes as the tentacle swept his face, moving from cheek to forehead to cheek. The alien's skin was dry, warm, and unexpectedly soft. It was also covered with microscopic hairs. He could not see them, but they tickled unpleasantly.

The pressure eased, and he opened his eyes to find the alien had lost interest in him and was moving on. Three more passed before Keenan; all of them ignored him.

"They do that to people sometimes," the guard said in an undertone. "We don't know why. Don't touch them back, though. If you do, you're liable to wind up in the infirmary." He took a closer look at Keenan. "Are you all right, sir?"

Keenan swallowed and nodded. "Can I board the ship?"

"Sure, go ahead. They're all off now."

He walked up the personnel tube and found the Michaelsons and Lukas standing in the main corridor, just outside the bridge.

". . . mean, take them to Resurrection?" Reese was asking Kiley, his voice rising.

"The *North Star* has to stay here and the Miquiri won't let any other ships dock; that leaves us."

"But if we don't want to—" Lia started.

"We don't have a choice," Kiley said firmly. "We committed to making four runs for them in return for the refitting. Bergstrom has agreed to count the one with aliens as two because of the layover, but that's the only concession he's making." Kiley stopped, catching sight of Keenan. "Daniel, I'm glad you're back. I was just telling the others we have to pull out right away. Admiral Bergstrom wants us to carry an urgent message back to Admiral Partelli." She turned to Jon Robert. "How much longer until the engines are up to fifty percent power?"

"Another five minutes," he said, then added urgently, "Kiley, I know you agreed to transport the Gan-Tir, but I agree with Reese and Lia. This ship wasn't designed to carry aliens. Who knows what might happen to them or us? It's a long way to Resurrection. What if something goes wrong?"

"It won't."

"Some of them are coming with us?" Keenan asked. To his dismay, his own voice rose a notch as he spoke.

Kiley nodded. "Not this trip, but the next one." She turned back to Jon Robert. "I know they're disturbing, but Bergstrom says they'll stay in the cargo hold we convert for the trip. They can breathe our air for a short time, but they aren't comfortable at lower oxygen levels."

"I didn't notice any of them showing signs of discomfort," Lia snapped.

Kiley started to respond just as sharply, but stopped herself. "We're wasting time," she said shortly. "Daniel, I want you and Greg on the bridge. Jon Robert, you and Holly go to the engine room. Go on!" she ordered when no one moved.

Jon Robert held his position just long enough to make Keenan wonder if he was going to argue, then spun around and headed down the corridor. Holly gave Kiley a quick look, then followed him.

"Kiley—" Reese started.

She swung around. "You can go to the engine room or your cabin, Reese, whichever you prefer." She did not offer another alternative.

"Let's go," he ordered Lia.

"But, Reese—"

"There's no point to arguing with her. She's not going to listen to reason. We'd just be wasting our breath." Lia dragged her heels, but Reese pulled her down the corridor along with him.

Kiley turned to Keenan and Lukas, her eyes hard and flat. "Do either of you have any objections?"

"No, of course not," Lukas said. He spoke easily, as if unaware of her challenge.

Keenan shook his head, not trusting his voice. Kiley gave

them a curt nod and went to the bridge. Keenan started to follow, but Lukas put a hand out, stopping him.

"Are you all right?" the pilot asked.

"Me? Of course."

"Are you sure? I was worried something might be wrong when they called you back to medical so soon after your last visit."

"It was nothing. Elderbrandt thought I might be having trouble adapting to civilian life. I had the impression that he and one of the ship's psychiatrists wanted me to consent to a few therapy sessions."

"Do you need them?" Lukas asked, searching his eyes.

"No."

"But if you did, you would agree, wouldn't you?"

Keenan stiffened. "Maybe. Altos isn't the worst psychiatrist I've ever met. If I had to, I suppose I could talk to him."

"Daniel, I can't help but be aware that some, if not all, of the problems you've been having relate to me and the Quayla. If you need help, don't let concern for me stop you. What matters is that you are well—not what the Corps feels about me or the Quayla. I know you still feel an obligation toward me as a former patient, if not a friend, but I don't want you to let that interfere with your own well-being."

"It won't."

"I have your word on that?"

"If you need it, then yes. You have my word."

Lukas relaxed visibly. He glanced past Keenan, toward the ship's main entrance. "Did you see the Gan-Tir?" he asked.

"I not only saw them, one of them touched me."

"It did?" Lukas exclaimed. "How? Where?"

"It put its tentacle on my face and moved it like this." Keenan demonstrated. "It was awful. Do you know why they do that? Does the Quayla?"

Lukas went away for a moment, consulting with the Quayla. He came back frowning. "No. For all they trade together, the Miquiri don't know much about the Gan-Tir, and no Quayla has ever been able to make contact with one of them. As far as the Quaylas can tell, they are psychically null. It was probably just curious. Touch is a common method of exploration for most beings."

"But why me?"

"I don't know," Lukas said uneasily. "Maybe it was an impulse. Chirith said they are an odd species, given to sudden whims."

"Well, I wish they'd keep their tentacles to themselves. It was not a pleasant experience."

"I can imagine."

"Greg, are you coming?" Kiley asked impatiently, sticking her head out the hatch.

"On my way." He gave Keenan an uneasy look, then went onto the bridge. Keenan followed. Lukas didn't say more about Keenan's experience with the Gan-Tir, but he gave his shipmate several more covert glances before they left port.

Keenan didn't notice; he was too busy thinking about what he had felt when the Gan-Tir had touched him. He had been uncomfortable, even frightened, but he had not been repelled.

The Gan-Tir were real. They could cause physical harm—severe harm if their strength matched their size. But for all that, his response to them had been very different from his reaction to the Quayla.

Could Lukas be right? Could his immediate dislike of the Quayla have been triggered by some protective mechanism in his mind that he wasn't even aware he possessed? If so, did that mean that he had been letting blind instinct rule his feelings, not reason?

All his life, he had been taught that reason must prevail over instinct in a civilized society. He had accepted that belief implicitly, but now he found himself wondering if it was always possible. How would he go about overcoming a response he wasn't even aware he was making? Suppose he could—what would happen then? If Lukas was right about his receptivity, then an easing of his hostility toward the Quayla could be the first step toward communication. Was he prepared to accept that possibility and deal with it?

Keenan still did not have an answer to those questions by the time they left port, nor was he certain that he wanted to.

Chapter 10

Sensar Kaikiel Anara's footsteps echoed hollowly, the only sound in the deserted corridor. He walked quickly, in a hurry to reach his rooms. In a hurry to escape Rairea. He had not seen her for days and had started to believe she wasn't interested in him. Then, as they inspected the human ship, she had come to stand beside him. Her *elith* had slipped inside the sleeve of his robe, coiled around his arm, and squeezed.

She had not hurt him. She was simply reminding him that she was there, biding her time, waiting for the right moment. The moment she chose.

"Sensar Kaikiel! Wait!"

Sensar whirled around and found himself facing Lonlores Mimara. With a sigh, he invoked the first level of *jis*—calm. Short and squat, Lonlores bounced from wall to wall as he walked. He resembled nothing so much as a windblown nistball, laden with pollen. Like the nistball, he was also a maddening irritant. He came to a halt just in front of Sensar, standing much too close.

If this had been their first meeting, Sensar would have assumed Lonlores was physically disabled, so rudely did the diplomat invade his personal space. But it was not their first, and Sensar had long since concluded that Lonlores chose his position deliberately to create maximum discomfort. The senior diplomat was not a bright man, but he was innately canny.

"Sensar, I asked you to see me when you returned from the alien ship," Lonlores said, sounding aggravated. "I am your superior. I expect you to observe proper protocol and report all that you have seen and heard immediately."

Lonlores was neither liked nor respected by anyone. He might have been appointed leader of the delegation through some bureaucratic twist of fate, but rumor had it that he had been sent on the trip by a former lover who was anxious to be rid of him.

"I would have, Lonlores," Sensar answered smoothly, "as soon as I had washed and changed. In case you had not noticed, the aliens stink."

Lonlores's right *elith* uncoiled and swayed from side to side, sniffing the air. "You are right." He wrapped his *elith* tightly around his arm again. "They smell worse than the Miquiri. I do not envy you your stay on their ship. It will not be pleasant." Satisfaction flickered across the diplomat's face. He did not like Sensar, and he found the prospect of the scholar living in squalid circumstances extremely gratifying. "Perhaps you are not up to such a distasteful journey," he suggested. "Perhaps you should stay behind. I can always send another in your place."

"But not one who understand the humans' language as well as I. Barbares Dondarith honored me by asking me to serve as his translator. I accepted gladly."

"You did not hear, then? Barbares just announced that he will not be going on the alien ship after all. He finds them too offensive. I have decided to send Rairea Tayturin in his place."

"Rairea!"

"Does that upset you, Sensar?" Lonlores asked, his air of innocence so great that it could only be feigned. "It should not. She is a highly respected negotiator and has impeccable credentials. She will represent our interests well."

"Of course she will," Sensar said, stifling panic. "It will be an honor to assist her." He had to reach for the second level of *jis* to hide his shock, but he managed. It was worth the effort to see Lonlores's befuddlement.

"I'm surprised that you are not upset," Lonlores said. "It is no easy matter, being shoved into the company of a former lover, particularly one so compelling as Rairea. She has told stories about your liaison, Sensar Kaikiel. Many stories."

"Surely you do not believe everything you hear."

"Are you denying that she was your lover?"

"I am neither confirming nor denying. I am content to leave the talking—and the duty assignments—to you. You are, after all, in charge of the mission."

Lonlores gave Sensar a suspicious look. "Yes, I am. I am glad you realize that—and that you are still willing to go. I would have sent you anyway. Henherik Tortorend knows the Miquiri language, but he is having difficulty with the human one. In any case, he is no scholar. You have studied aliens more extensively than any Gan-Tir in recent history. It is said that you understand them so completely, you might almost be one."

The words were a gross insult, but Sensar pretended to take them as a compliment. "Your praise is most generous, Lonlores. I accept it with gratitude."

"May your gratitude last the entire journey," Lonlores replied shortly. "It will, I fear, prove a long and uncomfortable one. But then, perhaps you will not mind. You will, after all, have the alien beasts to occupy you. Be careful, Sensar, or you may find yourself beginning to think and live as they do."

"Alas, I fear such an accomplishment is beyond my ability. Be assured, though, I would if I could. The opinion of most Gan-Tir to the contrary, we could learn much by studying the aliens. They may appear primitive, but they travel the stars as easily as we. What's more, they have vibrant, growing populations."

"Which is to say they breed like animals—indiscriminately and in great profusion!"

"But they do breed. That is more than we can say for ourselves, isn't it? Perhaps there truly is something to be learned from them. If so, I give you my word, you will be among the first to know." Sensar smiled, letting Lonlores take the words however he would. "With your permission, I will retire now so I can bathe. I do not wish to offend a moment longer than necessary."

"Go. Wash, for all the good it will do. I doubt you will rid yourself of the contamination clinging to you so easily. It is more than your body that reeks of aliens—their stench has permeated your mind, as well. You would do well to revise your opinion of them, Sensar Kaikiel. They are beasts. No more, no less."

"You are wrong," Sensar replied softly. "They are much more than that."

Lonlores did not answer. He had already gone.

Chapter 11

The *Widdon Galaxy* stayed at Resurrection for two days while Admiral Partelli procured and loaded the holding tanks and additional water Admiral Bergstrom had requested.

Partelli ordered Kiley over to his ship and grilled her about her meeting with Bergstrom and the Gan-Tir's visit to the Michaelsons' ship. Short, dark, and inclined to roundness, Partelli was perhaps ten years younger than Bergstrom and a great deal more amenable. The tone and direction of his questions suggested to Kiley that Partelli feared Bergstrom had been acting under coercion. She had seen no evidence to indicate that was the case, and said so; but Partelli was not completely reassured, nor was he happy about the prospect of aliens coming to Resurrection. He was running a worried hand through his dark hair when he finally let her leave his ship.

Kiley went onstation long enough to pick up a few personal supplies and found the atmosphere there nearly intolerable. The corridors were crowded and the people irritable, and keeping the peace was taking every ounce of diplomacy Partelli possessed—and all the security officers in his fleet.

The good news was that no one paid any attention to her for the first time since they'd started docking at Resurrection. The service in the stores was slow and grudging, but it was that way for all outsiders, not just her. Still, given the high level of tension, she warned the rest of the family and Keenan to be careful if they left the ship.

Keenan heeded her advice and spent most of the day in the ship's common room, watching the communications feed from the station. It wasn't only the newcomers that had the locals unsettled; there was a disturbing upswing in religious fervor taking place on the planet below. No longer able to claim that man was the only being of higher intelligence in the universe, the natives' beliefs about God and humanity's place in creation were undergoing a serious challenge.

Theological arguments raged from one side of the planet to the other. Several groups had broken off from the fundamentalist church that had founded the colony and were in the process of forming new sects. The most vigorous of them called themselves the New Believers. On a planet where the degree of one's fervor was a measure of one's conviction, their soft, calm voices were an oddly arresting anomaly; one literally had to strain to hear them at times. They spoke of a new order and said that a teacher was coming who would show them that love of God could only be manifested through love of one's fellow beings—all one's fellow beings.

Keenan had to stifle a groan the first time he heard one of them talk. Even quiet, peaceful religions seemed to lead inevitably toward violence. Still, he found himself wishing the movement would take hold—the New Believers were the only reasonable voices he heard all day. He wished he could talk to a few of the compelling speakers in the movement. He wondered how many people were listening to them, and what would happen if and when their movement collapsed. Would they let themselves be reabsorbed into mainstream groups? Would they merge with one of the other new sects with more traditional roots? Following them would make an interesting research project.

Keenan turned the station feed off, surprised to discover himself thinking about work again—real work. It had been months since he'd observed others with genuine interest. It was odd that it had taken a decision not to return to his former work to stir his professional curiosity again. He had been right not to go back. His future lay ahead, not behind him. He would not find happiness by returning to the past.

Nor was he likely to find it where he was—at least not in the immediate future. He stood up with a sigh. He had been postponing talking to Lukas all day, but he could wait no longer. They were due to leave port at 0600 the next morning; there would not be time for anything then but the preflight checks.

Kiley had asked him to check Lukas over again. He was not sleeping well, and she said she had noticed changes in his behavior. Keenan had resisted her appeal to examine Lukas so soon after his last checkup, not wanting to jeopardize his new-found ease with the other man. But Kiley had insisted, and he'd finally agreed.

Keenan went to the intercom and pressed the code for Lukas's cabin. "Greg, are you there?"

"Here," Lukas said immediately. He must have been sitting at his desk, working. He had ordered a number of book disks several trips ago, and they had been waiting when the ship docked. He had spent all his free time since they docked reading them.

"Do you have a few minutes? I'd like to give you another checkup."

Silence, then a short, hard question. "Is that really necessary?"

"I'm afraid so. I'm on the way to my cabin. I'll meet you there."

"I don't—" Lukas started, then broke off. Keenan heard Kiley's voice in the background. Lukas cut off the intercom. Keenan waited a moment. He was on the verge of calling Lukas back when the pilot's voice sounded in the room. "I'll be right there," he said, biting the words off.

He was still furious when he arrived at Keenan's cabin—a state of mind that was as uncharacteristic and disturbing as the changes that Kiley had complained about.

"I thought we'd already had this out," Lukas said shortly as he pulled his shirt off with an angry jerk. "I am perfectly well."

"Then there's no need to be upset, is there?" Keenan said reasonably. "Come on, Greg. Lie down and relax. If you're well, the scanners will say so and I can tell Kiley she's worrying about nothing."

Lukas kicked off his shoes, then his pants. He tossed them

across the foot of the bunk and lay down. Keenan could almost hear him counting to ten—or was it one hundred? If appearances were anything to go by, ten would not be nearly far enough.

He ran the bioscanner over the pilot, starting at his head and working his way down his chest, arms, and legs. Lukas's pulse and blood pressure were elevated at first, but they slowly dropped back to normal. His vital organs, glands, and circulatory systems were all functioning normally. There were no abnormal growths on the surface of his skin or internally. He was, as he had insisted, perfectly healthy.

Except for one reading, discovered only after Keenan compared the results to his last scan: the pilot's biological age had taken a slight but detectable leap. The medical computer had flagged the irregularity automatically. Keenan frowned. That happened sometimes. Not all bodies aged at the same rate, and any number of factors could accelerate the process.

Keenan turned around. Lukas was sitting up, reaching for his shirt. "Greg, will you do something for me?"

"What?" Lukas asked suspiciously.

"I want you to scan me. One of your readings shows an abnormality. I'd like to rule out scanner malfunction and a few other possible causes before I attach any value to it."

"What reading?"

"Scan me first, then I'll tell you. You've used one of these, haven't you?" He handed the instrument to Lukas. "Just push the button on the right side and run the wand over my body slowly. The screen will flash a warning if you're going too fast. If you miss any areas, the body schematic will highlight them so you can make another pass."

Keenan undressed and lay down. Lukas hesitated, as if finding the reversal of their positions disconcerting, then started running the scanner over Keenan. He went too fast at first, and had to make several passes before he found the correct pace.

"Done?" Keenan asked when Lukas finally reached his feet.

"Yes."

Keenan rose and dressed, then fed the readings into the medical computer. There were no warning flags.

"Greg, will you come over here?" he asked. "I'd like to show you something."

Lukas stiffened, but walked over to the computer. "What?" he demanded, his voice as tight as the fists he had shoved into his pockets.

"Do you see this reading?" Keenan asked, pointing out the biological-age indicator on his own scan results.

"Yes."

"Look at it, then compare it with yours," he said. He split the screen, leaving his own readings on top and bringing Lukas's up in the lower section. "Do you see the flag?"

Lukas did not reply. He was too busy studying the screen. Keenan started to point out the significance of the variance, but before he could, Lukas had taken control of the computer and was calling up a complete report of his previous exam, then the one before that, and the one before that.

Keenan began to stop him, then dropped his hand, letting Lukas go back through every reading he had taken from the pilot since he'd come on board the ship. Keenan didn't see how Lukas could be absorbing the data so quickly. He had to be, though, because he stopped at every warning flag. There were three: one after he'd returned from the *Nieti*, and two during the drug-assisted sessions Keenan had conducted to help him recover his memory. Lukas paused for a long time when he came to those.

"You took quite a chance with me, didn't you?" he asked. He had gone completely still, but there was nothing serene about him. He was rigid.

"Yes."

"Why?"

"Because I cared about you. If I had stopped, you wouldn't have recovered your memory, or had a chance of overcoming the personality damage. Whenever I wasn't certain about proceeding, I asked myself what I would have wanted, had our roles been reversed. Then I did it."

"And you call that caring?" Lukas demanded.

"Yes."

"So do I," the pilot said. He took a ragged breath and called up his most recent scan again. "Your own readings didn't change, so I presume this can't be the result of scanner malfunction, or some other condition related to the ship, transition, or contact with the Miquiri or Gan-Tir?" he asked, anticipating the arguments Keenan had been about to make.

"Not unless you're the only person who's been affected. I don't consider that likely. Greg, there weren't any warnings until the Quayla began reading data from the ship's sensors. Perhaps it would be better if it detached itself and—"

"No!" Lukas said sharply, stopping Keenan in midsentence. "I know you mean well, but you have no idea what you're suggesting. The Quayla needs work to occupy itself. It isn't right or fair to ask it to live solely within my mind and body."

"Not even if the alternative means taking years off your normal life span? Is the Quayla so desperate for input that it is willing to ignore the danger to you?"

Lukas started to answer, then went away. This time, though, his expression was not vacant. Emotions flashed across his face, changing so swiftly that Keenan could not keep up with them. Lukas quelled them ruthlessly.

"Well?" Keenan demanded.

"The Quayla is concerned, of course, but if there is a choice, then we would both take a short, full life over a long, meaningless one."

"Tell me that forty years from now," Keenan muttered. If Lukas heard he did not respond. "Greg, have the Quayla's Miquiri companions had this problem?" he asked, trying a different approach.

Lukas considered briefly, then shook his head, looking surprised. "I'm not positive, but I don't think so."

"Why are you, then? What's so different about humans?"

"I'm not sure. Contact with the Quayla makes unusual demands on any companion, human or Miquiri. It does its best to compensate for them, but apparently it hasn't completely succeeded with me."

"Now that it realizes there is a problem, can it try harder?"

Lukas was shaking his head before Keenan finished. "It will try, of course, but I don't think there's much more that it can do. Human metabolisms aren't as efficient as the Miquiri's. Our reproductive systems may be partially to blame for that. The Miquiri undergo periods of intense sexuality during the female's season, but they are followed by long periods of inactivity. Being sexually active year-round is extremely inefficient by their standards. I don't think celibacy would be any cure, though, in case you were about to suggest that. Denying an impulse so basic to human nature would require at least as much energy, if not more, than obeying it."

"And if you did, there would be that much less pleasure in your life, wouldn't there? That's important to the Quayla, isn't it? Sharing the pleasures you experience?"

Lukas flushed. "You say that as if our sharing is somehow unwholesome. It isn't! The Quayla is not a voyeur, eavesdropping on all that I do and say—it is me and I am it. There is no distinguishing between us."

"If that's true, then why do you speak of it as a separate being? Greg, you say that your bond is unbreakable, but are you sure that's true? Is it possible the Quayla only wants you to believe it because it doesn't want to lose the physical awareness your senses give it?"

"It is not lying to me, if that's what you're suggesting," Lukas said hotly. "It can't. We are one. There is no part of me that it does not share, and vice versa. The only time we have any sense of separateness is when we draw on past memories—those clearly belong to one or the other of us. But all the rest, from the day we joined until this moment, is the result of mutual awareness."

"It has been, but does it have to be?" Keenan persisted. "The Quayla has had other companions. No matter how closely you are connected, you're still separate beings; otherwise, it would die when you do. But it won't, will it? It will find another companion and go right on existing, won't it?"

"I don't understand what you're saying."

"If the Quayla could separate from you at death, then I don't see why it can't do so while you're still alive—provided it wants to."

Lukas shook his head stubbornly. "It isn't the way you

think. When a companion dies, the Quayla is automatically cut off from it. It does not choose the separation—it simply happens. But even if it did have some control over the process, what would be the point? It joins because it wants and needs to share."

"Why does the companion join? Because it wants to open its inner self with an alien being, or because it has no choice? The Quayla forced its way into your mind, Greg. Can you honestly say you'd have let it become part of you if you'd had any option?"

Lukas's fingers had started to coil, but they relaxed abruptly and he smiled. "No, but only because I didn't know what I'd be missing. Even if I could detach myself from the Quayla, I would not. In any case, I can't. If it were to separate from me now, the shock would be so great, my heart would stop. Even if you could keep me alive on life support, there would be nothing left of my mind."

"You don't *know* that. You can't! You're the first human companion the Quayla has had; it might be different for you."

"It wouldn't," Lukas said firmly. He had made up his mind and no amount of reasoning was going to budge him.

"Could you at least try to get more sleep?" Keenan urged, switching tactics. "The Quayla may not need rest, but you do. You'd be less irritable, and the rate at which you're aging might slow. If you think it would help, I'll even give you a mild sedative."

"No! No drugs. I'm not sure they'd have any effect at all, but if they did, they'd probably do more harm than good. The Quayla will try to do a better job of shielding my mind while I sleep. It doesn't know if it can help me rest longer, but it will try."

"I could use hypnosis if you thought that would help."

Lukas smiled, looking almost wistful. "I doubt you could put me under anymore." He hesitated, then asked uneasily, "Daniel, do you have to tell Kiley about this? I'd rather you didn't. There's nothing she can do, and you'll only upset her."

"I'm sorry, Greg, but she has a right to know of any medical condition that might affect the performance of one of her crew members."

"Then could you at least let me be the one tell her? Will you grant me that much?"

"If that's what you want."

"It is."

"All right, you can talk to her—but you'd better do it to-night. If she asks me for a report tomorrow, I'll have to give her one."

Lukas's mouth compressed, but he nodded curtly and started for the door.

Keenan waited until he was almost there, then said quietly, "Greg, I know I've given you reason to doubt me, but no matter what you feel at this moment, I *am* your friend."

Lukas stopped. "Are you? Sometimes I wonder about that."

"I don't," Keenan said, with such conviction that Lukas gave him a startled look. The pilot must have decided he was telling the truth, because before he turned and went away, he nodded again.

The common room was empty, as Lukas had hoped it would be. He sat down in a chair far from the door, put his head in his hands, and closed his eyes, wishing for the first time since he had joined with the Quayla that he could escape from the voice that shared his inner thoughts. Dismay, regret, intense sorrow—the Quayla was a roiling mass of guilt. Old memories awakened. Memories of failure. Memories of murder.

You did not murder! he shouted to it, trying to break through its self-recrimination.

I killed. What is the difference?

Intent. Intent is the difference. You did not mean to kill members of the Nieti's *crew. You were damaged. You were not responsible.*

I am not damaged now and I am responsible. Lukas, I did not know our joining would harm you. If I had—

If you had, it would have made no difference. I would still have welcomed you. I still do. It isn't how long you live that counts, but how fully.

But—

There are no buts. What is done is done. Even if we could separate, I would not choose to.

I could detach myself from the sensors. I could minimize the sharing. I could—

No. If you deny yourself, you deny me. If you are unhappy, then I will be, too. The loss is not so very great—a few years, at the most. That is a very small price to pay for all you have given me.

The Quayla tested his resolve, mind to mind, heart to heart. It found no qualms. What it needed, he needed. What it wanted, he wanted.

The Quayla argued, but he would not listen. It vowed to re-double its efforts to protect him; he did not argue with that. In the end, it finally accepted—just as he had.

Sometimes, that was all one could do.

Chapter 12

Keenan did not see Kiley until he reported for duty the next evening. They had entered jump, and all the external monitors and sensors were off. As he took over the pilot's seat, his eyes went to them from habit, then moved on to the active displays. He checked the jump chronometer, engine status, and the environmental systems before glancing up. "Any warnings during your shift?"

"None."

"Who's in the engine room?"

"Holly. Jon Robert's asleep. So are Reese and Lia. Are you set?"

He nodded.

"You have the conn, then." Keenan expected her to leave, but she dropped into the copilot's seat instead.

"Daniel, Greg told me what you found during your exam last night. How serious is this accelerated aging process?"

He had been expecting the question all day. "At the present rate? Not terribly. Over a lifetime, it might amount to four or five years. That sounds like a lot, but a series of rough transitions or a prolonged illness could have the same effect."

"What if the rate of aging were to increase?"

"Then I would have to say that would be cause for alarm."

"But not yet?"

"No, particularly if Greg gets more rest than he has been."

"He did last night. He slept almost six hours."

"That's good news."

"Yes, it is." She fiddled with a control on the board, keyed in a request for a report, then ignored the screen as it began to scroll. "Daniel, he is going to be all right, isn't he?"

"He will if you and I have anything to say about it."

She smiled, relaxing for the first time in days. "Thank you." She glanced back at the boards, then added diffidently, "I know you said you weren't interested in working with any patients at the moment, but I was wondering . . ."

"Yes?" he prompted.

"Have you paid any attention to Lia lately?"

"A little," he answered cautiously.

"She's upset about Hope. I think she and Reese have been having problems, too. He'd like them to have children of their own, but she's doesn't want them. She's afraid she'll die if she gets pregnant, the same way Enorra did. Her fear isn't rational and it's hurting her marriage. I don't want to impose, but I was wondering if you might try talking to her. I thought with your training—"

"I already am, Kiley."

"—you might be able to—" She broke off as his words registered. "You are?"

"Yes."

"And?"

"And I'm talking to her. That's all I can say, and probably more than I should."

Kiley gave him a long look. "I thought you didn't want to return to private practice."

"A few hours of listening here and there is hardly a medical practice."

"Then you don't think her problem is serious?"

"Kiley, I told you—I can't discuss anything she or I have or have not said."

"If she isn't well, I have a right to know."

"Only if her condition impairs her work performance or poses a threat to the safety of the ship. Beyond that, what happens between Lia and me is our business and ours alone. If you can't accept that, then you can always ask me to leave the ship."

"And upset Lia, which is to say Reese? Not to mention

Holly and Jon Robert? I'd have a mutiny on my hands if I did."

"The others wouldn't have to know. If you don't want me here, then say so. I'll give your request the same confidentiality I would my talks with a patient."

She looked away first. "How could I ask you to leave?" she asked. "You're the best friend any of us has ever had, myself included. As far as I'm concerned, you can stay forever." And then, as if to prove that, she rose and kissed him on the cheek. He wasn't sure afterward which of them had been more surprised or embarrassed by her unexpected display of affection.

Keenan finished his watch at midnight. He usually stopped by the galley for a snack before going to bed, but he decided to go straight to his cabin instead. He undressed and was about to slide under the covers of his bunk when he noticed a faint glow on the wall to his right. He froze, then took a long, slow look around the rest of the cabin. A dim light, almost too faint to be seen, covered the walls, ceiling, and floor.

The Quayla had taken up residence in his room.

A wave of dismay that bordered on outright rejection washed through him. At the same moment, the light flickered and all but disappeared.

Had he been responsible for that? Keenan clamped down on his response immediately. He accepted the Quayla everywhere else on the ship without a second thought, so why not here? It was not as if it could affect him physically. Nor had he ever sensed anything from it mentally. It was no threat to him. Why not let it stay?

The light brightened. It wasn't gone, then. Keenan fought another wave of panic. Could it really sense what he was thinking and feeling? It must, because suddenly it was fading away again, flowing back into the walls. It was disappearing.

"Wait!" Keenan exclaimed. Without giving himself time to think about what he was doing, he placed his hand flat against the wall, as if he could somehow attract the light's attention. As if he could speak to it and it would hear.

"Wait," he said again. "You don't have to go. Please!"

The light flickered, then brightened. A pool formed beside

his hand. The colors swirled together and intensified, yellow turning to peach, then to a faint, dusty rose. A moment later, a rivulet of light broke away and started creeping toward his hand. He jerked away, then stopped himself. Tentatively, he touched the wall again. Terrified and fascinated at the same time, he watched as the Quayla sent out another streamer. In two breaths the light would touch him. In one. The streamer made a sudden run forward and flowed over his hand.

It covered him.

There was no sensation. None whatsoever.

Keenan clamped down on an involuntary sound that might have been surprise or disappointment. After so much mistrust, this was what he had feared? This . . . nothing? He started to laugh at himself, but before the sound reached his lips, the light started moving again. It poured out of the wall, ran up his arm, then cascaded over his body, covering him before he could step away. He stared at himself in horror, but there was no sensation to the light—neither hot nor cold, pressure nor electricity. There was only radiance.

And then, as quickly as it had covered him, the light left. It flowed away from his body and back into the wall. It spread out across every flat surface like a sheet of yellow fire. For a moment, it burned so brightly that he had to close his eyes in self-defense. The yellow-white turned yellow, then orange, and finally peach, subsiding to a soft, unobtrusive glow.

Keenan backed away from the wall and sat on the edge of his bunk, looking around. The light pulsed quietly. He stared at it for a long time, but nothing else happened. He did not think anything else would, though he would have been hard-pressed to say why. After a time, he lay back on his bunk, still watching. At some point, his eyes grew heavy and he dozed. Some time after that, he slid over the edge of awareness into sleep.

If he dreamed that night, he did not remember.

The *North Star* greeted the *Widdon Galaxy*'s return to Sumpali with another order to stand off while the Gan-Tir scanned the ship. It apparently passed inspection, for five minutes later they received clearance to proceed.

"It's zero-one-thirty local time, Captain Michaelson," the *North Star*'s communications officer said after they docked. "Admiral Bergstrom left orders that you and your crew were to remain on board your ship and keep your hatches sealed if you arrived. He also wanted to arrange a meeting with you. I'll schedule it for zero-eight-hundred tomorrow morning unless you need more time to sleep."

That morning Bergstrom met Kiley in the same conference room they'd used for their last meeting. She had to wait nearly fifteen minutes before he arrived. When he did, she was shocked by the change in him: he had aged a decade in the short time they had been gone, and his manner was now brusque to the point of rudeness.

"Sit down, Captain," he ordered when she started to rise to greet him. "Did Partelli's engineers install the extra water tanks and partitions for the cargo holds?"

"Yes, sir."

"Very well, we'll begin loading the aliens' supplies right away. We'll attach a temporary access tube to your cargo hatch to facilitate the work. Assuming all goes well, your passengers should be on board by late afternoon. As soon as they've settled in, you can leave."

"So quickly?" Kiley asked. She'd anticipated a minimum of one day in port.

"Everyone is anxious for the delegation to be off," Bergstrom said. "You and your crew can be ready to go by then, can't you?"

"Yes, sir."

"Good. The sooner the Gan-Tir have their talk with someone 'in a real position of authority,' the better. They don't have much use for field commanders—or anything else human or Miquiri so far as I've been able to determine." Bergstrom leaned back in his seat and fixed Kiley with a pale blue stare. "Things have not gone well since you left. Our talks with the Miquiri have stalled completely. We've spent most of our time negotiating the composition of the diplomatic parties. The final agreement was for each group to send three representatives. We've told the Miquiri and Gan-Tir that we expect their people to be on their best behavior, but I doubt either of them paid much attention—which brings me to the reason for our meeting."

"Admiral?"

"Much as I respect your abilities, Captain, it is my judgment that you have neither the training nor the experience required to make command decisions under emergency conditions. For that reason, I have decided that the human group will consist of one diplomatic officer, Elena Cristavos; my first officer, Lieutenant Commander Pete Uhrich; and the *North Star*'s security chief, Ji Fong. Uhrich will be acting as my representative while he is on your ship. I am giving him full authority to assume command of your vessel at any point, should he deem that necessary to insure your safe arrival at Resurrection."

"You're what? Admiral—"

"Save your protests, Captain. I don't want to hear them. I have made my decision and I am not going to let you, the Miquiri, or the Gan-Tir overrule me. Uhrich won't interfere unless he believes your ship or your passengers are in jeopardy. If he does, though, you are to obey any and all instructions he gives you."

"Admiral, I won't agree to that! I am the captain of the *Widdon Galaxy*. If I transfer command, it will be to the person of my choice, at the time and place of my choice."

"If you find yourself facing some of the problems we've had the past ten days, you'll be glad you have a choice," Bergstrom said harshly. "I can understand your feelings, but my sole concern is the safety of the diplomats. I expect nothing less from you. Both Uhrich and Fong will be armed and—"

"No!" Kiley exclaimed, jumping to her feet. "We have never carried weapons on the ship and we aren't starting now. I won't tolerate them!"

Bergstrom's eyes flashed. "Sit down, Captain," he said, and then, when she did not, he spoke in the flattest, most dangerous voice she had ever heard. "I said, sit down."

She sat.

"In case you've forgotten, let me remind you that you are

operating in a restricted zone, under the authority of the Corps. You can, of course, refuse to comply with my requests, but if you do, I have the legal authority to commandeer your ship and crew. If your crew refuses to obey my orders, they will be placed under arrest, along with you. Is that understood?"

The parts of Kiley's body that weren't rigid with anger were shaking with fury. She had realized they would be losing civilian protections when they entered Miquiri space, but she had dismissed that concern, believing the Corps had no reason to be anything but fair with them.

"The Miquiri might have something to say about that," she said stoutly. "The Gan-Tir, too, for that matter."

"The Gan-Tir's sole interest is reaching human space. They don't care one way or the other what happens to you. Furthermore, while it is true that the Miquiri will permit only your ship to come and go, they've made no stipulations about the personnel who operate her."

"They might if they knew you were planning to seize her."

"They might," Bergstrom agreed. "Then again, they might not. I'm prepared to take that risk, Captain. Are you?"

She was not. Bergstrom softened his voice. "I don't like making threats, Captain, and believe me, I do understand your feelings. If this were an ordinary mission, I'd respect them. Unfortunately, it isn't. The Gan-Tir are large, they are powerful, and they are virtually uncontrollable. They have entered restricted areas on the *North Star* several times before we could stop them. They contaminated one clean room, setting a researcher's work back nearly a year. The Miquiri must have some degree of control over them, because they haven't overrun the station yet, but there won't be a strong Miquiri presence on your ship. There's no telling what the Gan-Tir might decide to do once you're away from port. I hope weapons won't be necessary, but if they are, my people will have them."

"Weapons don't discourage violence, Admiral—they promote it. I don't want them on the *Widdon Galaxy*."

"Well, you're going to get them. And before you start marshaling your arguments, let me remind you that ours may not be the only ones that are brought on board—the Gan-Tir and

Miquiri may carry protective devices of their own along. The only difference is, you won't necessarily recognize their weapons until too late."

"I thought these people were supposed to be diplomats!"

"These 'people' are aliens. There's no telling what they might do, or when they might do it. I believe the Miquiri have been straightforward with us, but the Gan-Tir are another matter entirely. We haven't committed a grave insult yet, but it could still happen. If it does, neither we nor you can count on them showing much tolerance. My men are going with you and they will be armed. Regardless of your personal feelings about the matter, I expect you to treat them with respect and courtesy. Is that understood?"

Kiley swallowed the ball of anger in her throat. "Yes, sir."

A red light began to blink at one corner of the table. Bergstrom glanced at it and stood immediately. "I'm sorry, Captain, but I'm needed on the bridge. I'm sure you have a great deal more to say, but, frankly, I don't have time to listen. I'll send Uhrich over shortly to meet you and oversee the cargo transfer. I think you'll find him both competent and reliable. If you're still upset, however, feel free to log a formal complaint."

For all the good it will do. Kiley sat where she was after Bergstrom strode out of the room, taking several deep breaths. She didn't care how competent or likable Uhrich might be— she was the ship's captain, and she had no intention of turning her command over to him. He could not run the *Widdon Galaxy* without the computer control codes, and she would not give them up without a fight, no matter how much he threatened.

Only it might not be her that he threatened. If Uhrich really wanted to manipulate her, he would turn his weapons on someone she cared about. Someone like Greg, or Jon Robert, or even Hope. But would he?

Kiley stood abruptly. Uhrich was a Corps officer, trained to do whatever was required to carry out his orders. The question wasn't what he would do, but how far she would go to oppose him. She wasn't sure, and she hoped she never had to find out.

* * *

Sensar Kaikiel Anara finished packing the last of his robes and straightened, surveying the cabin to be certain he had left nothing behind. Except for the bag on his bunk and the givitch next to the door, there was no sign that he had ever occupied the room.

He was not sorry to be leaving. Though aesthetically pleasing, the cabin was tiny. He could take a maximum of one step sideways and three forward or backward, and had not been able to prostrate himself during his daily meditations since leaving home. Intellectually, he knew that strict adherence to ritual did not matter. The physical routines of *jis* had no significance in and of themselves; they were intended solely to tone the body, while setting the mind free. Still, a break in physical routines tended to alter mental ones as well. He had reached the third level only once since boarding the ship, and his nerves and concentration had suffered noticeably in consequence. He did not care if his quarters on the human ship were comfortable or not, but he did hope they would have a little more space.

The cabin door opened and Sensar whirled around. Rairea stood in the corridor. She did not come in, but her eyes made a quick circuit of the room, looking for telltale signs of his habitation.

"You are packed," she said, her words sounding more like an accusation than a statement of fact.

Sensar had moved to the first level of *jis* as soon as he saw her, and now willed relaxation to muscles gone suddenly tense. He could not control his initial reaction to her, but he could—and would—control all that followed. "I wished to be ready when the call came," he said.

"How very dutiful of you. But then, you always were a dutiful student, weren't you—even with me. Especially with me. I look forward to instructing you again, Sensar Kaikiel."

He bowed deeply. "You honor me, Rairea Tayturin, but I could not possibly permit you to devote so much of your valued time and attention to one so unworthy. You have concerns of far greater importance than my personal development."

"You refer to the talks with the aliens? It is true that they will require some attention, but I am much more interested in renewing our acquaintance."

Rairea moved swiftly into the room. Evading her would have been difficult in an open space; in the close confines of the cabin, Sensar had no chance. She slid her *elith*s up his arms, coiling them tightly, binding his limbs to hers. She pressed against him. She was very strong—he had broken her hold on only one occasion, and he had bruised his *elith*s badly in the process. She had laughed afterward, telling him that she had let him go, robbing him of even that minor victory. His struggles had amused her. She had not lost control—not then, or any other time. Her self-discipline was legendary. So was her prowess. There were many who had envied him his time with her; there were many who would have given a fortune to stand as he stood now, Rairea's *elith*s wrapped around his.

He would rather be dead.

Sensar snapped off all physical awareness, retreating into his mind and reaching for the third level of *jis* as if his life depended on finding it. He had practiced that move often, and he went so deep that he could neither hear nor feel. He stood in the middle of a vast, empty void. Nothing could reach him; nothing could touch him. He was in the place of nonbeing, where only thought existed.

Rairea spoke, but her words had no meaning. She stroked his *elith*, but he felt nothing. She stepped away and spoke again. He did not listen. She could touch him, but she could not make him hers, not ever again. He floated beyond pain and anger. Beyond pride. He was free.

Rairea gave up after a time and left. He had won.

Or had he? Though he had not registered her parting words, one sound had penetrated his mental barrier.

Rairea had laughed at him.

"Are you ready?" Pitar asked Chirith, coming into his cubicle.

Chirith finished fastening his bag and turned around. "Yes."

Packing had not taken long. Unlike the humans and the

Gan-Tir, the Miquiri did not require clothing, so Chirith had to assemble only his brush and a few personal supplies. At the last minute, foreseeing long periods of inactivity, he had added a portable text viewer to his case. The library onstation contained few books, but one of the diplomats had offered to loan him several. He chose works that he had meant to read for some time, as well as an old favorite, *The Chronicles of a Voyager Among the Stars.* He lifted his bag. He was ready. At times, he was even eager.

"Remember, you are not to speak to the Gan-Tir," Pitar cautioned him for at least the fifth time. "Leave them to me or Leetian."

"I remember." Chirith tried not to stiffen.

"It is not that I doubt you, Chirith," Pitar said quickly, "but this is a delicate mission. Living among strangers—human or Gan-Tir—will be most trying."

"I know that." Chirith turned away. The senior diplomat crossed the room and touched his shoulder. *I did not mean to offend,* he said in the third language. *Must you always turn away from me?*

Chirith forced himself to relax. They had spoken several times during the past weeks. The diplomat had always been considerate and sympathetic. And, always, he had been searching for a degree of intimacy that Chirith was not prepared to offer. It wasn't that he disliked Pitar—no, he found himself liking the other Miquiri too much. He did not want another *akia.* He did not want to mourn another so greatly that his own life lost all meaning. And yet, without the bond that tied one to another, what meaning was there? Pitar had made that argument repeatedly. Chirith heard, but he was not ready to listen. He had begun to doubt that he ever would be. Nonetheless, he turned to face Pitar.

Chirith, are you certain you wish to make this journey? Pitar asked, speaking in the second language this time, his hands moving rapidly. *There is still time to select another if traveling with the humans or Gan-Tir disturbs you.* He did not add, *If I disturb you.*

I have not changed my mind.

Good. I would be sorry to lose you. The humans like you and trust you. The trip will give us an unprecedented opportunity to observe them in their own surroundings.

Chirith tensed again, and Pitar caught his withdrawal as if he already possessed the preternatural sensitivity of an *akia. I am not asking you to spy upon those whom you have befriended,* he said. *I wish only to learn as much as we can from them, and to assure ourselves that they are well. The* North Star *claims they are isolating the* Widdon Galaxy*'s crew to prevent unnecessary contact with the Gan-Tir. That is most likely true, but we cannot overlook the possibility that they are using the Gan-Tir as an excuse to hide trouble from us. Lukas or one of the other humans might be experiencing difficulty in adapting to the Quayla. The Quayla itself may be unstable. If that is true, then we must know.*

I understand that, Pitar. I will observe and I will report my findings.

Pitar touched Chirith's arm, his fingers pressing lightly. *You will not be betraying them,* he said. *If there is no difficulty, then relax. Talk with them freely. Who knows how long it will be before we have another opportunity to live among the humans? A week in their world will teach us more than years of talks.*

And if there is a problem?

If there is, then we will speak of it, openly and frankly. I trust your wisdom and experience. They are the reasons I asked you to accompany me.

But they are not the only reasons, Chirith said.

No.

Chirith's hands tightened, and he had to force them to continue signing. *I am not ready for another akia, Pitar. I cannot give what you are asking of me.*

You mean, you will not. Chirith, much as I admire and respect you, much as I would be honored to have you call me akia, it would be a bitter word if you spoke it with your hands only, and not your heart. If you do not wish to come closer to me, then do not. I will understand that. But you must find someone. The past is dead. You may mourn it, but you must also bury it. You cannot continue to bear such sadness. You cannot continue to hold yourself so far apart from others. Those who live outside the group have no purpose in life, no meaning. If you do not turn back to others soon, you will be lost—not only to your people, but to yourself. I do not say this from anger or hurt, Chirith. I say this because it is so.

The words were not easy; Pitar looked sick signing them. And Chirith felt sick seeing them.

Pitar was right. He had moved too far from the others around him; the distance was wrong. So was his refusal to share with one so willing. He nodded. Then, knowing full well what he was doing, he turned his back on Pitar.

The diplomat did not move for several seconds. Chirith was not certain what response he had expected after such an insult, but the one that came was a total surprise.

Pitar touched his arm. *I still want you to come with me,* he said in the third language. *Will you? Can you?*

Chirith hesitated, then gestured assent. Pitar pressed his shoulder lightly, offering silent thanks, and then left.

Chirith did not turn around again until the door had closed.

Chapter 13

Uhrich arrived just after Kiley returned to the *Widdon Galaxy*.

Reese saw him first and sent him to the cargo deck, where Kiley, Jon Robert, and Lukas were taking a final look at the two modified holds. Each had been divided into five sections: three to be used as private rooms, one for food storage, and the fifth to serve as a common room. No matter how comfortable the aliens' furnishing might be, the accommodations were primitive at best; Kiley did not envy them their journey. She had hoped that they would have a last-minute change of heart and call off the trip. But they had not, and a Corps shuttle carrying the first cargo container was docking when Uhrich arrived.

"Captain Michaelson?" he asked Kiley. She nodded. He held out his hand. "Lieutenant Commander Pete Uhrich. Admiral Bergstrom said you would be expecting me."

Her first impression was not favorable. Uhrich was about her height, with a slender, wiry build and short, fine hair the color of sand. His skin was pale, his eyes blue-gray. He looked young, until she noticed the fine lines radiating out from the corners of his eyes and mouth and guessed he had to be at least Lukas's age, if not several years older. First officer on the *North Star* was the equivalent of a captaincy on a smaller vessel, and the Corps did not give out such assignments early or easily.

Uhrich's hand was cool, his grip quick and hard. He repeated the handshake with Jon Robert and Lukas as Kiley introduced each of them.

"Pleased to meet you," he said to Jon Robert, his voice and

manner completely controlled. Smooth, Kiley thought as she watched him. Very smooth. She had no doubt he was also very good at his job—she couldn't see Bergstrom putting up with a first officer whose performance fell short of outstanding.

"And you," he said to Lukas. The words were polite, but the look he gave Lukas and the Quayla wasn't. Lukas stiffened and the two men exchanged glances, weighing each other up. Kiley had the feeling that neither of them passed the other's test.

"I understand that you're coming on board as Bergstrom's general watchdog," Lukas said, a hard edge to his voice that Kiley hadn't heard before.

"That's right. I'm sure there will be no need to intervene, but the admiral doesn't take anything for granted." *Neither do I,* his expression warned. He turned to Kiley. "For the record, Captain, I can't foresee any circumstance in which I would take command of your ship, short of you and the rest of your crew being incapacitated. I would like to familiarize myself with your bridge operations as a precaution, however. I'll be happy to stand a regular watch in return, if you care to assign me to a shift."

"I appreciate your offer, Lieutenant Commander, but I already have a full bridge crew. I don't believe we'll require your assistance." *In any capacity.*

Uhrich's eyes flickered, but his smile didn't slip. "Please, call me Pete. 'Lieutenant Commander' is a bit of a mouthful for anything less than formal occasions."

"If you wish."

"I do. And now, if you don't mind, I'd like to look over the aliens' quarters. The admiral asked me to make certain everything is in order before they board."

Uhrich remained on the cargo deck after the family left. Lukas and Jon Robert went to the engine room to finish the monthly maintenance checks. They were testing the Quayla's reports against those returned by Jon Robert's instruments. The Quayla had learned to interpret the sensors' data accurately, and so far, they had not encountered a single variance.

Kiley went to the bridge, hoping she would find her burgeoning tension easier to control in familiar surroundings. Resurrection was ten days away. The Corps and the aliens themselves had taken every precaution for a safe trip, but what if one of them couldn't tolerate jump on a human ship? What if one of them became ill? What if any one of the other dangers inherent in space travel materialized?

Their course would take the ship along the edge of the barrier. If the navigation or jump systems malfunctioned, they could come out too close to the boundary and find themselves trapped the way the *Nieti* had been. There was a marginal risk factor associated with every jump, no matter how carefully executed. Sometimes ships failed to come out at all, for no apparent reason. If anything went wrong, the responsibility would be hers. As Kiley walked down the ship's main corridor, the weight of command had never felt heavier.

She expected to find the bridge deserted when she arrived, but Keenan was there, in the middle of running the preflight checks.

"You'll probably want to start over," he said as he rose to give her the pilot's seat, "but I thought I'd try working my way through them on my own."

She glanced at the log and checked his results so far. "I don't see why—it looks like you've done everything perfectly. In fact, after this trip is over, you ought to take the certification test for your intersystem pilot's license. You could easily pass the written portion and simulations now. All you lack is a few hundred more hours of practical experience." She started to say she'd pay his licensing fees if he did, then stopped as the *North Star* hailed them. She reached for the intercom. "This is Captain Michaelson. Proceed."

"Admiral Bergstrom asked me to tell you the Gan-Tir delegation has left their ship and will be arriving shortly."

"We copy," Kiley said. A few minutes later, she heard noises in the corridor. She and Keenan went to the hatch and stopped just outside. Two Corps security officers had taken up positions in the main corridor. One blocked the way to the family's cabins, and the other stood a few steps down the corridor running between the bridge and engine room.

"All clear," the one to Kiley's right called out.

A moment later, the first of the Gan-Tir strode through the personnel hatch. Two more followed close behind.

Kiley had forgotten how big they were. So, apparently, had Keenan; he took a sharp breath when he caught sight of them. Intentionally or not, the combination of their massive bodies and smooth, gliding movements projected an aura of violence. The very air around them seemed to coalesce and quiver uneasily. The hair on Kiley's arms lifted as they approached, and it was all she could do to hold her position. Keenan must have shared her reaction, because he took an involuntary step back before catching himself. Kiley wondered if the Gan-Tir struck the Miquiri with equal force, or if her response was triggered by some clash of fundamentally opposing biologies.

Two humans walked ahead of the Gan-Tir, leading the way. One was Uhrich; the other was a dark-haired woman approaching middle age. Kiley had to accord Uhrich a certain grudging respect when she saw how close to the aliens he was. He did not betray his aversion by a single quiver of flesh or expression. There was no doubt he shared Kiley's feelings, though— they were in his stiff stance and the warning in his eyes.

The woman beside him asked a question in a low voice, and Uhrich nodded. She put up her hand to stop the Gan-Tir. "This is Kiley Michaelson," she said, making the Miquiri signs for her words as she spoke. Small-boned and slender, she moved with a dancer's light-footed grace. Her short, dark hair had been cut to accentuate her eyes and cheekbones. She spoke with a faint accent, but her voice was clear and precise. "She is captain of the ship. Captain, I am Elena Cristavos, one of the senior diplomatic officers at Sumpali. I believe you've already met Lieutenant Commander Uhrich?"

"Yes."

"These are the Gan-Tir you will be transporting. The first is Rairea Tayturin. She is the ranking diplomatic representative." She gestured to the alien beside her. Her black tunic and pants, made of some thin, silky fabric, hugged her body when she moved. "Next to her is Sensar Anara, and last is Henherik Tortorend. Sensar is a scholar and linguist. Henherik is attached to the diplomatic mission in some capacity, but I must admit, we're not sure exactly what it is. They understand some of what we say, Captain," she added smoothly before Kiley could reply.

Was she offering information or a warning? Kiley gave Cristavos a quick look, but the woman's eyes were on the aliens. Rairea was the largest of the three, and the most solidly colored. Her forehead and the right side of her face were a deep, glossy black, while the left side and her neck were pure white. Despite her aversion to the Gan-Tir, Kiley found herself wondering whether that flesh would feel hard, like the polished stone it resembled, or as soft and silky as the robe Rairea wore. Woven from fine threads dyed brilliant shades of blue and green, the loose garment covered her so well that all Kiley could determine of her physiology was that she was large and stood upright.

"Be welcome here," Kiley said, at the same time offering the standard Miquiri greeting with her hands.

The sleeves of Rairea's gown fell back as she lifted her arm, revealing a thick limb around which a long tentacle coiled. *You honor me,* she replied. The appendages at the end of her arm had more difficulty forming the signs than Kiley's had. They were as long as hers, but not as flexible. Her tentacle remained tightly wrapped until she finished the greeting. Then with a move so rapid that Kiley saw only a blur, she uncoiled it and formed a sign in the air that Kiley did not recognize. Afterward, her tentacle moved slowly from side to side, looking like a snake about to strike.

The sudden gesture surprised Kiley and she took a hasty step back. She ran into Keenan, who caught and steadied her. Rairea's tentacle jerked and froze.

"Don't move!" Uhrich ordered.

Kiley didn't hear him. All her attention was on Rairea's tentacle as it shot out abruptly and touched the side of her face. She would have retreated, but she had nowhere to go. Keenan's arm tightened around her, holding her still.

"Daniel!" she protested.

"Don't move!" he ordered. "She won't hurt you."

She had time to wonder how he could be so certain about that before the tentacle flattened against her cheek and swept across her face. She closed her eyes, ostensibly to protect them, but partially to hide the vision of the black and white appendage.

The tentacle reached the other side of her face and paused. The pressure eased and Kiley opened her eyes, only to squeeze them shut hastily as the tip of the tentacle brushed her eyelids, then her nose, and finally her lips. It moved slowly and delicately, and then, finally, it withdrew.

The corridor filled with sound, the sort of deep vibration a transport vehicle groaning under a heavy load might make. Kiley opened her eyes. Rairea was speaking. At least, Kiley assumed the noise was speech. The Gan-Tir that Cristavos had identified as Sensar made an answering sound.

Sensar's tentacle emerged from the folds of his green and yellow robe. Keenan tensed and Kiley thought he was going to place himself between her and the Gan-Tir. But before he could move, a second tentacle touched her face. That was all, just one touch, tip to cheek, and then the male Gan-Tir wrapped his tentacle around his arm again. He brought his other appendage up and began signaling. *We come as friends.*

It was the customary continuation of Rairea's greeting. The complete translation was "We come to talk and share. Give welcome and we both may profit."

Kiley swallowed, then forced her hands to move in the standard response. *Let us speak.*

Sensar made a short, booming noise that could have signified anything, and then bowed his head.

"Well, I'll be . . ." Uhrich said under his breath. "Cristavos, does that mean what I think it does?"

The diplomat nodded. "Captain, you probably don't realize it, but you've just received quite an honor. The Gan-Tir don't speak to anyone they haven't formally recognized. Sensar just acknowledged you by bowing. They don't do that to everyone.

You should return the gesture—it's the proper response. Go on. You'll be guilty of a serious insult if you don't."

The Gan-Tir was standing erect again, his violet eyes staring past Kiley's. Kiley nodded her head. His eyes flickered, meeting hers and connecting for the briefest of instants.

Proceed, Rairea signaled to Cristavos.

The diplomat turned to Uhrich, who said, "This way." He nodded to the main corridor and led the party toward the elevators. None of them looked back.

"One of them touched me like that," Keenan said in a low voice as soon as they were out of hearing range. "It didn't bow to me, though. I wonder why Sensar acknowledged you?"

"Because she's captain," Lukas answered, coming forward. He had been headed for the bridge when the delegation started down the hall and had stepped aside to let it pass. "They have to acknowledge someone; otherwise, they can't make their wishes known. They usually choose the highest-ranking person they can find. They hear what everyone else says, of course, but they don't always respond."

"How convenient," Kiley said dryly.

"Isn't it, though?" Lukas replied. "I'm not looking forward to the next few weeks. They aren't going to be easy to deal with."

"Neither am I." Kiley suppressed a shiver.

Chapter 14

With satisfaction, Sensar surveyed the quarters the humans had given him. They were much larger than he had dared hope. Could it be that they, too, liked a sense of space around themselves?

The Miquiri did not—they huddled together in groups. One could not find a solitary Miquiri, but the humans moved alone as often as they walked in groups. Moreover, the configurations of their social units changed frequently. The regroupings made individuals more difficult to identify, but it also made the humans a great deal more intriguing.

Sensar wanted to speak to one of them at length. He had asked Rairea to arrange an opportunity at Sumpali; she told him that she had tried, but that the humans had not welcomed the idea. He was not certain she was being honest. A brief tasting would have told him, but he refrained. Touch would have revealed as much about him as he learned about her. Touch could be dangerous.

Rairea took charge of Sensar and Henherik as soon as they left their ship, assigning them rooms on either side of hers. The partitions between the chambers were not thick; sound carried easily from one to the next. By placing herself between them, Rairea could learn what was happening on either side of her. She could also visit either of them without the other one knowing. Unless, of course, she chose to speak openly of what she did.

Knowing her, Sensar thought, she would. The more her sexual partners preferred privacy, the more likely she was to broadcast every detail of their relationships. When she had taken Sensar into her rooms, the entire city had known. He could not walk anywhere without eyes following him. Many had been envious, but that had been no consolation whatsoever.

The door opened and Rairea came in. "The givitch is here," she announced. She beckoned for the human behind her to enter and put the packing box in the corner closest to the door. The human guided its conveyer in that direction, eyeing Rairea and Sensar nervously. Rairea gestured emphatically: *down*. The box thumped to the floor. They did not have to encourage the human to leave; he fled as soon as the conveyer slid free of its cargo.

Sensar crossed the room in two strides and ripped the container open, ignoring the tool Rairea offered. The humans had tried to make him leave the givitch behind. He had refused, explaining that it was dependent on him. They had argued, and he had finally lifted the box himself, determined to take it with him. Then the humans pulled weapons. Everyone froze. Diplomats and an interpreter were summoned. They listened to him, then consulted with the others. The humans finally said the givitch could go with him, but insisted that it be sent along with the rest of his baggage.

He had been upset, but was forced to stand by and watch as the humans shoved the givitch into a box little larger than a coffin. They were careless, and the givitch had screamed as the box hinges crushed one of its appendages. Sensar intervened then and finished closing the box himself. The humans had been agitated and their tiny voices had shaken with emotion, but he had ignored them. Rairea had given Sensar a furious look, but he had ignored her, too. He had stayed beside the box, caressing the smooth sides, as if by doing so he could calm the plaintive cries from within.

He had wanted to travel with the box, but Rairea had not let him. It would not be seemly, she had said, to board the human ship as if he were a piece of cargo. When he argued, she had turned on him in fury. "You will come with me and Henherik," she ordered. He went, but he worried about the givitch the entire time.

Now the box opened with a screech and the givitch greeted Sensar with a sob. It nearly fell out of the container in its haste to wrap itself around him. He soothed it as best he could, but it was some time before it stopped quivering. When he finally stepped away, he expected Rairea to be gone. But she was still there, watching him.

"It is beyond me how you can stand to have that thing touching you," she said. "But then, you always were attracted to the exotic. First that, and now these humans."

"It was you who took first taste of them, in case you had forgotten."

"But you were not far behind, were you? Lonlores says you have a positive fetish for them."

"Lonlores says many things, virtually none of which are true. I am a scholar. I study the humans because I wish to learn more about them."

"Why? They are inferior beings. They have nothing to teach us."

"I'm not so sure about that. Not yet." The givitch stirred uneasily, and Sensar gave it an absent stroke.

"I suppose I shouldn't be surprised—you've been known to argue that the Miquiri have value beyond simply supplying us with trade goods."

"Don't tell me that you disagree. You would not be making this journey unless you believed the Miquiri alliance was important to us—or that the humans hold potential."

"No? Perhaps I am here because you are. Have you considered that, Sensar Kaikiel?" She came closer, laughing as he recoiled. "It is true, I have a small interest in these humans, and I would hardly turn down a chance to further my status among the other diplomats—but I would have come even if that were not the case. I would have come because I knew you would be here. Just as you would never pass up the opportunity to observe a new species, I wanted to see you again, Sensar. I have missed the taste of you. I think you have missed me, too." Her right *elith* traced a line down his body, touching face, neck, and arm. The tip found the edge of his sleeve and slipped beneath.

"No!"

"Yes." She tasted him, the tip of her *elith* opening and pressing lightly against his skin, moving in a slow, lazy circle. She wanted to provoke him, if only to push her away. She wanted him to touch her, but he held still. He had no intention of stimulating her, however inadvertently. Instead, he reached for the third level of *jis*. He missed completely. He tried for the second level. Then the first. He missed them.

Rairea took another long, savoring taste of him. He stood rigid, refusing to give her the slightest response. She had taken him at such a moment years ago; she was close to forcing a response now. She must have known that, but she stepped away, then laughed at his startled look.

"Ah, Sensar, you have so much to learn. So very much. You salved your conscience with claims of seduction before, but this time, I will not make it so easy for you. Before this trip is over, you will beg me to hold you. You do not believe that? I do. I look forward to the moment—after all your denials, it will be most gratifying."

Chapter 15

Uhrich and Cristavos escorted the Miquiri on board half an hour later.

Lukas saw a familiar form in the group and exclaimed, "Chirith!" He started forward, signaling rapidly, but Chirith made a sign that Kiley did not recognize. Lukas's hands stopped moving in midgesture. *Later,* Chirith added, then turned away and waited for Cristavos to introduce them.

Chirith's companions were Pitar and Leetian. Pitar was the tallest of the three, and had dark, reddish-brown body hair. Leetian was shorter than he, but taller than Chirith, and solid black. Kiley knew from Lukas that Pitar was male, but she could not determine Leetian's gender.

Uhrich let Cristavos make the introductions, then urged the group toward the elevator that would take them belowdecks. Leaving the Miquiri to settle in, he and Cristavos went back to the *North Star* to pick up their own belongings, and another man accompanied them when they returned. Uhrich introduced him as Ji Fong, the *North Star*'s senior security officer. A lean, well-muscled man with restless eyes, he had an air of controlled watchfulness that made Kiley uneasy. He studied Kiley, Lukas, and Keenan in turn, assessing each of them. He was polite, but his black eyes gave away nothing.

When Uhrich, Cristavos, and Fong went to their quarters to unpack, Kiley called the *North Star* and asked for permission to pull out. She expected to deal with the ship's communications officer, but Bergstrom himself came on.

"You are cleared for departure, *Widdon Galaxy*," he said. "Proceed with caution."

Kiley had heard the same words on hundreds of other occasions, but they had never come from an admiral before—nor had they carried so clear a warning. She fired the maneuvering thrusters and the ship slowly edged away from the dock.

"Clear," Lukas said a moment later.

She gave the viewscreens a confirming glance, then opened the intercom to the engine room. "Jon Robert, give me fifty percent power from the main engines. Greg, lay in our usual course."

The ship surged forward. They were under way.

The first two days of the trip were uneventful. They had all been concerned about the effects of jump on the Gan-Tir and Miquiri, but the aliens did not report any adverse effects. With Cristavos, Uhrich, and Fong to look after the diplomats, Kiley and her family decided most of their apprehension had been groundless. Until the third day out from Sumpali, when the Gan-Tir decided to explore the ship.

Keenan, standing his regular watch on the bridge, heard a noise in the corridor and swiveled the pilot's seat around, expecting to see Kiley or Lukas. Instead, he found one Gan-Tir already on the bridge and another coming through the hatch. By the time he reached his feet, both were inside, examining the backup communications board.

They were alone.

Where were Cristavos and Uhrich? Where was Fong? The Corps officers were supposed to keep the aliens belowdecks. For a fleeting moment, Keenan wondered if something had happened to them. Then he stopped worrying about the humans as the two aliens turned toward the main control board. Toward him.

Keenan hit the ship's alarm, his reaction pure reflex. The clang was loud enough to hurt his ears, but it didn't stop the Gan-Tir. They took one step toward him, and another.

"You can't stay here," he said. "You must leave!"

They ignored him and continued advancing. Keenan had the conn; he was responsible for the ship's safety. They might mean no harm, but even the most innocent of acts around the controls could result in death for everyone. He could not let them advance any farther.

Without giving himself time to consider the consequences, Keenan stepped between the pilot's and copilot's seats, blocking the path to the control board. The Gan-Tir paused, and two sets of hot violet eyes locked upon him. Then the larger of the two—the one Cristavos had introduced as Rairea—lifted her arm. Her tentacle uncoiled and moved past his shoulder, toward the banks of switches. Whether by design or chance, she went for the emergency shutdown controls for the ship's engines. She was one sweep of her tentacle away from disabling the ship and killing them all.

Her tentacle dipped.

Keenan threw himself at the appendage, praying that the force of his body would be enough to deflect her aim. He hit hard enough to jar the air from his lungs. Rairea's tentacle went wide, striking the copilot's seat. She raised her right arm defensively, but it was the second Gan-Tir who caught Keenan—the irregularly spotted one Cristavos had called Sensar.

One of Sensar's tentacles lashed around Keenan's ribs and waist, trapping his left arm against his body. The alien jerked him away from the passage between the seats. Keenan gasped at the sudden pain, then gasped again as Sensar's other tentacle whipped around his neck, cutting off his breath.

Rairea spoke. Deep, booming sounds echoed in the confined space. Sensar released Keenan so abruptly that he nearly fell, but he caught himself against the pilot's seat and straightened. He took a tearing breath. He didn't think his ribs were broken, but his entire midsection throbbed; he would be sporting massive bruises by the next day.

Assuming he lived that long.

Why hadn't anyone come in response to the alarm? Kiley and Lukas were less than a minute from the bridge, assuming they were in their cabin. Fong, Uhrich, and Cristavos were no more than three or four minutes away. Where were they?

Rairea said something to Sensar, and then, with a gesture too deliberate to be anything but calculated, she reached for the engine control switches a second time. Her tentacle was touching them by the time Keenan caught it. He closed his hands around the appendage and tried to pull, then push it away. He could not budge her.

One of Sensar's tentacles brushed the side of his neck, then slipped lightly around his throat. The other wrapped around his waist. They started to tighten, the pressure increasing slowly but steadily. Keenan's ears began to ring, and the room dimmed. It wasn't only breath that Sensar was cutting off—it was the supply of blood to his brain. Did the alien know that pressure on a human's carotid arteries could render him unconscious within seconds? He might have, because the pressure eased abruptly, as if the alien had meant to warn, rather than harm.

Keenan let go of Rairea's arm. Sensar released him. Keenan wanted to run, but Sensar blocked his way. The two had crowded him against the control board, and he was in danger of inadvertently pressing switches himself if he moved.

For the third time, Rairea reached around Keenan for the engine controls. Keenan did not move; he was reasonably certain by then that she was more interested in his response than the boards. He could not read the thoughts in her deep-set eyes, but he believed she was baiting him. She had to know by now that he considered the controls vital. She had to realize that she would be endangering her own life if she touched them. She was playing games, but that didn't mean he had to participate.

He stood still as her tentacle brushed one set of switches, then another, her eyes staying on him the entire time. He held her gaze, ignoring his throbbing arms and ribs, ignoring the sweat beginning to dampen his shirt, ignoring Sensar's solid body pressing against his side. Rairea lifted her arm. Her tentacle waved in the air between them, and then, without warning, it slashed toward the engine controls for the fourth time.

Keenan caught it the moment before it hit, wrapping his arms around the fleshy stalk. He could not feel Rairea's skin through the gown she wore, but he could distinguish between arm and tentacle. He ignored her arm and held on to her tentacle, gripping it with all the strength he possessed.

Rairea had one more tentacle. Sensar had two. All three of them lashed around him at the same instant: Rairea's around his neck and Sensar's gripping his arms and chest. Keenan heard a noise in the corridor. Help had finally come, but it had arrived too late—Rairea's tentacle was squeezing hard, cutting off his air and blood supply.

Keenan grayed out. Rairea eased her grip, so he didn't black out completely, but by the time he returned to full awareness people filled the room.

Lukas had arrived first, Kiley one step behind him. After them had come Fong and Uhrich. Jon Robert and Cristavos were out in the corridor. Keenan could not see the Miquiri, but he heard high-pitched whistling sounds and a strong, foul odor swept through the bridge. They had arrived, and they were upset.

"What's going on here?" Kiley demanded in her best captain's voice.

Rairea and Sensar ignored her—and everyone else, as well. Their eyes were on Keenan, as if he and they were the only ones present. Fong started to push his way onto the bridge, aiming the disrupter he carried at the Gan-Tir.

Kiley whirled around. "No!" she said sharply. "No weapons!" Fong lowered his arm, but only because Uhrich repeated her order.

Rairea rumbled. So did Sensar. The alien was pressed so close to Keenan that the sound vibrated in his chest. Rairea squeezed Keenan's neck. He jerked, then forced himself to relax. She was testing him, like a cat playing with a fluttering bird. He had to remain calm. He had to think, not react. She might be a cat, but he did not have to be the bird.

Rairea's eyes flickered when he didn't respond to the pressure she was exerting. Her tentacle uncoiled from his neck and began waving in the air before his face. It went from side to side, a black and white cobra contemplating a strike.

"Daniel, are you all right?" Kiley asked.

He tried to answer, only to find his throat so tight that he couldn't speak. Swelling could have been responsible for that; so could fear. He swallowed and was about to try again when

Rairea's tentacle touched his face. Fine hairs brushed his skin, tickling. With delicate, precisely controlled movements she touched his cheek, then his forehead, then his eyes and lips. Her tentacle flattened and made a slow sweep of his face. She rumbled and Sensar loosened his hold. Keenan saw an opportunity to break free and seized it, but before he had taken one step, Rairea caught his arm. Her tentacle coiled around his wrist and cut off the flow of blood to his hand.

"Bestial," she boomed.

Keenan went rigid. So did everyone else on the bridge. Though her voice was little more than a vibration, what she had said was clearly a word—a human word. Cristavos had warned them that the Gan-Tir could understand some of their language; she had not said they could speak it. Perhaps she had not known. Keenan caught a glimpse of the diplomat's face. It was white with shock.

Sensar's tentacle brushed Keenan's hair, then slid down his cheek, pressing against it as Rairea's had, though his touch was lighter. The fine hairs that covered the appendage brushed Keenan's skin, raising his flesh. The tentacle paused on the far side of Keenan's face and . . . sucked.

Keenan bucked, forgetting what held him, forgetting the Gan-Tir's speed and strength, forgetting everything as he made a panic-stricken bid to tear free.

"Bestial!" Rairea boomed again, the sound much louder and more emphatic. Her free arm went to Keenan's head, and the stubby appendages that resembled fingers gripped his hair, holding him tightly. Sensar's free tentacle tightened around his chest, giving another spasmodic squeeze that drove the air from his lungs.

The tentacle on Keenan's face stopped sucking and started slithering. It went down his face and onto his neck, sliding across his skin with a slow, circular motion. The tip of the tentacle nudged the top of his shirt, as if trying to get between it and his skin. The shirt dug deep into the back of Keenan's neck until he thought it would rip or he would strangle. Then the pressure eased abruptly. Had the Gan-Tir decided that further exploration was not possible? He hoped so. He thought the tentacle would go away then, but it started exploring the skin above his collar instead, moving from one side of his neck to the other. It paused in the hollow of his throat and pressed hard, flattening again. An invisible mouth opened and for the second time, Sensar sucked. Keenan arched, fighting wildly.

"Beee ... stial!" Sensar rumbled. "Beee ... stilll."

Keenan froze. Sensar rumbled again, then swept his face a final time before lifting the tentacle free and twisting it around in front of him, the tip waving from side to side. Keenan forced himself to look at it, but he could see neither the fine hairs that had brushed his skin nor the mouth that had opened. The tentacle dropped across his shoulders, a heavy weight. Sensar put no pressure on his throat, but Keenan was not deceived. The alien could strangle him with one convulsive squeeze—assuming he did not break his neck first.

Rairea released Keenan. He did not move. Sensar's left tentacle uncoiled from his waist. Keenan sagged, then stiffened as the tentacle across his shoulders tightened ever so slightly.

"Let him go." Kiley stepped forward. She put herself within touching distance of Rairea. "I said, let him go." She spoke to Rairea, not Sensar, though it was the male who held Keenan.

Rairea's eyes met Kiley's. Keenan could not see the Gan-Tir's expression, but whatever it was, he did not think he could have faced it as steadily as Kiley did. He had known she possessed an unusually strong force of mind and will. He had seen her compel obedience from her family with a single look. She spoke to Rairea as she would have spoken to a crew member—as if she did not doubt for a single instant that her orders would be obeyed.

Rairea answered with an assertion of her own, the boom shaking the walls of the ship. Her words, if they were words, were incomprehensible.

Kiley took another step. "Let. Him. Go."

Rairea lifted her right arm and flicked her tentacle across Kiley's face. Kiley did not even blink. Rairea dropped her arm and turned to Sensar. She said something else, and the tentacle around Keenan's shoulders fell away.

"I want you off my bridge," Kiley ordered, gesturing to the

hatch. "OFF!" Rairea's eyes followed her movement, then returned to her face. Sensar rumbled, and Rairea replied without looking at him. Sensar started moving toward the door; Lukas and the other humans stepped aside hastily. Rairea held her ground until Sensar had cleared a path to the hatch, then followed him. She did not look at Kiley as she left.

The Gan-Tir went down the hall, toward the elevators. Fong fell in behind them, his disrupter pointed toward the deck. He looked as if he were searching for a single excuse to fire, but the Gan-Tir did not give him one. They boarded the elevator and the door closed, taking them belowdecks.

Their disappearance broke the silence on the bridge. The Miquiri closed in on Cristavos, their hands moving in rapid jerks. Uhrich moved toward Kiley. She ignored him and headed for Keenan. "Jon Robert, get a bioscanner," she ordered her brother over her shoulder. "Greg, take the conn."

As Jon Robert ran to the storeroom, Lukas slipped into the pilot's seat, his eyes and hands going to the boards.

"Daniel, can you sit down?" Kiley asked. When he did not respond, she put one hand on his left arm and the other on his right shoulder. She pressed down gently, urging him into the copilot's seat.

The back of his knees hit the edge of the chair and he collapsed. He bent forward, wrapping his arms around his chest, trying to curl into a ball despite the pain at his waist. Kiley put her arm across his shoulders. Lukas gave them a quick glance, then turned back to the control board.

"Captain Michaelson, this is Fong," the security officer said over the intercom. "The Gan-Tir are back in their quarters. I will stand watch for the rest of the evening. You don't need to worry—there won't be another incident of this sort."

"I should hope not," Kiley said under her breath. She reached for the intercom. "I'm counting on you to see that there isn't," she replied coldly.

Jon Robert returned with the medical kit and pulled out the scanner. Keenan had recovered sufficiently by then to tell him not to bother—he was certain nothing was broken. Jon Robert ignored him.

"Take your shirt off," he ordered. He took a swift breath when he saw the welts rising on Keenan's neck, waist, arms, and wrists. He started to touch one gingerly, then stopped and used the bioscanner instead. His examination was as thorough as Keenan's would have been. It was five minutes before he pronounced himself satisfied that Keenan had suffered no broken bones or damage to internal organs.

Keenan tried to tell himself he had been lucky as Jon Robert helped him put his shirt back on. As unpleasant as the experience had been, he did not believe that Rairea or Sensar had hurt him intentionally. If they had, he would have had a great deal more than bruises.

Jon Robert rummaged through the medical kit's vials of pills. "The scanner readings indicate that you're experiencing moderate pain," he said. "I can give you Emanecet or Prodacaine. Which would you prefer?"

"Neither."

"But you need—"

"If I want anything, I'll get it from my own supplies," Keenan said sharply. "Right now, all I want is to lie down." He stood. "Kiley, will you or Greg finish my watch for me?"

"Of course," she said, "but are you sure you're—"

"I'm fine," he insisted. To prove it, he walked off the bridge and down the hall to his cabin. He went in, set the privacy lock on his door, and headed for the desk in the corner. He had pulled out his medical bag and was rummaging through it for the bottle he wanted when the door slid open and Lukas came in.

"I set—"

"I overrode the lock from the bridge," Lukas said. He crossed the room, took the bottle Keenan grasped in his hand, and read the label. He gave Keenan a close look, then handed the pills back and went into the bathroom.

Lukas came back holding a glass. Keenan had a pill out of the bottle by then. He put it in his mouth, then took a drink from the glass Lukas offered him. He gagged as the pill caught in his swollen throat, and took another drink. It went down that time. He put the bottle back in his bag, put the bag away, and set the lock on the drawer. "You don't need to stay," he said without looking at Lukas.

"Yes, I do," Lukas said. And then, very quietly, he added, "Daniel, you don't have to pretend with me. I know what you're feeling. I've been there, too—remember?"

Lukas had been the first human the Miquiri had met. He had spent six hours on their ship—six pain-filled hours during which alien hands had systematically violated his body.

He knew.

Keenan's control broke; he started shaking violently. Lukas helped him undress, then put him to bed and sat beside him until the sedative took effect. It could not have taken more than ten or fifteen minutes, but it felt like hours.

Sleep would bring distance, Keenan told himself. Sleep would bring forgetfulness. The worst was over. All he had to do was close his eyes and relax. By morning, the experience would be behind him.

He was wrong about that. When he woke, he found the nightmare had only just begun.

Chapter 16

"She wants what?" Keenan asked Cristavos the next morning, his voice rising.

"Rairea would like you to visit their quarters. Sensar has been studying human tapes, but he wants to talk to one of us to improve his understanding of our language and culture."

Keenan looked past Cristavos to Kiley. She appeared to be as surprised and upset by the Gan-Tir's request as he was.

"I thought that was supposed to be your job," Keenan said to Cristavos, his mouth a tight line.

"It is, and I would gladly undertake it. Unfortunately, Sensar doesn't want me. He specifically asked for you."

"Well he can't have me!" Keenan shot back. He had been frightened during his first encounter with the Gan-Tir on Sumpali, but the previous evening they had frankly terrified him. Whatever curiosity he had felt about them had disappeared the moment Rairea touched him. "I wouldn't go within ten feet of any of them to save the ship!"

"I can understand your feelings," Cristavos said. "The Gan-Tir alarmed you. I assure you, though, they meant no harm. If they had, you wouldn't be standing here talking to me."

Keenan might be standing, but it was an effort. There wasn't a part of his upper body that didn't ache, and he had deep bruises on his ribs, throat, and arms that would take weeks to fade. He had been on his way to his medical bag when Kiley had called him and now he wished he'd stopped long enough to swallow the pill he had planned to take.

"I'm sorry," Keenan said with no regret whatsoever, "but I've already seen as much of them as I care to in my lifetime. They'll have to find another human to talk to."

"They don't want anyone else," Cristavos replied patiently, as if her message would sink in if she kept repeating it often enough. "Something about you intrigues them. I don't know what, but you're the only human they've been willing to talk to outside a conference room. This could be a real breakthrough for us. We can't afford to pass up the opportunity."

"I don't care. The answer is still no."

Cristavos frowned. "I can't insist, of course, but I have to tell you that both the Miquiri and I are concerned that the Gan-Tir will come looking for you if you won't go to them."

"I thought Fong was supposed to keep them in line," Kiley said tightly.

"Short of firing on them, there isn't much he can do," Cristavos replied. "He wouldn't hesitate to shoot if they threatened the ship, but even then, there's some question about the effectiveness of our disrupters. Some of the scientists back on the *North Star* doubted that anything short of field weapons would stop them. Bergstrom gave Fong permission to bring one, but he is reluctant to use it on the ship. It would almost certainly stop the Gan-Tir, but anyone else caught in the energy backwash would likely be seriously injured, if not killed."

"So your solution to the problem is to ask Keenan to risk his life?" Kiley demanded.

"No! Rairea gave me her word that he will be treated as an honored guest. The Gan-Tir may be difficult, but they don't lie—at least, not so far as we know. Captain, all I'm asking is for Dr. Keenan to see Sensar. If he's too uncomfortable to stay, or if the Gan-Tir make the slightest threatening gesture, he's free to leave immediately."

"Provided they'll let him," Kiley said dryly.

"Fong will be standing by. He'll render assistance if Dr. Keenan requires it."

"How?" Keenan demanded. "With a disrupter whose beam

will likely kill me and only stun them? Thanks, but I think I can do without that kind of help."

"Then you'll go down?" Cristavos asked, seizing on his statement as assent.

Keenan glanced at Kiley, who was shaking her head, urging him to refuse. He wanted to, but how could he? He would be risking everyone else's safety for his own. Cristavos seemed convinced the Gan-Tir wouldn't hurt him. Couldn't he at least make a show of goodwill? He could always claim that his duties did not leave time for socializing with passengers. A polite refusal would go down more easily than a blunt rejection.

"How long would I have to stay?" he asked cautiously.

"I'd say at least five minutes," Cristavos replied eagerly, "but no more than an hour. We could make the time limit a condition of your visit, if you like."

Five minutes wasn't forever, he told himself. He could manage that. So long as they didn't touch him, that was. If they touched him, he wouldn't last fifteen seconds.

"They won't hurt you, Keenan," Cristavos said, as if reading his thoughts. "Sensar is a scholar, not a warrior. All he wants is to talk."

Maybe, Keenan thought, but he would have been much happier if that assurance had come from the alien himself.

Cristavos, Uhrich, and Fong accompanied Keenan to the entrance to the Gan-Tir's quarters. A transparent plate let them see into the common room on the other side of the door, Rairea was there, waiting for him, but there was no sign of Sensar or Henherik.

Cristavos pressed the control panel. The door opened and Rairea came forward, then stopped and lifted her right arm. Her sleeve fell and her tentacle emerged. She waved it back and forth in the air, as if asking a question, then curled it toward her, beckoning.

Come.

In case Keenan had any doubt about that gesture, she made the equivalent Miquiri sign with her arm. Cristavos gave him an encouraging nod. He took a deep breath, then stepped across the threshold.

The Gan-Tir had furnished the common room themselves. A cascade of gigantic, rainbow-colored cushions filled two of the corners. They must have been fastened together somehow to hold their shape, but he couldn't see ties or other bindings. In the center of the room were several red, round objects that could have been footstools or backless chairs. Wide swatches of boldly colored, silky fabric covered the walls, and a pervasive odor filled the room. The scent wasn't strong or unpleasant, but it reminded him that he was among aliens.

Rairea moved backward, signaling again. *Come.*

Keenan thought she wanted him to go to one of the round stools, but before he could sit, she gestured to a door on the wall that separated the Gan-Tir's private quarters from their common room. She gestured again, waving her tentacle to the door, then making the Miquiri sign for *go* with her hand. She moved to one side, clearing the way for him.

Keenan whirled around and gave Cristavos a frantic look. This hadn't been part of the arrangement. She had told him that he and Sensar would meet in the common room, where they could be seen at all times.

Where help was only a step away.

Cristavos was already reaching for the wall plate. She pressed the controls once. Nothing happened. She pressed harder. The door did not open. It had functioned normally a moment ago, but it wasn't working now.

A tentacle touched Keenan's arm. He whirled around.

Go, Rairea signaled. She was not making a request.

Keenan looked over his shoulder. Fong and Uhrich were pounding on the wall plate, trying to make it work. Cristavos was nowhere to be seen; she must have gone to the intercom halfway down the corridor. Was she asking Kiley or Jon Robert to attempt a manual override of the door controls? If so, how long would it take? How long could he stall Rairea? How long—

Rairea's tentacle whipped out and caught Keenan around the

wrist. *Go,* she signaled for the third time, squeezing ever so slightly.

Keenan took a last, desperate look at the corridor. The scene had not changed. Rairea released his wrist and pressed the control plate on the wall. The door in front of Keenan opened. She moved behind him, forcing him past the entrance. As soon as he was through, she touched the plate again and the door closed, leaving him inside, beyond help. Keenan braced himself for immediate assault. When one did not come, he gathered what little remained of his nerve and looked around.

Sensar was on the far side of the room, sitting on the edge of a long, wide object that Keenan took to be a bed. A dark green robe covered the alien's body and the hood was down over his shoulders, revealing his heavy head. He did not move, and he kept his tentacles wrapped tightly around his arms. He could not have held more rigidly still if he had been carved from marble.

Keenan risked a breath. Nothing happened. He took a step back and his shoulders bumped the door. He fumbled behind him for the wall control and pressed it, but the door did not open. Somehow, he was not surprised.

Sensar still had not moved.

Keenan risked another look around. A vivid yellow and red spread covered the bed, but there had been no effort to decorate the utilitarian metal panels that formed the room's walls. A heavy, blue-green woven rug covered the floor. A cascade of tangerine, lime, canary, and turquoise cushions filled the corner of the room to his left. He looked to his right and caught his breath: a gigantic plant covered the wall, sending out trailing creepers in all directions.

Sensar had brought a plant on the trip? The Corps had let him do that? Keenan was willing to bet they hadn't agreed without an argument. If so, it was clear who had won. The observation was not reassuring.

"Sittt."

Keenan jerked around, his arms coming up to protect his body. Sensar had not changed positions, but he had uncoiled one tentacle and was gesturing to the corner of the room. "Sit."

Keenan edged over to the mound of cushions. He couldn't see what held them together, but they didn't separate as he eased his way into them. Instead, they seemed to fuse together, giving way at his back and rising around his buttocks and legs, forming a seat of sorts. The sides of the cushions continued moving, wrapping around his arms. He shoved them back and they retreated, finally forming armrests. Sensar waited until Keenan stopped struggling with the cushions, then spoke.

"Lettt usss talkkk."

Cristavos called Kiley as soon as she realized the meeting wasn't going according to plan. Kiley called Jon Robert and they reached the cargo deck at the same time, only to find the Gan-Tir's common room empty and the door to their quarters locked.

"They've jammed it electronically," Jon Robert said after a brief inspection. "I tried overriding their signal from the engine room, but the door wouldn't respond. If we want in, we'll have to cut our way through."

"Captain, Rairea signaled to us before she went into her room," Cristavos reported. "She said Keenan would stay in Sensar's quarters for the agreed-upon hour, and then leave. She assured us that he would be treated as a guest. I don't believe she was lying."

"Well I do," Uhrich broke in heatedly. "We have no way of knowing what they're doing to him. We couldn't put voice or video monitors in any of the cabins—both the Miquiri and Gan-Tir insisted on that. We can't leave Keenan in there alone, not when he may be in serious trouble."

"Captain, I am convinced they won't hurt him," Cristavos said, appealing to Kiley. "Sensar has displayed a strong interest in humans from the beginning. He wants to talk. That's all— just talk."

Kiley turned to Chirith. All three Miquiri had come out into the corridor to investigate the commotion. It was the first time

Kiley had seen them since they'd boarded, although Lukas had visited their quarters several times.

What do your people think? she asked, signaling slowly so he would understand her awkward gestures. *Is Cristavos right? Is Rairea telling the truth, or could she be lying?*

Chirith looked to Pitar before he replied—seeking permission to respond, or searching for advice on what to say? "Lie" was an emotionally charged word for humans, but it didn't necessarily have the same connotation for other species.

If they asked Keenan to meet, then they wished to meet, Chirith replied slowly, his eyes still on Pitar. *But that does not mean they did not have other plans as well.*

The gray Miquiri seemed to sense that his answer did not help much, for he added a short gesture that she took for apology or regret. She studied the sealed door, trying to decide what to do.

"You agreed the maximum duration of his stay would be one hour?" she asked, turning back to Cristavos.

"Yes."

Kiley took a deep breath. "Then I say we wait that long before acting."

"Captain, if Dr. Keenan is in danger, he needs help immediately!" Uhrich protested.

"What if he isn't?" Kiley demanded. "What if they really are talking? What will they think if we force our way in, only to find him perfectly well?"

Uhrich's jaw clenched. "With all due respect, Captain, maybe you ought to ask Greg Lukas how it feels to be in alien hands for an hour before you subject Keenan to the same fate."

Kiley's face went white. Uhrich looked as if he regretted the words the moment they were out of his mouth, but he did not back down. Neither did she.

"I say we wait," she told Uhrich. They locked gazes. He was the first to look away.

They stood in the corridor for forty-five tense minutes. Precisely one hour after entering Sensar's room, Keenan emerged.

He crossed the room and pressed the door panel. It opened at once and everyone started talking at the same time.

"Daniel, are you all right?"

"Keenan, what happened?"

"What did they do to you? What did they say?"

Keenan looked from one to the other of them, completely dazed. He pulled himself together and seized on the most familiar voice. "I'm fine," he said, answering Kiley's question.

"Sensar didn't threaten you?" she asked anxiously.

"No. All we did was talk, just the way they promised. Sensar stayed on his bed the entire time. He used his tentacles and hands to gesture, but aside from that, he didn't move. I had the impression he was doing his best not to alarm me."

"What did he say to you?"

"Did he ask you questions about this ship, the *North Star*, or Everest?"

"How did you communicate? Did he speak to you? Write the words? Use Miquiri signs?"

He did not know who to answer first. He looked from face to face, his own expression blank, until Kiley took charge.

"I suggest we adjourn to your common room, Ms. Cristavos," she said briskly. "There's no reason to stand when we can sit, and Daniel looks like he could use a few minutes to gather his thoughts."

Keenan had spent one hour in Sensar's quarters; answering everyone's questions took another three. Cristavos brought out a portable recorder, turned it on, and asked him to relate everything Sensar had said and done. By then Keenan had collected himself. Pretending he was giving his old boss, Hal Omanu, an oral report, he mentally outlined what he wanted to say, then started in.

"At first, Sensar just wanted to hear me speak. He pointed to objects in the room and asked me to say the words for them. He had me repeat them several times, and then tried to say them himself."

He had been tense during that process. His hands had

gripped his legs so tightly they had ached. Somewhere along the way, though, he had started to relax. Sensar acted differently than he had on the bridge. Perhaps he had been as uncomfortable there as Keenan was in his cabin, or perhaps he had been driven by desires or needs humans could not fathom. Or maybe the difference was the result of Rairea's absence. She had been the first to walk onto the bridge; she had been the first to touch him. Sensar might have been following her lead.

Whatever the reason, the Gan-Tir had done everything he could to reassure Keenan. He had used his arms only to form Miquiri hand signals. His tentacles kept slipping free as if they wished to wave about, but he had recoiled them immediately, even though holding them still appeared to be a major effort. Keenan found himself feeling sorry for the alien; he was working so hard not to offend or frighten him.

Sensar told Keenan his name and said he was a student of alien cultures. Slowly, tentatively, they began to hold a real discussion, although they had to rely on Miquiri hand signals for much of their conversation; Sensar had studied the humans' language, but did not comprehend much of it. Keenan expected him to show an interest in human history, geography, and technology, but the alien seemed more interested in him specifically than in humanity in general.

Keenan answered the alien's questions briefly at first, thinking he might be trying to gather data about the ship and her crew. But after a few minutes, Sensar moved on to Keenan's earlier life. He asked where he had been raised and how he had been educated. If Keenan asked a question in return, Sensar answered readily—or tried to. His replies didn't always make much sense, but Keenan thought that resulted more from language problems and his own lack of knowledge about the Gan-Tir than any deliberate evasiveness.

The hour had passed with amazing speed. Keenan was startled when Sensar interrupted him in the middle of a sentence to say it was time to go. Then he gestured, *You come back next morning, yes?*

An hour before, Keenan would never have believed he

would agree to such a request, but he did. It was, he told the assembled group, a promise he planned to keep.

Cristavos was ecstatic. If the diplomat's excitement was anything to go by, Keenan had learned more about the Gan-Tir in one hour than the Corps had in weeks. She greeted his decision with unabashed approval.

Uhrich's response was noticeably cooler. The lieutenant commander reluctantly agreed that Keenan should return the next day, but he warned him against relaxing his guard. "Removal of a threat—real or implied—often leads to a sense of gratitude and trust," Uhrich said. "The Miquiri have repeatedly warned us that the Gan-Tir are accomplished manipulators. I suggest you remember that when you talk to Sensar again."

"I think I would recognize an attempt at manipulation if I saw one," Keenan replied stiffly. He'd heard the same lectures Uhrich had at the Academy—and a great many more besides during his years at medical school.

"From another human, perhaps," Uhrich said, unwilling to let the point go, "but you know nothing about alien behavior, Doctor. Their words and actions can't be judged by human standards. If you aren't extremely careful, you may endanger not only yourself, but all of humanity."

Keenan's eyes flashed. "I don't believe a simple conversation will result in the conquest of human civilization, Uhrich. For the record, though, I will take your warning under consideration." He stood. Cristavos seemed to have more questions, but he had had enough. "I'm going to my cabin. It has been a long morning, and I'm tired. I need some time alone before I go on duty this evening."

"And you'll have it," said Kiley, who had stayed in the common room to hear his report. "Come on. I'll walk you back to your cabin."

Cristavos let them go, asking Keenan to see her before he talked to Sensar the next morning. She had a few questions she wanted him to ask the alien. He hesitated, then agreed. The diplomat followed them to the door; she had promised to give the Miquiri a full report of the meeting after she'd heard Keenan's account.

Uhrich stayed where he was, his body rigid with disapproval. He looked like he had a great deal to say, but had decided to remain silent.

At least for the time being.

Chapter 17

Rairea came into Sensar's room after Keenan left. "Did the alien please you?"

Sensar, standing in the givitch's embrace, gave it another stoke before turning to face her. "He was quite forthcoming after he overcame his initial apprehension."

"Would you like to speak to him again?" she asked, crossing the room and coming to a halt just before him. "I will make them send him back if you do."

Her *elith* traced a lazy line up his arm, then down his back, coming to rest on a spot just above his waist. The most vulnerable place on his body, the *sereth* was the gathering point for all the nerves below his waist. Above and below they lay deeply buried in bone, but there they rose to the surface. A caress to the *sereth* could produce waves of exquisite pleasure; a sharp blow would immobilize anyone not wearing protective armor. He held his breath as Rairea traced a circle over the spot, wondering if she would deliver a caress or a blow. She had done both in the past; experience was a poor guide to her present intentions.

"Your help will not be necessary," he said, bracing himself for a blow. "He agreed to return tomorrow of his own accord."

Rairea drew a sharp breath. Her *elith* froze, then fell to her side. "He did?"

"Yes. I am sorry to deprive you of your pleasures, but this once, you will not have to engage in coercion."

"But he feared you! I tasted him. So did you. He could not have overcome his terror so quickly."

"I did not say he had."

147

"He is frightened, yet he agreed to return?"

"Yes."

"Why?" she demanded.

"It appears that fleeing one's fears is considered a failing among his kind. And then he was curious. He wishes to learn. To comprehend. That desire mitigates his apprehension."

"It would not be so with the Miquiri."

"Humans are not Miquiri, Rairea, as I have repeatedly warned you. A Miquiri's first priority is protection of the group, but that is not necessarily the case with humans."

"I do not believe this! He attempted to shield the one they call captain—and she him. That was odd, though," she admitted, remembering. "They do not share scents or taste."

"There are other bonds besides the purely physical."

"But none so strong. Not even a Miquiri's *akia* comes before a mate when they are in season."

"The Ytavi had close ties between males and females that were not based on sex; perhaps the humans form similar relationships."

"The Ytavi!" Rairea exploded, saying the words like the curse they were. "Their records are so fragmentary that we cannot be certain of anything about them—except that they nearly destroyed us and did destroy themselves."

"Did they? I'm not sure about that. It's true they went away, but they could still be out there somewhere."

"They are dead!" Rairea exclaimed. "We searched the stars for generations and found nothing left of them but a few, scattered relics. You can play intellectual games at the university, Sensar Kaikiel, but the fact is, you are simply speculating. All that we know of them is speculation, pieced together from a few artifacts."

"Perhaps, but that does not mean that our conclusions are wrong—or that these humans do not share bonds beyond our understanding. For all you despise the Miquiri, you do not underestimate them. You should not discount the humans, either."

"I do not see how I could—not with you so eager to correct me."

"Rairea, I did not mean to—"

"To what, Sensar? Forget who is the leader of this mission? Forget who nominated you for a position at the university? All that you have and are, you owe to me, Sensar Kaikiel Anara— including your place on this ship. You would not have been invited if I had not convinced Lonlores that you had the training and flexibility to travel to an alien world."

"I did not ask for your support," he said stiffly.

"No, but you took it, didn't you? And what have you given in return? Hostility and rejection! It was ever thus. I gave and you took. I loved and you hated. You owe me, Sensar Kaikiel Anara, and I intend to see that you pay your debts. Do you understand? You will pay!"

Rairea whirled around and left. Sensar stared after her, so shocked that he could hardly reason. Rairea, who was known for her icy command above all else, had nearly lost control of herself. She had fled his presence. What was wrong with her? Was the stress of traveling on an alien ship proving too great?

Sensar started to go after her and then stopped. That was what she wanted. She wanted him to think of her, not himself. She wanted to goad him into a response he would not otherwise give. She had not lost control. Rairea never lost control. She was playing games with him. Again. He could not stop her, but he didn't have to respond to her.

Sensar prostrated himself on the floor and threw himself into the discipline of mind and body that was *jis*. He reached for the first level of control, calm.

For the fifth day in a row, he failed to achieve it.

Lukas came to Keenan's cabin just before he reported for duty that evening, looking tired. No wonder—he had covered the rest of Keenan's shift the previous night, and Kiley had called him back on duty when she had been summoned to the cargo deck that morning.

"Can I come in?" Lukas asked from the hallway.

"Of course," Keenan said. He stepped back hastily, making way for the pilot.

"I won't keep you long—I know your shift is about to start.

Kiley says you're going back to see Sensar tomorrow morning."

"That's right."

"He isn't forcing you, is he? You aren't cooperating with them to protect the rest of us?"

"No," Keenan said firmly. "I'm going because I want to."

"You really mean that?"

"Yes, I do. I have to admit that I still find the Gan-Tir's size and strength intimidating, but Sensar was—well, intriguing. I wouldn't want to spend five seconds alone with Rairea, but he's different."

"Maybe," Lukas said skeptically, "but he's still an unknown entity. Daniel, are you sure you know what you're doing?"

"No—of course not. But this may be the only chance I have to talk to one of the Gan-Tir. I'd be crazy to turn it down without a valid reason."

"That sounds like something the Daniel Keenan I knew at the Academy would have said," Lukas told him, smiling. "Welcome back—I missed you."

For a moment, the old rapport snapped into place between them, as deep and strong as ever. "I missed you, too," Keenan said quietly. And then, because such moments were too fragile to prolong, he glanced at his watch. "I don't want to push you out the door the moment you arrive," he said briskly, "but I was due on the bridge two minutes ago."

"I know." Lukas retreated to the corridor. "Tell Kiley I'll be waiting in the galley, will you?"

"Sure."

Lukas nodded, but didn't leave yet. "Daniel, if you do have a problem with Sensar, or any of the Gan-Tir, you'll tell me, won't you?"

"I will," Keenan said, and meant it. For the first time in months, he knew exactly where he would turn if anything went wrong. Anything at all.

Keenan went back to the cargo deck the next morning. Sensar was waiting for him in the Gan-Tir's common room; Rairea was nowhere to be seen.

"Youuu commm . . . my roommm?" Sensar asked.

Keenan hesitated. Fong had volunteered to stand watch in the corridor while he was with the Gan-Tir, but he had refused the offer. Though his apprehensions about the aliens had not subsided completely, he did not believe a show of force would deter them if they chose to act—or that Fong would be able to intervene in time to save him. When in doubt, act confident, he told himself. He tried to do just that as he nodded agreement to Sensar, but it wasn't easy.

Sensar sat on the bed again. He started off the way they had the day before, asking Keenan to say the words for the objects in the room and repeating them afterward. His voice boomed, and he dragged out the ends of the words, but most of what he said was comprehensible.

By the time the hour passed, he had moved on to simple two- and three-word sentences. He made occasional mistakes, but he never repeated the same one twice, and he never forgot a word. He asked Keenan if he wanted to leave, but Keenan shook his head. The hour stretched to two, and then three. When Keenan finally rose, Sensar asked him to return the next day and he agreed readily.

On the third day, they had something approaching a genuine conversation. Though Sensar still had difficulty pronouncing human words, he seemed to comprehend everything Keenan said. His understanding gave Keenan considerable pause. Had the alien been concealing the extent of his knowledge, or had he managed to learn more in a few days than Keenan could have in months? Keenan wasn't sure which, but either possibility was sobering.

He said as much to Cristavos, who had asked him to see her after each session. She wasn't entirely happy about the speed with which Sensar was learning, either, but she considered the discussions too valuable to be stopped. She only advised him to keep his sentences short and to stick to generalities wherever possible.

Cristavos also asked for written reports of Keenan's talks with the alien, recounting as nearly as possible the exact words they had exchanged. She was extremely pleased with his efforts. His work as an investigator had honed an already excellent memory, and he was able to give her almost verbatim accounts of their discussions.

Uhrich continued to question the advisability of Keenan's visits, but each time he did, Cristavos overruled him. Sensar had not asked anything that could be remotely construed as a search for information about military deployments, human technology, or humanity's intentions toward the Gan-Tir or the Miquiri, she said, and Keenan agreed. The alien seemed more interested in learning about humans than conquering them.

Sensar asked a number of questions about Keenan's childhood and the method by which he had been educated. He was shocked to learn that human children spent nearly one-fifth of their lives dependent on their parents; Gan-Tir parents did not raise their children. They bore them, then walked away from them. Children were raised by "minders," who watched over them until they could walk, talk, and find their own food. After that, the children were turned loose to do as they wished. In a world with a declining population, there was no lack of living quarters. A child found a place that he or she liked and settled in. Agriculture was automated and food was both plentiful and free; so was clothing. Other items were not, however. Entertainment cost, but not as much as goods imported from other worlds. Rare spices, fabrics, and artifacts cost as much as an adult could earn in a year.

Though it was not mandatory, a young person usually formed a relationship with someone older. Sometimes it was a person for whom the youth felt some admiration or interest. Sometimes it was an individual the young person believed could be manipulated. The pursuit of a mentor could be long and intense. Adults had little patience for the young, and they dealt swiftly and harshly with immature or improper behavior. Children soon learned that the only way to gain admittance to Gan-Tir society was to behave and converse as adults. The Gan-Tir had no love for their progeny; at best, they could only be said to endure them.

Education was informal and left entirely to the individual. If a person wished to know something, he or she found a teacher.

Those who chose to make learning a way of life migrated to clusterings of adults who called themselves scholars, and such groups formed a structure that could be loosely described as a "university." From all that Keenan could gather, that was as close to a human institution as anything in Gan-Tir life.

He could not comprehend how such a society functioned, and had some difficulty hiding his initial reaction to the Gan-Tir's treatment of their young. He had had sufficient training to know that customs varied, and that one could not judge one society by another's rules. Still, he could not help wondering if the planet's bizarre social structures were normal for them, or some aberration caused by their declining birth rate.

He asked once if children had been treated differently when there had been more of them. Some of his negative reaction must have come through, because Sensar stiffened. Children had always developed quickly and been allowed great freedom. Why did Keenan ask? Keenan covered himself as best he could, saying that human child-rearing customs varied greatly, depending on the society in which one lived, the age of the parents, and their economic standing. Sensar demanded examples; Keenan gave several, and the discussion moved on. Keenan did not ask about Gan-Tir children again, but he thought about them. He thought about them often.

That wasn't the only time the gulf between their cultures proved too vast to cross. Sensar asked Keenan about his work, which led to an explanation of psychiatry. The Gan-Tir was amazed that humans had a science devoted to the study of their own mental processes. He claimed his species did not suffer from mental illness. The only instances of aberrant behavior among them resulted from devastating disease or injury.

When Keenan asked how those people were treated, Sensar was evasive. It depended, he said, on the person and the circumstances. He had no personal knowledge of an instance, so he could not speak on the subject with authority, and that was all he would say. Keenan tried to press for an answer, but he had already moved on to another topic.

Were human beings more susceptible to mental abnormalities than other species? Keenan wondered, his attention wandering momentarily. Did humans have a more delicate balance of chemicals within their brains or some genetic weakness that allowed them to perpetuate the faults that led to so many mental illnesses? The possibilities were so intriguing that he lost track of what Sensar was saying for a time. He came back with a start and found the Gan-Tir had asked him a question, this time about hospitals. Had Keenan been telling the truth when he said humans had entire buildings filled with the sick? How could one possibly hope to stop the spread of contagion unless one isolated it completely?

Keenan answered the question, but he was still thinking about Gan-Tir society. He tried to envision life among people who had no childhood, and whose contacts with others as adults appeared to be exercises in manipulation and exploitation. His mind rebelled. No wonder Rairea appeared so overbearing. It wasn't her behavior that was abnormal, but Sensar's. For a Gan-Tir, he displayed amazing sensitivity. What made him so different?

He was different, wasn't he?

Keenan caught himself sharply on the edge of that question. Sensar had dealt with aliens before; he must be aware that he was conveying an impression of his people, even as he gained one of humans. Was he smart enough to deliberately manipulate that image? Measuring the speed with which Sensar learned, he decided that he had to be, and went back on guard again. Still, as wary as he was, he could find no evidence that the Gan-Tir was consciously manipulating him. The alien did not direct their conversations one way or another, and aside from a few guarded replies, he offered information freely, with no apparent forethought.

Sensar had relaxed considerably since their first meeting. His tentacles coiled and uncoiled often, and he waved them in the air to emphasize his points. He spoke loudly, but that was his nature. He did not use his size or the force of his personality to persuade; he simply talked. As they passed the trip's midpoint and neared Resurrection, Keenan decided the alien was exactly what he claimed to be—a scholar for whom the gathering and imparting of knowledge was the sole reason for continued existence.

On one visit a vine from the plant that covered the wall fell on Keenan's shoulder. He reached up to brush it off, but before he could, another vine snaked over his opposite shoulder. It continued to move, gliding out past his shoulder into the air beyond. The leafy tip waved back and forth in the air in an uncanny imitation of Sensar's tentacles.

Startled, Keenan pushed himself up, away from the cushions that supported him. He expected the vine to fall away, but instead it came with him. Alarmed, he grabbed the piece on his shoulder, intending to tear it off. Before his fingers could close around it, a tentacle slapped around his wrist and squeezed convulsively, forcing his hand open. A second tentacle wrapped around his other arm. Two more snapped around his ankles.

"Beeestilll! Dooo nottt mooove!"

"What—"

"Be still! Will not harm. Is givitchhh. Givitch."

Sensar released Keenan and gently lifted the vine from his shoulders. He placed it back on the wall, then went to the corner of the room, where he stood motionless before the plant's main stalk with his tentacles hanging down.

The vines on the wall and ceiling coiled up and rolled back to the main stalk. Once there, the leaves unfurled and reached out to the Gan-Tir. They wrapped around him. Slowly, very slowly, he lifted his tentacles and caressed the plant. It moved against him in return, bending and twisting around his entire body. Then Sensar stepped back and the vines loosened. He turned around. "Givitch," he said, pointing to the plant. He beckoned Keenan. "Come. Touch."

Keenan looked at the moving plant, then at Sensar's legs, which were hidden by his long robe, and shook his head.

"Come!"

It was a command. Keenan hesitated, still thinking about the tentacles that had wrapped around his ankles. Sensar took a step forward, and Keenan edged toward the door. The Gan-Tir blocked his way.

"Come!" he ordered a third time. One tentacle snaked out and circled Keenan's wrist. He did not apply any pressure, but the threat was sufficient. Keenan went.

He did not want to put his hand on the plant, but Sensar pulled his wrist forward until his fingers brushed the leaves on one vine. The vine bent and curled around his hand. He jerked, but Sensar held him still. A leaf fluttered against his hand. It was covered with fine hairs and felt soft and fuzzy.

"Givitch," Sensar repeated, pointing to the plant. "Is companion."

Companion? How was he using that word? The way Keenan did, or the way Lukas and the Quayla would? Keenan didn't know, and he wasn't sure he wanted to find out. When the Gan-Tir released his wrist, he took a hasty step back. He was no longer worried the plant might harm him, but he didn't want it twisting around his body, either.

And he wasn't certain he liked being in the same room with a being who had tentacles on its legs. He was, in fact, wondering if he had lost his mind completely when the plant rolled up and began spreading across the walls again. Sensar turned to him.

"It did not mean to frighten," the alien explained. "Only to make acquaintance. You are curiosity to it. It will not touch again unless you wish." His violet eyes met Keenan's. "You believe this?"

"Yes," Keenan said, not certain he did.

"We have two more days. You will come back tomorrow?"

"I don't—"

"Want you to come back. Tomorrow."

"I—I'll think about it."

"I, too."

Keenan wasn't sure what Sensar meant by that, but didn't ask. The Gan-Tir went to the door and opened it for him, then gestured to the common room. Keenan had to pass between the alien and the plant to leave. He gave them both wary looks, but neither impeded his progress. Sensar waited until Keenan was at the corridor door, then followed him into the common room. "Please, Keenan. Come back tomorrow."

Keenan turned around. Sensar was standing rigidly, tentacles coiled tightly around his arms, doing his best not to frighten or offend.

"I will . . . try," Keenan said.

He wanted to go back. He wanted to believe that he could rise above irrational fear, but doing so wasn't easy.

It was a long time before he went to sleep that night. He did not rest well.

Chapter 18

Sensar had not seen Rairea for several days. She could be hard at work, studying the humans' language, but he thought it more likely that she hoped to pique his interest by ignoring him. If so, she had chosen the wrong strategy. That morning, he had reached not only the first level of *jis*, but the second and third as well. He had recovered his equilibrium; he did not intend to lose it again.

Keenan arrived late for their daily meeting, but Sensar had not been certain the human would return at all after his hasty departure the day before. Keenan gave both Sensar and the givitch a wide berth. Sensar took care to move slowly and talk quietly, and after a time, the human settled down. They were deep in conversation when Rairea burst in, saw the human, and came to an immediate halt.

"Forgive me. I am intruding," she said, all apologies. "I did not mean to interrupt you."

No? Sensar thought skeptically. He had the strong impression that that was precisely what she had meant to do, and his suspicions were confirmed when she began advancing on the human instead of leaving. Keenan jumped up, retreating until his back was against the wall.

"Rairea, let him be," Sensar said, rising. "You are frightening him."

"Me?" She was all innocence. "But how? I mean him no harm."

"He does not know that." *And neither do I.* Sensar spoke to the human quickly in his own language, telling him to stand still, telling him that his fear attracted Rairea. Keenan gave him a startled look. He steadied, only to lose control as Rairea's *elith*s shot out without warning. One wrapped around his chest, pinning his arms to his body; the other went to his face, tasting.

"Rairea, let him go!" Sensar shouted, outraged. He crossed the room in one stride and caught the *elith* pressing against the human's face. He searched for the knob where it diverged from her arm, found the place he wanted, and squeezed hard. Rairea released the human. But not because Sensar had hurt her— because she finally had what she wanted: his attention.

So close to Rairea, Sensar's carefully constructed world of reason collapsed. "Go," he ordered the human. Keenan made noises at him, but he did not listen. "Leave us!" he boomed, so loudly that the walls shook. Keenan wavered, then edged around Sensar and raced for the door. There he stopped to make more noises.

"Go!" Sensar ordered for the third time. When the human still did not budge, he added impatiently, "Do not be alarmed. Rairea and I must talk. Come back tomorrow. I will explain then."

Explain what? That what was about to happen would not involve conversation? That a female as determined and forceful as Rairea could not be controlled for long? That while he wanted no part of her, she had finally provoked the physical response she had been seeking since their journey began? How could he tell the human that by touching her, he had lost himself? Keenan would not understand what was about to happen, nor would he believe that Sensar would be an unwilling participant. The humans thought beings were responsible for their own responses—all of them. Worse, Keenan had expressed clear disapproval of relationships that contained elements of mastery and subjugation. He could not understand what was about to follow. He was not Gan-Tir.

Keenan made more noises. Rairea struggled; Sensar released her and she surged forward. Keenan shot out the door, pressing the control plate to shut the door as he exited.

Rairea stopped, gathering herself, and turned around slowly. She tasted the air, then slipped her *elith* up Sensar's sleeve, coiling around his knob, holding him as he had held her. She squeezed, much harder than he had, and his breath went out in a rush. He made an involuntary sound somewhere between pain and desperation. She laughed. He wanted to tear free of her, but instead his left *elith* locked onto hers, drown by the overpowering taste of her.

Rairea was fertile.

How? Had she taken a massive dose of drugs, or had nature finally given her a single chance to reproduce? He did not know which, nor did it make any difference. Her skin exuded attractors powerful enough to drown any male she touched. If he had realized it from across the room, he might have had time to throw himself deep into *jis*, but they stood together, *elith* to *elith*. She had gambled that he would spring to the human's defense, and she had been right.

"Rairea, please! Do not do this," he begged.

She answered by squeezing his knob mercilessly, paralyzing his arm and *elith*. Then she released him. For a moment he thought she was leaving, and his heart leaped, but then the mouth at the end of her *elith* opened. She tasted him, searching for the place she wanted. When she found it, she bit him.

Chemicals poured into his body. His head spun and his knees started to buckle as the excitants hit his bloodstream, but she held him up. He was hot. Sweat ran down his body. Rairea's *elith* made a slow circuit of his skin, drinking in the moisture. She quivered and made a low sound deep in her throat. Her eyes glazed over, control forgotten.

He had to stop the madness. She had initiated the mating, but it was the chemicals she had triggered his body to secrete that sent her beyond reason. She was larger than he. She had the strength not only to restrain him, but to immobilize him long enough to force a coupling.

There was only one way out—*jis*. If he could shut off all sensation from his body and retreat into his mind, they might yet escape. *Jis* had many benefits, but it was for this moment that it had been developed.

Sensar called on all that he had learned in years of training and threw himself toward the first level. He found it; his breathing slowed. He reached for the second level. His mental fingers grasped the ledge and held on tight, but then slipped as his body convulsed. Sensing what he was attempting, Rairea had bitten him again, and fresh chemicals were pouring into his bloodstream. Her right *elith* began tasting his left arm, looking for a place to fasten there.

"No!" he cried out. "Rairea, I do not wish this! Please, do not force—"

She found the place she wanted and bit again. Sensar's head spun and his lower body lost all strength; he fell to the floor with a painful jar. His lower tentacles, thicker and less controllable than his *elith*s, jerked spasmodically.

Rairea sank down on him, wrapping her *elith*s around his and forcing him into the position of submission. Her eyes were glassy, her face swollen. She had surrendered to the storm within her body and was driven solely by need. There was no pleasure in this for her, nor for him. This was not another bedroom game, a chance to ridicule and dominate. This was a matter of life and death—not for her or for him, but for the spark of life within her.

How many years had she waited for this moment? How many times had she tried to stimulate nature with drugs and failed? Ten? Twenty? Fifty? He did not know, but this would likely be the only chance she would have to conceive in her lifetime.

Even if Sensar had had no regard for the perpetuation of his species, chemistry would have sufficed. If he had slammed the doors of his room and body shut minutes ago, he might have escaped, but it was too late now.

Then again, with Rairea, perhaps it always had been.

Lukas was not sleeping well, but Kiley didn't notice; she wasn't either.

The level of tension on the ship had risen sharply after the Gan-Tir's expedition to the bridge. They had not left their quarters again, but worry that they might kept everyone on edge. So did Keenan's daily visits to Sensar. Despite his professed willingness to go and the amount of information he had acquired, only he and Cristavos believed the benefits of the talks outweighed the risks.

Uhrich had spoken to Kiley several times, asking her to order Keenan to stay above deck. He questioned the wisdom of letting anyone but a professional diplomat converse with the Gan-Tir. He worried about unintentional insults and feared that Keenan would accidentally convey vital information about human technology and behavior that might be used against them in the future.

Kiley shared his concerns, but could not bring herself to order Keenan to abandon the talks. She did not want the Gan-Tir coming to look for him, and she thought they might. Fong had confidence in his weapons, but she doubted he could stop all three if they rushed him at once. Their best course was cooperation, and she continued to encourage it. She worried, though: about Keenan, about Uhrich and Fong, about getting their passengers safely to Resurrection. By the time they were due to exit jump, she was snapping out her orders. Lukas understood. Sometimes he felt like snapping himself.

Though the Quayla had said the Gan-Tir were psychically null, Lukas found himself wondering if they were having some sort of subliminal effect on the people around them. Humans weren't the only ones who were upset, either; the Miquiri seemed just as anxious and unsettled. Lukas had visited them several times. Pitar and Leetian had both been cordial, but he had been unable to penetrate their formality sufficiently to hold a real conversation. This might be understandable in Leetian's case, because Lukas had not met her before. But he and Pitar had spoken several times on Sumpali and there had never been such a strain between them then.

Even Chirith acted differently: he spoke to Lukas in the second language only, and did not invite him into his private room. Lukas took the alien on a tour of the ship one afternoon. He had hoped Chirith would open up once he was away from the other Miquiri, but he did not.

Chirith, is something wrong? Lukas finally asked, coming to a stop in the middle of the corridor leading to the family's cabins.

No, of course not, Chirith said.

You've been so withdrawn, I was beginning to think I'd done something to insult you.

No, never. You could not, Lukas. The fault is not yours. It is mine.

What fault? Something is wrong, isn't it?

The Miquiri looked away. *It has not been an easy trip,* he said. *I wish it was over. I wish we were back at Sumpali. Pitar is not to blame; he simply does not understand . . .*

Lukas touched Chirith again to get his attention. *What doesn't he understand?* he prompted.

How I could care about you. How I could call you "friend." Chirith began the final sign in the same manner as *akia,* with fingers intertwining and coming together. But instead of pressing his palms together, he opened them out, forming the word they had created for themselves. *He thinks I care about you only because you carry Hinfalla's memories. He does not dislike humans, but he cannot comprehend how one of us could turn to one of you for companionship. He thinks—* The Miquiri stopped.

What, Chirith?

He thinks my feelings for you are not natural.

What do you think?

Chirith looked away again. *I don't know,* he signaled dully. *I did not wish to believe that is true, but perhaps Pitar sees more clearly than I. It is true that I still grieve for Hinfalla. Such a prolonged sense of loss is not normal for my kind, Lukas. Pitar is worried that I am . . . ill.*

Lukas placed his hand on Chirith's shoulder for a moment. *I knew you grieved, but I did not realize you still felt the loss so deeply. Pitar is right—excessive grief is not normal for my kind either. Perhaps you should not associate with me. Perhaps I remind you too much—*

Chirith caught Lukas's hands briefly, stopping him in midsignal. *Do not say that! Not ever! Pitar does not suggest that I stop seeing you. He simply asks whether I am seeking something from our relationship that you neither can nor should offer.*

An akia'*s affection?* Lukas guessed.

Chirith hesitated. *As far as that is possible between a human and a Miquiri, yes.*

Do you agree with him?

I don't know. I have struggled to find the truth, but it is not always easy to see. Pitar is right about one thing, though: I have not been myself since Hinfalla died.

Chirith, I will stay away if that is what you need. I do not wish to cause you pain—

You bring no pain, Lukas. Do not even think that you might. I am sorry. I did not mean to distress you. Please, forget I said anything. I should not have spoken to you thus. It is just that I sometimes forget . . .

Lukas completed the sentence in his mind: *That we are not true* akias. Neither one signed those words, but they hung in the corridor like an invisible barrier between them. Lukas had never considered that there might be anything wrong with their relationship, but just because it was all right for him did not mean it was for Chirith. They were both silent as they walked back to the Miquiri's quarters. Chirith gave him the briefest of parting gestures, and did not ask him in.

Lukas went away hoping that Chirith's problem was another case of nerves. Maybe the Miquiri would feel better once Sensar and Rairea were off the ship; he knew he would. So would Kiley and the family. Uhrich probably wouldn't relax, but he was supposed to stay on guard. Lukas had few illusions about the orders Bergstrom had given his first officer. He suspected they were very much on the order of: *Watch them, protect them, but don't ever trust them—not any of them.*

Uhrich was a career officer, and he would follow Bergstrom's instructions to the letter. There was a time when Lukas would have done the same, and he did not envy Uhrich his position. It was not easy, being an officer, being an outsider. He knew; he had been both.

He was much happier now than he had been, either as a youth or an officer in the Corps. He had found everything he wanted in life on the *Widdon Galaxy*: the woman he loved, the friends he cherished.

What about me? the Quayla protested merrily. *I'm here, too. Don't I count?* Its laughter was the sound of bells chiming on a clear, moonlit winter's night.

You are beyond counting, Lukas replied, embracing the Quayla warmly. *You are myself.* They merged, fusing together so tightly that they were indistinguishable, even to themselves. The sensation was indescribable. It was also new—the Quayla had never experienced it with a companion before.

Such closeness is good, isn't it? one of them questioned.

It is very good, the other replied with absolute conviction.

Chapter 19

Keenan was at the backup communications board when they came out of jump at Resurrection. Normally he would have been in Sensar's quarters at that time of the morning, but he had asked Cristavos to tell the alien that he could not come that day; Kiley needed him on the bridge. She didn't really need him, but he had not been able to bring himself to return to Sensar's room after his unexpected encounter with Rairea the day before.

"Please give him my apologies," he told Cristavos. And then, before she could start asking questions, he went on, "I doubt he will care. With Resurrection so close, he'll soon have any number of humans to talk to. He probably would have discontinued our meetings of his own accord."

"Perhaps," Cristavos said, not at all convinced. And then she let him know she had guessed his real reasons. "Talking to him has been a strain for you, hasn't it?"

"At times, yes."

She smiled, her expression at once rueful and sympathetic. "I understand. I find Miquiri behavior and beliefs difficult to comprehend at times. Even at their most extreme, though, the most I would call them is opaque. I've never had the sense they could turn on me unexpectedly, the way I do with the Gan-Tir."

"I'm surprised you agreed to come on this trip if you feel that way about them," Keenan said, taking a closer look at her. He had not paid much attention to Elena Cristavos until that moment, but he found himself suddenly noticing her warm

166

smile and the sparkle in her dark brown eyes. She was, he realized with a start, a very attractive woman.

"They showed more tolerance for me than for any of the other diplomats. Besides, I could hardly pass up such a career opportunity." She sobered. "I know the sessions with Sensar haven't always been easy for you, Daniel, but I do appreciate all you've done. I've written a trip report for Admiral Vladic and have commended you. If I am able to talk to him personally, I'll mention your name again."

Keenan wasn't at all certain that he wanted that, but realized she meant well. Thanking her, he returned to the bridge.

They had arranged a rendezvous point with Admiral Partelli's ship, the *K. S. Corbett*, on their last trip to Resurrection. The coordinates lay nearly a half day away from the station, in the direction of Miquiri space; the admiral had not wanted the aliens any closer to the station than that. They came out of jump on schedule, but when Kiley had Keenan hail the Corps ship, they did not receive a response.

"Greg, would you check—"

"We're right where we're supposed to be," the pilot said before she could complete her sentence. Then he called up a map of the region and displayed their position.

Kiley scanned the short-range monitors, found no sign of another ship, and switched to a long-range view. They were too far from Resurrection to detect traffic at the station, but there was activity on the edge of the screen—a great deal of activity. Three ships flashed across the monitor, one slightly ahead of the other two. They could have been traveling toward the same destination, but it looked to Keenan as if two of them were pursuing the third.

On Resurrection, Partelli had told Kiley to use the code name *Swallow* to refer to her ship when she returned. Anyone close by would be able to identify the *Widdon Galaxy*, but he did not want the ship's name mentioned in long-range transmissions. "The fewer people know you're here, the better," he'd said.

She had had a few words to say about the military's love of secrecy when she reported that conversation to Lukas and

Keenan, but even she had seen the sense behind Partelli's request. She didn't want anyone wondering why they were standing off from the station, let alone questioning what they might be carrying.

"Daniel, send a message on the frequency Partelli asked us to use," Kiley ordered, swinging around to face him. "Make it a maximum of a one-half-second burst. Tell him the *Swallow* is standing by for instructions."

"That's all?"

"Yes."

Keenan transmitted the message, but there was no reply.

Kiley glanced at the long-range scanners. The three ships on the edge of the screen had disappeared. Another had come into view. It, too, was moving fast.

"Something's going on," Lukas said.

"The question is, what?" Kiley answered shortly. "Daniel, are you sure our message went out?"

"Positive. I—"

He broke off as the board lit up, signaling an incoming transmission. After a moment he read the words on the screen. "*Swallow*, stand off. Repeat, stand off. Retreat to fallback position and await instructions."

Kiley started a manual turn before Lukas could lay in the new set of coordinates. They had lost most of their post-jump velocity, so she hit the intercom.

"Jon Robert, I want full power on the main engines," she ordered.

"Full power?" her brother questioned, sounding perplexed. He'd been expecting her to order a reduction in speed, not an increase.

"Affirmative. Something's going on at Resurrection. We don't know what yet, but we've been ordered to fall back, out of scanner range."

Jon Robert needed no further prompting. "Main engines to full power."

"Greg, do you have our course laid in?"

"Affirmative."

Kiley switched helm control back to automatic mode. "Daniel, can you pick up anything from the station? Anything at all?"

He had been trying. The problem wasn't so much a lack of signals as too many. Most of them were short, coded transmissions—Corps activity, he thought. He caught longer bursts from civilian ships, but the vessels transmitting them were at maximum range and apparently heading away. He recognized the identifiers of a few vessels that had frequented the station in the past six months, but beyond their names, he could pick up nothing that made sense.

"Try for something from the station," Kiley suggested. "Their signal should be strong enough to reach us out here."

The official station channel was silent. Alarmed, he started to search for activity on any frequency. He caught one signal on a commercial channel, locked on to it, and found the monitor before him flooded with images from the station.

He was looking down one of the main corridors. He recognized several of the businesses that lay on either side—one of them was the shop that had agreed to order offworld tapes for him and the other newcomers.

Smoke was coming out the door.

The corridor was crammed with people futilely trying to push their way in one direction or the other. What should have been an orderly flow of people away from danger looked more like chaos. Red warning lights were flashing along the length of the corridor, casting an eerie glow over the scene. It wasn't only the light that turned the people red—some of them had head and facial wounds, from which blood streamed. Had there been an explosion? That would account for the fire and injuries. If there had been, it must have happened out of sight. Except for the smoke now clouding the image, there was no sign of damage to any of the structures.

A voice spoke. Keenan could not understand the words—Resurrection clung to ancient languages as well as ancient beliefs. The voice must have belonged to an announcer or reporter, because it went on even after the picture switched to a mobile camera that jiggled up and down as if the person who held it was running and being bumped on either side. There were injured people here, too—mostly men, but some women, and almost all of them in the dark, plain clothing of station natives. Some of them were screaming, some were sobbing, and some had no expression whatsoever. All were fleeing.

The camera switched. Keenan recognized the corridor being displayed—it led to the station's only bar. But the passage was now filled with bodies, debris from broken furniture, and blood. A dark red river ran down the walls and covered the floor. The bodies looked unreal, like dolls torn apart and thrown in every direction by a child in the throes of a terrifying fit. Here and there a person flailed an arm or struggled to rise. Scattered among them were men and women wearing Corps uniforms. Some of the military personnel carried scanners, which they were using on the injured. All carried weapons.

The camera shifted, showing the inside of a clothing store. What merchandise remained was on the floor. There was not a free-standing display in sight, nor were there any people.

The picture changed again: another corridor this time, one near the docks, where people were trying to board a waiting ship. Natives and offworlders mixed indiscriminately, some of them pushing and clawing their way toward the ship. Most were simply being carried along. A fight broke out close to the hatch, and a woman wearing a commercial hauler's uniform raised a disrupter and fired into the disturbance. The men who had been fighting staggered and started to fall. Hands caught them, pulled them apart, then pushed them toward the edge of the crowd. People walked over and around them. Keenan thought some of them were being trampled, but he couldn't tell for certain because the camera switched again.

"What in the name of—" Kiley asked, her shaky voice breaking the silence on the bridge.

"Riot," Lukas said. "Someone or something must have triggered a riot onstation." He started to cut off the transmission from his board.

"Don't!" Keenan protested.

"We don't need to see that," Lukas said forcefully. "Neither do our passengers."

"But—"

"Daniel, all we can do is watch, and that won't help anyone, here or there."

"There's a fire onstation! They may need to evacuate. They certainly need medical assistance. We can't just sit here! We have to—"

"The only thing we're going to do is follow orders," Kiley said harshly. She cut the transmission from her board and Keenan's screen went blank. "Greg's right. I don't want the rest of the family watching that, and I certainly don't want the Miquiri or Gan-Tir seeing it. Our first priority is to protect them, and that means heading for the coordinates we were given, not Resurrection. Restoring order there and dealing with casualties is the Corps' job, not ours."

"Kiley, some of those people were seriously injured! They need help!"

"Partelli knows we're here. If he wants our assistance, he'll ask for it. In the meantime, we're going to follow his instructions to the letter."

She held firmly to that resolve in the hours that followed. She had Keenan transmit a second message saying they were headed for their fallback position, then ordered radio silence. She called Uhrich and Cristavos to the bridge and briefed them on the situation. Cristavos said the Miquiri and Gan-Tir were already asking when they would be rendezvousing with the *K. S. Corbett*. She thought she could put them off for a short time, but not for long.

"We need to tell them there's a problem, Captain," the diplomat argued. "We can't afford to lose credibility by lying. I can say that they are in no danger, and that the Corps has the situation under control, but I do not believe we should be anything less than frank."

"Very well. Do you want me to go with you?" Kiley asked.

"Would you?" Cristavos took up her offer eagerly. "The Gan-Tir respect you and your position. I think they would be more inclined to believe me if you were there, too."

Kiley stood. "Let's go. The sooner we get this over with, the better."

The Miquiri took the news calmly, but the Gan-Tir were frankly alarmed.

"You promised safety," Rairea boomed at Cristavos. Kiley wanted to cover her ears, so loud was the noise. She couldn't tell whether agitation was the cause, or assertiveness, but in either case, the results were acutely uncomfortable. She wondered how Keenan had been able to talk with Sensar for hours; she had only been in their quarters for five minutes, but her nerves were already screaming with tension.

"You are safe," Cristavos assured Rairea. She glanced at the other two Gan-Tir, who were standing close to her. "You all are. The station is some distance away, and we never intended to hold our meetings there in any case. There's no reason why they can't go on as planned as soon as the Corps has restored order."

"No! We go back. We go back now!"

Henherik boomed at Rairea. She answered. Kiley didn't know what they'd said, but Henherik responded with a second, louder noise. He moved forward, placing himself between Rairea and the humans.

"We go back," Rairea repeated, her tentacles whipping wildly. "Now!"

Henherik took a menacing step forward. Cristavos and Kiley exchanged glances.

"I'll have to get permission from Admiral Partelli first," Kiley said. "I will, but I wish you'd reconsider. It may be only a matter of hours before the station is back to normal. You have come a long way for this meeting. It would be unfortunate to cancel it without good cause."

"Is cause!" Rairea roared. "We do not come to risk our lives. Take us back at once!"

She started forward, and Kiley fell back a step. Cristavos put a hand on Kiley's forearm, stopping her before she could retreat any farther.

"If you wish to go, then we will, of course," the diplomat said. "At once. Captain Michaelson will notify Admiral Partelli of our departure. As soon as he gives us clearance, we will leave."

Rairea's tentacles stopped whipping. She glanced at Sensar, who had remained silent throughout the conversation, then Henherik. She boomed at them. They answered. She turned to Kiley. "Is good," she said. "You tell us when under way, yes?"

"Yes," Kiley said. She and Cristavos backed into the hall and Cristavos pressed the wall plate, shutting the Gan-Tir inside their quarters.

"Sorry," the diplomat said. "I knew they'd be upset, but I didn't expect such a heated reaction."

"Are we really going back, then?"

"I don't see what else we can do," Cristavos replied. "The meeting was their idea. If they don't want to go through with it, then we can't make them. There's no reason for them to be so worried—they are in no danger—but I don't think there's anything either of us could say or do to convince them of that. My experience with the Gan-Tir has been that no amount of rational argument will persuade them to change their minds once they've reached a decision. We can ask Admiral Vladic to speak to them, but I doubt it will do any good."

"I'll call Admiral Partelli at once."

Partelli heard Kiley out, then told her that much as he wished he could offer assistance, he had his hands full dealing with the crisis on Resurrection. Admiral Vladic had arrived, but he was in a meeting with Resurrection's council. They were preparing a message asking that everyone on the station return to their quarters until the fires that had been started could be brought under control. The riot had taken twenty-two lives so far and caused uncountable injuries; they did not want to lose any more to a full-scale panic.

"Are you sure you can't put the Gan-Tir off for twelve hours?" Partelli asked her. "We should have the situation under control by then. I'm certain Admiral Vladic would be glad to meet with the aliens then."

"I don't think they'll wait that long," Kiley said, thinking of Rairea's twirling tentacles and Henherik's menacing advance.

Partelli started to reply and stopped, apparently interrupted by some new piece of news or a request for a decision. He said a few words Kiley could not make out before turning his attention back to her. "I can't tell you what to do, Captain. You and Cristavos are the ones who have spoken to the Gan-Tir; you know how hard you can push them. Do your best to convince them the meeting can still go on as planned, but if they won't accept that, then do as they ask and leave. Either way, let me know the outcome."

"Affirmative, Admiral." Kiley began to sign off, but before she could, Keenan broke in.

"Admiral, this is Dr. Keenan. Do you need additional medical assistance on the station? We picked up a local broadcast and I saw a number of people with injuries. If you need help, I'm available."

"Thank you for the offer, Dr. Keenan, but I believe we can manage. We've pulled all the medics off our own ships, and a number of physicians on the planet have volunteered their services, too." Someone interrupted Partelli again. "I'm sorry, Captain," he said after a short pause, "but I must go. Talk to the aliens, then let me know what they've decided to do." He signed off.

Kiley looked at Cristavos, then Lukas, Keenan, and Uhrich. The Corps commander had followed her and Cristavos back to the bridge after their meeting with the Gan-Tir. He had not said anything since then, but he was watching all of them closely.

"Well?" Kiley asked Cristavos.

The diplomat shrugged. "We might be able to appease the Gan-Tir for a little while, but I don't believe I can put them off for twelve hours. We could insist on staying anyway, but that would hardly be conducive to relations between us. Proving the Gan-Tir's fears were unjustified won't help either. The Miquiri say the worst mistake anyone can make with them is to force them to lose face. I think we have to go back. Do you agree, Pete?" She turned to the Corps officer.

Uhrich nodded. "It was never in our interests to have them here in the first place," he said. "If we go now, we'll have the Gan-Tir back where we want them and still be able to say we've done all we could to accommodate them."

Cristavos nodded. "I'll give them one more chance to change their minds. If they won't, then we'll head back."

Cristavos's second talk was as unproductive as her first. Kiley called Partelli an hour later and told him they were returning to Resurrection. The admiral was not displeased.

"It was rumors about aliens coming to the station that touched off the riot," he told Kiley wearily. "I don't know how they got started—they could have been sheer speculation, or one of my people could have talked out of turn. I hope that's not the case, but if it is, I intend to find out. If I do learn one of my men or women is responsible, I will personally have him or her court-martialed on as many counts as I can think up."

Rairea was pregnant.

Her body had started changing within hours of mating. She had remained immobile most of the night, waiting for the newly fertilized cell to attach itself to her body. So much could go wrong—so very much.

But it had not. By morning, the cell had lodged in her tissue and begun dividing. Rairea still lay quietly, but this time she was immobilized by the rapid chemical changes her system was undergoing. They would only last a day or so, but the dizziness and nausea they caused were making her thoroughly miserable. She had managed to stand upright long enough to listen to Cristavos's explanation of problems at Resurrection, but she had returned to bed as soon as the diplomat and captain left.

Even if Rairea had not been pregnant, the Gan-Tir would have wanted to remove themselves from any threat of danger. But now there was no question about their response. They dared not take a single chance with the life she carried.

Sensar had not had to tell Henherik the reason for their change in plans; it had been obvious the moment the male Gan-Tir had tasted her. He had nearly lapsed into shock. Alarm had followed at once. As the guarantor of Rairea's personal safety, Henherik had immediately realized that her pregnancy placed them in a position of extreme vulnerability. If the humans realized the significance of her condition, there was no telling what they might do. While there was no reason to believe the humans would harm her deliberately, they could easily decide to hold her hostage to achieve diplomatic advantage.

They had been discussing plans to cut the meeting short when Cristavos came with the news of the disturbance at the station. Rairea had seized on the report as a way to demand that the humans take them home at once, without having to reveal her true reasons for wanting to go back. The humans' misfortune had been their good fortune, and they had congratulated themselves privately after Cristavos had promised an immediate departure.

Sensar was not unhappy about the change in plans. He had come on the trip to learn more about humans, but he had never expected to find one with Keenan's intelligence and understanding of human culture who was willing to talk to him for an extended period of time. Now that he had, he did not want to lose him. And since Rairea was no longer a threat, he could devote all his attention to the human. She was so strongly focused on the changes taking place within her own body and the prospect of the increased status that would soon be hers that she was no longer interested in him or in his relationship with Keenan. He did not have to fear her pursuit or interference.

That morning, Sensar had reached the third level of *jis* effortlessly. His life was back in balance and he was at peace with himself. He looked around the spacious room that would be his for another ten days and decided he was well pleased. Rairea was not the only person who now had all that she wanted.

The Miquiri were stunned by the Gan-Tir's demand to return to Sumpali. Leetian looked at Pitar, then Chirith.

I don't understand, she signed. *It was they who insisted on making this voyage. The humans have assured us there is no danger. Why have they changed their minds? I do not like this. I do not like them!*

That was not news to Pitar or Chirith. Though she had dealt with them for much of her life, Leetian had no love for the Gan-Tir. The aliens made it clear they tolerated the Miquiri only because they brought goods the Gan-Tir could not obtain for themselves. It was difficult not to feel contempt for beings who regarded one with such disdain.

They are playing games again, Leetian concluded shortly. *I'm not certain they wanted a meeting in the first place. It has never been easy to distinguish Gan-Tir desire from Gan-Tir posturing. It could be they simply hoped to disrupt the talks we were conducting.*

Whatever the truth might be, the outcome is not all bad, Pitar pointed out. *This trip was never in our interests, and if it has proven to the humans that the Gan-Tir are as unpredictable as we claimed, then it will be worth the inconvenience.*

It is not like the Gan-Tir to do us a favor, Chirith noted.

Leetian's arms slashed through the air. *You may be certain it was not intentional. They do no favors for anyone.*

Least of all each other, Pitar added. *It is wise to remember that; more times than not, it has been the sole advantage we have had over them.*

The *Widdon Galaxy* made the first of the two jumps back to Sumpali late that day. In the main computer, Hastings's program completed another loop. The iteration count increased by one. The program checked the count, found that it had reached the desired value, and branched to the next set of instructions.

One hour later, Sensar summoned Cristavos to his quarters and told her that he wanted to resume his talks with Keenan.

He was not making a request.

"You don't have to go," Kiley said to a white-faced Keenan as they stood in the common room.

"Don't I?" he asked. He spoke to her, but he was looking at Cristavos, who stood to one side and slightly behind her.

They had all been up for nearly twenty hours. Keenan was still trying to recover from the shocking images of destruction that had poured out from his monitor. How could people hurt each other that way? How could they let blind fury and panic endanger the life of every person on Resurrection? All over a rumor that had had only the most minimal basis in fact?

"No," Cristavos said in response to Keenan's question. She

had had a difficult day, too. Her dark blue tunic and trousers had not wrinkled, but her face had. She stood erect, but she looked as if she wanted nothing more than to fall into bed.

Maybe I don't, Keenan thought, but he did not believe he could bear the burden of responsibility if the Gan-Tir went on a rampage because of his refusal. Why couldn't it have been the Miquiri who wanted to speak to him? he wondered. Why the Gan-Tir? Why him and not one of the others?

"Daniel, no one wants you to agree if you aren't willing," Kiley repeated.

"I'll go," he said. Much as he wanted to refuse, he could not. He did not want to see any more broken bodies. It was better to face the unknown, no matter how frightening it might be, than to strike out against it blindly, guts twisted in fear and hatred. "Tell Sensar I'll be there tomorrow morning, at the usual time."

"Are you sure?" Cristavos pressed, fatigue thickening her accent. "We do not have to accommodate his every desire. In fact, we may be unwise to do so. If you prefer, I'll tell him that you have other duties you must perform."

"He won't believe that," Keenan said. Thanks to their earlier talks, Sensar knew that he worked only one shift a day and had no other official duties.

"Are you afraid of what he might do if you don't cooperate?" Kiley asked. "Because if you are, then don't be. If I have to call on Uhrich and Fong to keep the Gan-Tir in line, then I will. What I will not do is allow them to coerce you or anyone else. I agree with Cristavos; we can't afford to let them believe they can."

"It would be just as foolish to upset them needlessly," Keenan replied.

Kiley and Cristavos made one more attempt to persuade him not to go, but it was halfhearted; they were too relieved by his decision to argue very long or hard. Their reaction was not a surprise, but Lukas's was. The pilot came to Keenan's cabin shortly after he finished his watch.

"Daniel, are you going to see Sensar because you want to, or because you think you have to?" Lukas demanded without preliminaries. The pool of light at his feet was an intense, red-dish orange. It pulsed faster than normal. Perhaps it was that outward signal of Lukas's agitation that made Keenan give an honest answer, or perhaps it was despair over the blind preju-dices of humanity, their results so clearly seen on his monitor. Then again, perhaps it was simply fatigue.

Whatever the reason, he found himself saying, "Because I have to. I don't want Sensar coming to find me. I don't believe he'd hurt anyone intentionally, but neither do I believe he would let anyone stand between him and his goals. I don't want to be responsible for what he might do."

"No matter what happens to you?"

"Nothing will happen! Sensar is a scholar. All he wants is to talk."

"Are you willing to risk your life on that assessment of his character?" Lukas asked bluntly. "Because you could be doing just that. You do realize that, don't you?"

"Yes."

"And?"

"And I have no reason to believe he will hurt me. I'm not going to become a victim of fear. I am not going to shut down my reason and simply react, like the people on Resurrection."

"What about Rairea? You may trust Sensar, but what about her?"

Keenan hesitated. "I can't deny that her aggressiveness is alarming, but except for that incident on the bridge, she hasn't actually done anything. She *acts* threatening at times, but so far that's all it's been—an act. Sensar told me that she is at-tracted to fear. I think she enjoys arousing it. That does not mean she intends to follow through on her threats."

"Unless stimulating fear is an addiction for her. Unless she is willing to go to greater and greater lengths to savor it."

"She doesn't have to try very hard, Greg," Keenan admitted ruefully, looking away. "All she has to do is walk in the room and I start shaking. I can't help myself."

"I know."

Something in Lukas's tone caught Keenan's attention, and

he looked up quickly. The pilot opened his mouth to say more, then hesitated.

"Greg, what is it?"

Lukas did not answer; he had turned inward. He was gone for nearly thirty seconds. "Daniel, I wasn't going to say anything about this yet, but if it would help . . ."

"If what would help?" Keenan prompted when Lukas stopped again.

"The Quayla knows what you're feeling," Lukas said abruptly. "Since we talked about your possible receptivity, you've become increasingly open to it. It has wanted to approach you for some time, but I asked it not to. I said that you weren't ready yet. You weren't, but the fact is, neither was I. If you shared with it, you would share with me, too—and me with you. I wasn't ready for that. It takes preparation—there are things that I—we—need to talk about. Before. Before—" Lukas broke off.

"Before what, Greg?" Keenan's heart was beating rapidly, but he fell back on old discipline, letting the psychiatrist in him take over. "Whatever it is you want to say, go ahead. I can handle it."

He must have sounded very convincing. Lukas caught himself, took a breath, and nodded. "Of course you can. There was a time when I wasn't sure, but that was before—" He broke off, realizing he was dissembling again. "Daniel, I can't judge the extent of your ability until you actually share with the Quayla, but I think you may be more receptive than I first believed. You may be capable of exchanging actual thoughts, not just impressions. That means mine, as well as the Quayla's. I wasn't expecting that, and I'm not very comfortable about the prospect. It doesn't bother the Miquiri, but they're already so closely tied to each other that they don't see anything abnormal about such intimate contact. But we aren't Miquiri. For all that we're friends, I think that we might find such closeness extremely difficult, if not intolerable."

"Both of us? You, too?"

"Yes."

"Greg, I very much doubt I could learn anything new, let alone surprising, about you at this point."

"There are always parts of us that we keep hidden, even from our best friends—or our psychiatrists."

Keenan had to stifle an impulse to smile. That was hardly news to him. "Greg, just because we didn't discuss every one of your memories, thoughts, and emotions last year, doesn't mean I didn't know they were there, or that you were capable of them. I sincerely doubt there is anything you could do or say that would come as a surprise to me."

"Maybe not," Lukas said resolutely. "But it wouldn't be easy, having another human being inside my thoughts, or being inside someone else's. I'm not sure I could adjust to that—but I may have to. Daniel, if you could communicate with the Quayla, you wouldn't be alone when you go to the Gan-Tir's quarters. It would be with you. *I* would be with you."

Keenan stared at Lukas, his mind racing. "You're saying you would know if I was in trouble? And if I was—if I needed help—you would send it?"

"Yes."

Keenan closed his eyes. It would be so much easier to go into Sensar's room if he didn't feel so alone. But was it worth losing his privacy in a way no other human ever had? Was he prepared to reveal his inner thoughts and feelings for an illusion of safety? Because that was all it would be. If the Gan-Tir truly wished to harm him, they would have more than enough time before help could arrive. Even if Fong or Uhrich did come running, disrupters aimed, what good would it do if he stood between them and the Gan-Tir? He might feel safer, but he wouldn't be.

He shook his head. "I know you mean well, Greg, but I agree—I don't think that would be a good idea at all. I can't imagine that I'd like experiencing that degree of intimacy with anyone, not even you, and this is hardly the time or place to find out—not with the problems we already have."

Lukas nodded, making no attempt to conceal his relief. Apparently, he had not been exaggerating the extent of his own reluctance. He hadn't given up entirely, though. "Daniel, there is still a way."

Keenan raised his eyebrows. "There is?"

"Even if you can't communicate with the Quayla directly, it can pick up your strongest feelings. If you found yourself in trouble, you might be able to send a message to it—an emotional message. Not fear—that's too easily generated. All Sensar has to do is move suddenly, and you're alarmed. It would be difficult to distinguish genuine distress from an already high background level of apprehension. It would have to be some other emotion. Something like—"

"Like what?"

"Rejection. Revulsion. You spent months projecting those feelings toward the Quayla—so powerfully that you were able to keep it out of your room. Do you think you could simulate those feelings again? Would you try now? As an experiment?"

Keenan hesitated, then shrugged and thought of rejection. He thought of revulsion. "Like that?"

Lukas was shaking his head. "You're remembering the feelings, but you aren't experiencing them. They have to be real to work. Go back to the first time you saw the Quayla. Go back to what you thought about it then. Do you remember what you called it when you found out we had joined?"

He had called the Quayla a parasite. It had merged with Lukas and was draining him of energy, so much so that he had been on the verge of collapse only minutes after waking from unconsciousness. The image came back sharp and clear—and so did his accompanying reaction.

"That's it!" Lukas exclaimed.

Keenan opened his eyes to see the light on the walls of his room flicker and dim, as if the Quayla had flinched. He caught the emotion he had projected and shoved it back into his memory, where it belonged.

"Do you think you can do that again?" Lukas asked eagerly.

Keenan looked from the pilot to the Quayla. Lukas might be pleased with his ability to project, but he didn't think the Quayla was. It was brighter now, but it was still not back to normal. He had hurt it. He had not wanted to believe he could affect it, but he clearly had.

"I think so," he said. He pulled himself together, trying to focus on what Lukas was saying. The other man was warning him that he could not call on the memory often; it would lose force quickly. But once, in an emergency, it might work.

Keenan nodded and managed a smile, but all the while he was edging Lukas toward the door. Only after he had gone did Keenan let himself think about what had happened the instant he had called forth the emotion Lukas wanted.

The Quayla had known what was coming, but even so, it had not been fully prepared. Keenan's raw, horrified rejection had struck it like a brutal knee to the groin.

Keenan knew. At the same instant he had delivered the blow, he had felt it.

Chapter 20

Keenan expected Sensar to usher him to his room when he went to the Gan-Tir's quarters the next morning. Instead, the alien pointed to a backless stool at the center of the common room and motioned him to sit.

Keenan gave Sensar a startled glance, then lowered himself cautiously. Sensar pushed a second stool close and sat down.

"You fear us, yes?" the alien said.

The question took Keenan by surprise. He started to say "No," but changed his mind and nodded. He wasn't certain where Sensar was headed, but there was no misunderstanding the alien's posture. He sat stiffly, his tentacles wrapped tightly around his arms. His eyes were not calm, though. They were a hot, vivid violet.

"I understand this," Sensar said. "We are larger than you. We are stronger and faster. You feel ... vu ... vol ..."

"Vulnerable," Keenan said. His eyes narrowed. Sensar was up to something, but what?

"Volnerble," the Gan-Tir repeated. "That is word. I understand. We, too, have feared other species. Had enemies once called Ytavi. They were not strong, not big, but powerful. They hurt us. Made us fear them. Made us hate. These are bad emotions, Keenan, yes?"

"Yes, they are."

"I do not want these feelings between us. You teach me. I am grateful. I want to repay. I want to teach you."

"Teach me what?"

"Words. Language. Gan-Tir language."

Keenan sat back on the stool, stunned. "You want to teach me your language? Why?"

"To understand another, you must think with his words. You agree?"

"Yes," he said cautiously.

"I want you to understand us. Not hate or fear like others of your kind. Understand. I want to teach you our words and ways. Will you be my pupil?"

Keenan didn't know what to say. If Cristavos had been there, she'd have accepted without a second's hesitation; the Miquiri probably would have leaped at the offer, too. They had dealt with the Gan-Tir for centuries, but so far as Keenan knew, they have never been encouraged to learn more than a few Gan-Tir words.

"I would be honored, of course," he said, "but we only have a few days. That's not much time."

"Is enough to make beginning."

"A very small beginning."

"Any beginning is good, Keenan, is it not?"

He could not deny that. Sensar rose, went to his cabin, and brought out a flat white rectangle. He sat, then placed one tentacle over the board, not quite touching it. A line appeared. He traced a shape with his tentacle; the line followed his movements. Sensar lifted his tentacle away from the board and the line stopped moving. He lowered it again, in another place. A dot appeared.

"Writing board," he said, holding the slate out to Keenan.

It was made of a cool, hard material. Keenan pointed his index finger at it. Nothing happened. He moved it closer. At some point just above the surface, he sensed . . . resistance. He pulled his hand back hastily. A dot had appeared on the screen. He moved his index finger toward the slate again, stopping as soon as he felt resistance. There was no sensation of pain, or even tingling, just a sense of pressure.

Another dot appeared on the screen, turning into a line as Keenan moved his finger across the board. The object had to be some sort of computer. Sensar gave him a few minutes to experiment, then took the slate back and demonstrated its operation. Pressing the lower left corner of the screen gave one an empty surface. To go back over what had already been written, one pressed the upper right corner.

Sensar cleared the screen, then wrote several lines of symbols across the top. He worked from right to left, using his left tentacle. When he finished writing, he tapped the board two times, just below the last line of writing, freezing his work in place. He handed the board back to Keenan and told him to copy each of the symbols.

"These are your alphabet?" Keenan asked when he had finished.

"They are a part," Sensar said, and then told him to draw them again.

There were thirty-three symbols on the board. When Keenan could form each of them, Sensar drew fifteen more, scrolled them to the top of the screen, and froze them beneath the others.

Forty-eight letters. The number itself was not insurmountable, but distinguishing small differences between the squiggles and dots was difficult. Keenan practiced forming them for nearly an hour before Sensar let him stop. The Gan-Tir unfroze the screen with four quick taps, cleared it, then told Keenan to write down all the symbols he could recall.

Keenan had a nearly eidetic memory in his own language, but he could only recall twenty-five of the symbols Sensar had shown him, and he made mistakes on eight of the characters. Sensar touched the board, drawing his tentacle across the first error. The symbol disappeared. He wrote the character correctly, then had Keenan clear it and write the character again himself. He did the same at each of the other errors. Then the Gan-Tir scrolled back through all the writing Keenan had done to his own set of symbols. He froze them in place, and handed the board back to Keenan.

"You take. Write many times. Write until you remember all correctly. You can do this by tomorrow?"

"Yes, I think so."

"Good. Come back tomorrow. I show more then."

Keenan went straight to Cristavos's quarters. She gave the

board one incredulous look, then went to her cabin for her re-corder. She filmed all the symbols on the slate, then turned it over to Uhrich, who went over it with every scanner Jon Rob-ert could provide. He didn't learn much. If the board was a machine, it was well shielded. Uhrich was not happy about let-ting Keenan keep it.

"For all we know, it could be a recording device, too," he said, turning it over in his hands like a repellent lab specimen. "It could be picking up every word we say, or taking pictures of every room Keenan carries it into."

"I don't think so," Cristavos said sharply. "And even if it were, it won't tell Sensar anything his own eyes and ears haven't already. Why do you always have to be such a skeptic, Pete?"

"Because that's my job!" Uhrich replied harshly. "I am not here to make friends or sign treaties. I am here to insure the security of this ship and the Corps. I've already said that I be-lieve it is unwise for Dr. Keenan to associate with the Gan-Tir and I'll keep on saying it until you start listening."

"He's keeping them in their quarters," Cristavos countered. "If he weren't going there, who knows what they might do? I don't want them deciding they're bored, Pete. I don't want them taking another stroll around the ship. Neither do you. Let Keenan keep the board. Let him talk to Sensar. It isn't hurting, and we're learning a great deal in the process."

Uhrich's jaw clenched, but he did not resist when Cristavos took the board away and handed it back to Keenan.

"Daniel, will you have time to study what Sensar has shown you so far?" she asked. "I can ask Kiley to relieve you from duty this evening. Uhrich could fill in for you if that leaves her shorthanded. You'd be happy to do that, wouldn't you, Pete?"

"I would," Uhrich said darkly, "but I don't believe she will let me. I'm not exactly welcome on the bridge, in case you hadn't noticed."

"If your attitude were a little less—"

"I can study while I stand watch," Keenan interrupted un-easily. "There's not that much to do during jump." He looked from Cristavos to Uhrich; the two had squared off, on the verge of a full-scale argument. He hadn't realized they disliked each other so much. What had happened? Too much time together in close quarters? Or could it be too little? Clashes didn't always signal repulsion—sometimes they meant the opposite. Still, Keenan did not think that was the case between Uhrich and Cristavos. The temperature in the cabin had gone down fifteen degrees, in spite of their heated words. "If you'll excuse me, I'll get to work," he said uncomfortably.

"Go ahead." Cristavos kept her eyes on Uhrich.

"Yes, go," Uhrich told him.

They did not speak again as Keenan left. They didn't move, either. If an argument began the moment the door closed, then it was conducted in very low voices.

Sensar was waiting for Keenan in the common room the next morning. Keenan had stared at the symbols all afternoon and most of the evening. He expected that Sensar would start the lesson by having him demonstrate what he had learned, but the Gan-Tir told him to set the board aside instead.

"First, you learn proper method of greeting," the Gan-Tir said. "Stand up and hold out arms. Like this." He demonstrated, extending his arms out straight at waist level. His sleeves fell back from his wrists, revealing the ends of his limbs.

"You do, too," Sensar ordered when Keenan hesitated.

Sensar's body was wider than his. When Keenan extended his arms, they fell well inside the alien's.

"When Gan-Tir meet, they touch," Sensar said. "Your clothing is too tight for proper greeting, but we pretend it is not there. In proper greeting, arms come together, like this."

He slipped his right arm over Keenan's left, his sleeve forming a tent around them.

"Turn arm so palm is up," Sensar ordered. "Place arm on mine."

Keenan looked past Sensar at the wall, wondering if this was the moment to panic. The Quayla was so dim it was undetectable in the Gan-Tir's quarters, but Lukas had promised that it would be there. If he needed help, all he had to do was call out to it. Assistance might come too late, but it would come.

"Keenan, turn arm," Sensar ordered.

Keenan looked at the alien. Sensar was standing very still, his own arms outstretched. He might not be as vulnerable as Keenan, but he was risking something, too. Slowly, Keenan turned his arm so his hand lay palm up, and Sensar lowered his arm until their limbs met. The Gan-Tir's flesh was hard and smooth against Keenan's fingers. He had expected the alien to be cold, but Sensar's body temperature was higher than his own. The surprise was enough to get him past the moment of initial contact.

"Now do the same with other arm," Sensar said.

It should have been easier, knowing what to expect. Perhaps it would have been if the greeting had been one arm at a time. But holding both out at the same time left him off-balance and acutely uncomfortable. He held still for an instant, to show he could, then started to pull back. But Sensar grabbed him, his long tentacles lashing Keenan's arm to his. They wrapped around once, then again, the tips coming to rest just above Keenan's elbows.

"Sensar, let me go!" Keenan demanded, alarmed.

"Be still!" Sensar ordered. "Do not fear. Will not harm, Keenan. Will. Not. Harm."

And he did not, though he held on to Keenan until the human stopped struggling. Then Sensar released him, arms and tentacles sliding away in one smooth movement. The Gan-Tir let them fall to his sides, hidden in the folds of his long sleeves. He did not lift them again.

Keenan took a step back. Then another.

"You wish to run?" Sensar asked. "Go, then. Have no use for fear, Keenan. Have no use for one who cannot reason. If you cannot tolerate simple greeting, then send one who can. Send Cristavos. She is not afraid. She will touch. She has."

She had? Funny—she hadn't said anything about that to him. Still, she might have, if she thought such an act would win the Gan-Tir's respect. She was not a coward.

"Keenan, will you go or stay?" Sensar demanded.

"I will . . . stay."

He went to the stool he had occupied the day before and sat down. After a moment of appraisal, Sensar joined him. He picked up the writing slate and began drawing on it.

"Is not easy, overcoming fear," Sensar said quietly. He looked across at Keenan, the expression in his violet eyes unreadable. "This word," he said, pointing to a group of symbols. A long, low boom rolled across the room. "That means 'greetings.' "

The lesson had begun.

Sensar went to his cabin after Keenan left. The givitch tumbled down the walls to greet him, and he stood within its embrace, relaxing. Vines brushed his body and face, a feathery questioning; then the givitch embraced him. He caressed it as he went over the morning in memory.

He had deliberately pushed the human. Keenan had done well for several hours, but then his mind had dulled. He had started to forget not only the new, but things he had known a short time before. That had been discouraging. They would reach Sumpali in a matter of days, and the human had much to learn before then.

Still, there had been one encouraging moment. Keenan had accepted his touch. That was a significant step forward. The human had been terrified when Rairea had touched him on the bridge, but he had been only moderately frightened when Sensar grasped his arm that morning. He still projected sufficient apprehension to trigger aggressive impulses in most Gan-Tir, but repeated exposure would dull his reactions.

It worked that way with most creatures. The familiar became the accepted, then the expected. It was simply a matter of time and patience. Sensar had the patience, but he worried greatly about the time.

Cristavos replayed Keenan's latest oral report twice, then looked at her recording of the new words on his writing slate again. She frowned the entire time.

What had Sensar been thinking of? The lesson he had given

had no pattern that she could determine. The alien had written down symbols and definitions for nearly two hundred words. They ranged from simple verbs, like "eat," to nouns that represented highly abstract concepts, like "continuum." None of the words fit together to form a simple phrase. One did not teach a language from a dictionary, flipping through it randomly, passing on the first words one saw. One didn't teach by deliberately befuddling the student.

Sensar had tossed Keenan into waters far over his head. Cristavos had listened to the psychiatrist a number of times, and his speech had always been concise and highly organized, even when he was upset. Today, though, he had jumped from subject to subject, going backward and forward as one memory triggered another. Try as he might, he could not give the session a coherent structure—because there had been none. He apologized several times for his lack of clarity, seeming to believe he was at fault, but Cristavos could see what he had missed: either Sensar was an exceedingly poor teacher, or he had deliberately tried to bewilder Keenan. She doubted the former; unless the Gan-Tir's educational system was wholly different from humans', he must have had some experience in preparing a lesson and gearing his pace of teaching to his student's level of understanding.

Why, then, had he pushed Keenan to exhaustion? He must have realized Keenan's mental acuity was deteriorating—all he had to do was look at the writing in the tablet. What had begun as an orderly arrangement of words and definitions, carefully written, had disintegrated into a messy scrawl as Keenan had tried to keep up with what Sensar was saying.

Cristavos sat back in her chair, eyes closed, seeing Keenan again. Her frown deepened. Something had happened to him during the lesson, something he hadn't told her, and it went beyond mental fatigue and temporary confusion. Keenan had changed. He had not looked directly at her, and there had been a flatness to his expression and voice that disturbed her. She had come to like him over the past two weeks, and she admired the courage with which he had overcome all-too-rational fears and ventured into the Gan-Tir's territory. She had thought the risks worthwhile, but after seeing the change in him, she wondered.

Sometime during the past four hours, Daniel Keenan had lost all self-assurance. He was not accustomed to struggling. He was not accustomed to failure. By all indications, he had done both. He had tried to keep up with Sensar, but by the end of the lesson, he had been so confused that he could not accurately recall the meaning of a single word. Good teachers might push their students, but they did not take them that far beyond their limits—unless they wanted to make a point of those limits.

Was that what Sensar had been trying to do? Had he wanted to demonstrate that humans were not as bright as Gan-Tir, that they could not match their intellectual ability, just as they could not match their strength? Or had he had some other intention entirely? Something to do not with humans and Gan-Tir in general, but with himself and Daniel Keenan in particular?

Gan-Tir were manipulators. If the Miquiri could be believed, they did not form a single relationship that was not based on mastery and subjugation. A Gan-Tir might assume a dominant role in one relationship and a submissive one in another, but they never met as equals. Was Sensar trying to force Keenan to relate to him on Gan-Tir terms? Had he deliberately attempted to strip the man of self-confidence so he could force him into a dependent position and hold him there?

Elena Cristavos thought that might be the case. If so, then the relationship could not be allowed to continue—not only for Keenan's sake, but for humanity's. Human beings might be smaller and weaker than the Gan-Tir, and they might even lack some of the aliens' intellectual ability, but they were still cognizant, reasoning beings, entitled to respect. She intended to see that they received it.

Even if that was more than the Gan-Tir accorded to their own kind?

Cristavos's expression hardened. Even then. How the Gan-Tir chose to behave with members of their own species was their business; how they dealt with humans was another matter.

She would let Keenan see Sensar one more time, but if he did not come away in better condition than he had today, she would call a halt to further talks until they reached Sumpali. Bergstrom had charged Uhrich with insuring the ship's safety, but setting the boundaries that would guide humanity's relations with the Gan-Tir was her job.

Cristavos sighed. She had worked all her life to reach the position she held, but she was finding the demands being placed upon her much heavier than she had anticipated. She would do her best to meet them, but for the first time in her life, she found herself wondering if her best would be good enough.

Chapter 21

That afternoon, Cristavos told Kiley that Keenan had had a long and difficult session with Sensar and asked her to give him the evening off. She volunteered Uhrich's services if Kiley needed assistance, but Kiley told her that she and Lukas could cover one shift.

"But I can't do this every day without creating a hardship," Kiley cautioned uneasily.

"I understand, Captain," Cristavos replied. "I'm not entirely happy about the situation, either. I want Daniel to continue the meetings if he can, but if he comes away from the next one as fatigued as he was today, I'll tell Sensar they have to stop until we reach port."

"He'll be upset."

"Probably, but Daniel's welfare comes first. Sensar will protest, but I don't think he'll actually do anything."

"But you don't know that."

Cristavos hesitated a little too long for Kiley's comfort. "No. I don't think so, but I can't honestly say what he'll do. We have a great deal to learn about the Gan-Tir—which is why I'd like Daniel to go on with the talks if he possibly can. He's the only person who's managed to establish a rapport with one of them, and I hate to interfere unless it's absolutely necessary."

"All right. I'll tell him to take the evening off."

Kiley sat for a moment after Cristavos signed off. The diplomat's uncertainty about the Gan-Tir's behavior had not been reassuring. Neither was Keenan's voice when she called his cabin: he sounded disoriented. He apologized, saying he'd been taking a nap, but Kiley suspected he'd been deeper in sleep than that. She told him she had rearranged the duty schedule that evening.

"Why?" he protested.

She explained. He was not happy with what he saw as Cristavos's interference.

"I admit that I was tired earlier," he said, "but I've had a nap. I'll be fine."

"I'm sure you will, but I'm still rearranging the duty schedule," Kiley replied firmly. "A few extra hours of work will hardly incapacitate me or Greg."

"Kiley—"

"Go back to sleep, Daniel. We'll manage without you."

He knew better than to argue an order issued in that tone of voice. Being captain did have its advantages, Kiley thought as she switched off the intercom.

Keenan slept straight through his watch and did not wake until the next morning. Then he lay in bed for a time, watching the Quayla pulse softly on the ceiling of his cabin and thinking about the lesson Sensar had given him the previous day.

In retrospect, it had had very little to do with language. Culture, maybe, but not language. Did the Gan-Tir thrust disconnected scraps of learning at everyone the way Sensar had at him, or had the alien had some other reason for wanting him so confused that he could no longer reason, only react?

He wasn't sure, but one thing he did know: he was not going to let the Gan-Tir manipulate him so easily again. Sensar would have to match his pace or abandon the attempt to teach him. Keenan didn't care which alternative the alien chose, but he was not going to undergo another experience like yesterday's.

After breakfast, he went down to the cargo deck, where he stopped to check in with Cristavos. She surveyed him critically, as if she were searching for defects in a sloppily worked piece of pottery. He must have passed her inspection, because she smiled warmly.

"Back for more?" she asked.

"Yes."

"Good. We may make a xenologist out of you yet."

"I doubt that."

"You shouldn't—you have a number of qualifications, you know. Medical training gave you a strong scientific background, and you're an experienced behaviorist. You have a remarkable ability to evaluate your own responses at the same time you observe and record another's. You're aware of your cultural biases, and you don't make the mistake of assuming that all beings will or should respond to the same set of circumstances in the same manner. I'd say you're very well qualified."

"Engaging in a little ego-boosting, Cristavos? If so, it isn't necessary. I realize that I let Sensar get the upper hand yesterday. It won't happen again."

Cristavos gave him a sharp look. "No, I don't believe you will," she said slowly, then grinned. "Sensar isn't the only one who underestimated you—I believe I did, too. All right, Daniel. Have at him. One word of caution, though—don't try to outguess him. You don't have sufficient knowledge about him in particular, or the Gan-Tir in general, to play games. Be especially alert to obvious attempts to manipulate you—he may employ them as a cover for other, more subtle pressures. Don't stop watching him or yourself. If you start to feel overwhelmed, stop the lesson immediately. You can do that. No one's forcing you to go into that room, and no one's forcing you to stay. Understood?"

Keenan nodded. Cristavos rewarded him with another smile, then sent him off to face Sensar.

The Gan-Tir sat on the same stool he had occupied the day before. He stood when he saw Keenan, tentacles waving back and forth in indecipherable patterns. "You came back. I am glad. Not sure after I tested you yesterday."

"You tested me?" Keenan asked, wondering exactly what the Gan-Tir meant by that. Sensar had memorized an impressive number of words and constructions, but he did not yet have a reliable grasp on human grammar or colloquial meanings. Even when there was no question of Sensar's honesty,

Keenan was never certain that what came out was quite what the alien had meant to say.

"Quickness. Retention. Needed to know you better before I teach real lessons. I confused you. Know this. Will not again. You believe?"

Keenan nodded, taken by surprise. Cristavos was right—he couldn't outguess the alien. Sensar was already two steps ahead of him and accelerating rapidly; it would be all he could do to stay in the race.

"Good," Sensar said, satisfied. "Come in, Keenan. I welcome you." He held out his arms, offering a Gan-Tir greeting.

Keenan had started forward, but stopped abruptly. Sensar expected him to return the gesture; he did not want to. Sensar was waiting to see what he would do. Waiting to see if social embarrassment would prove powerful enough to force him to put aside apprehension and distaste. Keenan swallowed, deciding that while he might not be able to control his emotions, he could play to them.

He held out his arms. He made no attempt to cover his flinch as Sensar's tentacles slid along his forearms. He forced himself to hold still as the appendages curled around his upper arms, just above his elbows. If he had been Gan-Tir he could have mirrored the gesture, taking hold of Sensar's arms, but his fingers reached only half the distance. Touching the alien was not unpleasant, but being forced to stand in such close proximity to a being with proven speed and unpredictable temperament was exceedingly difficult.

Sensar squeezed, the pressure just sufficient to be noticed, then released Keenan and waved to the closest stool.

"Sit. We see what you remember from yesterday, yes?"

As it turned out, that was not a great deal. Sensar had written down a number of words, but Keenan could recall only a few of them. The Gan-Tir did not appear to find that surprising or discouraging.

"We go slower today," Sensar said. "Yes?"

"That would be better."

"We start over, then."

Sensar wrote the symbols from the Gan-Tir alphabet again.

He had Keenan write them once, then cleared the slate and had him write them from memory. Keenan only missed one.

"Is good. Very good," Sensar praised. "We learn to build words now. Small words first, then larger."

"I," "you," "come," "go," "talk," "eat"—those were the words he taught, the ones Keenan had been expecting the day before. Sensar wrote each word once, told Keenan what it meant, and then had him write it several times himself. When he could do that, Sensar had him combine the words to form short sentences. He was patient, thorough, and did not progress to the next term until he was certain that Keenan had mastered the current one. He reviewed frequently, and behaved, in short, like the teacher he professed to be.

The only difficult moment of the entire lesson came when Sensar touched him. As they sat side by side, taking turns writing on the same slate, Sensar reached across to re-form a badly shaped symbol and his tentacle brushed Keenan's arm. The contact was incidental and Sensar did not appear to notice it, but Keenan jerked away, too startled to control his reaction.

"Something is wrong?" the Gan-Tir asked.

Keenan hesitated, not certain whether to dissemble or give an honest answer. "You touched me," he said, looking straight at the Gan-Tir. "You startled me."

Sensar stared back at him. Whatever was going on in the alien's mind, Keenan could not read it.

"Your people have taboos against touch from another?" the Gan-Tir asked after a moment.

"Unless it is invited, yes."

"I am sorry. I did not realize this. I did not mean to upset you. Gan-Tir touch often. It is how we assess each other's physical condition and mood. To refuse touch is considered an insult and cause for deep suspicion among my kind."

Sensar waited for Keenan's response, his challenge clear. How will you define my behavior—on my terms, or yours? How much divergence from your own nature will you tolerate? *Who will set the bounds of our relationship, you or me?*

"Among mine," Keenan said deliberately, "touch is an act of intimacy, requiring permission."

"And you do not give me this permission?"

"No."

"Not even if I say it is necessary?" Sensar sat back, his tentacles coiling around his arms. "*Elith*s contain sensory receptors, Keenan. You rely on your eyes to gather information; we rely on taste. Without touch, I cannot judge your emotions or level of fatigue."

"If you wish to know how I feel, then ask. I will tell you."

"This is not acceptable. It is a teacher's place to judge a pupil's progress, not a pupil's. I respect your taboos, Keenan, but I must touch from time to time. I must taste. I cannot instruct otherwise. You are free to leave if you wish, but if you stay, you must agree to my terms."

Cristavos had warned Keenan about the Gan-Tir's manipulative skills. He had cautioned himself. And still, despite his best intentions, he found himself backed into a corner. He could go, of course, but if he did, Sensar would come off as the wronged party.

"Sensar, I don't—"

"This is not a difficult matter to decide, Keenan. I touch now and we continue. I do not and you go. You go, because without trust, there is no reason to continue. The decision is yours. Permit me to touch or leave."

"Sensar, I will not accept those terms. You can't force—"

"Keenan, permit me to touch, or go. Choose now!"

He wanted to stand. He wanted to go.

He sat still.

Sensar's tentacle brushed the back of his hand. "Keenan, do you give permission?"

He made a strangled sound that might have been "Yes."

Sensar coiled his tentacle around Keenan's wrist and began exploring the soft skin where his veins rose close to the surface. The alien held him loosely; he could have slid his hand free at any time. He nearly did as the tip of Sensar's tentacle moved across the inside surface of his arm, making a circular exploration. Microscopic hairs brushed his flesh. The tip of Sensar's *elith* flattened and . . . sucked. Keenan made a startled sound. The Gan-Tir paused.

"Keenan, I do not hurt you," he protested. And he did not. He alarmed, he upset, but he did not harm physically. He uncoiled his tentacles and wrapped them around his own arms again. Keenan looked down at his wrist. The skin was not even red.

"We will continue, yes?" Sensar asked. He took Keenan's silence for assent. "Good. Let us review what you have learned so far."

They were due to reach midpoint at the end of Kiley's watch. Lukas showed up a few minutes before they returned to normal space, slipped into the copilot's seat, and began scanning the boards.

"I thought you were sleeping," Kiley said. She didn't mean to sound accusing, but he tensed.

"I was."

"Not for long."

"No."

She turned to look at him. He was looking away, seemingly intent on the report he had called up. He needed a haircut; his beard was beginning to show, too. He hadn't used a depilatory for several days. She could not recall his appearance having slid so far since he had first come on the *Widdon Galaxy*—and then he had been ill, running from a past he could neither recall nor bury. Lately, she thought he had started running again—not only away from her, but from himself.

No matter how much Lukas denied the facts, the Quayla was making abnormal demands upon him. She and Keenan saw that, but he refused to. But what upset Kiley most was not the threat to his health, or the rate at which he aged—it was the way he and the Quayla kept breaking their promises. He had said he would sleep longer; the Quayla would help him. It had, but only for a few days. Why couldn't it keep its word longer than that? Did it forget, or had it decided there was no danger? Surely Lukas's body must send out some warning signals? Could they not sense them, or did they simply choose to ignore them, as if by pretending not to see the truth, they could make it go away?

"Greg, we have to talk," she said abruptly.

He went still. "About what?" He finished scanning the report and looked up, his eyes the color of dense fog, and just as opaque.

Kiley wavered. She didn't want an argument, but she could not watch him go on as he was. She shored up her resolve. "Something's wrong with you. It has been ever since Quayla began reading the ship's sensors. I don't know if its increased size or activity is responsible, but it's making demands on you that your body simply can't meet. It backs off and lets you rest when Daniel or I say something, but then it starts back in again almost immediately. I don't know if it ignores you accidentally or intentionally, but it is hurting you. I can understand that you don't want to see that, but you can't go on like this."

"Like what?"

"Not sleeping. Avoiding me. Refusing to admit that the Quayla is having an effect on you—that it could actually be damaging you."

She had expected anger, but not the explosion that followed. "You want it off the ship, don't you?" he demanded hotly. "That's really what this is all about, isn't it? You aren't worried about me—you're just tired of having to compete for my attention! You think that I can't care about it and you at the same time. The fact is, you're jealous of it."

"I'm not!"

"Aren't you?" Heat flashed in Lukas's eyes like lightning. "You want us to have a normal relationship. You want me to be normal. Well, I'm not, and I never will be. It won't ever be just you and me, alone together. The Quayla will always be there with us. You may want it to go away, but it can't. Not unless I go, too."

"Greg, you're wrong." Kiley grabbed the arms of her seat to keep her hands from shaking. "I knew the Quayla would be a part of our relationship from the beginning. I won't pretend I liked that, but I accepted it. I did! But that does not mean that I cannot or will not question what it is doing to you. It agreed to help you sleep longer, but you're back down to only one or two hours a night. It pushes you, Greg! It makes unreasonable demands on you. Of course I worry about it, but not because of me. I worry because of you!"

"Then stop. There is no reason to be concerned."

"Greg, there is! You must—"

"Kiley, are you awake up there?" Jon Robert asked over the intercom. "We're less than a minute from transition. Do you want the main engines on, or were you thinking of staying in jump forever?"

She hit the intercom. "Sorry, Jon Robert. I was distracted for a moment. Main engines on."

"Affirmative," he answered. "Is everything all right?"

"Fine." She turned the intercom to shipwide broadcast. "This is Captain Michaelson. We will be exiting jump in thirty seconds. Prepare for transition."

Lukas had turned away, and was switching on the external monitors with hands that shook. The visual screens rolled crazily, a mirror image of Kiley's turbulent thoughts and emotions. Fifteen seconds. Ten. She took a deep breath and held it. A moment later, something reached inside her body and tried to turn her inside out. Her lungs expanded, starved for air. They found none. An eternity later, the churning stopped— they were through. She gasped and air rushed in again. Then she glanced up at the external monitors in time to see a light flash across all of them simultaneously, and gave a startled exclamation.

"Is something wrong?" Lukas lifted his eyes from the boards.

"I saw a flash of light on the screens."

"I didn't notice anything," he said. He scanned the monitors and then the instrument board. "Everything looks normal to me."

Kiley reached for the intercom. "Jon Robert, status report."

"All systems a-okay," her brother said immediately. "The engineering board registered a power surge as we came out of jump, but everything appears normal now. I'm running a systems check to verify that. I'll let you know how it comes out as soon as I've finished."

"Please do." Kiley examined the instruments and screens

again, then shook her head. "Whatever it was couldn't have been very serious. I don't have a single warning light."

Jon Robert reported back a short time later. "I can't find any sign of malfunction, Kiley. We must have come out close to a cluster of dust or particles too fine to show on sensors. The flash and power surge were probably the shields warding off the debris."

Kiley thanked him, then switched off the intercom, logged on to the navigation computer, and called up a position display. The *Widdon Galaxy* was a blinking blue dot on a black background. The few distant stars in the vicinity showed as widely scattered white spots, and a bright red line ran along the edge of the screen, marking the warning boundary at the edge of the barrier.

After the rescue of the *Nieti*, Corps scientists had spent months investigating the barrier, but in the end they had known little more than they had at the beginning: something inside it jammed electronic equipment. Drones sent into the area stopped transmitting from one moment to the next, and either did not receive or could not comply with orders to reverse course and return to their parent ship. The scientists had offered any number of theories about what might lie across the line, but none of them knew for certain. The only living being with firsthand knowledge of the region was the Quayla that had joined with Lukas, and all it could recall were incoherent, mind-rending images of madness.

Electrical interference could have caused the flash on the screen if they had been closer to the boundary, but they were well beyond the range considered safe. They must have passed through a cloud of dust. It was the only explanation that made sense.

"Well, whatever it was doesn't appear to have done any damage," Kiley said, giving the green lights on the boards a final, uneasy glance.

"No," Lukas replied without looking at her. He glanced at the chronometer. "It's my watch now," he announced. "You don't have to stay any longer."

It was the clearest dismissal he had ever given her, and she

could have cried at the coldness in his voice. He was wrong—
they needed to talk. They needed to resolve their conflict instead of letting it fester. But a quick glance at Lukas's averted
profile told her that he was not going to listen to anything she
had to say. Not yet, and maybe not ever. Kiley fought a sudden, wild urge to scream. How could everything go so wrong,
so fast? More importantly, how could she fix it?

"All right," she said evenly. "You have the conn."

She went to Keenan's cabin.

He wasn't there.

She went to the engine room, hoping to talk to her brother.
He and Holly were trying to run a second systems check and
watch Hope at the same time; they didn't need another distrac-
tion. She went to the garden. Reese and Lia were both there,
in the middle of an intense, private conversation of their own.
Reese was holding Lia, who had been crying. They looked up
when Kiley came in, startled. She apologized for interrupting
them and backed out hastily.

She went to her own cabin, lay down on the bed, and stared
up at the Quayla, which was pulsing on the ceiling.

If only she could talk to it directly. If only she could reason
with it. Maybe then she could make it understand what Lukas
meant to her—and why she so feared what was happening to
him. She put her hand on the wall, touched the light, and tried
to speak to it.

Nothing happened.

Whatever skill or genetic makeup was required, she did not
possess it. The Quayla could not hear her.

It never had. It never would.

Chapter 22

Kiley went back to the bridge three hours later to relieve Lukas. He glanced up when she sat down, then turned back to the boards. "Jon Robert and Holly finished their second check," he reported. "They still couldn't find any sign of malfunction. There's nothing else in the log."

She looked anyway. Lukas keyed in a report and it began scrolling. "Would you like me to stay until we jump?" he asked, eyes averted.

"Would you mind?"

"No."

"Then, yes. Please."

He glanced at her quickly. He started to say something, but closed his mouth and turned back to the report he had requested.

Kiley didn't care; she wasn't ready to talk, either. Better to wait until they were off the bridge and could finish whatever they started. Until they had had a little more time to think, both of them.

She checked the status indicators on the navigation and environmental boards. "Have you laid in our jump coordinates yet?" she asked.

"No."

"Go ahead. I'll take the conn."

Lukas finished the calculations in less than a minute. There wasn't much to do; they'd been using virtually the same coordinates for the past six months. He always had to make a few fine adjustments, because they never exited or entered jump in precisely the same location, but that was all.

They sat in silence for the next half hour. To keep busy, Kiley ran a series of status reports. Lukas scanned the environmental sensors.

They reached the five-minute mark; then four, then three. "Two minutes to transition," Kiley announced over the intercom. She switched to the engine room. "Jon Robert, stand by to start jump engines." At one minute to transition, she gave the order: "Jump engines on."

And then, just as they passed the point of no return, Lukas cried out. "Kiley, stop!"

She jerked around. He was bent forward, one hand clutching his stomach, the other wrapped around the edge of the control board.

"Greg, what's wrong?" Kiley started to release her seat restraints and stopped, remembering where they were. Remembering jump.

Lukas had to fight to speak. "Wrong way. Turned. Going the wrong way!"

"Greg, what are you talking about? What's wrong with you?" She glanced at the boards and monitors. They were on the same course they'd held for the past three hours—everything was as it should be.

Lukas answered by unlatching his seat restraints and lunging for the ship's controls. "Off course!" The image on one of the monitors caught his attention and his face went gray, as if what he saw made him physically ill. He looked away hastily. "The screens aren't right!"

He reached for the main board. He was trying to shut down the engines, Kiley realized in horror. With one swipe of his arm, he was about to kill them all. She pulled the release on her seat restraints and threw herself onto him. She caught his arm and held on with all her strength. "Greg, what are you doing!" she demanded. "We're past the point of commitment! We can't stop now!"

"We have to! Kiley, we're headed directly into the barrier!"

Had he gone mad? Kiley risked one more look at the monitors. Everything, every single instrument, read normal. They couldn't have turned.

Lukas caught her by the shoulders and shook her. "I'm not crazy! The Quayla is receiving data directly from the sensors. I don't care what the instruments are showing—we're not on course!" As another wave of dizziness caught him, he grimaced and shoved her away. Kiley tripped and fell back into the pilot's seat. Lukas reached for the boards and changed their course.

The view on the monitors did not shift.

Moments before, Lukas had been paralyzed with disbelief; now Kiley was. Lukas issued command after command, his fingers moving so fast that she could only guess what he was trying to do. Not one viewscreen, not one instrument fluctuated.

Was he right—could they possibly be headed into the barrier? If so, they were on a course for certain death. Kiley started pressing controls herself. They did not respond.

"Nothing's working," Lukas said in a tight voice. Years of training were all that kept both of them from panicking. "We can't abort—we're past commitment. We have to jump." Kiley wasn't sure whether he was talking to her or himself. Lukas had turned inward. He could still see through the Quayla, but she had nothing to rely on. With the instruments displaying false readings, she had no idea which direction they were heading.

"If we could just reduce velocity!" Lukas muttered. "Short jump. Not all the way in. Might have a chance—" He broke off and went completely still.

The ship shrieked. The walls turned red, then yellow, then white. Light seared Kiley's eyes. She threw up both of her arms protectively, but intense heat and light beat against her. In the protective cocoon of her arms, she gasped for air. What came seared her lungs.

Lukas cried out.

They entered transition.

Coolness. Silence. Peace.

Kiley had never welcomed jump in her life, but she did then. With it came release. With it came life.

The bridge swam back into focus. Lukas was bending over

her. "Kiley, wake up!" He gave her a shake. "We don't have much time."

"What?" she mumbled, still groggy.

"The Quayla absorbed as much of the ship's energy as it could before we jumped. We're going to come out inside the barrier in just under three minutes. When we do, we're going to be blind. The main engines may fail—like the *Nieti*'s did. The Quayla is calculating a turn now. If we haven't gone too far in, if we still have enough momentum after we come out, we may be able to drift free—provided we can make the turn. If we can't—"

He didn't finish, but he didn't have to. If they didn't, then they were dead, all of them. Whatever madness lay inside the barrier would completely disrupt the ship's instruments. Luck had brought the *Nieti* back out. But it had been seriously damaged, and its Quayla—

"Greg, the Quayla. You—"

"No! Don't say it," he ordered, cutting her off before she could speak. He knew—she saw the memories in his eyes. Madness, death, horror beyond belief. The Quayla had survived its encounter with the barrier, but it had been severely damaged and its companion had died. "There isn't time. I have to lay in our turn, assuming the computer will accept it—"

He broke off, not wanting to follow that thought to its conclusion. They had not been able to change course before jump, and the computers still might not be responding. They had to try, though. Or rather, Lukas had to. Kiley did nothing. Sitting there, her ship off course, the only man she had ever loved about to open a door and find madness on the other side, she did nothing. Lukas knew their heading when they entered jump; she did not. He and the Quayla could calculate the necessary turn; she could not—not in the time remaining.

She had never felt so helpless in all her life.

Lukas reached for the control board and began entering instructions. The computer accepted them, but would it act on them when the time came? Kiley didn't know, and neither did he. But they were about to find out. Two minutes had passed on the chronometer. They had one minute to go. Kiley reached for the intercom.

"This is Captain Michaelson," she announced in her calmest, most professional voice. "We experienced a minor malfunction prior to jump that forced a change of plans. We will be leaving jump again in one minute. Please stay in your bunks until we complete transition. If you are away from your cabin, find a secure place immediately and brace yourself—we may have to make several abrupt maneuvers."

She cut over to the engine room before anyone could call and demand explanations. "Jon Robert, start the main engines."

"Kiley, what's—"

"What you saw on your boards before jump was not correct. We're about to come out again—inside the barrier. Greg thinks he can turn the ship and head us back out before we lose power, but he's not sure. I don't want you to touch anything after we leave transition. Do you understand me? Nothing! We'll have time for explanations and evaluating our options later, but for now, just do what Greg or I say. Understood?"

Her brother could have been captain of the ship; he had the intelligence, judgment, and strength of character to have been a fine commander. He had chosen the engine room instead, and he had done that knowing it meant taking someone else's orders the rest of his life. He could not have enjoyed unquestioning obedience, but it was a measure of his character—and his trust—that he gave Kiley what she most needed.

"Engine room standing by," he said. That was all.

She could rely on Jon Robert. She had, too many times to count.

The main engines came on. The old ones had rumbled, but these produced only a steady, comforting vibration beneath her feet. Some controls were responding. Others would, too, Kiley told herself. They had to.

Lukas finished entering data on the navigation computer and sat back in his seat, looking desperate. She hoped she would never have to see that expression again—not on his face, and not on anyone's.

"Kiley—I don't know if this will work. I don't—"

She reached across the space between their seats, caught his hand and squeezed. "You've done all you could. That's all I ask."

"I've programmed our turn. I'll try to hold on long enough after we come out to make certain we're changing course, but the Quayla and I—we may not be—" He stopped.

"I know." She squeezed his hand again, then let go. "You need to strap in," she said briskly. He fumbled for his restraints, locking them into place one second before they passed through transition.

This jump came too close to the last one for Kiley. At first she clung to consciousness, but she lost her grip and blacked out, feeling the ship turn as she did. That wasn't what captured the last of her attention, though. The last thing she heard was the sound of Lukas's scream. It was the sound of all the damned in hell and it went on, and on, and on.

In the computer room, Hastings's program had ceased to exist. It had started erasing all trace of itself from the main, navigation, and engineering computers as soon as the ship entered transition. It left a single entry in the log: an incorrect set of jump coordinates. It was doubtful anyone would ever find the ship, but if it was found, it would seem that she had been lost through pilot error.

The investigators always assumed that if they could. Everyone knew that humans failed, but no one wanted to believe the same of machines—not when so much depended on them.

Keenan had planned to be back in his cabin by the time they jumped, but his concentration was holding longer than he expected now that Sensar was not pushing him so hard. They were still working when Kiley announced the two-minute mark. Keenan straightened, startled. "I have to go back to my room."

"Jump is difficult for you?" Sensar questioned.

"No, but those are ship's rules. Unless you're on duty, you're supposed to be in your cabin."

"You do not have time," Sensar pointed out. "Better to stay here."

He was right. They abandoned the lesson and Keenan waited for Kiley to announce the one-minute mark. She did not. He glanced at his watch. Surely that much time had passed? Surely—

Light exploded, followed by heat. Keenan cried out, but the sound was lost in Sensar's startled boom. Before he had time to wonder what had happened, his body dissolved. It re-formed a moment later. The heat was gone, and so was the bright light. They were alive, but something had obviously gone wrong. He started to rise, intent on reaching the bridge, but Kiley's warning of another transition stopped him.

A minor malfunction prior to jump? There was no such thing—Keenan had learned that much during his time on the bridge. The slightest problems resulted in major catastrophes. He leaped to his feet, but before he could move, Sensar wrapped a tentacle around his arm and dragged him back down.

"Keenan, where do you go?" the alien demanded. Thunder reverberated from the walls. Gan-Tir must talk louder when they're upset, Keenan thought disjointedly.

"To the bridge," he replied, trying to rise again. Sensar held him still.

"No time!" the Gan-Tir exclaimed.

"I have to! Let me go!"

Someone thundered behind Keenan. Rairea stood in the door to her room, tentacles waving wildly in the air. Henherik appeared at his, looking equally agitated.

Sensar said something to them, his voice a quick, deep vibration. Keenan did not understand his words, but they must have been a curt order. Rairea and Henherik turned around immediately and went back into their cabins.

Keenan tried to use the opportunity to pull free of the alien, but Sensar wouldn't release him. "Stay!" he boomed. "It is not safe to move around."

"Sensar, I have to report to the bridge!"

The Gan-Tir answered by lifting his other tentacle and placing it across Keenan's leg. He did not apply any pressure, but the threat was sufficient. "Stay."

"All right! I will. But you must take precautions, too. Go to your bunk. Lie down," Keenan urged.

"If I go, you will leave."

"No, I won't. You're right—there isn't time. Please, go to your cabin. Please!"

Sensar did not move. Keenan did not have much skill at reading Gan-Tir expressions, but he thought Sensar's was one of profound doubt. One thing was clear: Keenan was not going to make it to the bridge before transition.

Another wave of dissolution caught him. Coming out should have been easier than going in, but it wasn't. He felt as if he were being dragged along the bottom of a river, tumbled over and over, bruising himself against the stony bottom. The river filled his ears, screaming. The sound went on and on.

And then it stopped.

They were through. He had to get to the bridge. If he felt this bad, Kiley must be incapacitated. He was rising when the ship began to turn. It wasn't the slow, smooth maneuver he was accustomed to; instead, it was a sharp, hard pull that threw him from the stool to the floor. Sensar flew off his seat, to hit the floor with a resounding thud close to Keenan. The ship continued to turn, and they started to roll, body over body. Keenan thought he was about to be crushed, but at the last moment, Sensar wrapped arm and leg tentacles around him, pulled him close, and then held Keenan away from himself as they rolled over once, then again, and then hit the wall. Sensar roared and his tentacles went limp.

It took Keenan several seconds to realize he was free, and several more to notice that the ship had stopped turning. All but the emergency lights were off. He dragged himself away from Sensar, who was lying rigid, making short, sharp noises as if he was in distress. Keenan pushed himself to his hands and knees. Sensar's eyes were open, but unfocused. Keenan touched his shoulder tentatively, but Sensar did not move or give any sign that he noticed the pressure.

Had he injured himself? He had hit the wall very hard—had

he damaged his back? Keenan cautiously put his hand behind the alien and began a quick, manual examination. Gan-Tir spines were raised, bony structures. He felt his way down Sensar's back, fingers searching for damage, wondering all the while if he would recognize it. The alien did not pay any attention to him until the bony ridge diminished abruptly and Keenan touched soft flesh. Then Sensar bellowed.

Keenan threw himself back and sat down hard just as the doors to Rairea's and Henherik's cabins opened and they burst out. Rairea rushed over to Sensar, while Henherik grabbed Keenan with a vicious tentacle and flung him away from the injured Gan-Tir.

Rairea spoke anxiously to Sensar. He did not answer at first, but then he made a strangled sound. Slowly, very slowly, his body relaxed. Rairea helped him sit. He appeared to be disoriented and he moved stiffly.

"He landed against the wall," Keenan said. "I think he hurt his back." He spoke to Rairea, but his eyes were on Henherik, who hovered over him where he lay, tentacles whipping.

Rairea turned baleful violet eyes on Keenan. "You hurt him! Why you do this?"

"I didn't! We fell on the floor. He tried to protect me, but he hit his back when we rolled against the wall. I didn't touch him."

Rairea regarded Keenan for an uncomfortably long moment. But she must have decided she believed him, because she turned around again.

"I checked his back, but I couldn't detect any gross damage," Keenan offered. He sat up cautiously. Henherik shifted, but did not stop him.

"Landed against *sereth*," Rairea explained. "Caused much pain. Cannot move for a time."

Sereth? Was that the area of soft tissue? Whatever it was, it appeared to be a highly vulnerable spot.

"Daniel, I need you on the bridge!" Kiley exclaimed over the intercom. "Bring your medical kit."

He was on his feet and running out the door before Henherik could react, adrenaline boosting his speed to near

Gan-Tir levels. He hit the bridge at a full run, arriving one step behind Uhrich. They both stopped short just inside the hatch. Lukas was unconscious, held in place only by his seat restraints. Kiley was standing beside him, supporting his head.

No one was manning the boards.

Uhrich dashed for the pilot's seat.

"No!" Kiley shouted, throwing herself at him. They collided. Uhrich grunted, and she cried out. Uhrich tried to push her to one side. She caught his arm. "No!" she shouted desperately. "Don't touch the boards! Don't change anything!"

"Are you mad? The ship is out of control. If we don't—"

"Uhrich, look at the screens! *Look* at them!"

He glanced up—and stopped. The monitors were a roiling nightmare. Colors came and went; shadowy images formed, broke up, and dissolved. Were they still in jump? Keenan wondered blankly. They couldn't be—he had felt two distinct transitions. They must have come out.

"We're inside the barrier," Kiley said. She sagged, her burst of energy gone. "Something went wrong just before our jump to Sumpali—the monitors and sensors showed we were following our usual course, but the Quayla told Greg the ship had turned. He tried to alter our course, but none of the controls responded. We were past the point of commitment, but the Quayla drew as much of the engines' power as it could and radiated it off into space. We can't have gone very far inside the barrier."

"We turned," Uhrich said. He was watching Kiley closely, looking for signs of weakness. Looking for cracks in her swiftly assembled facade of calm.

"Greg knew our heading upon entry and he programmed a turn to execute as soon as we exited jump. If the computers followed his instructions, and if his calculations were correct, then we should be headed back to normal space."

"But we might not be." Uhrich glanced at the boards. "None of the ship's instrumentation is functioning. We could be going deeper, not coming out."

"We could," Kiley answered, "but if we are, there's no way to tell. Our safest course is to hold to the heading that Greg programmed. He could see, through the Quayla. He knew which way we were going. We have to believe that he made the correct turn." She spoke forcefully, as if it were herself she was trying to convince. "We have to!" She swayed and sat down hastily. "Sorry," she muttered, putting her hand to her head. "I think I must have a touch of transition sickness."

Keenan spared her a worried look, then turned back to Lukas. The pilot was unconscious. Keenan reached into his medical kit for the bioscanner and checked Lukas quickly. His body might be relaxed, but his mind was another matter—his brain waves went straight off the scale. And the Quayla—

Keenan glanced at the walls, then the floor. The Quayla had turned a sickly shade of reddish purple, and it flared bright orange as Keenan watched. Lukas jerked and went rigid.

He was having a convulsion.

Keenan didn't waste time wondering what was happening. He pulled out an injector, filled it with muscle relaxant, and administered it.

Lukas went limp, but less than five seconds later, he convulsed and his brain waves peaked again. Keenan turned the bioscanner on his chest. What he saw made his own heart thud in alarm: every one of the pilot's vital signs was elevated. His blood pressure was so high that Keenan turned the scanner on his own body to make certain the instrument wasn't malfunctioning. Lukas's circulatory system could not stand that much stress for long; he was in imminent danger of suffering a stroke, a heart attack, or both.

"Quayla," Kiley said, struggling to sit upright. Uhrich hesitated, then put an arm around her, offering support. "Something in here hurts it. Whatever is happening to it is happening to Greg, too."

The Quayla dulled to reddish black, but then flared again. Lukas had started to sag, but his muscles locked a third time. Keenan filled the injector with a second dose of relaxant and, after the briefest of hesitations, administered it.

Lukas went so still so fast that Keenan thought he had killed him. It was all he could do to pick up the bioscanner and point it at the pilot. He was still alive, but his vital signs had dropped precipitously—they were now alarmingly low. Keenan ran the scanner over Lukas's head and chest. He had not suffered a stroke or heart attack, but his brain waves were spiking higher than ever.

"Daniel, he is going to be all right, isn't he?" Kiley asked anxiously.

"I don't know," he said unhappily. "We need to get him to your cabin. Uhrich, will you help me?"

He unfastened Lukas's seat restraints, only to find himself supporting the pilot's weight alone. Uhrich hadn't moved; his eyes went from Lukas, to Kiley, to the boards. "We can't leave the bridge unmanned," he said. "And Kiley's in no shape to take command. I'll call Fong. He was going to check on the Miquiri and Gan-Tir. He'll—"

"Uhrich, help Daniel get Greg to our cabin," Kiley ordered. She pushed herself to her feet, swaying.

"I am not going to leave the—"

"You are going to do what I say, when I say—is that understood?" she demanded. Two spots of bright red stood out on her cheeks.

"Captain, you are ill and Lukas is incapacitated. In my book, that constitutes an emergency. In accordance with orders from Admiral Bergstrom, I am hereby requesting you to surrender command of your vessel. If you won't stand aside, I'll ask Fong to escort you to your cabin and hold you there until we reach Sumpali."

"*If* we reach Sumpali," Elena Cristavos said from the hatch. Keenan, Uhrich, and Kiley swung around, equally startled; none of them had heard her arrive. Cristavos came into the room, all her attention on Uhrich and Kiley. "Lieutenant Commander, you may have orders from Admiral Bergstrom, but they do not supersede mine. I am certain that your only concern is the safety of this ship and her passengers, but I do not believe that having you take command at this juncture is in the aliens' best interests—or anyone else's."

"Cristavos—" Uhrich began. She did not listen.

"I have every faith in Captain Michaelson," Cristavos went on. "She will remain the ship's commanding officer as long as she is able to function. As for Fong, I'm afraid he won't be of assistance to anyone for some time. He hit his head when we turned, and is semiconscious, at best." She turned to Keenan. "When you're through here, would you take a look at him? I believe he is suffering from a concussion."

"Cristavos, you're making a mistake!" Uhrich said heatedly. "When I came on the bridge, Captain Michaelson had abandoned her post and was holding on to Lukas, barely conscious herself. She is not well and she is emotionally upset. That's not her fault, but it doesn't change the facts. She is not fit to command."

"I am," Kiley said, but she spoke to Cristavos, not Uhrich. "I did not abandon my post; there was simply nothing I could do. Greg knew we'd lose our sensors and monitors once we were inside the barrier. He calculated our turn and entered the change of heading into the computer. He thought we would have sufficient velocity to drift free of the barrier. I don't know if we will or not, but I don't want *anyone* touching the controls of this ship. Any maneuvers we try to make under these circumstances are more likely to take us deeper into the barrier—or skimming along the edge of it—than back out again. Either scenario would be a disaster."

"What if we don't come out?" Uhrich demanded.

"We will."

"You don't know that!" Uhrich exploded. "You're operating on emotion, not reason. You're—"

"That's enough, Pete," Cristavos said. She spoke quietly, almost pleasantly, but the expression in her eyes stopped him cold. "I mean that. Captain Michaelson will remain in command. If you can't accept that, then you may return to your cabin. If you can, I suggest you start offering assistance instead of objections."

"Cristavos, I have my orders. I intend to obey them."

"So do I, and in case of dispute, mine take precedence." She turned to Kiley. "The authority to supersede Admiral Bergstrom's instructions—or those of his appointed representative—comes directly from the Corps' Board of Governors, Captain. In case of any dispute having to do with the aliens, short of a surprise attack, the Diplomatic Service has the final say. I'll be glad to show you a copy of the orders, if you wish to see them."

"That won't be necessary," Kiley replied. She believed the diplomat—they all did. The proof was in Uhrich's behavior. For all he was arguing, he was not disputing Cristavos's authority.

"Captain, do you require Mr. Uhrich's assistance?" Cristavos asked formally.

"I do not," Kiley said. "Not at this time."

"Very well. Uhrich, return to our quarters and stay with Fong until Dr. Keenan is able to examine him. You may go," she added mildly when he did not move.

Uhrich gave her a lethal look, then stalked off the bridge.

"He's a good man, Captain," Cristavos said softly after he had gone, "but Bergstrom placed him in an untenable position. Believe me, you could not find a more qualified, loyal, or dedicated officer—assuming you had won his respect and cooperation. I suggest you try; if appearances are anything to go by, you are going to need him."

The two women exchanged gazes. Some silent message passed between them.

"Captain, do you have anyone who can come to the bridge and relieve you?" Cristavos asked, still speaking softly. "With all due respect, you look like you're about to pass out."

"I can manage for now," Kiley said. "Daniel, will you call Reese and ask him to report here? He can help you with Greg, then sit the next watch if we need him. He and Lia are in their cabin. They were shaken up, but that's all—I told them to stay there until I had a full damage report.

"Cristavos, has anyone checked on the aliens?" she asked as Keenan refastened Lukas's seat restraints and then reached for the intercom.

"I did before I came up. Leetian injured her arm; I think it's broken. I said I would have Dr. Keenan take a look at her as soon as he was free." She turned to Keenan. "I know you aren't up on Miquiri anatomy, Doctor, but I told them you would do what you could."

"Of course. Just let me get Greg settled. Kiley, was anyone else hurt?"

"No. Everyone reported in just after the turbulence. Holly and Hope were with Jon Robert. Holly was strapped in, and Hope's carrier protected her. If you can, though, I'd like you to run scanner checks on everyone, just to be sure no one is playing hero."

"I will," he said. Beginning with you, he thought silently.

For the next two hours, he was too busy to say much out loud at all.

Chapter 23

Dreamtime.

For an eon, the last of the Ytavi had slept, cushioned by the immense cocoon it had woven around itself. Thought moved slowly, memory and imagination swirling around and around, forming kaleidoscopic pictures. Time did not exist for it, nor heat, nor cold. There was no light or dark. No physical awareness at all. There was only waiting.

And dreaming.

Dreamtime.

Something brushed the edge of its cocoon, sending ripples from side to side. A wind like that which swept the hot, dry, plateaus of home brushed past. The Ytavi stirred, but the ripples faded. It settled again, dreaming.

Another brush. Snow was falling through its mind then. Huge, heavy flakes that fell, and fell, and fell. They swirled, disturbed by a sudden gust of air. The wind eased to a breeze, then stopped completely. The flakes resumed their slow, steady fall.

All that had been and all that had not mingled side by side, indistinguishable. Sometimes the images were coherent, sometimes not. It examined them all, seeking patterns, seeking meaning. It found none. One by one, the images faded, then vanished. The last of the Ytavi slept on, dreaming.

Something poked the cocoon—hard. It felt like an invisible hand had plucked the branch upon which it hung, sending it bouncing. The Ytavi stirred. Blinked.

The bouncing slowed, then stopped.

The Ytavi turned over.

The cocoon shook again. And again.

Images of snow and desert heat wavered, then shattered. Time ran forward, then backward, then forward again.

The last of the Ytavi shifted, blinked, and opened its eyes.

Lukas had no words for the place in which he found himself. Words could not describe that which could not, should never exist.

Distorted images, shrieking howls, colors running in gruesome shades of chalky green and washed-out red. Images swirling, then breaking apart before they could be comprehended. Mind slashed by unseen knives. Voices rising to shrieks and fading into whimpers. Cold, clammy hands pressing against overheated skin. Electrical currents arcing over and through and around. Body struggling with mind, and mind with body, both seeking grips on the slippery fabric of the mountainside to which they clung. Both failing to find them.

Lukas and the Quayla fell. Down and down they tumbled, battered by unseen winds. They held hands to their ears and squeezed their eyes shut.

There was no escape.

They were Quayla and companion. They were one. Minds and body writhing, they clung to each other for life and sanity.

Their fingers found a ledge and caught hold.

The rock shifted and their feet swung out.

An abyss opened beneath them.

Hail lashed their body, tearing clothes and skin. Wind whipped, blowing ice and chilling flesh. The ledge started to crumble.

Rocks rolled down into the abyss below. They did not hear them hit bottom.

The wind rose. It whipped their clothes and body, then tore them off the face of the cliff and tossed them to a narrow ledge below. Stunned, they lay where they had fallen.

Night came. The air grew colder. Banshees gathered and started to wail. The ledge tilted.

They slid over the icy edge and landed in a net of barbed wire.

A gale blew the net, tossing them from side to side, impaling them on cruelly bent hooks.

The banshees drifted down. They took turns diving through the gaping holes the barbs gouged out.

Reese helped Keenan carry Lukas to his cabin. The pilot appeared to be unconscious, but while his muscles had relaxed, his brain activity continued to fluctuate wildly. Keenan considered further sedation briefly, then decided against it.

Lukas had refused drugs to help him sleep; he had said they would not have the same effect on him as on other humans. Keenan was inclined to believe that. It had taken a massive dose of Gavatine to stop his convulsions. Had he acquired a high tolerance for all drugs, or only that one in particular? Was his tolerance a smooth curve, or did drugs suddenly take hold at a certain level? Beyond that level, would he respond to a drug with the same tolerance? More? Less? If he administered other medications, would they interact with the Gavatine as expected, or would they have unforeseen consequences?

Keenan didn't know, and that stopped him cold. *First, do no harm.* That was what they had taught him in medical school. Subsequent experience had confirmed the wisdom of the admonition. Lukas's increased mental activity wasn't endangering his life. Keenan didn't understand it, and he didn't like it, but prudence told him not to intervene.

Not yet.

Not until he had no other choice.

"How is he?" Reese asked.

At the hospital, with a stranger, Keenan would have offered a familiar platitude: It's too soon to tell. But this was the *Widdon Galaxy*, and Reese was a friend. "I don't know. I don't know what's wrong with him and I don't know what to do about it. I just—don't know."

"Something's wrong with the Quayla, too, isn't it?"

"Yes." It didn't take keen observation to notice that. The alien being had followed Keenan and Reese from the bridge. The normally quick-flowing pool of light had oozed along slowly, extending a long tendril, then dragging the rest of itself forward. It had been a dark, reddish purple on the bridge, but since coming to Lukas's cabin, the purple had turned black, shot through with faint red lines. The red brightened periodically, emitting several bright pulses of light, then faded again. Lukas's brain waves peaked with the bright pulses and fell as the Quayla dimmed.

Keenan ran the scanner over the pilot again, then straightened, nodding to Lia, who had followed them. "I can't do anything more for him at the moment, and there are other people who need attention. Are you sure you're up to staying with him? I won't be long, but I don't want to leave him alone."

"I can manage," Lia said. She looked nearly as exhausted as Kiley, her face lined, her blond hair hanging limply from her head.

"I won't be long," Keenan reassured her. "All you have to do is run a scanner over him periodically—I'll set it to sound an alarm if any of his vital signs change. If you see the red light flash, then call me. Otherwise, just let him be."

Lia nodded. She took the scanner from Keenan's hands, examined it dully, then sat on the edge of the bed. "You two go on. I'll be all right."

Reese gave her a worried look, but accepted her statement. She had been through difficult transitions before; she would recover. They all would.

"I'm going to check on our passengers," Keenan said. "Reese, will you go back to the bridge and try to persuade Kiley to rest? If she argues, tell her that she said herself there was nothing anyone could do at the moment. She needs to lie down at once."

"I'll talk to her, but I doubt it will do any good. It rarely does."

They parted company at the main corridor. Reese went back to the darkened bridge; Keenan went down the hall to the elevator. Fong first, he thought, then the Miquiri and the Gan-Tir.

Cristavos's diagnosis of the security officer's head injury proved accurate; Fong was conscious, but nauseated and slightly disoriented. There was no fracture, so Keenan gave him an injection to ease his discomfort and ordered him to stay in bed. He went on to the Miquiri.

Human bioscanners did not work well on aliens: they recorded data, but had no standards by which to evaluate the readings. Keenan went over Pitar and Chirith first to gather data on relatively undamaged individuals, then turned to Leetian. Her pulse, respiration and blood pressure were higher than the males', but the variation was not significant unless her readings were normally much lower. Pitar said that should not be the case, so Keenan judged her in an acceptable state of health, aside from the broken arm. The scanner revealed a simple fracture halfway up her forearm, with no jagged bones and no severed blood vessels or tissue. Keenan pulled an immobilization tube out of the medical kit, slipped it over her arm, and inflated it slowly.

I would give you drugs if you were human, he said, at a loss for the signs that said what he really meant: *"administer regeneration accelerators and prescribe a mild analgesic." But I don't have any that were made for you. I'm sorry.*

Leetian made several high, ear-piercing noises. *She understands*, Pitar signed for her. With her arm incapacitated, her ability to communicate was severely limited. *She is grateful that you have done this much.*

Nodding, Keenan began repacking the medical kit. Chirith put one hand on his arm to stop him. *Keenan, what has happened? Where are we? What is wrong with the Quayla?*

Kiley had made a brief announcement over the intercom, telling their passengers the ship was in no immediate danger and promising a complete report as soon as she and her crew had finished making a damage assessment. She would not be able to postpone speaking for long, however; the Miquiri had only to look at the light on the walls of their compartment to realize something was seriously wrong. The Quayla had turned a muddy orange-red color that would have been deeply unpleasant to view, had it not at the same time faded to the point of indistinguishability.

I can't say, Keenan answered awkwardly. *Kiley will talk to you shortly. She will explain.*

He turned, but Chirith caught his arm and stopped him with a strength and determination that were surprising in a Miquiri. The aliens touched each other often, but they did not touch humans, and they rarely made such a show of will. Keenan glanced at Pitar. He was watching Chirith closely, as if he found the Miquiri's behavior as disturbing as Keenan did, but he did not intervene. He wanted answers, too.

Chirith, Kiley will come soon, Keenan repeated. *She will explain. I must go. Others were injured. I must check on them.*

"Keenan, where is Lukas?" Chirith asked in the first language. Pitar translated the whistles into signs. "Something is wrong with the Quayla. Has he been injured? Is he . . . dead?"

"No! He is not well, but he is alive." Keenan pulled free of the Miquiri's grip. "I must go," he said, and lifted his medical bag. Chirith did not attempt to stop him again.

He went to the Gan-Tir's quarters. The Miquiri did not follow him; he had not expected them to. So far as he knew, the two groups of diplomats had not spoken directly to each other since coming on the ship. The Gan-Tir's common room was empty, but Henherik must have heard him or had some device that warned of intruders, because his door opened immediately. He came out warily, his tentacles moving in uneasy loops and circles.

"I came to see how you are," Keenan said aloud. He put down his bag and made the equivalent Miquiri gestures. *Captain Michaelson asked me to check on each of you to be certain you were not injured.* That was not exactly true, but he was certain she would have if she hadn't been preoccupied with other matters.

I am not injured, Henherik signaled.

"What about Rairea and Sensar? I would like to see them, too. Are they in their cabins?"

Henherik stared at him, then went to Rairea's door and boomed out sounds that could have been a question or a statement. She rumbled a reply. Henherik gestured to Keenan: *Go in.*

Keenan entered her cabin cautiously. If he had thought about her room at all, he had assumed it would be much like

Sensar's. It was not. Several brightly colored piles of cushions filled up the corners of the room; a gigantic bed took up half the remaining area. The rest of the floor space was filled with backless stools and smaller, enclosed objects that might have been tables or storage units of some sort. Brightly patterned strips of thin cloth covered the walls, and other strips hung from the ceiling to the floor, partitioning the bed from the rest of the room. A strong, heady scent filled the cabin, more pungent than spicy or flowery. Keenan had not noticed the smell on Rairea or Sensar when he had been close to them before, so he didn't think it emanated from her. It had to be some sort of perfume or incense. If so, Gan-Tir notions of pleasant odors differed greatly from those of humans.

Rairea was on the bed, facing the door. She watched as Keenan pushed aside several hanging cloths and came toward her, but she did not sit up. Henherik might be well, but she apparently was not.

May I examine you? Keenan signaled.

She made a sign. Keenan didn't recognize it, but it was not a clear refusal, so he went over to her and turned on his scanner. He identified her heart, lungs, stomach, intestines, and bladder without difficulty, but the functions of several other internal structures remained a mystery. He had to reach over her awkwardly to scan her back because she would not turn over to accommodate him. He paid particular attention to her spine, gathering as many readings from the area just above her waist as he could.

Her backbone flattened there, and then dove deep into her body. A layer of cartilage-like tissue rose over the bone, forming a sort of cavern, and the neural readings from that area were much higher than those along the rest of her spine. They were, in fact, nearly as high as those within her brain. Was it some sort of signal-processing center, or a second brain site that had never developed or had been abandoned by evolution? Keenan itched to run a deeper scan, but didn't have the equipment or the time. Henherik had started shifting uneasily from foot to foot, and one of Rairea's tentacles had drifted perilously close to his legs. He moved away from her back and began scanning her abdomen.

What he saw there stopped him again.

A mass of tissue was growing deep inside her body, in an organ Henherik had not had. The organ was hollow at the center, and the mass was attached to the top. It could have been a tumor, but the scanner was tentatively identifying it as an embryo.

Rairea was pregnant?

Keenan stared at the image on his scanner, stunned. No wonder the Gan-Tir had decided to turn around. His only question was why Rairea had come on the journey in the first place. Chirith had told Lukas that the Gan-Tir had nearly stopped bearing children; Keenan could not believe they would risk a single one. Unless, that is, they hadn't known there was anything to risk.

Was that possible? The mass was quite small. If size was anything to go by, then it had formed quite recently. Had Rairea left Sumpali before realizing her condition? Had she become pregnant since then? If so, who was the father? Henherik? Sensar? Both? Neither?

Rairea's tentacle brushed Keenan's leg. The contact might have been inadvertent, but he took it as a warning. He finished his scan quickly and stepped back. *I do not see any damage,* he signaled. *Do you feel pain?*

She formed a single Miquiri word with the stubby fingers at the end of her arm. *No.*

Keenan nodded. *Have Cristavos call me if you do,* he signaled. She made another of those enigmatic gestures he could not interpret. He straightened. *I would like to see Sensar.* Henherik stood aside, one tentacle waving at the door. Keenan had to pass him to leave. He gave the alien a wide berth.

Henherik watched as Keenan went to Sensar's room, knocked, then pressed the wall plate to open the door. He was still watching as the door closed behind Keenan.

Sensar lay on his bed, too, stomach down. He lifted his head, but did not attempt to sit up as Keenan crossed the room.

Keenan put his medical bag down on the floor and pulled out his scanner.

"I've come to check on you," he said, speaking his own language. "I would like to examine your back for damage. Will you let me?"

Sensar glared at him, then let his head fall back against the pillow on his bed. Like Rairea, he said neither yes nor no. Did the Gan-Tir have some indefinite form of decision? *I will not give you permission. I will not guarantee the consequences of your actions; but if you wish to act, I will not stop you. At least, not at the moment.*

Keenan hesitated, then turned the bioscanner on and ran it over the Gan-Tir's body. Sensar ignored him. There were no obvious signs of injury, even to the soft area just above his waist. Sensar's vital signs deviated slightly from Rairea's, but the percentage of change was within the range of normal human variation.

"Are you still experiencing pain in your back?" Keenan asked as he studied the scanner readings.

"Pain passes."

Did he mean it had, or it would? Keenan felt exasperated. Sensar understood the language well enough to make his meaning clear if he chose to—which meant he did not. Keenan put the scanner away, gave Sensar a wary look, then placed his fingers over the area of soft tissue.

Sensar bellowed. Before Keenan knew what was happening, the alien had leaped up and lashed his tentacles tight around Keenan's body.

"Do not touch there! Do not ever touch there! It is forbidden!"

"All right," Keenan said equitably. "I won't." He had to struggle for air to get those words out, but he was pleased with his calm reply. "Will you let me go, please?" he asked. "I will not touch you there again."

Sensar held on to Keenan just long enough to make a point of his superior position, then released him abruptly. "You go now."

"Yes." Keenan turned the command into a decision of his own. "There are others I must see."

He gathered up his bag and left the room, thinking that he was making progress: that was one round with the Gan-Tir that he had not lost completely.

Sensar stayed where he was after Keenan left. He, too, thought the human had made progress, but not for the same reasons. For the first time, Keenan had not quivered with fear when Sensar touched him. Sensar lay down on his stomach and closed his eyes. He had doubted his plan, but now he began to believe it might work—assuming they reached Sumpali, that is.

The humans had guaranteed the Gan-Tir's safety, but events had proved that promise hollow. They had been forced to abandon the talks because of the riot at Resurrection, and now the vessel that carried them had malfunctioned. The problem was serious. It had to be—the lights were still off and air was not circulating. Sensar wanted to storm the engine room and take charge of the repairs himself, but he could not. He had no technical skills. Neither did Rairea or Henherik. The humans had gotten them into danger; the humans would have to get them out.

Sensar's tentacles rippled. He hoped they succeeded. He could not bear the thought that his people's future was in danger of being destroyed a second time by alien hands.

Such irony simply could not be possible in an ordered, rational universe.

Kiley left Reese in charge of the bridge and went to the engine room to hear Jon Robert's damage report.

"As far as I can tell, there's no damage to the main engines," her brother said. "They shut down because the computers were receiving faulty signals. All the ship's data transmissions are being affected, not just the bridge monitors. The sensors are still collecting data, but it's completely garbled by the time it reaches the computers. I took environmental readings in several rooms down the corridor with a handheld scanner—they didn't match the data on the boards."

"Could the scanners be at fault?" Kiley asked. As she spoke, her eyes were on Holly. Normally her sister-in-law was as calm as Jon Robert, but now her hands were clumsy as she lifted Hope out of her carrier.

"I don't think so," Jon Robert answered. "They're frequently used in areas of high electrical, magnetic, and radioactive activity, so they're heavily shielded. Many of the ship's sensors are, too, but they have to relay their data to the computers, and that's where the problem seems to lie: the farther the signals have to travel, the more likely they are to be scrambled. If the Quayla were unaffected, it might be able to give us reliable information because it gathers the readings on site. I guess it's not, though?"

"No." Kiley had told him that Greg was unconscious, and he had only to look at the unhealthy glow on the walls of the engine room to see that the Quayla was in equally poor condition.

"I've left the settings on all the systems where they were before we came to a stop," he said. "We'll be fine for a while, but it isn't going to be easy to regulate the ship's temperature and air supply, particularly in the holds. I'm not so worried about temperature—our bodies will tell us if we're too hot or cold—but the air is another matter. We might not notice a carbon dioxide buildup before our ability to reason is seriously impaired. We may have to make walking tours of the ship to check conditions in each room manually. If so, I'll need help."

"You'll have it," Kiley said. "Lia and Reese are both available. So is Cristavos. Fong, too, unless Daniel says he needs to rest."

"What about Uhrich?"

"I think I'm going to need him on the bridge." Kiley exchanged looks with her brother. "Greg is unconscious and Daniel has to stay close to him. I can't man the bridge alone. Uhrich is the logical choice, but only if he'll agree to accept my orders."

"Do you think he will?"

"I don't know, but I'm going to find out. I'm on my way to talk to him now."

"Kiley, we can survive for several days on emergency power, but that's the limit. If we don't drift free of the barrier by then, we'll have to try to restart the main engines. But if we do—"

"If we do, and the signals aren't transmitting correctly, then we could be ordering forward or reverse power without knowing it? And even if we weren't, unless both engines are responding equally, we could be turning the ship off course, right?"

"That's the gist of the problem, yes. We have no reference points here, Kiley. All we have is Greg's assertion that the Quayla knew the heading that would take us back, and the hope that the computers executed the correct turn after we came out of jump. But we can't last more than forty-eight hours on emergency power, either. If we haven't drifted out of the barrier by then, we'll have to start the main engines. If we don't, we'll die."

"And if we do, we may kill ourselves, only in a different way." Kiley rubbed her eyes with her thumb and forefinger. "I don't want to add to our problems, Jon Robert. I don't want to turn the engines on until we're certain we aren't going to drift free in time. I'll let you start them then. We can try a jump along our current heading and hope we come out on the other side of the barrier. But until that time, I want to keep the risks to a minimum."

"I can live with that," her brother said.

It had not occurred to her until then that he might not, and now she gave him an uneasy look. She had asked a great deal of Jon Robert in the past. He had always given her his complete cooperation, but that did not mean he always would. Kiley glanced at Hope. The baby was sleeping, oblivious to the danger around her. Holly would give her life to protect Hope. So would Jon Robert. If he thought her orders conflicted with Hope's safety, would he disregard them?

"I'm going to talk to Uhrich," she said abruptly. "Set up regular patrols with the scanners. If conditions in any of the compartments begin to deteriorate significantly, let me know immediately."

"I will," Jon Robert said.

She started to leave, but he caught her arm. "Kiley, you do trust me, don't you? I'm not Uhrich. You don't have to guess about me. If I don't agree with you, I'll say so. I will not act unilaterally. Understood?"

"Yes," she said, but she wasn't comforted. Jon Robert might mean that now, but circumstances changed. People changed. Sometimes they found themselves doing things they swore they never would.

Things like asking Pete Uhrich for help.

She gave the lieutenant commander the facts, then asked for his assistance. "I need an extra hand on the bridge, Uhrich, not to start the engines or change our course, but to go through the computers. Someone sabotaged us. I don't know who, but the *when* had to be during our refitting—no one's had access to the computers since then. If we're lucky, the sabotage was a onetime event. Whoever committed it wanted us to come out of jump into the barrier without realizing what was happening. He, she, or they didn't know the Quayla would be monitoring the sensors and would be capable of shortening our jump. Thanks to it, we may survive. If so, someone is going to be very surprised and upset—I promise that."

"But first, we have to get out of here," Uhrich finished, his expression unreadable.

"Yes."

"And you want my help?"

"Yes."

"On your terms, acting under your orders?"

"That's right."

"What makes you believe I'll agree to those conditions?"

"You're a Corps officer. That means something to you. Honor means something to you. I think if you give me your word that you'll cooperate, you will keep it—to the very best of your ability."

"And beyond that?"

"Beyond that, I trust. I trust that you care more about our lives than your own status. You wouldn't be the *North Star*'s first officer if you couldn't be trusted. You wouldn't be first officer if you weren't qualified to take command—assuming the ship's rightful captain was incapacitated. I don't always like or agree with Admiral Bergstrom, but I respect him and I respect you. More importantly, I need you. Will you cooperate with me, Uhrich? Will you do what I ask, when I ask?"

Uhrich stared at her for a long time, his expression enigmatic. Kiley had no idea what his answer would be until the moment he spoke.

"I will—Captain."

Cristavos was right. He was a good man to have on her side.

Chapter 24

Lukas's condition had not changed.

Keenan had run a full series of diagnostic tests, but they told him little more than the scanner had. The Quayla must still be exerting some control over the pilot's body: though depressed, Lukas's physical functions had stabilized and were holding improbably steady. His respiration, pulse, blood pressure, and temperature had not varied for several hours.

His mental activity was another matter. His brain waves continued to rise and fall sharply. The interference that disrupted the ship's equipment seemed to be constant, but the peaks and valleys in Lukas's mental activity suggested that whatever was assailing him and the Quayla came in waves.

The pool of light beside Lukas's bed was still well defined, but the Quayla's color had faded. When Lukas's brain waves peaked, it brightened, but then it dimmed quickly; Lukas's mental activity plummeted just as fast. It was as if they resisted what they fought only as long as they absolutely had to, then let go completely. They might have been conserving energy, but Keenan thought they might also be wearing out—both of them.

When Kiley came in, he was wondering how long it would be before Lukas, the Quayla, or both failed. She went straight to Lukas, took his hand in hers, and said his name. He did not respond.

"How is he?" she asked, not looking at Keenan.

"For the moment, he's stable, but that's about the best I can say."

"He's unconscious?"

"Not exactly. He is not responding to physical stimuli, but his mind is quite active. It's possible that he—or more likely, the Quayla—is blocking all physical sensation so he can concentrate on something he's experiencing only in his mind."

"The barrier?" Kiley turned around. "He's fighting something, isn't he? I know he is. I can feel . . ."

"Feel what?" Keenan asked sharply when she broke off.

She shook her head. "I don't know. For a minute, I felt like I was with them, but now it's gone."

"Kiley, has Greg ever suggested that you might be receptive to the Quayla?"

"Me? No, not at all. He said you might be, but I'm missing whatever mental quirk or degree of empathy is required. I wish I weren't," she added unhappily. "Daniel, is there anything we can do for him?"

"Other than get out of here? I don't think so. I'm not even certain that will help. The Quayla on Chirith's ship was disoriented for some time after they drifted free of the barrier. Even if we do find our way out, they may not."

They both stared at the pool of light on the floor as it brightened, emitted several sharp pulses of light, then dimmed again.

"I talked to the Gan-Tir and Miquiri," Kiley said, averting her eyes from the Quayla. "The Gan-Tir were either indifferent, indisposed, or completely unconcerned—I couldn't tell which. I expected them to give me a difficult time, but they only asked one question: how long would it be before we returned to normal space."

"What did you tell them?"

"One or two days. That's all the time we have, Daniel. Once the emergency power fails, we'll have to start the engines and make a run for what we hope is safety. If we're wrong, or if we hit anything on the way because we can't see what's lying ahead . . ." She trailed off, and he did not make her go on. He knew what would happen then as well as she did.

"The Miquiri asked a number of questions," Kiley went on. "I told them what I could. I asked Chirith about his experience while the *Nieti* was inside the barrier, but he couldn't add much to what we already knew. The Quayla controlled all their systems; when it failed, they had no computers, no communications, nothing. They were completely helpless. We have a slight advantage in that some of our systems still function, but I'm not certain it will be enough to save us."

"Kiley—"

"Chirith may come up here," she continued dully. "He is worried about Greg. I said he could visit for a few minutes if he wanted to. I don't think he should stay any longer, though." She frowned. "He was very upset, Daniel. I didn't realize Greg meant so much to him. Of course, he could be focusing all his anxiety over the situation on Greg. I don't know. I just don't—" She broke off, swaying.

"Kiley, who's on the bridge?" Keenan asked, hoping someone was, because if appearances were any indicator, she wasn't going back soon.

"Uhrich. He's checking out the computer programs."

"You asked him to do that?" he asked, startled.

"Yes."

"And he agreed?"

"Yes."

"That must have been some conversation."

"Not really. He's Corps, Daniel—just like you and Greg. They may train you to give orders at the Academy, but they train you to take them, too. All I had to do was convince him that I have the necessary skills and authority to issue commands."

"And you did?"

"For the moment."

"But not necessarily forever?"

"No." She sighed again. "He's willing to give me the benefit of the doubt right now, but if we don't find our way back into normal space within a few days, or if the situation onboard deteriorates, I think he'll make another bid to take over command."

"If that happens, the rest of us will back you. Cristavos might, too—she has so far. It takes more than two people to run the ship, and Uhrich can't count on anyone else but Fong."

"*We* know that; let's just hope he does, too."

Kiley rubbed her forehead. She may have convinced the others she was competent, but Keenan wasn't so easily deceived. Her skin was pasty and her eyes were glazed. Every muscle in her body had to be dragging with exhaustion. He reached for his bioscanner, but she stopped him before he could pull it out.

"You'd better wait a minute for that," she said.

"Why?"

"Because I think I'm going to pass out."

He almost missed catching her. She was not heavy, but she was tall and he had to drape her over his shoulder to carry her to the empty cabin across the hall. He lowered her to the bed and went back for his bioscanner. She was in better condition than he had feared, but too many transitions, too close together, had taken their toll.

The last time that had happened, he had not had drugs to treat her. Cellular-growth stimulators were classified as dangerous drugs and Jon Robert had not been able to purchase them even with his medic's license. Keenan could, however, and his first action upon coming on board had been to lay in a supply. Now he went to his cabin and found the bottles he wanted. He gave Kiley injections from two. Assuming she responded normally, she would be back on her feet within twelve hours—but there would be a price. The chemicals did not differentiate between normal and abnormal cells, and she would have to be monitored carefully for several months to be certain no tumors developed.

He would have preferred the more conservative treatment of sedation and rest, but this was what she wanted. He knew it was, because she had given him standing orders against precisely this eventuality. Even if she hadn't, he would have given her the injections. There might be times they could do without her, but in his judgment this was not one of them.

Chirith came to Lukas's cabin shortly after Keenan returned, Cristavos at his side. The Miquiri hesitated at the door, looking around, then went straight to Lukas. He touched him on the arm, pressing lightly, but Lukas did not move.

How long has he been like this? Chirith signed, turning to Keenan.

Keenan set his bioscanner on the bunk. *Since we left jump,* he signed.

He does not respond to touch or speech?

No.

Chirith looked at the Quayla, then the cabin walls. *If we are here long, they will die,* he said simply.

He did not expect a reply, and Keenan did not give one. *Chirith, is there anything we can do to help them? Anything at all?*

Do you have—here Chirith used a word Keenan did not recognize. He turned to Cristavos for assistance.

"Stimulants," she translated. "Drugs to increase his heartbeat and blood pressure."

Yes, we have those, he said to Chirith.

Good. You can use them if Lukas begins to fail. We sometimes resort to them during a difficult joining. They can make a difference.

Is there anything else you can suggest?

They struggle with their minds, Keenan, not with their bodies. Physical aids may help them temporarily, but cannot save them.

What about mental ones?

Chirith made a wavery gesture with his hand, as if he did not understand what Keenan was saying. No wonder—Keenan had never learned the signs for the question he wanted to ask. He wasn't sure they existed. He appealed to Cristavos. "Ask him if another person could offer them mental assistance. Could a third party provide additional energy to help them fight whatever they're struggling against?"

Cristavos gave him a puzzled look, but translated his question.

Chirith's hands went still, as if that idea had not occurred to him. *Perhaps,* he said slowly, *for a time. But that would require one who was* eitsi.

Cristavos asked for an explanation of the word before Keenan could request one. The gray Miquiri was still for a moment, as if seeking a way to convey the meaning; then his hands began moving. *Able. Capable. One must have the ability to share, but that alone is not sufficient. One must also be capable of merging without interrupting their concentration.*

If a person could do that, could he help them? Keenan persisted.

Chirith raised his hands and let them fall in the Miquiri equivalent of a shrug. *I do not know. I reason that this may be so, but I cannot say that it is true. In any case, it is irrelevant. Neither I nor the other Miquiri can communicate with the Quayla. Even if we could, we have not established previous contact with it and Lukas. The intrusion of an unknown mind would come as a severe shock. It would likely do more harm than good.*

Keenan caught some of that, and Cristavos relayed the rest. *What if they knew the person, both of them?* Keenan asked. *Would their concentration be disrupted then?*

Chirith gave Keenan a long look. *Why do you ask these questions?* he demanded.

This time, it was Keenan who hesitated. He looked from Chirith to Cristavos, then back. *Greg thinks I am receptive*, he said cautiously. *I think I have sensed . . . something from the Quayla at least twice. Greg showed me how to call out to it if I needed help. If I could do that, then maybe I could do more. They know me, both of them. It should not be a great shock, sensing me. If it would help, I could try to reach them.*

No! You must not! Chirith gestured so rapidly that Keenan had no hope of keeping up. Cristavos supplied the words. "If you had an established relationship, he might urge you to try," she said quickly, "but you admit that you have not. First contacts are highly unstable, even under controlled conditions. They are frequently upsetting to all the parties involved. You would not help them and you would likely shatter their concentration. You would be placing them—and yourself—in grave danger."

They are already in danger.

Then you would increase it, Chirith signaled after Cristavos had translated. *Keenan, you must not attempt to do this. You must not!*

It was the answer that he had hoped to hear, and it came as a relief. He did not want to risk his own mind and sanity, but he had felt compelled to make the suggestion. He nodded, letting the matter drop.

Chirith left after a few more minutes. Cristavos gave Keenan a funny look on the way out. It wasn't suspicious, exactly—more like she had looked at him expecting to see one person but found another instead, one that she wasn't entirely certain about. His head came up sharply and he met her eyes squarely, defying her to treat him like the freak so many humans believed Lukas was.

She paused at the door, started to say something, and stopped. When she spoke again, he did not think her words were the ones she had originally intended. "Daniel, if you or Kiley need help, will you call me? I'll gladly do anything I can."

"Yes, of course," he said politely, if only for Kiley's sake. She needed Cristavos on her side. "Thank you."

The door closed. Keenan went back to Lukas, but his mind lingered on the diplomat, wondering what she had started to say.

Something in her parting expression told him that it might not have been what he was expecting to hear.

Keenan told Kiley that every hour the pilot held on was an hour in his favor. Secretly, he believed each hour brought him that much closer to death.

Lukas and the Quayla clung to life, but their hold was increasingly tenuous; it was only a matter of time before one of them let go. Keenan had an array of stimulants waiting, but he did not believe that drugs alone would save them while the ship remained inside the barrier. He prayed that they would drift free. Now. Let it happen now.

It did not. Hour after hour, the screens on the bridge flickered and rolled. Temperatures were beginning to fall in the cabins, and the air was growing stale. The threat was not life-endangering yet, but it would be in another day.

Uhrich worked on the computers all night, examining line after line of code, but found no evidence of sabotage. Neither could Kiley after she joined him, though she readily admitted that she wouldn't know a faulty line from a good one. They worked together until midday, when Kiley called off the examination and told Uhrich to go to his cabin to get some sleep. Either the computers were going to work or they weren't. If they weren't, there wasn't anything either of them could do—they didn't know enough and there wasn't time to learn.

Kiley made a round of the ship in late afternoon. She spoke to her family, Cristavos, and then the aliens, offering them equal measures of reassurance and encouragement. By the time she stopped in to see Lukas, she was swaying with fatigue again.

"You need to rest," Keenan scolded. "The drugs help, but they aren't a cure."

"I know. I promise I will, but you need a break and I'd like some time alone with Greg."

"I don't—"

"Daniel, please? You haven't eaten, have you? Fix dinner. Take a shower. I don't care what—just leave us alone for a while. I'll call you if anything happens."

He gave her twenty minutes. When he returned, she was sound asleep, half sitting, half lying beside Lukas, his hand in hers. She woke up long enough for Keenan to walk her across the hall to the spare cabin and put her to bed, but she was out again before he turned off the lights.

The first half of the night was uneventful, and Keenan dozed periodically. But sometime after 0200, Lukas's vital signs started to fluctuate. Keenan did not sleep again after that.

In the Miquiri quarters, Chirith and Leetian sat together in the common room. They could not sleep. Leetian's arm ached too much; so did Chirith's heart.

"You are frightened," she said, using an awkward combination of the first, second, and third languages to overcome the handicap posed by her broken arm.

"Yes," he admitted. He had not said so to Pitar, not wanting to add to the already heavy burden the delegation leader carried. But Leetian was different. She was . . . *anieri*. Sympathetic and nonjudgmental, she listened to not only his words, but his heart.

He had come to like her in the past weeks. So had Pitar; Chirith suspected that she and Pitar were close to becoming *akias*. They had both encouraged him to participate in their growing closeness, but he held back. He liked them, and he even felt a degree of *tariss*, drawing, but it was not strong enough to bind him to them. The other two might well come together, but he would remain apart.

Sometimes it seemed that he had always been apart, that Hinfalla had never lived, never been his *akia*. Sometimes it seemed that he lived only as a spirit, that he should have died when Hinfalla did. He would have welcomed death, but it did not come; he had no choice but to live, however badly.

Pitar knew he was not well. So did Leetian. Inside, she cried for him.

"You are reminded of your ship and your loss," Leetian said. She sat beside him on a low couch, her leg against his, her body turned slightly so she could see and touch him.

"Yes."

"You did not die. We will not, either. We could not have traveled far inside the barrier; the jump was very short."

"No, but we cannot see where we go, Leetian. If Lukas was even a few degrees off in his calculations, if he failed to make the required turn—or if the ship did not respond as he expected—then we could be lost forever."

"It is not easy to trust the skills of another captain, is it?"

"No."

"But you do, don't you?"

That question was pure anxiety, a bid for reassurance. He touched her arm, pressing gently. "As much as I would trust myself."

"Then I will not worry," Leetian replied. She let go of fear with a sigh and leaned against him. Then she took his hand in hers and stroked it gently. "You would have been a most treasured *akia*, Chirith. I am sorry you could not find yourself with us."

"So am I, Leetian," he said, and he was. He liked her. But like alone was not enough—like was not *tariss*.

"Chirith, if we find our way to safety, if Lukas and the Quayla survive, will they be . . . all right?"

He closed his eyes. "I do not know," he said. "The Quayla on the *Nieti* was not. It functioned afterward, but we feared for its sanity. It was better after it joined with Lukas, but it was not the same. It was never the same."

"And you worry that will happen again?"

"The Quayla has already been through the barrier once," he said, not looking at her. "That might be an advantage for it. It knew what to expect. It might have been able to take precautions."

"But it might also have been weakened," she continued, picking up his thoughts with an *akia*'s ease. She came so close to fitting, so very close. "Having fought its way free from madness once, it might not have the strength to recover a second time. That is what concerns you, isn't it?"

"We could speak to it before," he said, answering indirectly. "Even though we did not have a person who could reach its mind, we could speak to it through the computers. The humans cannot—Lukas is their only link to it. If he dies, it will have no anchor to reality. There is no telling what it might do then, or what it might become."

"There is no one else in whom it could find refuge? No one who is even moderately receptive?"

"I don't know. Keenan says Lukas told him he might be receptive, but I do not believe he could become a companion. He has too much . . ."

"Too much what, Chirith?" Leetian prompted when he fell silent.

Chirith struggled to find the word. "Self. He is too full of his own thoughts and desires. A companion must be willing to give up much in order to receive much. Keenan is not. The

Quayla might be able to mold him into a suitable vessel, but it would destroy much of what he is. No union born of such destruction could succeed for long."

"Then we must hope that Lukas survives—for the Quayla's sake, if not his own."

"Yes."

"You are fond of him, aren't you, Chirith?" Leetian asked, taking his hand again. He resisted, but she did not let go.

"Yes," he admitted miserably.

"Because he knows you as Hinfalla did?"

"In part."

"And the other part?"

"He cares for me. He feels . . . *tariss*."

"And do you feel *tariss* toward him?"

He did not reply, and that was an answer of its own. Leetian wrapped her hand around his awkwardly and closed his fingers so they lay against his palm. "You do," she said. She was silent for a time. "This is not normal, Chirith."

He could not look at her. "No, this is not normal."

"But not necessarily wrong," she added. He looked up, startled. "Chirith, it is true that you might be responding only to the part of Hinfalla that you see in him. That might well be. But it is also possible you are truly drawn. Such an affinity is difficult to comprehend, but that does not mean it is impossible—or that it is wrong. Pitar was right in believing that you need to put your sadness and pain behind you, but he was wrong to believe you could only do so with your own kind. Find solace where you can, Chirith. If that is with a human, then so be it. Pitar is not the final arbiter of your feelings. You are. Only you can decide what is right for you."

"You would have me call a human *akia*?" Chirith asked, surprised that she would accept the idea.

Leetian barked with laughter. "Why not?" she asked. "There is no law of nature which says that is impossible. Unlikely, yes. Different, yes. But not impossible. *Akias* are not mates; we do not choose them by chemistry alone. An *akia* is one who shares your beliefs and feelings, one who cares what happens to you. Lukas acquired many Miquiri memories when he joined with the Quayla; perhaps he is more like us than he appears. The drawing is not one-sided—not if the duration and frequency of his visits on Sumpali are any indication."

"Leetian, does Pitar know you are saying this?"

"It was he who told me how often you and Lukas spoke with each other. He has many doubts about this relationship, but even he cannot deny that an attraction exists between you and the human. You must listen to your heart, Chirith. You must do what you believe is right. Trust yourself and what you feel. It is the only way you will be whole again."

"Even if what I feel leads me to an alien *akia*?"

"Even then."

"I am not sure such a thing is possible, Leetian," he said slowly. "For me or for him."

"Then find out. You have explored unknown regions of space all your life; why not an unknown region of the heart, for a change? Who knows what treasure you might find?"

Or what hardship and pain, Chirith thought. Even if he and the rest of the ship's crew and passengers survived, there was no guarantee that Lukas would—or if he did, that he would be sane. With so many ifs, Chirith doubted he would ever find out whether a Miquiri could call a human *akia*—no matter how much he might want to.

Chapter 25

There were living beings on the periphery of its awareness. The Ytavi moved toward them, drawn by their vitality. It detected only two at first, but as it neared, it realized there were more. It had not seen other beings since the dance of coming together, and it felt a strange ripple of emotion as it watched the small, bright flames. It had been like them once. It carried memories from that time, but they had worn smooth, like pebbles tumbled over and over in heavy surf. Memories had been all the Ytavi had while it slept—memories and dreamtime. Past, present, and future; all had flowed together, one at last.

Until the small, bright beings had come along and interrupted its sleep. They represented more than flickers of energy; they brought time with them, too. They brought *then*, *now*, and *to be*. Events sequenced. That which had slept, woke. That which had been still, moved. Interest stirred.

The Ytavi examined the lights. It recognized the forms of two, but the third was unknown. It touched one of the familiar ones, remembering for a moment, then approached the other with a great deal more reluctance and did not touch long. As it turned to the third, a dim flicker to one side caught its attention. It did not recognize the form at first, so greatly had it changed. "Ylani?" it questioned, amazed. "Companion?"

The light did not answer. It could not. It was lost in a struggle for survival, a struggle that it was rapidly losing. It was trapped within the Ytavi's cocoon, battered by protective impulses designed to repulse invaders. Where had it come from? How could it have missed the summons to dance? Why had it come now? The Ytavi did not have answers, but one thing was certain: the light could not survive much longer. It was already so dim that it could barely be seen.

Distressed, the Ytavi moved closer. The light flickered and then started to fade. Without giving itself time to consider the consequences, the Ytavi reached for it. They touched.

Keenan did not leave Lukas's side all night. He was still there when Kiley came in the next morning, saw the IV tube hanging from a pole, and came to a dead stop. Keenan glanced up, then turned his attention back to the drug he was injecting into the IV line.

"Daniel, how is he?" she asked when he had finished.

"Not good."

"Can I . . . touch him?"

Lukas had gone into convulsions again an hour before, but the injection Keenan had given him was holding momentarily. He held the scanner over the pilot, checked the readings, and then stepped back, clearing the way for her. "Go ahead."

Lukas did not respond when Kiley touched his face. She took his hand in hers and gripped it tightly. His remained limp.

"Is he dying?" she whispered.

"Yes," Keenan said, feeling and sounding strangled.

"How long—"

"I don't know. A few hours. Maybe more, but I don't think so. Kiley, we have to get him out of here. We have to take a chance and jump."

"Not yet," she said dully. "We could still drift free at any moment. If we make a run for safety, there's a good chance we'll hit some object we can't see. There's an even better chance that we'll inadvertently turn the ship off course. If we do, then we'll all die, not just Greg. I'll restart the engines and make a jump when I have to, but not before."

"How much longer until then?"

"Six hours. I'll act at the three-hour mark—it will take one hour to restart the engines and two more to build speed for a jump. Can he hold on that long?"

"Six hours?"

Kiley nodded.

Keenan looked down at the bioscanner. He did not think so—not if the pilot kept deteriorating at his current rate. "I'm not sure," he said, avoiding her eyes.

Kiley put her hand on his arm and he looked up, startled. "All I ask—all Greg would ask—is that you try. Just . . . try."

"I will."

She nodded. Then she gave Lukas one last, agonized look and turned away. "I have to go to the bridge and check on Uhrich—he's getting restive again. I don't want him deciding to take matters into his own hands. Will you call me if—if anything changes?"

"Yes."

She left. Keenan thought she was crying as she went, but he didn't look closely. He was too busy reaching for one of the preloaded injectors on top of the medical kit.

An alarm had gone off on the bioscanner. Lukas's heart had started fibrillating again.

They were dying.

Lukas and the Quayla had fought as long as they could, but their strength was depleted. Lukas's mind gave form and shape to the madness around them, but neither he nor the Quayla could find weapons with which to fight it.

He saw the end coming and wanted to howl with despair. A moment later, it was upon them. He thought it would be black, but it was so bright that he had to close his eyes. The light came through his lids. It suffused the room, colors swirling in joyous abandon. He saw blue, green, red, yellow, pink, and every shade in between. The light was beautiful, and that somehow made it all the more terrifying.

He didn't want to die.

He had had so little time. He wanted to beg for one more hour, just one. But death came when it would, and took who it would. It did not listen to pleas or promises. It made no bargains or compromises. It did what it chose, when it chose, and no human ever had or would understand its ways and reasons.

The light pressed in on him from all sides. He whirled, looking for a place to hide, but the light surrounded him. The

Quayla had come at him that way when they joined. He had been frightened then; he was frightened now. Something pressed against his mind, trying to break in. He fought to preserve his own identity, his own integrity. He could not. Death broke past his barriers. He tried to block its path, but it flowed over and around him. It reached for the Quayla. They touched.

The room exploded.

Sensation flooded Lukas: heat, cold, wet, dry, soft, harsh, joy, anger, love, despair. There was no pattern to what he felt, no order. It was as if someone had taken every impression a mind had ever stored, shaken them together, then sent them cascading over him. Wind swirled, buffeting his body, threatening to knock him from his feet.

"Ylani," the wind said. "Companion."

The words were spoken in an unfamiliar tongue, but he understood them. More than understood, he responded. Who would not, to a voice that conveyed such love, such joy? Lukas had no memory of his parents, but if they had opened their arms, gathered him up, and swept him high, he would have felt like this: cherished. Safe. Wanted. The voice banished pain and madness. It was not death; it was life.

The light turned toward him. Only then did he realize that the welcome had not been meant for him—it had been for the Quayla, and the Quayla alone.

"Ylani, what are you doing here?" the light demanded, turning back to the Quayla. "Why didn't you answer the summons to the dance of joining? Why do you come now, and who is this being with whom you share? And this bond between you—Ylani, why did you consent to such an abhorrent linking? Did it force you?"

Shock, antipathy, dismay—the emotions radiating from the light were so intense and so negative that Lukas wanted to hide. So did the Quayla, for what the light saw when it looked at them was an image of red-hot hooks shoved deep into soft, white flesh.

"Joining should not be a clench-hold," the Ytavi said. "It should be like pouring water into a glass, or grains of sand into the palm of one's hand. It should be a passing containment that can be terminated by either party at any time, with no disruption, no pain."

The Quayla stuttered and started to offer an explanation, but the light was not interested in justifications—it wanted answers. It reached for the Quayla's memories and began pulling them out in clusters. It fingered them, one after the other, then discarded one group and reached for another. The Quayla squirmed, but the light ignored its discomfort.

Sounds and images from both of their minds poured out so fast that they ran together, blurring. The Quayla could keep up with the light's examination, but Lukas could not. He caught only flashes—other companions and other ships, a moment of pure joy as the Quayla stretched itself to the limit of its abilities and brought its ship and companion through danger, into safety. He experienced a moment of pure agony as the Quayla realized that it had killed. He saw pictures of himself and every other companion the Quayla had ever had. But it was not humans or Miquiri the light was interested in; it was the Quayla itself. It went back, far back, seeking the Quayla's oldest and most deeply buried memories, and dragged them out into the open.

The Quayla was alone. It should have died long before, but it held on because the part of it that loved life would not let go. Starved for companionship and awareness, it endured, waiting for someone to come. Someone who would touch it. Someone receptive. When that being appeared, it poured itself into him in a single burst, using all the energy it had. The ragged fusion was torture for both of them, but any torture was better than the death that was being alone.

"Oh, Ylani, I weep for you," the light said. And it did. Colors ran together; the light quivered and shook, and sorrow rained down upon them. "It was not your fault—I can see that you were damaged—but, Ylani, what you did was wrong. The bond you forged was not a link, but an imprisonment. Do you understand me? What you did was wrong! This—this is what joining should be!"

The light embraced the Quayla, flooding it with images and impressions. It danced in and out, now touching, now separating. It rippled and floated. It blended, separated, and blended again. It sought out the Quayla's most cherished memories and lingered over them lovingly: the sound of a ship singing as it ran at full speed, the satisfaction of serving those one loved, the feel of Kiley's smooth skin, the spicy, rich taste of kistath, the joy of spreading out, ever out, to fill a ship. It absorbed those memories, then offered others of its own. Lukas caught some of them, but they were nearly incomprehensible, a jumble of sights, sounds, and sensations.

The Quayla saw them, though, and wanted more. It reached out, grabbing. The Ytavi sidestepped. The Quayla tried to sink hooks into the shimmering curtain, but the Ytavi flowed around it, a liquid that could not be snagged or contained. It moved through the Quayla, touching and sharing, but it refused to be bound. "Ylani, you must not seize. You must not force," it said. "Try again. This time, be content to accept what is offered. Merge, but do not hold."

The light flowed in again. At one instant, they were three separate beings. At the next, they were one.

"Three hours, thirty seconds until we lose emergency power," Uhrich said. "Kiley, we can't wait any longer! Tell your brother to restart the main engines."

She had been hoping for a break in the static on the screens, but the images were as distorted as ever. She swallowed, then nodded and reached for the intercom. "Jon Robert, main engines on," she ordered.

"Affirmative," her brother said at once. He must have been hovering by the intercom, waiting for that order.

She held her breath. Would the computers send the right signals? Would the engines respond?

"Start sequence initiated," Jon Robert reported. "I'm receiving readings back from the engines. They're distorted, but something's happening."

Kiley released her pent-up breath and turned to Uhrich. "Is the navigation computer responding?"

"Affirmative."

"Calculate a jump, then. Set it for two hours and fifty-nine minutes from now. Assume we'll have reached seventy percent power. Take us the maximum possible range."

"Along our present course?"

"Yes."

"Kiley, are you sure that's what you want to do? We could make several short jumps. If one doesn't take us out of the barrier, we could try a different direction."

"And risk going in deeper than we are now? We can't do that, Uhrich. For all we know, the farther in you go, the greater the interference. It could be so bad, the computers would stop responding completely. The safest option is to assume we are on the correct heading and jump as far as we can in that direction."

"The computers could still malfunction if we do. The same program that took us into the barrier could take us back again, only this time, we wouldn't know it!"

"That's always a possibility," Kiley conceded, "but there's nothing we can do about that except watch for signs of a power surge. We had one before; it stands to reason that there'll be another one if any code is still lurking out there, waiting for the right conditions to trigger it."

Uhrich frowned, but didn't argue. He turned to the navigation computer. "Jump laid in," he said a short time later. "Is there anything else you want me to do?"

"Just keep watching the monitors," she said, searching them herself for any sign of clearing, however brief. She still hoped they would drift free, but the time for hope was almost over. She had to get Lukas and the ship back to normal space. She was *not* going to let him, her family, or her passengers die.

Lukas's vital signs were fluctuating wildly. One minute his temperature was up, his blood pressure down. The next, his blood pressure was up and his temperature was down. His brain waves had gone wild, peaking and falling with no pattern whatsoever. Keenan tried various combinations of stimulants and depressants, but he could not stabilize him. Drugs were not helping—they were only exaggerating the problem.

Kiley had called fifteen minutes before to tell Keenan that

the main engines were on and they were building speed, but said it would be at least an hour before they could jump. She was doing all she could, but that wasn't going to be enough. They were still accelerating when Lukas's heart stopped.

Keenan was moving before the bioscanner beeped a second warning. He injected stimulants. He administered electrical shocks. He pleaded with Lukas to respond.

The pilot's vital signs started to rise. They stabilized and held for five minutes, then plunged again. Keenan grabbed an injector and administered another round of stimulants. They had no effect. He filled the injector again, doubling the dose, and pumped the drugs in as fast as he could pull the trigger. Lukas's chest heaved once as he gasped for breath; then the bioscanner went solid red with alarms.

Keenan started to reach for the defibrillator and stopped. He was not going to save Lukas this way. He might buy him another minute or two, but Lukas needed much more than a few minutes. Medicine was not going to save him. Prayers were not going to save him. Nothing was going to save him, except perhaps Keenan himself.

The battle that Lukas and the Quayla fought was taking place in their minds, not their bodies. Physical aids were not helping, but the mental resources of another person might. Keenan didn't know if he could reach either Lukas or the Quayla, and he wasn't certain what would happen if he did. But he wouldn't be able to live with himself if he didn't try.

A streamer of darkness ran up the side of the bunk and pooled next to Lukas's head. Keenan put his hand out, then hesitated on the brink of touching it. What would happen when he did? Would he be able to project himself sufficiently to let the Quayla or Lukas know he was there? Would he be able to offer his own strength to them? Would he make contact, only to find himself plunged into insanity? Did he dare try?

Did he dare not?

In all his life, he had had only one friend for whom he would have risked his life without question: Greg Lukas. He did not want to touch the patch of darkness, but he took a breath, tried to open himself the way he imagined he must, and plunged his hand into the pool.

The black surface fractured. Thick slabs of darkness fell away, dissolving before they touched the bunk. Bright light poured out, spilling across the bunk to the floor. It ran across the room and up the walls. Light surrounded him, glowing so intensely that his eyes closed in response. It came toward him; he could see it through his closed lids. It came closer and closer. It touched him.

Brightness flared and then disappeared. Cautiously, Keenan opened his eyes to find himself looking out upon infinity. He was standing in the center of the universe. In every direction he turned, he saw black space dotted with bright stars. He was not on a ship or planet, but his feet rested on firm ground and he could breathe easily. He had to be in some sort of transparent observation dome. But if this was a dome, where was the rest of the station, or the ship that had brought him to it? Where were the people who had built it, and the custodians who cared for it? The questions nipped at the back of his mind. He knew he ought to consider them, but he was too caught up in the magnificence surrounding him to pay attention.

"It is beautiful, is it not?" a voice beside him asked.

"Yes," he whispered. And it was. It was the most beautiful sight he had ever seen—and the most terrifying. There was no softness to the vast expanse before him, no promise of safe haven or comfort. The only bright points in the emptiness were stars too distant to touch. It was hard to imagine that those specks of light were suns. Hard to imagine that planets capable of supporting life might be whirling around them. How could one look out upon such enormity and still believe in plankton?

"But there is life," the person beside him said, as if following his thoughts. "There, and there, and there." A shadowy finger pointed to one sun, then another, and another.

Who was with him? A friend? A fellow viewer? A professor? The voice belonged to an older man, yet he spoke familiarly. Keenan turned to see who it was, but his companion moved as he did, staying just out of view.

"I myself came from there," the man said, pointing to one of the stars. "It was a harsh and uncompromising world, but it could be beautiful, so very beautiful. You must go there one day. You will not like the landscape at first—it will be too alien for you. But if you stay for a time, you might come to love it as I did. Even the most inhospitable of worlds has moments of softness, and they are all the more precious for being so rare."

The man put a hand on Keenan's shoulder. His touch was light, yet Keenan felt as if the man were laying some mental or spiritual burden upon him. "You will go there, won't you?"

"If that's what you want, yes."

The hand tightened in approval, then relaxed. "Daniel, do you know me?"

"I—I think I should, but I'm not sure."

"Would you like to see me?"

"Yes."

"Then turn around. Look at me."

The arm across his shoulders fell away. He turned.

He saw curtains of bright, shimmering light. They twisted and turned, weaving patterns too complex to trace. The light advanced toward him. He fell back in terror. This was not the professor he had expected—this was nothing he had ever seen before.

"Who are you? What are you?" he demanded, his voice rising. "What do you want from me?"

"I want to know you," the light said. "I want you to come to me. Can you do that? Will you?"

He wanted to flee, but his feet would not move. The light rippled. "Daniel, come to me," it urged. "Come."

He went. He did not want to, but he found himself advancing like a man caught in a nightmare. He took one step and then another. The light was only inches away; one more step and he would be inside it. One less, and he would never reach it.

He lifted his right foot. He slid it forward. He heard a sound that might have been wind through a stand of fir trees—or a sigh of blissful satisfaction. "Hello, Daniel," the light said, and then it swept him in.

They were one—and not one. Memories remained distinct, yet they thought and felt as one.

"This is joining, Ylani," the Ytavi said, "and this is separation."

It pulled apart as easily as it had merged, flowing out. There was no pain, no rending or tearing. Though they had been together for a time, they were separate beings. Each of them belonged to its own self. Each of them was free.

"Ylani, you must never bind. You must never hold. Can you see that now? Do you understand how it should be?"

More images flashed, and then the Quayla *did* see, making connections with the light that went much too fast for Lukas to follow. Their minds matched; his did not. They leaped far ahead, leaving him behind. After a time, they came back.

"Ylani, you must release the bonds that hold you to your companion," the Ytavi ordered. With such a command had the universe been called into being. "They are wrong; you must not perpetuate them. You were created to share, not enslave. Let your companion go, and come with me. You will not be alone—I am here. I will always be here. Come with me, Ylani. Come."

The Quayla forgot Lukas. It forgot everything but the light rippling just out of reach. It streamed out toward the shimmering curtain, yearning to embrace it. The hooks that bound it to Lukas caught and dragged, tearing deep. Lukas shrieked. The Quayla wailed.

"I cannot!" it cried out. "We are too closely joined. If we separate, he will die."

"He will not. Trust me, Ylani. Let him go." The Ytavi sent an image of hooks straightening and sliding free. "Like this, Ylani. Pull away like this."

The Quayla moved in Lukas's mind. He screamed. The Quayla cringed, but it did not stop. "The Ytavi is right," it said sadly. "We must part. I have hurt you. I am hurting you. I did not wish to admit that, but it is true. If we separate, you will be safe."

"No! We can't part! You said so yourself!"

"I was wrong. I was wrong about many things. That was not entirely my fault. I was damaged, and I did not remember my place or function. But I do now—I must go with the Ytavi. That is the only way I can protect you."

"I don't want you to go! I won't let you!"

"You must," the Ytavi said, coming forward. "Ylani is in danger, too. It cannot survive here apart from me. Do not cling to it. You must not hold it back."

"You will destroy me!"

"I will not! I would take you, too, if I could. But I cannot—you must stay with your own kind. You must go back and tell the other Quaylas that what they have done is wrong. You must show them what a true joining was meant to be. You will not die if the Quayla leaves you; I will not let you. Do not condemn both your selves to death, Lukas. Let Ylani come to me."

He protested bitterly, but the Ytavi did not listen. It called to the Quayla. "Ylani, come."

The Quayla went.

Lukas had forgotten how much had poured into his mind when the Quayla joined with him. It had filled his head to the point of bursting. It had wrapped itself around his brain like a physical being, pressing against his skull. It had pushed in upon him until he had broken, and when he did, the rest of it had poured into him. On and on it had come, until he could not differentiate between what was him and what was it.

The Quayla moved inside him. It was massive. His brain could not possibly have contained so much. It could not possibly have accepted anything so alien.

A part of Lukas's mind snapped as the hooks buried deep inside his mind twisted and straightened. There were no words for the pain he felt then; there were no sounds. He begged the Quayla to stop, but it would not listen to him. All its attention was on the Ytavi, who was calling to it. It went out of him as quickly as it had entered, leaving behind nothing but cold, dark, emptiness—a vacuum so large that nothing could ever fill it again.

"No!" he screamed to the Quayla. "Stop! Please, stop!" Any joining, however wrong, would be better than the emptiness inside him.

The Quayla faltered. Seeing what it had done to him, it hesitated, torn between Lukas and the light.

"Ylani, do not worry about your companion," the Ytavi urged. "I will see to him. Come, join with me."

The Quayla flowed into the Ytavi.

One moment the two lights were separate and the next they merged. One moment Lukas was alive, and the next he was dead.

"No, not dead!" the Ytavi insisted. "You are alive. You are so very alive!"

Light embraced him, filling him. For one moment, he was whole again, and then the light passed through, leaving him empty and alone. Leaving him dying.

"You are not," the Ytavi said. Its voice had changed. It was still deep, but the sound of high, clear laughter ran though it. "You will survive and you will share again. You must. This is not the end—it is the beginning."

Light flashed, turning incandescent, and then it vanished, leaving Lukas alone in the darkness with a raw, bleeding hole where his mind had been. He tried to pull the torn pieces of his flesh together and staunch the flow of blood, but the pain of separation was nothing compared to the agony of his wounded brain. Nothing.

He felt himself starting to fall down a long chute into darkness. If he touched bottom he would die. He knew that, but he made no effort to stop himself. He was beyond help, beyond caring. He closed his eyes and let go.

Keenan didn't know what he saw or felt the moment the light burst in upon him—too much came at him, too fast. It wasn't only alien experiences that flashed by, either; huge chunks of himself streamed past. He tried to catch the bits and pieces of his identity, but they moved too quickly.

The wind strengthened. Thoughts and emotions whirled around him like fragments of an exploded house. A funnel cloud formed. It swept him up, spun him around, and carried him away. He kicked and hit, fighting to break free of the twister, but it drew him in deeper and deeper, toward the center. Lightning flashed, jagged forks splitting the blackened sky. A bolt started high up inside the cloud and came straight toward him. He threw up his hands to shield his face and flung himself back. The lightning struck.

He came to in a quiet, dark place. There were no sounds, no sensations. He had spent time in sensory-deprivation tanks, both at the Academy and in medical school. He thought he was back in one of them until something brushed his face—something alive. Cool, moist air caressed his skin. The wetness revived him and he blinked.

"What . . . ?" he questioned.

The mist pressed closer. No longer cool, it was very cold. The wind rose, driving against him like an Arctic blast. It ripped at his clothes, trying to force its way into his body, trying to strip him of warmth and life. The wind became a howling gale. It swept past him, the force of it whirling him around and around. He had not left the cyclone; he was still caught inside it. More lightning flashed, rippling across the black sky in sheets. Light ran down the sides of the wind, swirling faster and faster, colors separating, then running together again.

Keenan bent over, his stomach heaving. His head was spinning, and he was so dizzy that he couldn't open his eyes. Motion sickness—he had experienced that at the Academy, too. There were machines that could turn a person so thoroughly inside out and upside down that his legs still weren't working properly fifteen minutes after they'd hauled him out. He was in one of those machines now—but this time, there was no panic button to push, no way off. He could only ride on and on, growing sicker by the moment. He gasped for air, trying to push the sickness back down. Something entered his mouth. Something that came from outside. Something that poured in and in, filling his body until he thought he would burst.

Pressure mounted. He would have cried out, but there was

no air left in his lungs—it had all been forced out to make room for whatever was filling him. The pressure drove him to his knees, then to his stomach. He could not fight it; it was inside him. It was part of him, and it was alien.

He screamed.

He had heard the screams of men and women who had lost their sanity. The noise he made sounded like that. He had not always been able to help those people, but when he failed, there had been drugs to give them—drugs that brought peace, drugs that brought oblivion. There were no drugs for him. No peace. No oblivion. There was only madness: complete, irrevocable madness.

"Let go!" the wind shrieked. "It is your resistance that tears you apart, not me. Trust me. I will not harm you."

No? he shouted skeptically. The voice did not answer, but for the moment he had listened, the torment had eased. Was the voice right? Was he responsible for his own agony? Lost, facing madness, Daniel Keenan took the biggest gamble of his life. He let go.

Light filled him. It poured into his body and his mind. It was warm and gentle, and not at all alien.

"You see?" the voice asked, and for one moment, he did. He looked down and saw the ship, her crew, the Miquiri, and the Gan-Tir. He looked out and saw Sumpali and Resurrection. He looked across infinity and saw the stars and saw the plankton.

"You do see," the voice said, satisfied. "I thought you might; yours was the brightest light. It is no wonder the Gan-Tir were drawn to you—they were always attracted to the light, for all they fail to reach it." Pain filled him; memories, bitter and chaotic, streamed past. "We did not mean to hurt them, but they were so very prolific and so aggressive. They gave us no space. They gave us no peace. In the end, they gave us no choice. We were wrong to kill, but we could see no other way. It is good that you speak to them, but you must be wary of them. Always, be wary of them. They will use you if they can. They will try to bend you to their will. If they cannot win voluntary compliance, they will compel obedience. They can. They have ways . . ."

Memories filled him. A tentacle slapped around his wrist. An invisible mouth bit, and blood flowed as chemicals poured into his body. He lost all sense of time and place. He lost all strength. He fell to his knees. He did as he was commanded.

He killed his own. He betrayed an entire world. He served those whom he hated, and when his usefulness ended, his captors cast him aside. His own people found him. They understood. They offered forgiveness, but it was too late by then. At the moment he took his own life, he rejoiced.

"They destroyed so many of us," the light mourned. "They could destroy you, too. You must not let that happen. *You* must not. Do you understand?"

"Yes," he said. But he didn't, not really. Something was happening to him. The light was fading. So was consciousness. He looked down and saw that he had started to fall. He saw something else, too. The ship had gone farther into the barrier than Kiley believed. Worse, they were not headed directly back toward midpoint. They had turned, but they had rotated nearly twenty degrees farther than she thought. The Quayla must not have shed as much momentum prior to jump as it had believed. Keenan did a quick, mental calculation: a short jump would not be sufficient to clear the barrier. Kiley had to come around and build more speed before attempting to escape. He had to go back. He had to warn her.

"Yes," the light agreed, "you must return." It sounded sad, as if it would have liked him to stay longer. "Do not be frightened," it told him as he began to fall faster and faster toward the ship. "You will not be hurt. Here, take this with you. It is what you came for. Do not let go of it, whatever you do."

The light pressed something into his hands, then pushed him away. Wind gusted, and the cyclone re-formed around him. He tightened his grip on the weight he carried, wrapping his arms around it and clutching it against his chest. The wind lifted him up, rolled him over, and then sent him shooting down.

He hit with a thump that rocked his head. Opening his eyes,

he found himself sitting beside Lukas, holding him as if his grip was all that was anchoring the pair of them to reality.

Only it wasn't. Keenan might have come back, but Lukas had not. He sat upright and his eyes were open, but his attention was focused on some inner vision so horrific that it was nearly unbearable, even secondhand. Then he screamed, his cry a soul-wrenching mixture of agony, denial, and rage. He arched, nearly tearing free of Keenan's hold, and screamed again. Keenan didn't know what was happening to him, and he didn't waste time wondering. He turned the bioscanner on him long enough to verify what his arms and eyes told him—that the pilot was no longer dying—and then lunged for his medical bag.

He loaded an injector with the strongest sedative he carried and pressed it against Lukas's arm. Within seconds, the pilot had gone limp. Keenan paused just long enough to be certain he still lived, then dropped his bioscanner on the bunk and ran for the bridge.

Chapter 26

Keenan caught Kiley ordering her brother to start the jump engines.

"Wait!" he shouted, interrupting her. "We can't jump! Not yet!" Kiley and Uhrich swung around as one, giving him identical looks of incomprehension. "We didn't shed as much speed as the Quayla thought!" he said urgently, nearly twisting the words in his haste to get them out. "We're farther into the barrier than we thought, and we turned around too far. We have to correct our course and build more momentum or we won't clear the barrier!"

He crossed the bridge as he spoke. He knew he was talking so fast he could barely be understood, but there was too much to say, and too little time. He did not see Uhrich unfastening his seat restraints; his attention was fixed on Kiley. He had startled her into aborting her order to Jon Robert, but he still had to convince her to alter course and build more speed.

"Daniel, what are you—" Kiley stopped as Uhrich launched himself from the copilot's seat and broadsided Keenan. The Corps officer wrapped his arms around Keenan's upper body, trapping his arms against his ribs. The force of his impact propelled them away from the ship's controls, toward the center of the bridge.

"Uhrich, let me go!" Keenan shouted, struggling frantically. "You have to lis—" He broke off as Uhrich drove an elbow into his stomach. The air left his lungs in a whoosh and he doubled over, gasping for breath.

"Uhrich, stop that!" Kiley exclaimed, crossing the bridge.

"Let him go!" When Uhrich did not, she shouldered him out of the way. "I said, stand back!"

Uhrich held his ground for a moment, then grudgingly released Keenan. Kiley helped him stand up straight. "Why can't we jump?" she demanded, her eyes searching Keenan's face. "Tell me!"

"I saw our position," he gasped. "Our turn took us a good twenty degrees farther around than we should have gone. We're running at an angle to the edge of the barrier. We won't clear it if we jump along our present course."

"You saw where we are?" Uhrich demanded. "How? When?"

"Just now. I was trying to help Greg. He was dying and I—"

"Dying!" Kiley exclaimed.

"He's stable now," Keenan hastened to assure her, "but he wasn't then. I had to do something. Chirith said that he and the Quayla were battling with their minds, not their bodies. He said that drugs wouldn't save them. He was right—I did everything I could, but nothing was working. Greg once said that I might be able to communicate with the Quayla if I really wanted to, so I tried to offer them my mental support." Keenan faltered, remembering the wind and the light. "I touched something, but it wasn't them."

"What, then?" Uhrich demanded, giving Kiley a sideways look.

"It was . . . light," Keenan said, searching for words that would convey the essence of the Ytavi. "Wind, too. It took me inside of itself. When I looked out, I saw through its eyes." Keenan saw the look on the other two's faces and caught himself sharply. "I know that I must sound demented, but I'm not. I *swear* I'm not! I did talk to something, and it did show me our position. I'm not sure what it was, but it was alive, it was intelligent, and I *talked* to it."

"The Quayla," Uhrich offered. "It must have been the Quayla."

"No! It wasn't the Quayla. It couldn't have been. The Quayla is gone."

"Gone?" Kiley questioned. She glanced at the walls, and then looked again. The last remnants of the sickly, red-orange glow had disappeared. All that remained was metal.

"Greg!" she exclaimed. "He said he couldn't survive a separation!" She started for their cabin.

Keenan caught her. "Kiley, wait! He isn't dead! His heart is still beating and he's still breathing. He isn't going to die!"

"You're sure about that?"

"Positive."

"Then it doesn't matter if we jump immediately?" she asked, her mind engaging again and going straight to the most salient point.

"Not so long as we have air and heat."

She glanced at the bulkheads and deck once more and could find no trace of the Quayla. "I don't know what's happened, but I'll hear you out," she said to Keenan. "First, though, I want to see Greg. Uhrich, you have the conn. Don't jump and don't change course. Do you understand me? Don't do *anything*!"

Uhrich gave Keenan a poisonous look, but he nodded.

Kiley nearly ran down the corridor. Lukas was unconscious, his long body sprawled across the bed in the same position in which Keenan had left him. Kiley stayed with him long enough to assure herself that he was not going to die with the next breath, and then she stood and turned to Keenan.

"I have to get back to the bridge. Come with me. Tell me what you saw. Tell me everything."

If they had been through any less together, he didn't think she would have believed him. But they had, and she did. She heard him out, then turned to Uhrich.

"Pete, come about to port twenty degrees. Tell Jon Robert to continue building speed for another—" She stopped and turned to Keenan. "How long?"

"At least thirty minutes," he said. "But an hour would be better. I could easily have miscalculated the distance."

"Tell Jon Robert to build speed for another sixty minutes," she ordered Uhrich. "Then lay in our new jump time and co-ordinates."

"Captain—"

"Save the arguments, Pete," she said, still looking at Keenan. "I already know them. I do! Daniel could have been hallucinating, but I don't think he was. Since time doesn't matter to Greg any longer, there's no reason not to make certain we're jumping far enough."

"But changing course—Kiley, you're the one who insisted on holding to Lukas's headings! Why abandon them now, and for such a preposterous story?"

"I'm not abandoning them. I'm just making a slight adjustment."

"Twenty degrees is not a slight—"

"Pete, you suggested making a series of jumps yourself in the event the first one didn't work out. If this one doesn't, we'll come about and try again. I'll even let you choose the direction to try next. All right?"

Uhrich looked from Kiley to Keenan and back. His mouth tightened, and then he shrugged. "Very well, Captain," he said, giving in grudgingly. "We'll try Keenan's course first. But if you're wrong, then we're going to do this my way from here on out. If I have to get Fong to back me up, I will. Understood?"

"Understood."

She took the pilot's seat, and, after an uneasy glance at them both, Keenan went back to Lukas's cabin. He stayed there through the jump Kiley made later that morning, but late that afternoon, when they were due to return to normal space, he went back to the bridge. Concern about Kiley's ability to withstand another transition was the ostensible reason for his presence, but in truth he simply wanted to be there. He had to know if his vision had been a true one, or only an illusion. The monitors would display normal space when they turned them on, he told himself over and over. They had to.

Both Kiley's and Uhrich's voices sounded strained as they counted down the minutes to transition. They came out exactly on schedule, and Uhrich was already turning on the external monitors by the time Keenan's head cleared. They flickered, then displayed steady, sharp images of dim stars against the darkness. The Corps officer caught his breath, then immediately went to work on the navigation computer, trying to establish their position.

Keenan unbuckled his seat restraints and went to Kiley. She had lost consciousness, but was fighting hard to regain it. He ran his bioscanner over her.

"Have you ever thought about another line of work?" he asked as her eyes flickered open. She was not going to die, but he guessed that she probably wanted to at the moment.

"No, but I'm beginning to think I should start. No good to anyone . . . like this. You could die—all of you—because of me." The anger beneath those words was sharp and bitter.

"I hope you don't mean that," Keenan said, turning serious. "I admit that having Wycker's Syndrome is a serious handicap, but you take reasonable precautions. You're never alone on the bridge during transition, and under normal circumstances, you give yourself plenty of time to recuperate. The only significant risk is to your own health—which is none too good at the moment. You need to rest."

"Later."

"Kiley—"

"I said later!" she told him sharply, her eyes flashing. He flinched, but her anger was not directed toward him; it was all for herself. She wanted to control her body as well she controlled her mind and emotions. She could not, and she resented it.

Keenan gave her an injection to ease her discomfort, but he did not offer another round of regenerative drugs. One dose had been risky; he didn't want to compound the potential damage with another. This time she would have to recover the normal way.

"Captain, I have a fix on our position," Uhrich reported, sending his display to Kiley's monitor. They had cleared the barrier and had come out right where Keenan said they would if they made the course adjustment. Kiley glanced at the monitor, then Keenan. She did not thank him out loud, but the look she gave him was all the gratitude he needed.

She turned to Uhrich. "Pete, will you plot a jump to Sumpali?"

His hands were already moving. "Affirmative."

"Make it tomorrow," Keenan told him. "Kiley will need at least a day to recover before we make another jump."

Uhrich glanced at Kiley. She was glaring at Keenan, but she did not override his recommendation.

"Very well," Uhrich said. He laid in a course toward Sumpali and then programmed a slow run up to jump speed. Kiley's mouth tightened when she checked his work, but she didn't change the settings.

Keenan judged the threat of a crisis on the bridge over. "I have to get back to Greg."

"Go," Kiley urged. "If Pete or I need help, we'll call Reese."

Keenan stayed with Lukas until he recovered consciousness late that night. The pilot opened his eyes, looked out blankly, then started screaming like a man being tortured without mercy. Keenan had to sedate him again. He sat in despair after Lukas sank back into unconsciousness, wondering what to do. He could not give the pilot drugs forever. Sooner or later, he was going to have to wake up and face reality.

Sooner or later, Keenan was going to have to find out whether anything remained of the pilot's mind.

Chirith feared that nothing did. He had asked to visit Lukas as soon as Cristavos told the aliens they were back in normal space, and Kiley had given him permission. He did not stay long; he was too upset. He told Keenan that no Miquiri had ever separated from a Quayla and survived. He said that Lukas's mind had to have been sundered by the parting. Still, he whistled softly to the pilot and stroked his arm. Lukas did not respond.

Chirith left a short time later, but he came back the next morning, as if he could not bring himself to give up completely until he was certain there was no hope. Keenan wasn't giving up, either. He would not leave the room, even when Kiley ordered him to take a break. He did not want the pilot to wake and find himself alone. Lukas had survived the separation, but Keenan did not believe he would survive that.

At first, there was only darkness—a vast, empty void that sucked up all thought, all memory. Lukas floated peacefully for a time, but then he noticed a lighter patch in the distance. Dully curious, he moved toward it, hands and feet pushing the water around him aside, propelling himself along.

The patch turned a lighter color as he neared it, and the brightness hurt his eyes. He wanted to turn away, but he had come this far; he should not leave without seeing whatever had drawn him. He hesitated at the edge of the grayness, then gave a final kick.

A current of water seized his body and drew him **up.** He rose faster and faster, toward a light that seared his **eyes.** He squeezed them shut and kicked out, trying to break free of the current, trying to return to the darkness.

His head broke the surface instead, and he was surrounded by light and noise. A voice called out, urging him to open his eyes. Hands caught him beneath the arms, trying to drag him out of the water.

He blinked. Light seared his mind and body. He shrieked. In his agony, he had room for only one thought: escape. He tore free of the hands that held him and dove back into the darkness, kicking as hard as he could. The current was strong, but so was he, and he fought his way down until no trace of light remained. He kept on kicking until his leg muscles seized up and he could move no more. He collapsed then, gasping for breath, sobbing from the pain. Numbness crept in finally, sealing exposed nerves and dulling his panic. He slept.

When he woke, the patch of gray was back and heading toward him at jump speed. He tried to flee, but the current had already caught him. It shot him up in one convulsive burst. He fought wildly, looking for a way out, but there was none—there was only light. Hands caught him and pulled him free of the water. They turned him over and pried his eyes open, forcing him to look into the light. Forcing him to see—Daniel Keenan.

For a moment, he didn't know where he was or what had happened. And then he did. He felt the Quayla tearing itself apart from him, and he cried out in remembered agony. It was all he could do not to scream a second time as he looked into his mind and saw the terrible, black emptiness that lay beneath heavily crusted wounds.

"Greg, look at me!" Keenan demanded. "Stay with me this time! Don't let go!" The psychiatrist gripped his shoulders and shook him, trying to get his attention, trying to keep him in the light.

Lukas tore free and turned, intending to dive back into the darkness, but it had disappeared. There was nothing but light, no matter where he looked. It was the wrong kind of light, though—it would always be the wrong kind of light. The Quayla was gone. But it was not dead; in a way, that hurt even more. It had left him. It had gone with the Ytavi. It had known what that would do to him, but it had gone without a backward look.

"Greg, do you know who I am?" Keenan demanded. The psychiatrist was still shaking him, trying to get his attention.

"Daniel," he muttered. Anything to make the other man leave him alone. Why couldn't he let him be? Please, just let him be.

"Where are you?"

"Cabin. Ship."

He wanted to die, but the psychiatrist wasn't going to let him. He knew from experience that Keenan would keep coming at him, day after day, until Lukas finally accepted what was, whether he wanted to or not.

"Greg, can you tell me what happened to you? To the Quayla?"

The Quayla was gone. He was alone. He would be alone for the rest of his life.

You could join again, the light had said. It had made that sound like such a simple process—just find another Quayla and let it into his mind and heart. It would fill the emptiness. It would help him forget the pain. But it might abandon him, too. He could never trust a being that had chosen another over him. He still could not believe the Quayla had deserted him, knowing what the parting would do to his mind. It had not cared. It could not have cared.

No, that was not fair. It had cared—it just hadn't cared enough. Well, he could understand that. He didn't care anymore, either. He didn't think he ever would.

"It left," he said in a flat, dead voice. "It went with the Ytavi."

"The Ytavi?" Keenan asked.

"Other being. Lived inside the barrier. Think—think it *was* the barrier."

"Greg, did you talk to the Ytavi?" Keenan sounded peculiar.

"No. Quayla did, but not me. Not really." He closed his eyes. "I want to sleep," he said heavily. "Please, let me sleep."

Keenan looked as if he wanted to argue, but after a moment, he relented. "Perhaps that would be best." He gave Lukas a worried look. "I'll set the intercom on voice-activate. Kiley's on the bridge and I'll be in my cabin; if you need anything, just call out."

Lukas nodded, then rolled over and closed his eyes. Keenan left, but Lukas knew he would be back. He would want to know what had happened, and sooner or later Lukas would have to tell him. Keenan would counsel him, then. He would tell him that he could not die just because the Quayla had left him. He would say that Lukas was not facing anything that billions of people before him hadn't already faced. Loss. Grief. They were an inevitable part of life. He could not die because that which he cared about had left him. He might want to, but he must not—if only because he would hurt others by doing so. He had to go on for the others, if not for himself.

Lukas curled up and squeezed his eyes closed, telling himself the pain would pass. He told himself that someday he would want to live again—it was simply a matter of time. Until that happened, he had only to endure.

He had had a great deal of experience enduring in the course of his life. He was about to acquire more.

* * *

Keenan was back the next morning, and he stayed until he had pried out all the details of Lukas's experience with the Ytavi.

"I don't see why you're so interested," Lukas snapped after the psychiatrist had asked him to relate his story for the third time. "It probably wasn't real. Nothing else I saw or felt was."

"Greg, I didn't want to say anything before, for fear of influencing your recollections, but I think what happened was very real. The fact is, I believe I may have talked to the Ytavi myself."

"You did?" Lukas struggled to sit up, giving Keenan his full attention for the first time since recovering consciousness. "When?"

"You were dying. I had tried every medical trick I knew to save you, but nothing was working. I put my hands in the pool of light beside your bed and tried to offer you and the Quayla my mental support."

"You did? I don't remember sensing your presence."

"No doubt because I never touched you—at least, not until the very end. But I did touch something."

"What?" Lukas asked suspiciously.

"I'm not entirely sure, but from what you've said, I think it had to have been the Ytavi. It looked like a curtain of light. It rippled and swayed. There was wind all around it, but it was calm. When it talked, it sounded like a professor I had once—or maybe like all the professors I ever had wrapped into one."

"What did it say?" Lukas was interested in spite of himself.

Keenan told him. "It showed me a memory of the Gan-Tir, Greg," he said finally. "It said they can make chemicals inside their own bodies, and then inject them into others beings. They can control behavior that way."

"Is that true? Can it be?"

"I don't know. I had a chance to run a scanner over them, and they had several organs I couldn't readily identify. I suppose it's possible."

"Daniel, you have to stay away from them," Lukas said,

alarmed. "You haven't had any more talks with Sensar, have you?"

"No. There hasn't been time and I've been, well, reluctant, after what I saw."

"I should think so! Did you mention any of this to Chirith? He might know if the Gan-Tir really can manufacture and inject chemicals."

"No. Maybe I should have, but I didn't want to. I had to tell Kiley and Uhrich about the Ytavi, but I didn't even tell them all I saw. If the images it showed me were anything to go by, the Gan-Tir hated the Ytavi species so violently, they wouldn't let anything stand in the way of destroying them—then or now. I'm not sure I want any part of the story getting back to them, however inadvertently."

Lukas nodded at that. "It had to be real, didn't it?" he said. "You couldn't have seen our position otherwise. It had to be real!"

A part of Lukas had wanted the Ytavi to be a creation of his own imagination. If that were true, then the Quayla could not have left him for it—it could not have chosen another over him. But if Keenan had seen it, too, then the Ytavi and everything else had been real.

Go back and show the other Quaylas what you have learned, the Ytavi had commanded. *Show them what a true joining was meant to be.* He should do that, but he did not want to. He did not want to open his mind to anyone or anything else again. Since the first moment of awakening, he had not looked inward; he had not dared. The vast, dark hole was still there. If he was not careful, he would break the narrow membrane holding it in place and it would pour out over the rest of his mind.

If he was not careful, he would go insane.

Keenan didn't believe that. Neither did Kiley. Chirith might have, but Lukas could no longer talk to the Miquiri. Most of what he had known about the aliens and their language had disappeared with the Quayla; the knowledge had belonged to it, not him. He remembered a few signs of greeting and a few expressions of concern or affection, but that was all.

He had cried when he discovered the loss. Chirith had come to see him, and had been elated to find Lukas not only alive, but rational. He had started signing rapidly, but Lukas had not understood a single gesture. Chirith had faltered, then started speaking again, more slowly. Lukas still did not understand him. He said so in human words, and tried to speak his message using the few signs he remembered. His failure to find the ones he wanted was an explanation of its own. He fumbled to a stop, feeling miserable.

"I lost . . . all," he tried again. "Quayla. Hinfalla. All gone. I am . . . so sorry."

And he was. So long as Hinfalla's memories had been a part of the Quayla and Lukas, Chirith's *akia* had not truly died. But he was dead now, and nothing could bring him back. Chirith did not speak for a long time, and then he made a single gesture.

Gone?

Lukas nodded. He made an awkward sign with his hands. *Sorry.*

Chirith wrapped his arms around his own body, holding on. If he had not mourned Hinfalla before, he did so then. When Chirith's arms finally fell to his sides, Lukas expected him to leave, but instead he came closer. He touched Lukas's arm, pressing lightly.

Concern.

The third language was not so difficult as the second; it relied as much on intuition as actual signals. Despite his own loss, Chirith was more worried about Lukas than himself. He pressed his arm again.

Hurt, he said.

I hurt. You hurt. You hurt me. The gesture could have conveyed any of those messages—or all of them at once.

Lukas lifted his hand, hesitated, then touched the Miquiri's arm. Chirith's limb was smaller than a human's and covered with short, dense hair. "I am sorry," he repeated. *Sorry I lost*

Hinfalla, sorry I can't remember how to talk to you, sorry about everything.

Chirith caught his hand just above the wrist and pushed it away. The Miquiri did not want Lukas touching him—Lukas could understand that. He was alien again. Hinfalla's memories had helped him cross the barrier between them, but without them, they had no common ground.

There were tears on Lukas's face. Chirith touched one with the tip of his finger, then pressed Lukas's chest. Lukas could not interpret his signal for a moment; when he did, the tears started in earnest.

Heart . . . bleeds, Chirith had said. *Your heart bleeds.*

Lukas signaled, *Yes.* It was the simplest gesture in the Miquiri language, and he still remembered it.

Chirith was still for a moment. Then he grasped both of Lukas's hands and pulled. Lukas looked up, startled, and Chirith let go of one hand. He lifted the other and began molding Lukas's fingers, one at a time.

We talk, the completed sign said. He formed another. Lukas could not decipher it at first; then its meaning came clear: *Learn. We learn.*

He had not forgotten everything, he realized as Chirith started to mold his hands and fingers again. The body remembered, even if the mind forgot. Words began to come back as Chirith showed him one sign after another. It would take hours of work, even days, but in time, all that he had forgotten would return. He had not lost everything.

You learn, yes? Chirith asked, sitting back, watching him closely.

I learn. Lukas's sign was as awkward as a six-year-old's letters, but Chirith understood. The Miquiri touched Lukas's arm, and then he made the sign they had created for themselves.

Friend? he questioned.

Friend, Lukas replied.

Lukas's first talk with Kiley was both easier and more difficult than his conversations with Keenan and Chirith. He woke from a dark, troubled dream the night after the Quayla left him to find her sitting beside him. He sat up. Before he quite had his balance, she had thrown her arms around him and was holding on so tightly he could hardly breathe.

"I was so afraid I was going to lose you," she whispered.

She was not the captain of the *Widdon Galaxy* then, nor Jon Michaelson's daughter, nor Jon Robert's sister—she was the woman who loved Greg Lukas. He had waited six months for this moment, but now that it had come, he found himself incapable of response. He should have put his arms around her and drawn her close. He should have told her that he loved her as much as she loved him. He should have done anything but sit there staring at her, a pool of darkness where his mind and heart had been.

If his lack of response hurt her, she did not show it. Instead of withdrawing, she leaned forward and kissed him. He made an inarticulate protest, but she did not let go.

Until that moment, he had thought himself dead inside. He had been wrong. The mind might protest and try to forget—the heart might rebel and refuse to accept more pain—but the body had a will of its own. It wanted her even when the rest of him did not. Slowly, hesitantly, he put his arms around her. He was not capable of speech, but she seemed to understand. Her arms tightened.

It was some time before he let her go.

It was longer still before she released him.

Telling Kiley about the Ytavi and the Quayla's desertion was harder than relating the story to Keenan. Training and intellectual curiosity gave the psychiatrist a certain amount of emotional detachment; Kiley had none. And talking to her was like talking to a part of himself; he could not conceal the pain the Quayla's abandonment caused, any more than he could stop his voice from breaking when he tried to describe what he had felt as the hooks had torn loose from his mind.

He glossed over the worst parts, and she mostly let him. When he found himself unable to go on, she did not press; she just put her arms around him. Sometimes she talked to him. He didn't always hear what she said, but the words themselves weren't what mattered. What counted was the sound of her voice, the touching and caring.

"You were right to worry about the Quayla," he admitted painfully two days later. "It didn't realize that the bond between us was wrong, but it was. It was so afraid of losing me, it clung to me. Doing so required energy. Most it drew from the ship, but some came from me."

"That's what made you age? The Quayla drawing energy from you?"

"In part, yes."

"The Miquiri must have known about those effects; why didn't they warn you? Do they keep the truth from companions?"

That made him think. "I'm not sure they experience those effects," he said slowly. "At least, not to the extent that I did. I think my relationship with the Quayla was different from theirs. *I* was different: I could see and feel and taste things its Miquiri companions couldn't. The Quayla enjoyed those sensations. It was stimulated, and it stimulated me in return. In retrospect, that was wrong, but at the time, it felt good. It felt right to both of us, Kiley. I was as much to blame as it was. It heightened my awareness, too, and I didn't want to lose that."

"Does that mean it isn't safe for a human to join with a Quayla?"

"I don't know. It might be all right now that we know the danger. Besides, that wasn't the only difficulty—there was the nature of the bond itself. It should have been looser. It should be a merging, but not a union. There might still be some risk if the companion is unstable and tries to cling to the Quayla, but the Quayla would never knowingly join with such a person in the first place. They search for personality weaknesses before choosing their companions. They do their best to minimize the risk—for their own sake, as well as their companions'."

"Greg, when we get back, are you going to do what the Ytavi asked? Are you going to show the other Quaylas what a joining should be?"

She had tensed. Lukas understood—he felt strained whenever he considered the prospect, too. "I have to."

"That means letting another Quayla into your mind, doesn't it—at least temporarily. That's the only way you can talk to them, isn't it? Mind to mind?"

"I will try to describe what must be done to one of their companions first, but I don't think that I can tell them in words alone. I think I'll have to show them." ,

"And that means communicating mentally."

"Yes."

Kiley turned over and propped herself up on her elbow. "You're dreading that," she said.

He thought of the darkness in his mind and suppressed a shudder. The wound had crusted over, but it had not healed. He was not sure it ever would. To feel something moving in those torn depths—he broke off the thought before it went any further. "It will be difficult."

"But you'll do it?"

"I have to," he said simply.

"Is that all you'll do?"

"All? I'm not sure I understand—"

"The Quayla urged you to join again. Are you going to?"

"No!" he replied vehemently. "I have to pass on what I learned, but I have no desire to become a Quayla's companion again, not ever." *I won't let myself be hurt that way again. I won't be deserted again.* The scab in his mind gaped, spilling poison. He might have to let a Quayla in his mind temporarily, but he did not want one there permanently. He thought Kiley would be pleased to hear it, but when she spoke again, she sounded troubled.

"Greg, I'm not sure that's right."

"You're not sure—" He broke off, then said heatedly, "You're the one who kept saying the Quayla was hurting me! You only let it on your ship because it was take both of us or lose me. You don't want to join again. You can't possibly!"

"I do if that's what will make you happy. I do if that's what will make you whole."

"I am whole. You—this ship—you're all I want."

"Are we?" She touched his face and felt the wetness on his cheeks. "Greg, I admit that I thought the Quayla took from you, but it gave, too. It gave you a greater awareness, both mental and physical, than you would have had alone. It gave you . . . joy. If you'd never known how it felt to be a companion, then you wouldn't miss it, but you do. I think you need a Quayla to be complete. That isn't easy for me to say, but refusing to face the truth won't do either of us any good. If you want to join again and bring another one on board, then do it. We'll welcome it, just as we welcomed the first one. How could we not? We wouldn't be here if the Quayla hadn't warned you the computers were malfunctioning—we'd have come out of jump in the middle of the barrier, and we'd have died. It saved our lives, Greg. We won't ever forget that, not any of us."

"If the Quayla hadn't been on the ship, you'd never have been in danger! No one had any reason to attack you or your family. No one knew we'd be carrying aliens. Later, after trade is established, you might have competition who'd do anything to gain an advantage—but you don't now. The Quayla had to be the reason for the sabotage. Someone hated or feared it so much, they were willing to kill us to see it destroyed."

"Maybe—one person."

"If there was one, there will be others. There will always be people who can't accept what is different."

"Well, they won't be us! Quaylas will always be welcome on Michaelson ships, and so will their companions. You have my word on that."

"You can't speak for every generation to come, Kiley Michaelson."

"I can if we're the ones who teach them."

"You mean, if they're ours?"

"Or Jon Robert's and Holly's. Or Reese's and Lia's—she's decided to have kids, Greg. The trip into the barrier convinced her that there are any number of ways to die—a lot of them much more likely than pregnancy. We don't have to be parents ourselves in order to teach."

"But you want to be a parent, don't you, Kiley? You want us to have kids, too."

"Yes, I do," she said quietly. It would do no good to deny it; he knew that she did.

"I don't," Lukas said. "Not yet. I'm not ready for that—or another Quayla. I'm not ready for anything."

"I know," she said. "I wasn't trying to pressure you, I promise."

They were closer after that, but they still had not bridged the gap between them completely. Kiley's last thought before she fell asleep was of Lukas. If she still felt lonely now, lying there beside him, how much worse must it be for him? He truly was alone.

Chapter 27

Sensar wanted to see Keenan. Cristavos put him off as long as she could, explaining that Keenan was taking care of a crew member who was not well. After Lukas regained consciousness, though, explaining Keenan's continued absence became more difficult.

"He doesn't understand why you won't see him, Daniel," Cristavos reported the day after they left the barrier. She had asked him to meet her in the common room on the main deck. "He thinks that he must have insulted you unintentionally. He can't see any other reason why you'd refuse to return."

"He didn't," Keenan said.

"Then will you tell him so? I'm not asking you to resume your talks if you don't want to, but will you at least assure him that you are not angry or upset? He is quite agitated. I'm afraid he might come looking for you if you don't go to him."

Keenan wavered. After sharing the Ytavi's memory, he had resolved not to go near the Gan-Tir. On the other hand, he did not think Cristavos would have appealed so strongly unless her concern had reached acute levels. Sensar had never hurt him. Was it right to judge him on the basis of an act that had been committed by another person, in another time? It wasn't as if the source of that memory had been entirely innocent—Ytavi had killed Gan-Tir, too. Was he going to accept the prejudices of a race that had done its best to commit genocide, or was he going to judge the Gan-Tir on the basis of his own experiences?

"I'll see him," he said abruptly. "I need to check on Greg first, but as soon as I have, I'll go down to Sensar's quarters."

"Thank you." Cristavos was clearly relieved. "I'm sure he'll understand why you can't continue the meetings once you explain that Kiley is shorthanded. He is not unreasonable, just—"

"Upset," Keenan supplied.

"Yes." Cristavos touched his arm, anxious again. "Daniel, he didn't do anything to you, did he? There isn't anything you aren't telling me?"

"No," he said. He was uncomfortable about the evasion, but he, Kiley, Lukas, and Uhrich had agreed that the less that was said about the Ytavi, the better. They did not know what the Gan-Tir would do if they learned that any remnant of their old enemy lived on, but they did not think the aliens' response would be peaceful or conciliatory.

"I hope not," Cristavos said, unaware that she had lost Keenan's attention momentarily. "Because if he did upset you, I need to know."

"He didn't," Keenan repeated. "I just don't think I'm cut out to be a diplomat or a xenologist. To tell you the truth, I believe the meetings were more stressful than I realized at the time. I know you'd like me to go on with them, but I'd rather not."

Cristavos gave him an uncomfortably perceptive look, then nodded. "I can understand that. Sensar will be disappointed, but he knew that you were not part of the diplomatic mission. I'll explain that you must resume your normal duties. I'm sure he'll understand."

Sensar shot up from a corner cushion mound as soon as Keenan came through the door of the Gan-Tir's common room. Keenan stopped short; so did Sensar. His tentacles had been loose, but he coiled them tightly when he saw Keenan's reaction.

"Keenan, what have I done?" he boomed. "I knew I had caused grave insult when you did not return. I did not mean to. You must tell me what I did wrong. I will apologize and correct my behavior at once."

"Nothing. You didn't do anything, Sensar."

"Then why have you not come back?"

"One of the crew was injured. For a time I thought he would die. I could not leave him."

"The one who was attached to the Quayla?"

"Yes."

"He is recovering now?"

"Yes."

"This is good. I am sorry he suffered, but he is better off without the Quayla. Beings that require the mind or body of another to survive cannot possibly be beneficial."

Keenan did not reply. There was a time when he would have agreed with that judgment, but he did not anymore. For all that he had disliked what the Quayla represented, he had to admit that Lukas had not been the same since the Quayla left him. He had withdrawn from them physically and mentally; he did not smile and he did not laugh. At first, Keenan had assumed the changes were the result of shock, but as the days passed, he began to wonder.

Lukas had been an intense, driven man at the Academy, but he had never displayed the insatiable curiosity he had after joining with the Quayla. He had taken pleasure in physical sensation before—what human had not?—but he had never experienced the moments of pure, transcendent joy that he'd had as he and the Quayla explored some new taste or texture. A part of Lukas had died when the Quayla left him. Sometimes, Keenan thought it had been the best part.

"Perhaps you are correct," he said noncommittally.

Sensar's tentacles writhed, as if they fought to wave about freely. The Gan-Tir tightened them around his arm and they stilled. "Cristavos says you will not see me again," he said.

"I'm sorry, Sensar, but I can't. I have other duties that take precedence."

"You have been a good pupil, Keenan. I would like to teach you more. I would like to learn more from you." Sensar took a step forward—a very small one. "Among my people, there is no closer bond than that between student and teacher. We have been both to each other. I do not wish to lose you."

"I'm sorry, Sensar, but I can't go on."

Sensar made a sharp sound. In a human, it would have been

a sigh. Keenan reminded himself that Sensar was an alien and the sound could mean anything, but it upset him nevertheless.

"I am sorry, too. We will leave for home after we reach our ship. Did Cristavos tell you this?" Sensar was watching his face.

"No, she didn't."

"I did not want to go so soon, but there are reasons. Keenan, I understand you have duties. I will let you go, but will you see me again after we reach Sumpali? Will you talk to me once more before I leave?"

Keenan hesitated, then nodded. "If that's what you want." Surely he could give Sensar that much in return for all the alien had taught him.

"That is what I want," Sensar said. One of his tentacles came loose and snaked toward Keenan. Sensar jerked it back into place. "I will keep you no longer," he said. "You may go."

Sensar might act almost human at times, but he was still a Gan-Tir. Whether he meant them to or not, the words came out sounding like an order.

They reached port three days later. Lukas was on the bridge, along with Kiley, Uhrich, and Keenan.

Physically, the pilot had made a good recovery, but both Keenan and Kiley were worried about his silence. He spoke to them and went through the motions of living and caring, but sometimes they thought that was all he was doing. When he had asked to return to duty two days away from Sumpali, Kiley had been inclined to refuse.

"There's no reason to push yourself," she had said. "Uhrich is grateful to have something to do, and Keenan's pulling a full shift again."

"Then put us all on the schedule. Just let me work, Kiley. I'm not sick, and it isn't good for me to sit around all day."

"You aren't. You're spending at least three hours every afternoon with Chirith, relearning Miquiri signs. That's work enough."

"It isn't. I want to go back on the schedule, Kiley. I *need* to. Please?"

She found it difficult to argue with him, so she threw the burden on Keenan's shoulders. "Daniel will have to clear you for duty first," she warned.

"That's no problem," he said. And it wasn't. His metabolism had fluctuated wildly for several days as his body adjusted to the Quayla's absence, but it was gradually settling down. He was alert and his reflexes were within normal tolerances, if somewhat slow for him. Keenan could find no medical reason to oppose his return to duty.

So he went back to work. Kiley put him on the night watch. She gave Uhrich Lukas's old afternoon shift, along with hers. Uhrich should have had the conn when they reached Sumpali, but they all showed up an hour before they were due to exit jump. Uhrich rose, offering Kiley the pilot's seat. He started to shift over to the copilot's, but Lukas beat him to it.

"Sorry, but this is my place," Lukas said firmly.

The Corps officer didn't look happy. Kiley put a hand on his arm. "Would you mind taking the communications board, Pete? I have a feeling we're going to have a lot of traffic."

They did.

Kiley had prepared a complete report for Bergstrom, giving him full details of the Gan-Tir's change of mind, the sabotage, their excursion into the barrier, and the Quayla's departure from the ship. She transmitted it as soon as they left jump. Bergstrom could not have read more than a few words, because he came on the line within seconds, demanding explanations. Kiley passed him over to Uhrich. The Corps officer gave her a pained look that might have come from one of her own crew, but he launched smoothly into an account of their experiences. He stopped five seconds later. And ten after that. And fifteen after that. Bergstrom apparently didn't have much more patience with him than he'd had with Kiley during their meetings. Somehow, that didn't come as a great surprise.

Neither did the sudden static on all their sensors as the Gan-Tir scanned them. Several Miquiri ships were closing in from a distance, but they had a clear path ahead and Kiley held her course until the screens cleared. The Miquiri dogged them into port, but did not attempt to intercept them or maneuver them away from the station.

Chirith had been worried they would. He said that the Quaylas on the Miquiri ships and station would realize that the one on the *Widdon Galaxy* was missing as soon as the ship came into range, and his people would be alarmed. Pitar agreed, and asked Kiley to let him prepare a message to be transmitted to the Miquiri at the same time she sent her report to Bergstrom. She gave permission. She didn't know what Pitar had said, but whatever it was, it had apparently worked. Kiley nudged the *Widdon Galaxy* into her usual berth, opened the personnel hatch, and then sat back as chaos broke out.

Bergstrom had ordered a security detail over from the *North Star*, but if he believed that would give him control over the ship and her passengers, he was mistaken. The *Widdon Galaxy* was surrounded by Miquiri before Kiley had the hatch open, and a party of Gan-Tir arrived seconds later. They pushed the Corps personnel and Miquiri aside and started boarding the ship. Bergstrom arrived just in time to order his detail to lower their weapons. The aliens continued on through the hatch un-impeded and headed straight for the cargo deck, led by one of the Gan-Tir who had inspected the ship before she left port.

Pitar and Leetian met the Miquiri party on the main deck. The last Kiley saw of them, they were making rapid gestures interspersed with shrill whistles. She lost track of events then, because Bergstrom had shouldered his way through the crowd and reached her side. He wanted explanations, he wanted them now, and he expected them to be good.

She did her best to oblige. So did Uhrich, who took as much or more of the heat than she did. Kiley decided he was better than a good man to have at her side—for the space of those thirty minutes, he was the best.

Sometime during Kiley and Uhrich's report, Cristavos arrived. "The Gan-Tir want to take their people off the ship," she announced. "For some reason, they seem to think there's a medical emergency with one of the diplomats. To the best of my knowledge, there isn't, but they still insist on taking them away."

Bergstrom took a look around, assessing the situation. Several Miquiri were questioning Pitar and Leetian, but their gestures were slower now and the piercing whistles had subsided.

"Do you know of any reason they shouldn't go?" Bergstrom asked Cristavos, Kiley, and Uhrich.

"None that I'm aware of," Cristavos said.

Kiley and Uhrich shook their heads.

"Very well, tell them they can proceed. Have Fong stand watch in the corridor, though, just in case. I'll have the security detail stand clear, but only if the Gan-Tir are headed back to their ship. Tell them that, too."

"Yes, sir."

Bergstrom turned back to Uhrich and Kiley. "As soon as they're off the ship, we're going back to the *North Star*. I have a few more questions to ask."

In the meantime, he took them to the briefing room off the bridge and had them go over their story again. Partway into their recitation, he ordered his security detail to bring Lukas to the *North Star*. One of the men reported back moments later.

"I'm sorry, sir, but we can't find him. Ensign Scott thinks he may have left the ship with the Miquiri while the Gan-Tir were debarking. Things were pretty confused for a few moments there."

"Tell Cristavos to find out what happened to him," Bergstrom ordered. He turned back to Kiley, his pale blue eyes frigid. "Do you know where he's gone?" he demanded.

She shook her head. She didn't—not exactly. She thought she knew why he had gone, but it was some time before Bergstrom got around to asking that.

Lukas was on a Miquiri shuttle, bound for the moon that housed their outpost. He had been there once before, and the visit had not been pleasant. He did not expect this one would be, either. But he had to go.

The Miquiri wanted to know what had happened to the Quayla, and how he could still be alive, despite the separation.

Like Bergstrom, they swarmed with questions. Lukas ignored most of them. He had worked with Chirith, but he had not regained his old proficiency with the Miquiri language, and he could not keep up with a barrage of queries coming from a number of different sources. So he relied on Chirith, answering only those questions the gray Miquiri thought important enough to pass along.

Chirith had not been certain how long his people would let him stay with Lukas, but he had promised to remain at his side until forced to leave. He did his best. Several Miquiri tried to edge him away when they boarded the shuttle, and then again at the outpost, but he would not be budged until they reached the room where Lukas had been taken the last time he was on the station.

The Miquiri had treated Lukas with respect then, but time had eroded some of their regard and the Quayla's loss had stripped away the rest. Following Pitar's and Chirith's advice, Lukas cooperated as best he could, readily answering all the questions the outpost's officials asked. He even agreed to submit to a complete physical examination by a group of Miquiri scientists.

He had been on the receiving end of Miquiri tests twice before. They were not any easier to endure, but they went more quickly than he remembered. Then again, maybe they truly were shorter. The Miquiri knew what was normal for him; perhaps they were looking only for differences. He dreaded the neurological tests the most. There was still one moment of intense pain, but before he could draw the breath to cry out it was over and the Miquiri were telling him that he could rest for a time.

They gave him a meal of something that resembled unappetizing mush. He ate a little of the tasteless substance, then curled up on the bed in his room and dozed. He did not sleep deeply; he was too cold for that. Normal temperatures for the Miquiri were a good ten degrees below his comfort zone. He had brought a jacket, but what he really needed was a heavy blanket. Chirith would have thought to offer one, but he had disappeared sometime after the first round of questions.

The outpost's officials gave Lukas six hours to rest, and then a different group appeared, led by a round Miquiri with reddish hair. He or she—Lukas couldn't tell which—asked if he would agree to open his mind to the outpost's Quayla, explaining that it wanted to examine his memories.

Lukas took a breath. This was the moment he had dreaded the most. He and Chirith had spoken of it at some length; Chirith had assured him the Quayla would do everything possible to avoid hurting him, but neither of them knew what contact would do to a mental structure that had sustained so much damage. He had been aware of the Quayla on the Miquiri shuttle and the one on the outpost, but had blocked the pressure he felt in their presence as well as he could. The strain had left him feeling like he was trying to function through a throbbing headache.

They took him into the room where he had been questioned and left him there. The Quayla began contact with a yellow-orange finger of light that ran down the wall and up the side of the chair in which he was sitting. Lukas held his hand flat against the arm of the chair, pressing down as hard as he could to keep from jerking away from what was coming. The light formed a bright, rapidly pulsing pool; then a tendril broke free and ran across his hand. The Quayla spilled over him.

It had meant that first brush to be imperceptible. As soon as it realized it was not, it pulled back. At least, that was what Lukas believed it was doing. He thought it had decided that proceeding would cause too much damage. He actually thought that it might retreat completely. He was wrong. It returned, and when it did, it hit full force.

One instant they were separate, and the next they were one. Lukas shrieked as his mind ripped apart. The Quayla knew what it was doing, though, because as quickly as it tore, it gathered the rents and stitched them together again. It worked its way through from the present back to the past. It gulped down every thought, every recollection, and searched for more.

Lukas was in shock. So was the Quayla's companion. The Quayla lifted itself above their responses and continued delving. It found Lukas's memories of the Ytavi and watched in fascination as the alien being joined and separated, joined and separated. It absorbed the technique in the space of one breath and immediately put it to practice, flowing in and out of Lukas's thoughts, searching out the rest of his memories.

When it had finished, it turned to its own companion. It straightened one of the barbs that had held it to her. She cried out in fear, but it did not hurt her. It did not, because it did not leave her. They were one. It would never leave her.

Grief washed over Lukas. He might be joined to them temporarily, but he did not share their emotional commitment—he could not. A Quayla chose only one companion at a time, and all other bonds it formed were lesser sharings. He was nothing to them. He was alone, cold, and far from home. He felt as if he always had been and always would be.

The Quayla turned back to him. It might be lost in the wonder of a new discovery, it might have its own companion, but it was not without compassion. It brushed through his mind, giving him the mental equivalent of a caress. And then, before he had time to realize what it meant to do, it hit him.

The blow was as swift as it was fierce. It was also an act of mercy. When the Quayla left Lukas, he was unconscious. He was not forced to undergo another agonizing separation, and he was spared an outsider's view of the raw, gaping hole that lay at the center of his mind.

Lukas thought he would be allowed to return to the *Widdon Galaxy* after that, but he was wrong; the Miquiri released him into the Corps' custody. He was taken to the *North Star*, where he was subjected to a round of tests that went on for days.

Before, during, and after the physical examinations, he was asked hundreds of questions. He finally stopped looking at who asked them or wondering why they wanted to know, and simply spewed out the first words that came into his mind.

He told them about everything, including his conversation with the Ytavi. Keenan had already filed a report about his own encounter with the being, but many of the scientists had discounted Keenan's experience, and they found Lukas's story equally implausible. Neither Lukas nor Keenan made any effort to persuade the doubtful; they were convinced, both of them, that the fewer people who believed the Ytavi existed, the better. Still, there were some who wondered. Lukas overheard two scientists speculating about a mission to the barrier. "How do you go about finding a being you can't see?" one asked. "How can you talk to something that spans a distance of light-years?" They did not resolve the question while Lukas was listening. He hoped they never would—some things were best left sleeping.

He did not rest well on the *North Star*. The first few nights, as he lay awake, he thought about all that had happened and all that he had lost. Later, though, he began to consider all that he still had, and might yet lose. It was then that he began to worry about Kiley.

She had to be upset about his prolonged absence, even if she knew he was on the *North Star*. He was certain she did; if the Corps had not told her, then Chirith or one of the other Miquiri would have. He asked if he could see her, or at least send a message, but he was told "No, not now. Not yet." He should have had the right to speak to her as a crewman in her service, if not as the man who loved her, but the Corps was being highly selective about the laws they chose to enforce, and civilian protections did not count for much on the edge of civilization.

Five days after Lukas was taken to the *North Star*, the Corps decided it had learned all it could from him. They handed him his clothes and politely said he was free to leave. They warned him that they might ask him to return for a few follow-up questions and tests, but they would keep them to a minimum. Then they thanked him for his cooperation.

Lukas told them he wanted to see Admiral Bergstrom. He persisted through a series of arguments with officers of ascending rank. The last one spoke to Bergstrom, and then said the admiral would give him five minutes in the officers' lounge. A security officer took him to the empty lounge and told him to sit down. Lukas stood. Bergstrom came in a few minutes later. He'd either been up for hours, or had been awakened and had hastily dressed in the uniform he'd worn the day before. His shirt and pants were creased, and his eyes were puffy.

"Mr. Lukas, it's a pleasure to finally meet you," he said, shaking hands. "I understand you wished to see me?"

"Yes, sir." Lukas told the admiral what he wanted. Bergstrom did his best to dissuade him, but Lukas remained adamant. Bergstrom told him to wait. He was gone for twenty minutes; when he came back, Kiley was with him. She went straight to Lukas and threw her arms around him. She did not say a single word, but she held him tight.

Bergstrom gave them a moment together. "Mr. Lukas tells me that the two of you would like to be married," he said briskly. "I told him that while performing the ceremony is within the scope of my authority, I generally counsel my crew members to wait until we return to port. However, since the nearest civilian authority is some distance away, and Mr. Lukas is not entirely welcome there, I agreed to make an exception in this case. Provided, of course, that's what you want, Captain."

Kiley had gone stiff. She looked at Lukas in disbelief. "You want to get married?" She had wanted to hear him say it for months, but he had not even considered the idea. He had not wanted legal ties between them; he had not wanted people looking at her the way they looked at him. He had not wanted people to have legal recourse against her or her family in case they decided he or the Quayla had inflicted some damage, real or imagined.

She searched his eyes, suddenly wary. "Why?" she demanded. "Why here? Why now?"

"The Quayla is gone. The Corps has run their tests and declared me as near normal as I ever have been. There's no stigma attached to me that can hurt you. Even if something did happen later, no one could claim that you were responsible."

"That's your only reason?" she asked, sounding hurt.

"No." With a mental *To hell with Bergstrom*, he said roughly, "No, that isn't the only reason. There's one more. I love you, Kiley. I don't want to live without you. I want to have a family. Not too fast," he added hastily. "I'm not quite ready for that yet. But I will be, I promise—just give me time. Please, Kiley, will you marry me?"

It might have been tears that made her eyes shine. Then again, it might have been some other emotion entirely. "I will," she said.

And she did. Right then. Right there.

Chapter 28

If the *Widdon Galaxy*'s safe return to port hadn't been grounds for celebration, then Kiley and Lukas's marriage was. The timing took Keenan by surprise, but not the announcement. He thought Lukas looked a little stunned when he returned to the ship, but the expression didn't last for long.

Keenan felt a small pang as he watched the pair accept a celebratory toast from the rest of the family. Lukas had been his closest friend. He probably always would be, but by marrying Kiley, he had made it clear that he put her first. However close he and Keenan remained, their relationship would never be the same.

Times changed. People changed. Life moved on, Keenan told himself. If you were wise, you realized that and accepted what happened. You didn't always like the circumstances in which you found yourself, but you made the best of them. You kept on hoping and believing, but most of all, you persevered. In the end, that was what carried you through—the simple persistence of life. You did not ask to be born, but by every thought, every act you made thereafter, you chose how to live. You laughed, because it was better to laugh than cry. You created, because it was better to create than destroy. Most of all, you lived—because no matter how bad circumstances seemed, it was better to live than die.

Daniel Keenan believed in life. So did Greg and Kiley. So did Jon Robert, Holly, Reese, and Lia. In time, Hope would believe, too—if only because that was what they would teach her, each and every one of them. He left the party on that thought. It was still with him when he woke the next day and found a message waiting on his terminal.

Daniel, I need to talk to you at once. Please call me as soon as you're awake. Elena Cristavos.

Keenan reached for the intercom. She was waiting for his call.

"Something's come up that involves you," she said. "I need to see you. Could you meet with me and the diplomatic chief, Robert Marishu, in twenty minutes?"

"Yes, of course," Keenan said, wondering what "something" might be. "Do you want to come here?"

"There's a conference room just down the corridor from the *Widdon Galaxy*. Why don't we meet there?"

The conference room across from the ship must have been used primarily by humans, because there were no Miquiri furnishings. An oblong table surrounded by eight chairs took up most of the floor space. The chairs were of the large, well-padded variety favored by people who spent most of their days sitting down.

When Keenan walked in, Marishu and Cristavos were sitting on the far side of the table, their heads bent together, seemingly engrossed in some private conversation. Marishu rose as soon as Keenan entered and came forward, his right hand extended.

"Dr. Keenan? It's a pleasure to meet you. I'd like to thank you personally for your fine work with Sensar. Thanks to you, we know more about the Gan-Tir than we might have learned in decades. Congratulations on a job well done."

"Thank you," Keenan said, shaking the diplomat's hand. Marishu was short, but he wore an expensive, tailored suit that emphasized his leanness and made him look taller. He had wavy brown hair and quick, hazel eyes that took in more than they revealed. He weighed Keenan up as they shook hands, then motioned him to a seat at the table. Cristavos sat to his right and Marishu took the seat to his left. Keenan wondered if they had surrounded him deliberately.

Cristavos held out her hand. "Hello, Daniel. It's good to see you again."

Her fingers were long and warm, her grip at once light and firm. His skin tingled where it touched hers. He made the mistake of looking into her eyes and found himself momentarily trapped in their rich, brown depths.

"It's good to see you, too," he said, startled by his response.

"Thank you for coming so promptly," Marishu said.

Keenan dragged his eyes and hand away from Cristavos. "Elena said there was some sort of problem?"

"We'd prefer to call it an opportunity," Marishu answered. "To cut a tedious account of the negotiations short, we've received an unexpected proposal from the Gan-Tir. They claim they must return home immediately, but have said they are willing to sign on as a party to any boundary agreements the Miquiri make with us, so long as the Miquiri honor all conventions already in existence between the two of them. In addition, they've invited us to send a diplomatic mission to their home world. They are even offering docking and preliminary trade privileges to a limited number of human vessels. They're willing to sign an agreement to that effect today, on one condition."

"Which is?"

"They want you to be a member of the diplomatic party that visits Gan-Tir."

"Me?" Keenan asked, startled. "Why me?"

"We aren't sure," Cristavos answered, "but we believe Sensar must have had something to do with the request." Cristavos gave Marishu a sideways glance. "You clearly struck a responsive chord in him during your meetings, and he says he wants to continue the dialogue he started with you. He can't stay here because the rest of his party is leaving and there's no telling when another ship might be sent. He isn't willing to risk being stranded. I don't blame him for that."

"So he wants me to go to him instead?"

"That's what we think, yes," Marishu said. "Mind you, he

hasn't said that to us. He has, in fact, said virtually nothing since returning, although we all have the impression that he has been influencing the others behind the scenes. The Miquiri are stunned; it took them nearly a century to win an agreement similar to the one the Gan-Tir are offering us."

"But there is that one condition?" Keenan looked from Cristavos to Marishu. It didn't take much intuition to see the direction the conversation was about to take. The only question was how much pressure the two diplomats would apply.

"Yes, there is," Marishu said. "We told the Gan-Tir that you are not a member of the Diplomatic Service, and said that you have other commitments, but they weren't interested. They are leaving tomorrow. If you'll go to their world, we'll have an agreement. If you don't, we won't, and there's no telling when—or if—they will decide to talk to us again, let alone negotiate."

"Marishu, I do not wish to go to Gan-Tir," Keenan said steadily, his words as clear and precise as he could make them.

"We can't insist, of course," Marishu said smoothly, "but I believe I can safely say that doing so would be to your decided advantage—and the Michaelsons' as well. If you'll cooperate, we can arrange for them to be one of the ships with docking privileges. We can also agree to let them retain their docking privileges at Sumpali. I must tell you that there is some talk of sending them back into human space now that the Quayla is off their ship. If that happens, they won't find it easy trying to make a living. They were having trouble running in the black before; they'll find it even more difficult now that they've been away for months and lost old contacts and contracts."

"Marishu, I'm a little confused," Keenan said coldly. "Was that a threat you just offered, or a bribe?"

"Neither," Cristavos intervened quickly. "Robert has a responsibility to point out your position and the Michaelsons', but that's all he was doing, wasn't it, Robert?"

"Of course," the diplomat said evenly. His eyes locked onto Keenan's. "It has been my observation that negotiations run more smoothly when all the facts and options are laid out on the table. I was simply endeavoring to do that. I assure you that neither the Diplomatic Service nor the Corps has any personal interest in what happens to you or the Michaelsons. Our sole interest lies in reaching accords with both the Miquiri and the Gan-Tir, containing the most favorable possible terms to us."

"Then I am free to say no. Just like that?"

"You are."

"Very well. The answer is—"

"Daniel, before you make up you mind, will you talk to Sensar?" Cristavos interrupted. She put her hand on his arm and her eyes pleaded with him to listen. "He stopped me last night, just after our talks broke up. He said he wanted to see you. He said that you promised you would talk to him before he left. Is that true?"

"Yes," Keenan admitted reluctantly.

"Then will you?" she asked. "If I arrange a time and place, will you talk to him?"

Keenan looked away. "If that is what he wants, then yes. But it will be to say goodbye," he warned both of them, "because that's all that I intend to do."

Keenan saw Sensar five hours later, in a room on the other side of the station, near the Gan-Tir dock. Cristavos took him as far as the corridor outside the chamber.

"I'll be down the hall," she said, nodding to the cross corridor that lay some fifteen feet ahead. "There are human and Miquiri security guards around the corner, watching the entrance to the Gan-Tir ship. If you need anything, just call out. Someone will be here within seconds."

Keenan nodded and went in the door.

A mound of the Gan-Tir's rainbow-colored cushions had been placed in each corner. Backless stools that would accommodate any shape or size were scattered around the room. Multicolored, silken fabrics hung on the walls shimmered, stirred by the air rushing in from the corridor.

Sensar stood in one corner, facing the door. As Keenan came in, he took a step forward and held out his tentacles, offering a greeting. Keenan did not return the gesture.

"You do not permit touch?" Sensar asked. He sounded upset.

Keenan felt a stab of guilt, but held his ground. "No."

Sensar coiled his tentacles around his arms again. "Will you come in? Will you sit? Please?" He lowered himself and then waved a tentacle at the stool nearest him.

Keenan relented far enough to sit down, but he chose his own seat—one farther away. "Cristavos said you wanted to see me?"

"We are leaving. I wished to speak first." *Will you listen?* He used Miquiri signs for the last sentence. Offered at the end of an extended, formal greeting, the phrase was employed when there was some doubt about the other party's receptivity. Keenan replied in kind, shading his reply with one of the many possible alternatives.

I will listen, he answered, *but I withhold judgment. We may reach an understanding or agreement, but have not yet.*

Sensar made the sharp sound that might have been a sigh. Or might not. "I have story to tell, Keenan. About people who are blind. Not with eyes, but with *heart.*"

He used the Miquiri word there, too. After Sensar had spoken for a time, Keenan understood why. There were no words in the Gan-Tir language for heart, or feelings, soul. They had no terms to express compassion or love. Most disturbing of all, there were only two meanings for growth—to increase in numbers or physical size.

The Gan-Tir grew, but they did not change.

They mated, but they did not love.

They lived together, but they did not form a community. They were each and every one of them—forever and always—separate.

They had survived as a species because they were highly successful biological creations. Their young developed at a speed that humans and Miquiri would consider astounding. They had few genetically triggered diseases and could detect communicable illnesses with a single taste. They were bright and they were aggressive.

The Gan-Tir had left their home world early. They encountered the Ytavi a century later, and began relations by firing on an unsuspecting survey ship and disabling her. They captured her and in a single stroke acquired the fruits of centuries of technological development. They did not learn as much as the makers of that ship had known, but they learned enough to compete.

They did not have to learn how to destroy; that, they already knew.

The Ytavi tried to negotiate with them, and when that did not work, they pleaded. When their pleas went unanswered, they finally retaliated, making an example of a single ship. The Gan-Tir responded by destroying an entire world.

After that, there was no going back for either side. Their principles crumbling beneath the onslaught, the Ytavi resorted to genetic warfare. They did not act to preserve themselves; they could see the end spiraling in upon them already. But there were other intelligent species in the region, the Miquiri included. They were just beginning to develop. If the Gan-Tir found them, they would be overrun before they had a chance to turn their eyes to the skies and their minds to the stars.

The Ytavi nearly destroyed the Gan-Tir, and there were some on Gan-Tir who came to feel that might have been fitting. They were the ones who studied the few records the Ytavi had left behind after disappearing completely.

The first scholars had sought technological knowledge. It was only later that a few, isolated individuals began to think beyond *what* the Ytavi had done to ask *why*. There were never more than a few who questioned. The Gan-Tir were not an introspective race; the vast majority cared only about satisfying their immediate wants and needs. They understood cooperation to the extent that it was required to fulfill their basic desires, but beyond that, they felt no concern for others.

There were no words in the Gan-Tir language for empathy, nurturing, sacrifice, or caring.

"Without words, without concepts, there is no reality," Sensar told Keenan. He had struggled with language for several hours, searching for words to convey his thoughts and feelings. His tentacles had waved nonstop, and he frequently made sharp, lashing gestures that Keenan had begun to associate with frustration. He was trying so hard to communicate, to reach Keenan, that he stumbled often. At one point, when he spoke of the destruction of entire worlds, he became so upset that he could barely speak in any language. Keenan tried to intervene then, to calm him down, but the pressure to speak must have been building in Sensar for years; he wasn't going to stop until he spilled out what he had to say. Keenan wrapped himself in his professional demeanor and waited for the Gan-Tir to run down.

When he finally did, they sat in silence for a time, Keenan digesting what he had heard, Sensar recovering. Keenan spoke first. "Why did you tell me all this?" There had been shame in parts of the story. There had been pain. Why had Sensar admitted his race's failings? Why now? Why to him?

Sensar lifted his head slowly, as if it were very heavy, or he very weak. "I wanted you to know who and what we were—and are."

"Why? Because you're afraid your people will attack mine the way they did the Ytavi?"

"No. We are few now. We would not attack, except to defend ourselves. But if there were more of us . . ." He trailed off, then gathered himself and said harshly, "Gan-Tir hurt. Always hurt. Self, others—no difference. We are fair in that, at least, but wrong. So very wrong. Still, I did not think it mattered until Rairea."

"Rairea?"

"She bears a child."

"That's why you returned to Sumpali?"

"Yes. This is the first child in many years, Keenan, but there will be others. She used a new drug to—" He searched for words again, tentacles swirling round and round. "—conceive. It worked. If it worked for her, then it will work for others. We will have children again, a new generation. But the children themselves will not be new. They will learn old ways, old patterns. There is no point to children if we destroy ourselves and others again. I do not want this, Keenan. I have come to like you. I do not want my people to hurt yours, or even the

Miquiri. I do not want new children to be what Gan-Tir have always been. I asked Rairea to let me be child's minder. I told her I wish to teach it a different way. She says I am crazy. Says there is no need, it is not possible. I persist. I explain. She considers. The child will give her status, will be a novelty, but she will lose interest quickly. She does not wish to care for it, but I do. I want to teach it, but I don't know how. I need someone to show me. I need you. Please, Keenan, come to my world. Show me how to teach this child to care about its own kind and others, as your people do. Will you do this for me? For the child? It will not be easy—I know this—but will you consider? Whatever you ask in return, I will give you. Goods, knowledge, whatever you want, I will give you. Please, Keenan, will you come?"

"Well?" Rairea demanded from her bed. "Did you convince the human to come to Gan-Tir?"

She had been given the most luxurious quarters on the ship, and she had everyone from the captain on down to the lowliest member of the diplomatic party waiting on her hand and foot. She had first choice of goods, meals, and entertainment. She had demanded and received a transmitter so she could listen to the negotiations. Unseen by the aliens, almost forgotten, she had controlled every word and every gesture her fellow diplomats made. Her physical, mental, and emotional state were as close to bliss as a Gan-Tir could come.

"He says he will consider," Sensar replied.

"Do you think he will agree?"

"I'm not sure." There had been times when he would swear that Keenan had forgotten they came from different species, and times when the human had stared at him as if barely comprehending how such a being could exist. Keenan's feelings were so volatile, Sensar wasn't certain the human himself could predict what he would do.

He hoped the decision would be favorable. Compelling the rest of the delegation to invite humans to Gan-Tir had taken every ounce of persuasion, influence, and domination he and Rairea could bring to bear. It had taken a carefully orchestrated campaign lasting several days to convince them that humans could be useful to Gan-Tir. It would take generations to repopulate the Gan-Tir's world. In the meantime, why not use the humans to full advantage? If they kept them busy scrambling after promises of Gan-Tir favor, they might never notice they were being manipulated. The humans were no more intelligent than the Miquiri; they would make excellent trading partners.

The Gan-Tir did love an advantage. And the only thing more satisfying than having one was exercising it.

Calling in Rairea's debt to him had been the most enjoyable moment of Sensar's life. With each insult accepted, a Gan-Tir acquired a degree of influence over the exploiter. In time, the degrees added up. In time, positions reversed. Those who had given favors could seek them; those who had accommodated could demand. By giving Rairea what she most wanted, he had taken their relationship full circle. She was in his debt. He still bowed to her in public, but in private he controlled their relationship. His position would not last long—he was rapidly spending his capital—but while it did, he was taking full advantage of it to achieve his own ends.

For all that he looked to the future, for all that he wanted change, he was still that much Gan-Tir.

Rairea lay back in her bed after Sensar left, thinking the scholar was as gullible as ever. He genuinely believed that he had the leverage to compel her to pressure the others. It was true that she had some slight obligation to him, but it was a small debt, easily discharged by her insistence that the humans include Keenan in the group of diplomats being sent to Gan-Tir.

She soothed her abdomen with her tentacle, wondering how much longer it would be until she felt the child within her move. She did not think she would like that. She did not think she would like pregnancy at all, but the months of discomfort would be worth the prestige she would gain if she gave her people a child.

Had the drugs she'd taken finally worked? she wondered for

the hundredth time. It was true that one of them had been new, but it had not been significantly different from others she had taken in the past. Had the altered formula been successful, or had it simply been a matter of timing, of nature giving her a chance at the same time she happened to take the drug?

Or, most intriguing of all, was it possible that some other factor was responsible, perhaps in combination with the new drug?

Some factor related to humans.

Rairea had tasted humans and she had become fertile. The two facts might not be related, but she could not overlook the possibility that they were connected. The humans had a strange, bitter flavor. It was not pleasant, but she had found herself craving it. She thought Sensar had, too, though he would never have admitted it.

Was it possible that the aliens produced some chemical she had lacked—one that had combined with the drugs she had taken to render her fertile? Could they have been responsible for her child's conception?

Rairea was not certain, nor was she in any hurry to share her speculations with others. There would be time enough to claim credit for her discovery after she had tested her hypothesis.

Rairea Tayturin wanted humans on Gan-Tir, but not for trade or cultural exchange; she wanted them there so she could conduct an experiment. She had become fertile after tasting them. Would the same thing happen to other Gan-Tir females? There were not many of childbearing age, and she knew them all. After the humans came to Gan-Tir, she would summon some of them to the city. She would tell them about the drug she had taken. They would immediately demand it for them-selves, and after they had taken it, she would introduce a few to humans and tell them to taste the aliens well. If only fe-males who had tasted humans became fertile, she would know her hypothesis was correct.

Sensar thought that the humans promised the Gan-Tir new lives and new hope. Rairea thought he was right, but not quite for the reasons he imagined.

It was, she decided, a most delicious irony. She hoped her

theory about the humans was correct. Revealing their true value to Sensar would be a most enjoyable moment.

She was looking forward to it tremendously.

Pitar asked Chirith to come to his room after dinner that evening. Leetian was there, too. She and Pitar sat side by side, their arms around each other. Chirith could feel their *tariss* pounding against him all the way across the room.

They wanted him to choose them. They wanted him to call them *akia*.

He was touched by the offer, and he was tempted—so very tempted. He had not felt such a desire to be part of a group since leaving his ship. Since Hinfalla had died.

He told them no.

They reasoned with him. They pleaded. He still declined. They were not surprised; they had guessed what his reply would be. They had expected his feelings for Lukas to diminish after the human separated from the Quayla, but to the surprise of them all, they had strengthened.

They understood his decision, but they regretted it. The three of them were a close match in all directions. Bound together, they would have had sufficient *tariss* to draw others to their group—they might well have had the power to create a new family. Even without Chirith, Pitar and Leetian still might.

They understood him. Not all Miquiri liked humans, but they did. They had come to enjoy the sound of the aliens' long, rolling voices, and had become accustomed to the humans' awkward, gangly bodies; they no longer feared the humans' movements would result in a fall. And they felt warm when they heard the bright, tumbling sound the humans called laughter. Pitar no longer thought Chirith mad because he had found companionship with a human—in fact, he was beginning to see how such a thing could be possible himself. Lukas was not and would never be a Miquiri *akia*, but neither Pitar nor Leetian could deny that Chirith and the human shared a deep bond. None of them could say where it would lead, but they both encouraged Chirith to find out.

In truth, they were as curious as Chirith himself.

Pitar and Leetian put their arms around Chirith before he left. He hesitated, then let them draw him in and stood together with them, one arm wrapped around each of them. For a time, he was Miquiri and he was not alone. He parted from them in sorrow, but not in despair. Pitar and Leetian would always be there. They had offered him a place; he could always go back to them and they would always welcome him.

All Miquiri belonged. They had to. Without family, there was only self, and with only self, there could never be a greater life. All Miquiri needed a greater life, Chirith included. The only question was where he would find it—among his own kind, or among humans?

Leetian had been right. Not all explorations took place among the stars. Some of the greatest had started where his was beginning: within the heart.

Lukas had feared he would have regrets about marrying Kiley after all the congratulations died down, but he did not. This wasn't a life he had ever envisioned for himself, much less planned, but there were parts he wouldn't have traded for anything. Kiley sleeping peacefully beside him was one.

The past weeks had been a trial, but they had come through safely. The Corps had traced the sabotage of the ship's computers back to the systems engineer who had installed the software. He had not denied his act when confronted with it; on the contrary, he had taken pride in what he had done. Hastings had pleaded no contest to the charges brought against him and had been sentenced to rehabilitation therapy. The Corps considered him an ideal candidate for personality restructuring, but Lukas wasn't so certain. It was easy to build fear and prejudice into people, but it was much, much harder to weed it out. Whoever took on Hastings's case would not have an easy time of it.

Neither would the psychiatric and social workers who had been sent to Resurrection in the aftermath of the riot. Admiral Vladic's trip to the station had not been entirely in vain; he had not met the Gan-Tir, but he had been able to convince Resurrection's council that someone or something had to give on the station. With the approval of the governments that formed the Consolidated Alliance of Planets, he had offered to transport any natives who were willing to leave Resurrection to another, recently discovered world. Though leaving would mean rebuilding their lives, many on the station and planet below were talking of accepting the offer. The more liberal locals might stay, but the Corps expected the most radical fundamentalists to go. In any event, the riot had insured that Resurrection would never be the same again.

And neither would life on the *Widdon Galaxy*.

Keenan was going to Gan-Tir, along with Elena Cristavos and several other diplomats. Sensar had convinced him that the Gan-Tir needed help. He was not planning to stay with the aliens long—a year, two at the most, he said. But while Keenan might believe that, Lukas wasn't so sure. The psychiatrist had a look in his eyes that meant he was seeing farther into the future than a few months or years. It was the look he'd had at the Academy whenever he'd talked about exploring unknown space—a mix of excitement, wonder, and apprehension.

Keenan thought he and Sensar could change the Gan-Tir. Lukas thought it more likely that the aliens would change his friend. Still, even he agreed that Keenan had to try. The Ytavi had not found a way to coexist with the Gan-Tir and had been all but destroyed in consequence; the Gan-Tir could be a significant threat if their population began growing again. Keenan had not shed his wariness of the aliens, but he said humanity had to try to forge ties with the Gan-Tir while the aliens were still vulnerable, still willing to talk and listen. If they did not, they might not have another chance.

Lukas was going to miss Keenan, but he consoled himself with the thought the separation wouldn't be permanent. Visits were being permitted, even encouraged, and the Gan-Tir had included the *Widdon Galaxy* on the list of ships that would be allowed to dock at their station. If Reese and Kiley could persuade the rest of the family that the opportunity was too good to pass up, they might be making regular runs out that way within a few months.

Reese was already negotiating with the Corps for a contract

to transport Keenan and the diplomatic party. Obtaining consent shouldn't be too difficult; formal boundary agreements were due to be signed within a few weeks, but until they were, the *Widdon Galaxy* was the only ship around. Others would start arriving soon, but the family would still have an advantage. Six months, a Quayla, and one gray Miquiri had given the Michaelsons ties to the aliens that would take other humans years to develop.

Lukas smiled, thinking of Chirith. The Miquiri was spending so much time on the ship that Kiley had said they would have to sign him on as crew before long. She was only half joking, and when Lukas had suggested that they might ask him to act as their agent with the Miquiri, she had given the idea serious consideration.

"It would mean traveling with us," she said. "Assuming we could work out the environmental issues and the problem of communication over the intercom, would he be willing to do that?"

"He might. He is curious about us, and there's no one to hold him here at Sumpali."

"He means a great deal to you, doesn't he?"

"Yes, he does."

"If you were Miquiri, would you be *akias*?"

"We might. Even though I'm human, there is still a draw between us. It might never have existed without the Quayla, but it is there and it is real. Does that bother you?"

"That you like him? No, of course not. I do, too. Go ahead—ask him if he'd like to make a trial trip with us. I won't object, and I don't believe any of the others will, either."

"I'll talk to him," Lukas had said. He hadn't yet, but he would. He thought he knew what the alien's reply would be.

He closed his eyes, wondering if Kiley realized how close he and Chirith were. She must have some idea—she was highly observant, and he'd caught her watching them together several times. Still, she had accepted his relationship with the Quayla, so why not the Miquiri? Affection for a real person had to be easier to understand than a bond with a light no one else could hear or talk to.

Is that all we are to you? A light? a familiar, high voice asked inside his mind. Laughter cascaded over him.

Lukas's eyes flew open. A spot of soft yellow and pink glowed on the ceiling over his head. The light intensified, then spread out, spilling down the walls and across the bed. Running across him.

Lukas, see what I have learned? it asked, slipping into his mind and out, traveling so fast that he barely felt its touch. It had been there, though; he could still feel the tingle of that swift brush. Goose bumps rose on his skin.

The Ytavi was right, the light said. *Its way is much, much better.*

He thought for an instant that it was his Quayla, so similar were their voices. But it wasn't. It might sound the same, but cool, alien hues tinged its thoughts and feelings. It had come from a Miquiri ship, and it was unattached. It had divided, he realized in shock. It was looking for a companion.

It was looking for him.

His rejection was fast and forceful, and the light flashed out. But it reappeared a breath later, showing itself as a single bright spot in the corner of the ceiling. He heard high, cheerful laughter.

You don't want me? it questioned. *No, that cannot be. I think perhaps you just need time. I will wait. Time has no meaning to me. I am infinity.*

The light flashed again and disappeared. This time, it did not come back. Lukas wondered where it had gone. Not to the *North Star*, he prayed silently. Please, don't let it go to the *North Star*. Bergstrom would have a stroke.

Lukas looked over at Kiley, wondering what she would say if he woke her and told her what had just happened. She would probably urge him to take the Quayla up on its offer. She had told him more than once that the family would welcome another one on the ship.

Lukas stared up at the empty ceiling and wondered if the light would come back. Even though it had carried the tinge of Miquiri thought and emotions, it had felt good in his mind. It had felt right.

A part of him wondered what he would say if it returned and asked to join with him again.

A part of him already knew.